FIREBLOOD

FIREBLOOD

JEFF WHEELER

47N✦RTH

Text copyright © 2013 by Jeff Wheeler

Published by 47North
P.O. Box 400818
Las Vegas, NV 89140

Cover illustration by Eamon O'Donoghue

ISBN-13: 9781612187204
ISBN-10: 161218720X
Library of Congress Control Number: 2012944549

To David Pomerico,

Dream Fulfiller

FIREBLOOD

T he final embers of sunlight cooled against the pale sky, coloring the clouds orange and purple. From the north, massive thunderheads loomed—seemingly tranquil yet swollen and ribbed. It would rain within the hour. A humid breeze rustled the nest of brittle oak leaves, crackling and snapping as the invisible rush shook the branches and a hail of dead leaves came down, swirling like ashy flakes of snow. A penetrating bark reported somewhere in the distance within the maze of trees, and then the bark turned into a keening howl. The howling was joined by short fits of barking. Tyrus heard the sounds, tightened his grip on his cloak, and started to run again. If the storm did not break soon, he knew he was going to die.

Tyrus of Kenatos was not a small man. He was hardy and younger than the streaks of gray at the edge of his amber beard implied. Drenched with sweat, shivering with fever, and bleeding from claw gashes all over his body, he moved as quickly as he could manage without stumbling. In all likelihood, he was delirious, and he recognized the possibility that he was walking back toward the creatures that hunted him instead of away from them. Every twisted, stunted oak looked the same, covered with moss and black with disease. Mushroom spores abounded instead of grass or wytherweeds. Were they also affecting his mind? He had not dared to eat one, despite his ravenous hunger. The acorns would be poison as well. Everything in the Scourgelands was poisoned.

Tyrus was a fool. He had believed he was strong enough, wise enough, skilled enough to face the horrors past the northern borders and not only survive, but triumph. He had convinced himself—and others—that it was their destiny to destroy the murderous Plague that ravaged the lands every generation. How many cities had fallen victim to them? How many centuries had passed where once, twice, four times the culling had happened, dwindling the population of the races down to the few hunkering within fortresses and strongholds? It was his dream to end it at last, to banish the cursed Plague and stamp out its source, both root and branch, and end the vicious cycle of death and stagnation. His companions had trusted him. They had believed in his goal and shared in his vision. And with him, they had entered the Scourgelands only to find themselves caught in a maze of horrors, hunted and stalked and killed one by one. They had not even breached the inner core of the maze of trees. Nor had they seen the face of the enemy who commanded its precincts. But it had seen them, and its fury was incalculable.

The fetid air scorched Tyrus's lungs as he ran. He was exhausted. It had been days since he had slept, days since he had tried to wander free of the maze of oak trees. South was impossible. East was impossible. West was impossible. Somehow, he kept getting turned around, and found himself moving closer to the inner core of the maze, instead of fleeing it. It did not matter how hard he tried to focus or concentrate. The woods had a way of tricking him, sending him back the way he had come. Back toward the death that hunted him in a thousand forms. Clenching his teeth, he shoved through the woods, struggling to stay ahead of the creatures hunting him. His strength faded. Madness threatened him. He almost welcomed it.

In his mind, he thought of his study, high within the Paracelsus Tower in Kenatos. A cup of honeyed tea in his hand, soothing a sore throat or warming him before bed. There were books to read—so many books to read. Books written by the Vaettir on plants and spirit-life. There were obscure tomes by the Cruithne on the proper construction of furnaces or the gemcraft that would trap a spirit and bind it to obey for ten years. Even more obscure, the writings of the Preachán on lurid trading or the gossip of kings and thrones in distant lands—of queens and killers and the diplomacy of poison. But his favorite works were the writings of a hundred generations of Paracelsus, each more cryptic and awe inspiring than the last. Another twenty-five years and he would still not have read them all, but he desperately wanted to. It was that desperation, in the end, that kept him moving, preventing him from collapsing in gibbering fear and accepting his approaching death.

Tyrus of Kenatos—one of the wise ones of the city. A Paracelsus without peer. He wanted to laugh with bitterness. He had matched his mind against the best the island city had produced and had never found anyone who could win an argument with him save the Arch-Rike. And yet Tyrus could say he had never lost an argument either. He had persuaded the Arch-Rike to let him go. It was almost worth accepting death instead of admitting how wrong he had been to venture into the Scourgelands. How foolish he had been. How unprepared he was to face the wicked beings permeating the maze of oak trees known as the

Scourgelands. There was blood on his hands. So much blood. They had trusted him and he had failed them.

A snap from the side alerted him to danger. Already he started to summon power to defend himself. The fear was so sudden that he nearly abandoned the words that would tame it. He realized with horror how close he had been to unleashing it untamed—an act that would have resulted in irrevocable madness. Had not the Paracelsus writings warned of it? Discipline. Self-discipline. It was the only way to stay sane.

Tyrus swung his fist around and then saw her. It was Merinda. The Druidecht was alive?

"Tyrus?" she gasped. Her face was white, her robes soaked in blood. Dead leaves were tangled in her hair. Her left arm pressed against her side at an awkward angle, likely broken.

"Merinda," he said in amazement, stopping. "Are you...are you alone?"

She nodded in exhaustion, her eyes fluttering.

"Are you really Merinda Druidecht?" he demanded, studying her face. He could not trust anything right now, least of all his senses. The black ring on his finger burned with heat.

"I am," she answered and the ring throbbed. "Who did you think I was? Your sister?"

There was pain at the word. He clenched his teeth, trying to control it. "She died long ago, Merinda. Long ago. Do you know where you are?"

Merinda nodded, approaching. She doubled over in pain. "I am weak, Tyrus. But I know how to escape. I know the way out. But they hunt me. They are coming again. I lack the strength."

"Where is Aboujaoude?" Tyrus asked. "He would not have left your side unless..." He choked, unable to say it. Aboujaoude was a Bhikhu. The most talented Bhikhu in a generation, a natural with any weapon or with his hands and feet alone. Surely he would have survived the Scourgelands. Tyrus had assumed Merinda would have fallen first.

"Dead," Merinda said flatly. "I am tired, Tyrus. So tired. Will you…will you walk with me a ways?"

"I am hunted as well, Merinda," he said, pained by her plea. If he slowed for her, they would both die. He had to live. He had to live to describe what they had found. Perhaps someday, another Paracelsus would read the words and see something that he had not seen. The claw wounds would heal, though they were poisoned. He knew the cures for poisons. The guilt would possibly drive him mad. Yet one of them had to survive. One had to warn the Arch-Rike of the next Plague that was coming.

"I know, Tyrus. I can help you if you help me. I know the way out. I can help you escape. But you must promise me. You must help me."

He wanted to laugh, his mind giddy with dread. A way out? "Where, Merinda?" Tyrus asked, listening for the sound of their pursuers. The howling had stopped. That was not good. It meant they were still on the trail, trying to box them in. They would attack from three sides at once. "What is the way?" Tyrus seethed, grabbing her shoulder and shaking her.

Merinda looked back at the woods, her face twisted with grief. "They come."

"Tell me!"

"You must not look," she said. Her voice came as a whisper. "They live in the trees. Inside them, Tyrus. Inside these sick trees. You see their faces and they make you forget. You must not look at them, Tyrus. Walk south. Look at the ground. Do not look at the trees. The faces—you will see them. And then you will forget. They rule these woods. The faces. So beautiful. So twisted. They hate us, Tyrus. Especially our blood. Yet they will help us. Only us. Please…I have shown you the way out. It is the way of the

Druidecht. It is our lore. You would not know of it. Do not write it, Tyrus. There are secrets which cannot be written. Please…you must save me. You must…"

His heart pained him. He tried not to feel it or let it influence him. "I cannot *save* you, Merinda. I may not even be able save myself. If I stay with you, they will reach us, and I cannot protect you from them. They are without reason. They hunt and they kill. Even fire barely hurts them."

"I know," she said, nodding like a puppet. "I will stop them. I will unleash all of the magic. I will save you. I will sacrifice my mind. But you must save me."

"There is no way to cure the madness!" Tyrus hissed, trembling with fury. "I could not save Missy and I cannot save you from it. Have you unleashed it already? Are you already lost, Merinda? Say it!"

"No," she answered, and the ring on his finger pulsed with life again. "No, not yet. But I will. I will to save you. You must… in return…save me. Not my mind, Tyrus. Not for long. You must save my body. I must live…longer."

His heart skipped when he realized what she meant, and the pangs of guilt hit deeper. "No…Merinda…is it true? I had seen you and Aboujaoude look at each other, but never more than that. I never suspected…"

She reached and clutched his tunic front with her free hand, the one that was not angled crookedly against her side. "We were careful that no one knew. We were wed in Kenatos by the Arch-Rike in secret. We did not want anyone to know, least of all you. I am with child," she whispered. "His child. He sacrificed himself that I might escape. Now the madness will take me so that you will escape. But you must save me, Tyrus. Not for my sake, but for the child's sake. There are so few of us, and our blood is sacred. It will save many during the Plague that comes. The Plague that *we* have caused by coming here. This forsaken land. This wilderness of our wrongs. Save my child, Tyrus."

He saw the shapes emerge from the woods, coming from three sides at once. They were swift as shadows, slinking in the fading light, eyes luminous and full of hate. They were enormous, yet the bulk deceived. They were supple and graceful, beings from another realm of existence, let loose to guard and destroy. They were colorful, yet of no color, like glass.

Tyrus felt the first drops of rain on his face and the wind kicked up another cascade of brittle leaves. The leaves would burn. The entire grove would burn.

Merinda turned and faced the nightmares caging them. Her eyes were flat, devoid of emotion. "If a boy, name him Annon. If a girl, name her Hettie. That was my mother's name."

In his mind, Tyrus repeated the words to tame his magic. He would try to destroy them alone, but he was too late. Merinda raised her good arm and flames gushed from her fingers, sweeping the attackers with a plume of heat that turned them into white ash.

It was not enough. A new wave of attackers bounded in from behind them. Tyrus had just enough time to turn and send flames hurtling into them. He brought down three before the fourth launched at him and sent him toppling backward. Claws raked down his lips and chin, furiously and ferociously trying to rip out his throat. He felt its hind claws on his bloodied legs and he twisted reflexively. Its teeth snapped near his ear. He could feel its panting breath, its saliva spattering on his neck. Then suddenly he was bathed in flames, and the being vanished with the heat. Merinda stood over him, her crooked arm held out, sending more fire into the new attackers. Smoke trailed from his cloak.

Tyrus saw her eyes. They were gleeful.

"Stop!" he shouted at her. "Merinda, stop!"

She let the flames out like a flood, engulfing the area in blazing sheets, catching another group as it tried to flank her. Then she smiled, experiencing a euphoria so powerful that it stole everything from her.

Tyrus saw another pack lunging at her from behind. Pulling himself up to one knee, he straightened his arms and sent a whirlwind of fire at them, though more focused and controlled. There were so many! One dodged his attempt to destroy it and vaulted at Merinda. It struck her from behind, smashing her to the charred earth. It raised a terrible paw and Tyrus tackled it, grabbing its outstretched limb and sending flames through it all in one burst. He felt his hold on sanity slipping. He wanted to free the magic completely, to create a forest blaze so massive that nothing but he and Merinda would be safe to walk in it. He nearly gave into the craving.

Merinda was back on her feet again, her face twisted with hatred and rage. Another pack loomed in, circling them from all sides, more cautious this time, but no less determined. She did not hesitate. Her jaw looked swollen. It was probably broken. Her eyes focused and then the very trees around them exploded with flames, sending shards of bark and flaming wood into their midst.

Tyrus had never seen the fireblood unleashed so fully, not even when his sister had done it.

"No," he whispered hoarsely. It was too late for Merinda.

The storm broke at last, flooding the trees and woods in a deluge. The rains would stop the burning eventually. Tyrus led the Druidecht girl through the maze, eyes down on the dirt. He could sense the beings in the trees now, he could feel them grabbing at his mind, commanding him to look at them. He walked feverishly, pulling Merinda after him. She sang softly to herself, a lullaby broken with intermittent giggles.

In the end, it was the rain that saved Tyrus's life. It was not something he had planned on or accounted for in his thinking. It was a random bit of luck, a vagary that made the difference between life and death. It was the rain that disguised his trail just long enough for the two of them to slip away from the maze of oak trees, a maze that had murdered the twelve who had entered it with him.

"There is a saying among the Druidecht order: Faith is to believe what you do not see; the reward of this faith is to see what you believe. They harbor the peculiar notion that our world co-exists with another realm, a realm of spirit which they call Mirrowen. The denizens of Mirrowen cannot be seen with mortal eyes and often play pranks on us. They are firm in this belief, often wearing a token of their discipleship—called a talisman—around their necks. The world beyond the walls of Kenatos is full of strange and peculiar traditions. I do not pass judgment on them. My intent is merely to describe them fully and let my readers judge for themselves. I would add, however, that the Druidecht are known to ingest copious quantities of mushrooms."

– Possidius Adeodat, Archivist of Kenatos

II

It could be said, and rightly so, that Annon was a Druidecht. It could also be said that he preferred the company of raccoons, wrens, and the millions of unseen spirits roaming the woods to any conversation with people. He had spent most of his eighteen years wandering the vast woods of the Kingdom of Wayland, though on occasion he had journeyed as far west as the woods bordering Stonehollow. The life suited him perfectly. He had never been comfortable in thronging crowds or rude cities. The secluded hamlets and villages of Wayland fit his reclusive personality. Being a Druidecht, he was offered respect from nearly anyone he met. He had no home or dwelling place, carrying all his possessions in a large pack slung around his shoulders, but he was never deprived of shelter when he needed it.

A Druidecht was always welcome in a hut, no matter how small, and he was given the best portion of meat or a heaping bowl of vegetables and broth. He was revered because of his knowledge of the world and its many unseen inhabitants. The knowledge of the Druidecht was secret and only passed along from one to another, without books or written words, and Annon hungered to learn it all. He secretly hoped that by doing so, he would finally learn to control his anger.

Anger was a part of his life, like his walking staff, the dagger in the sheath at his belt, and his hands. Especially his hands. It was anger that made them tingle with heat. He had much to be angry about. The King of Wayland was a fool, and his reckless laws endangered the woodlands, threatening the creatures that lived there—secretly, dangerously. Lumber was needed to build his cities. Chalk from hills and sand from the rivers were removed, damaging the spirits that hid there. The creatures retaliated, of course, causing bizarre accidents amidst the workers. Some of the accidents were fatal. Deliberately so. The Waylanders were a superstitious people, yet they never learned to read the mood of the spirits in the shift of the winds. They never seemed to know when they had gone too far.

Annon ducked beneath a low-hanging maple branch and increased his stride, walking briskly through the woods and trying to make it to the hovel before the sun set. Dame Nestra would have baked fresh bread that day, and he longed for a slice drizzled with white honey. Her husband was a woodcutter; Annon had taught him which trees were safe and which were sacred—and how he could tell them apart. He was not wealthy because he was selective in his trade, but his lack of riches was balanced by the lack of harm and accidents in his work. Their little hovel was a haven, and they did not even realize it. But how could they? Only the Druidecht held the knowledge. Only another Druidecht could be taught about Mirrowen.

Light drained from the sky, showing small tufts of clouds that promised a balmy summer's eve. He smoothed the hair from his forehead and watched the signs of life surrounding him. Not just the dragonflies and the ravens, or the nervous gaze of a doe and her young. No, the woods were full of spirits as well, and they could not be seen unless one knew what to look for or unless one had been touched by them. They lived in an invisible realm called Mirrowen. It was in the world, but it could not be seen. Glimpses of it were fleeting.

Sometimes he had stared long and hard at a sacred oak, stared at it for hours, and in the moment of a half-breath, he saw it. Teasing him. Luring him. Mirrowen. The Druidecht were the intermediaries between the beings who dwelled there and those who lived and breathed and died. Occasionally there were Druidecht so accepted by the spirits that they were invited to dwell in Mirrowen. There was no death there, or so it was told, unlike the world he lived in—a world where death met his gaze often. Where the slightest misstep of chance could end a life. The worlds were opposites. One full of life. The other of death.

Annon smelled the smoke before he saw the hovel and smiled with relief that it was nearby. Through a thicket of maples and witherberries, he spied the small, cramped structure and heard the grating rasp of a whetstone and blade. There were voices drifting in as well, and Annon pursed his lips, surprised to find another visitor already there. His annoyance flared, but he shoved the emotion aside. He had not expected another guest to have found this place. It was one of his favorite haunts.

The feeling melted away when he saw the older Druidecht sitting on a stump, mouth open over a bowl of stew, savoring the blend of flavors. It was Reeder. Annon emerged from the copse of trees, sweating slightly, and beamed when he saw his mentor sitting with the couple he knew so well. Reeder was tall and had copper-colored hair that flowed down to his shoulders. It had receded from his scalp significantly since their last meeting. A small gray-flecked beard covered his sturdy jaw. He looked up as Annon approached. It had been several years since they had seen each other.

Reeder swallowed another bite from the stew bowl and then stood, towering over Annon like a bear, and set the bowl down on the stump. "Look at you, Annon. A child no more, but a man grown!"

"It is good to see you, Reeder," Annon said warmly. "You found one of my favorite places to eat."

"I know! I was telling these good people that I can see why you visit them so often. The bread is especially tasty. Now, if I were not journeying to Silvandom at the moment, I might stay and learn the secret of their white honey." He grinned as he gripped Annon's shoulders, smiling genuinely. "Look at you. It is good to see you again."

Dame Nestra smiled pleasantly. "I told Reeder we might expect you for supper, Annon. He waited all afternoon for you, but I made extra stew for you both."

"That was thoughtful of you," Annon replied. "How is your ax, Master Woodcutter? Worn it to a nub yet?"

"Well used, but sharp as the whetstone gets it." He reached out and shook Annon's hand with a grip as sturdy as his tool. "I have some more cutting to do, but don't forget the tunes you promised us, Reeder!"

"Yes, you said you would sing for your meal," Dame Nestra insisted, a pleasant look on her face.

Both she and her husband were much older than Annon, but they had been unable to have children and doted upon him as if he somehow made up for that fact.

"Songs you will have, after I've talked with my good friend. I was his mentor, you know, though he has proven my equal already."

Annon smiled and felt embarrassed. "What brings you westbound, Reeder?"

"Some mischief afoot in Silvandom. I learned of it while in Kenatos. I'll go and see if my old bones may do any good in the conflict. Likely not, but it is a pleasant country to visit besides."

Nestra returned with another bowl full of broth and vegetables and brought it carefully to Annon, bowing as she handed it to him. He smiled his thanks and inhaled the aroma.

"You eat another bowl if you are hungry," she admonished him.

"The young are always hungry," Reeder said, motioning for Annon to eat. "I'd like to finish mine as well. It's nearly as tasty as the bread. The couple says you wander here often. I'm not surprised," he added with a wolfish smile.

They supped together, finishing the stew and two generous helpings of Nestra's bread, sweetened to perfection. Reeder had a healthy appetite and did not refuse a third slice. His face glowed with warmth and humor. "You have a good reputation in these woods, Annon," he said after finishing the bread and brushing the crumbs from his lap. "Among the spirits. It was not difficult finding you. Do you think you will choose to dwell here longer? Or are you ready to move to another land?"

Annon shrugged, staring at his empty bowl. "I had not given it much thought. There is much still to learn here."

"I am much older than you," Reeder said, "and still that is true. Yet the woods of Silvandom have different breeds of spirits. And so do the mountains of Alkire. Each land has its own troubles." He stared into the darkening wood, his face turning serious, the smile fading. "And then there are lairs where even the Druidecht fear to tread." He looked down at his hands and then at Annon. "North, for example."

"Kenatos?" Annon asked wryly.

Reeder pursed his lips. "You know what I mean, Annon. I mean beyond Kenatos, beyond the mountains. The Scourgelands are safe for none of the races."

Annon smirked and stretched, loosening his weary limbs. "So you have told me, and so I believe you, old friend. What reason could I possibly have to wander in that forsaken place?"

But Reeder was serious. "A warning twice given is a warning still. It does no harm to repeat it. I was bid to come south and find you quickly."

Annon's stomach lurched and his mouth went dry. He was quiet, so quiet he could hear the fire snapping inside the hovel and the occasional clang of pots and dishes. "Who bid you, Reeder?"

"I said I was recently in Kenatos. That should be your clue."

Annon was stunned. For a moment, his ears started ringing and anger and hurt surged in his heart. Black, seething anger. The kind that made his jaw clench and his eyes squint. It was difficult to squelch it. But beneath that anger was pain. The pain of being abandoned. The pain of never measuring up. "My uncle?" he asked through a swallow.

Reeder nodded. "He is a powerful man in that powerful city. He is known by one and all. Tyrus of Kenatos. Tyrus Paracelsus. They say his power rivals the Arch-Rike's. When he learned I was there, he sent word for me. I left his study not two days ago. We had tea together actually."

Annon could feel the bitter feelings swirling inside him like black waters. His uncle. Tyrus. The blackness brought a feeling of loathing and defiance. It was a sore wound still, a wound that had never healed. He tried to speak but found himself hoarse. He coughed against his fist, trying to tame the wild surging in his heart. "And what did my uncle bid you tell me?"

Reeder was wise, and he looked at Annon with compassion. He knew of Annon's festering feelings. His disappointment. He knew that Annon had waited years for an invitation to join his uncle at Kenatos and that it had never come.

"He wishes to see you," Reeder said softly.

"Why?" Annon demanded, too hotly. Then he felt ashamed of himself. He stared down at the ground, resisting the impulse to pace and rant. Control—he needed to learn to control his resentment.

"He would not say. You know him better than that. He guards his thoughts like a Preachán guards his coins. He broods and plots and asks for no one's counsel, and he accepts none but his own." He reached out and rested his hand on Annon's shoulder. "I know you once wished he would send for you, but I do not think he bids you to join him and learn his ways. I cannot even guess why he asked to see you. But I knew that you would want to know he called for you, so I did not delay. It is your choice, Annon. I am bound for Silvandom. You can go with me there if you choose. Or you can see your uncle first and make your decision later. A Druidecht builds his reputation by traveling far and wide. You are known in Wayland already. It may be time to move on."

Reeder dropped his hand and stared at his empty bowl. He sighed heavily. The look he gave Annon next was piercing. "But if he bids you go north, tell him no."

Annon stared, confused. "Why would he do that?"

"I am old enough to remember. I outlived the last Plague. You know that. There were whispers back then. Word that your uncle led men into the Scourgelands to their deaths. Only he survived. They say it started the Plague anew. Now I do not know what to believe, Annon. Men are false by nature. I have had experience with many who wished to deceive, but not one who wished to be deceived. Since they are unwilling to be deceived, they are unwilling to be convinced that they have been deceived. They are jealous and petty and suspicious, save for the Vaettir, who distrust no one and serve all. And so they are robbed and cheated and wronged and consider themselves blessed in the bargain."

Reeder grinned and chuckled lightly. "But I have looked your uncle in the eye. I have seen the scars on his face and his hands. They have mostly healed and are tiny to the eye. But he has the look about him—of one who is well acquainted with death and all of its faces. He has no compassion for anyone. Even his own kin."

Annon grunted. "I know."

Reeder slapped his knees. "I have done my part. I have given you the message. Since I told these wonderful people that I can sing in three languages, they begged me to share a song from each of the kingdoms. You know I love to sing." He stared up at the sky and yawned. "I'm getting old and perhaps had too much bread. I'll depart in the morning for Silvandom. You decide what you will do, Annon."

The young Druidecht nodded, staring off into the distance. It surprised him how much of the hurt was still in his heart. He thought he had buried it long ago. Yet the pain of the memory suddenly was fresh, and tears pricked his eyes. He refused to give in to them, though. Memories could torment like poison.

His uncle had finally appeared. It was ten years before, when he was not yet a boy of eight. How young he had been. How softhearted. Uncle Tyrus loomed over him, an obelisk of iron will, his amber beard grizzled with gray. He looked uncomfortable being with Annon, as if the boy's presence caused him pain that he was determined to endure. It was so long ago, but he could never forget that moment of hope. His uncle had come for him at last. Tyrus had taught him about his anger. He had warned Annon what it could do. He had even shown him, and Annon remembered with guilty pleasure the look of his hands as the flames leapt from his fingertips. Most importantly, he had revealed the Vaettir words that could tame fire. *Pyricanthas. Sericanthas. Thas.*

Annon stared at his hands, struggling to subdue the disappointment of lost hope.

As a young boy, he craved to learn the lore of the Paracelsus. He wanted to learn it desperately, to prove to his uncle he was smart and determined. He assumed his uncle wanted to teach him the ways, to bring him as a student to Kenatos, and open the library corridors stuffed with all the recorded knowledge from all of the races. Annon practiced over and over, learning to control the flames, to control his anger. The invitation never came. A year went by. And another. And yet another. Disappointment turned to shame. Why had his uncle not thought him worthy to learn? Shame turned to guilt. He had done something wrong in his uncle's eyes. He had failed to act in some way to earn his uncle's trust. Guilt turned to resentment.

When Annon was twelve, he gave up hope of ever being invited to Kenatos. Four years was long enough to waste on an empty dream. So Annon had redoubled his commitment to learning the Druidecht ways, to immerse himself in the lore. He rose quickly, earning the right to wear a talisman at age sixteen. It was rare for one so young to be so recognized by the inhabitants of Mirrowen. Reeder had not worn his until he was twenty.

He began to pace, his heart rushing with conflicting emotions. Not even Reeder's singing could distract him from the hive of his thoughts. An outside fire pit crackled and spat, the smoke warding off flies, but Annon stared at the coals, the orange pulsing coals, and he could only think of his hands, his child's hands cupping a flame. He could reach into that nest of fire and pull out a burning log and it would not harm him so long as he had uttered the words in his mind. *Pyricanthas. Sericanthas. Thas.*

It had been several years since Annon had summoned that power. When he had rejected his uncle, he had rejected his uncle's teaching. It was not Druidecht. He should never have been taught how to do it. Annon never told Reeder—or anyone—what happened. He carried it in his memory as a secret shame.

Staring into the eyes of the fire, he wondered if he should obey his uncle's summons. He did not need to think about it very long, for Annon knew in his heart that he would wonder about it for the rest of his life if he did not. He was no longer that hopeful little boy. He was no longer bound to the past.

Annon was a Druidecht.

"The city of Kenatos was founded centuries ago on an island lake. The location was proposed by an advisor to the Arch-Rike for its proximity to the adjacent kingdoms as well as its defensible position. It took twenty years to build the shipyards on the southeastern shoreline; there, the ships were constructed to ferry the stone and timber and animals required to begin the construction. To this day it remains an icon of cooperation between the races and kingdoms, a monument to the knowledge that wise rulers can band together and work for the good of civilization. I believe that in the end we shall see that those individuals and kingdoms that learned to collaborate and adapt most effectively have prevailed."

– *Possidius Adeodat, Archivist of Kenatos*

III

Annon had a solid stride and could cover leagues without getting tired. The further north he went, the more sparse the woodlands became. Thinning pockets of boxwood and maple stretched before him, revealing glimpses of the undulating hills, thick with heather and fern. Jays swooped and glided nearby, and he nodded to them in greeting. There were fewer signs of spirits as well, giving the land a dead feel to it that Annon found worrisome.

As he walked, he encountered forsaken farmlands. The fences had rotted and collapsed. Little cottages with gaps in the thatch showed the years since the inhabitants had been decimated by Plague. It was a common sight, even in Wayland. Homes were abandoned, never to be reclaimed. Many had abandoned fortunes hidden beneath hearthstones, but money was of no consequence to Annon. Often the greedier spirits laid claim to treasures and harmed those who wandered too close. They did not need the golden coins—they just fancied pretty things, and the minting of coins was a curiosity to them. A tiny pent had the same value to them as a ducat.

He spent the first night nestled in the grass on a hillock, and he summoned a shain-spirit to guard him while he slept. In return, he promised to feed it with dew-filled berries that he would leave in his wake the next morning. That was the way of Mirrowen. Some favored a song; others wanted riddles. Some could be coaxed with mortal food and others with promises of service. This was beneficial to the spirits, especially when their lairs were disturbed by mortals. A Druidecht would always try to be fair-minded in any case. And by wearing a talisman that had been spirit-blessed, he had proven himself reliable.

As the morning wore on and afternoon passed, Annon wondered if he had missed his destination by traveling too far to the west. He was uncertain whether he should turn east or not. Fortunately, he discovered a gull loping high in the air and soon after that, he could smell the odors of the waters. It was an unhealthy smell. Kenatos.

He walked with a mixture of nervousness, excitement, and dread. Since spirits did not typically dwell in cities, he would be particularly vulnerable. His reputation might shield him, but it was enough to cause some alarm and nerves. The anticipation of what his uncle wanted teased his imagination.

Annon encountered a paved road and joined it, taking it west. There were multiple docks along the coast serviced by fer-ryboats. He was tired from the hard pace he had kept and was not surprised to see the first set of docks empty. Sitting down, he rested himself and ate the last of the bread that Dame Nestra had provided. He remembered her face for a moment as he chewed, wondering how long it would be before he returned that way. Dame Nestra and her husband were good people. He would miss them. By the time Annon's simple meal was over, the water began lapping against the dock posts, announcing the arrival of the ferryman.

He was a middle-aged man with the signs of pain in his back. He nodded to Annon as he berthed the ferry and stepped off, groaning in pain and stretching his arms. His face was full of whiskers that were as peppered as his hair; he shook his head mournfully at the thought of ferrying again.

"A Druidecht, is it?" he said, a little sharply. "What business have you in Kenatos? There are not many of your kind in the city."

"What is your fare?"

"I will not even take a pent from a Druidecht, you may be assured of that. Some ferryman think it right to charge everyone, regardless of rank or station, but that is foolhardy in my reckoning. It is the Druidechts and Rikes that save us from the Plague. You ought to have deference."

"That is kind of you. Please rest before you take me."

"I may, but tell me your business."

"What concern is it of yours?"

"I earn an extra pent from the Arch-Rike's coffers if I bring an answer." He leaned over and picked up the pole.

"So you take coin for my travel regardless." Annon was riled. "I come at the bidding of my master. He is a Druidecht."

The ferryman shrugged, grateful to earn the extra pent and not caring about the quality of the answer—only the lack of it. He motioned for Annon to board.

"Hold!" shouted someone coming up the road, a younger man than the ferryman, clutching a small chest in his hands. He was older than Annon but still quite young.

He arrived panting. "Thank you! I need to reach the city before nightfall."

"Five pents," the ferryman said, and the coins were dropped in his hand. "What is your business?"

"No business of yours."

The ferryman shook his head. "Come on, lad. We aren't going until you tell me."

He looked askance at the ferryman. "I am seeking work as a scribe." He patted the box. "My quills and ink. Do you need to see them too?"

"No, lad. Why the rush?"

"I didn't want to sleep on the plains again. No offense, Master Druidecht, but there are noises at night." He shook his head and shuddered. Annon smiled and shrugged.

They embarked and soon the skiff was maneuvering across the lake. Because of all the fires burning in chimneys and shops, there was a constant ring of haze around the island city. Swarms of gulls floated above, sending eerie shrieks ghosting through the mist.

"You loathe sleeping in the woods," Annon said to the younger man. "But I dread sleeping in the city."

"This is your first time to Kenatos?" the ferryman asked between grunts.

"Yes," Annon answered. "Wayland is my country."

"Mine as well," said the young man. "My father was a grave-digger in Wayland. Busy work with the Plague, you know. But I learned to read and write, and I hear you earn more in Kenatos if you can. Always records to transcribe."

The ferryman chuckled. "Gravedigger boy then. You must be good with a spade. Want to take a turn at the oars?"

"Want to give me my five pents back?" he asked archly, nodding to Annon at the man's rudeness and offering a look of disgust.

"This is my third trip today, stripling. I can keep going all night too. My calluses are like rocks. Don't be tart, or I'll box your ears."

The younger man rolled his eyes. "Friends call me Graves," he told Annon. "When we reach the dock, watch out for the

Preachán. They'll try and sell you moldy bread or bruised apples. I used to come here once a year with my father. Watch your purse."

"Watch your tongue, lad," said the ferryman between groans.

"Pardon," he said. "Where are you staying? Is there a Druidecht place in Kenatos? I didn't think so."

Annon shook his head. "I won't be staying long. Are you a good scribe?"

He winced. "It helps if you know more languages than just one. I know Aeduan and a little bit of Preachán. Knowing Vaettir pays the most, but how can you learn that?"

The lake was vast and the waves rippled against the skiff. It was the island-city's greatest defense. Kenatos possessed a fleet of sturdy warships that brought the food and grains from the mainland. Annon wrinkled his nose as they drew nearer to the smell of the city; he hunched down, pulling his cloak more tightly.

The ferryman paused to rest a moment. "Since you are new to Kenatos, remember that for every Preachán who will steal your purse, there is a Bhikhu who will chase him down and box his ears for it."

"A Bhikhu?" Annon asked.

"You'll recognize them when you get to the city. They dress in gray tunics and sandals. The men shear their hair down to the nubs. You'll see them on the street. If you get lost or have any troubles, seek one out. They won't take a pent from you. Good advice for a newcomer, and it cost you nothing." The docks of Kenatos were hulking and swollen with people arriving into different slips and disgorging their cargoes. Annon thanked the ferryman and Graves and gritted his teeth at the commotion as he advanced down the docks into the throngs filling up at the mouth of the outer gates. He felt practically naked being so far from the woods. Not even a mutter from a spirit creature. He had not expected to hear any, though.

Within the portcullis, there were a dozen black-robed Rikes of Seithrall speaking to everyone who entered and exited. They had rings on their fingers with dull black stones, which purportedly allowed them to divine falsehoods uttered in their ears. Annon wondered if the powers of the rings were just legends to frighten the people into being honest. The crowds jostled him. He waited sullenly in line until it was his turn to speak to one of the Rikes, anxious to get past the throng.

"A Druidecht, excellent. Seithrall's blessing be upon you." This was said with a wry and discourteous smile. There was no love between the Rikes and the Druidechts. "Have you ever been to Kenatos, Druidecht?"

"No."

"What is the purpose of your visit then?"

"I am here to see my uncle."

"What is his profession?"

Annon smiled blandly. "I believe you may know him. He is called Tyrus of Kenatos."

The Rike started, his eyes widening with shock. He blinked several times, as if he was not sure he had heard Annon correctly. "Indeed," came a curt reply. "Your uncle may be found in the Paracelsus Towers. Do you see it there, to the west of the temple? There?"

Annon did. The city was built on a hill in the middle of the lake, as so it rose before him in a crisscross of streets and buildings. Despite the plumes of sooty smoke, the air was clear enough to see an enormous keep with four ornate spires rising from each corner, the capstones forked. It stood prominently by itself, rising up from the island like a torch. It certainly lacked the massive bulk of the temple, which was the dominating presence of the skyline at the crest. But it was only barely inferior in intricacy and design. The temple was made of glistening white granite, full of sculpted walls, towers, interconnecting bridges, and iron-capped parapets. How many from Stonehollow had been hired to build it, he wondered. How many centuries had they labored?

Annon nodded and was bid to enter the city.

Kenatos teemed with life, a mix of all the races together. Most were young, his age, born after the last Plague. There were Cruithne and Preachán, easily seen. The Cruithne were big and sturdy, each weighing nearly as much as a horse, so they never rode. They were not overly tall, nor were they short. Their skin glistened grayish-black. While their skin was all the same color, their hair varied from pale blond to coarse brown. Never red and never black. They were an inventive people, creating machines powered by fire or water that milled grain. They were slow and ponderous in their walking, but incredibly strong. Their footfalls rattled the ground.

The Preachán were a contrast, with fair skin and ruddy hair. They were not a tall race, nor were they heavy like the Cruithne. They were lithe and quick, slipping through the crowds like quicksilver, hawking goods and huddled in clusters, casting dice with each other. They were incessantly talking, trading, bargaining, and most often, deceiving, as Reeder put it.

Not far after crossing the gates, one Preachán had tried to sell Annon a new pair of boots since his looked so worn out. Moments after shooing him away, another had come offering to buy his talisman for five hundred pents, then quickly doubled and then tripled the price. He was accosted third by a Preachán who offered to guide him to his destination since he was new. Graves was right about them. Annon was a newcomer, but he was no fool. He ignored them and used the distinctive spires of the towers as his guide.

There were also Vaettir in Kenatos, though they were few in number; most of them were Bhikhu. They wore the traditional gray garb of their order, and they patrolled the streets of Kenatos, looking for wrongdoing and offering assistance to those in need. The Vaettir were a tall race, dark-skinned and black-haired, but they did not have the same ashy complexion as the Cruithne. Those who were not Bhikhu wore their hair long and straight, their eyes slightly pointed, always dark. Some had high cheekbones. Others had flat noses. There were varieties that Annon could not understand because he was not from Silvandom. Only the Vaettir could live there permanently.

With the advent of nightfall, Annon was surprised when light appeared suddenly from atop tall posts with domes of glass. The light was bright, and all of the posts illuminated together at the same moment. There was no smoke. Annon was amazed. All throughout the city, the lights had illuminated at once, turning the hazy dusk into a new dawn. More interestingly, the domes of glass did not give off any smoke or steam. Annon approached one, staring up at the light, trying to determine the source. But it was too tall to see. The light did not shimmer or waver, like a flame would. It was cold and beautiful, like spirit magic.

He observed some Preachán watching him, and he quickly went on his way before they found something else to try and sell him. He was curious about the lights that glowed all around him. The whole of Kenatos was an impossible jumble of lopsided houses, some built of stone and some of rotting timber and pitch. Chimneys jutted into the sky, spewing smoke. Reeking garbage cluttered the cobbled streets. Carts clacked and rumbled, accompanied by shrieks and warnings, jangling harnesses, and the distant peal of bells. The light from the domes cast away the thickening shadows. Kenatos never slept, it seemed.

Annon wandered the city slowly, realizing that he was not making good time to the Paracelsus Tower. When he finally reached it, the doors were locked and no one answered after he pounded with his fist. The tower had a portcullis for a gate; Annon could see a shriveled oak tree in the courtyard beyond. It was dead, the heavy limbs barren of leaves, the bulky branches spiky and thick with clumps of mistletoe. It was a sullen-looking tree, and Annon pitied it. It was strange to find such a mature oak in the middle of the city.

Leaving the tower behind, Annon sought a nearby inn off of the main road and was not as fortunate as he was with the ferryman. He did not have to pay for the lodging as long as he slept in the common room, but he was required to pay for his meal. He did, without complaint, and had an ill night's sleep on the floor.

During the night, a Preachán ventured too near him, testing to see if he was asleep. Annon heard the other approach and opened his eyes, staring at him coldly. The fellow studied him, wondering if it was worth the bother to rob a Druidecht, and then decided to move on, slipping from person to person for something to steal. Annon's hands tingled with heat, but he kept a tight rein on his disgust and waited for the passion to subside. In the woods, a spirit would have protected him and frightened the intruder away. He could not wait to leave.

In the morning, Annon vacated the inn and returned to the Paracelsus Tower. The portcullis was open and he passed beneath it warily, staring up at the sharp spikes as he passed. He paused at the oak, running his palm across the husk-like bark. It looked decayed and withered, a sad replica of a once-mighty tree. To the Druidechts, the oak was a sacred tree. Why was it there? How had it come to be in the courtyard? Or had the tower been built around it? There were four simple walls surrounding it, rising up with huge towers in each corner. Which one belonged to his uncle?

"Hold there, friend. State your business."

A Cruithne guard had been waiting on the inner side of the portcullis, his skin and armor so dark he blended in with the shadows until he spoke. It startled Annon that the tree had distracted him so much.

"I have no business, only matters to discuss with Tyrus. He is expecting me."

The Cruithne was no taller than Annon, but at least twice as wide. His upper body cast a shadow across Annon. "Your name?"

"Tell him his nephew is here. Thank you."

Annon tried to calm his nervousness. It had been ten years since they had met. What would Tyrus look like? How would he act around his nephew? What possible reason could he have for sending Reeder to find Annon? There were more questions than answers. Had Tyrus tried to contact him earlier and failed?

The Cruithne lifted a jeweled ring to his mouth and spoke to it in low tones.

"Greetings, Druidecht. Are you lost?" said a voice from behind him.

Annon turned sharply, angry that another person surprised him. It was an older man with well-silvered hair and an elaborately embroidered black tunic. A chained amulet hung from his neck with a green gem fastened to the front that shimmered like glass. He was tall and rose-cheeked. He was an Aeduan, like Annon was. That was how one referred to his race, which was a mix of all the others and lacked the innate magic of the Vaettir, Cruithne, and Preachán.

"No, I am here to see my uncle. Tyrus Paracelsus."

The older man looked startled. He glanced at the Cruithne guard, who nodded in the affirmative. "Your uncle, you say? Strange indeed. He is in the northeast tower. That one."

Annon nodded his gratitude and walked toward the stone entryway at the base of the tower. He was greeted by an assistant there who used a mallet to sound a single tone on a metal gong at the base of the stairwell. The sound echoed up the shaft. After a moment, a bell chimed from the blackness above, and the assistant motioned for Annon to ascend the steps.

Sweat beaded on his forehead as he mounted the steps, going higher and higher into the vast tower. There were no windows, but the way was illuminated by little vials of light inserted into the walls. It was the only way to describe them. The vials were glass and were stoppered with little copper footings, sculpted by artisans. Each one illuminated the way to the next and then extinguished after Annon passed, leaving him in a small cone of light as he went. Annon stopped and studied a vial, sensing spirit magic as he had in the city the night before.

When he reached the top of the steps, he confronted a heavy door, gouged with knicks and scratches. In several places, it seemed it had been hacked at with an ax and then sanded down and varnished again. Annon fingered one of the gouges, but as soon as he touched the door, it swung open from within.

And there was Tyrus, seated at a work desk that was crowded with globes of glass of every size and shape, river stones, and glittering gems. There were vials propped within iron stays. Some orbs of glass seemed to contain trapped smoke that writhed and seethed. The room was lit by smokeless orbs and one ornate window, which was open to allow in natural light. There was a cushioned window seat, full of stacks of worn leather books that prevented anyone from sitting there.

"Hello, Uncle," Annon said as nonchalantly as he could, hoping fervently that his uncle would not notice his trembling hands.

"Don't you believe that there is in some men a deep so profound as to be hidden even to them in whom it is? I believe this for I know those who are called by their order—Paracelsus. Even they cannot fully explain how they understand the arcane lore that they have recovered. Only that they know it in their bones. The very first known of their order was a deep and brilliant man called Celsus, a Cruithne man from the deserts beyond the mountains of Alkire. The record he wrote is still contained in the Archives of Kenatos."

– Possidius Adeodat, Archivist of Kenatos

IV

Tyrus looked up from the globes on his worktable, meeting his nephew's eye. Annon thought he saw a glint of satisfaction—like one a fisherman would display after discovering a fish had swallowed the bait.

"Annon," Tyrus said, dipping his head slightly while fingering a vial and setting it back on the ironwork. He looked almost exactly as Annon remembered him from the last time they had met, the same amber-brown hair and beard flecked with gray. He was a rawboned man, a giant of a man, his very presence intimidating. His hands looked strong enough to crush Annon's, yet they handled the glass with a deftness that belied his size. His eyes were piercing and greenish-gray, a mix of dawn and grass that probed Annon instantly, measured him, and found him lacking. "Get the door, will you?" he commanded, returning to some work on his desk, sorting a tray of gemstones by size.

Annon's temper began to simmer at the contemptuous greeting. But he was eighteen, not eight. A man now. He pushed at the nicked door and it slid shut with a firm thud.

The floor was made of stone tiles, arranged in a complicated succession of angles, but Annon noticed obvious scorch marks throughout. It was swept and showed no dust. He expected the air to smell musty, but instead it contained a strange mix of fragrances— like cooking spices and flowers he could not name, as well as the hint of wood wax. The books on the window seat were of various sizes, but all bound in leather with ornate gold fluting at the corners. Some were quite hideworn and others relatively new. Annon could not discern a speck of dust except for on the windowsill.

Annon approached a bronzework brazier, admiring the craftsmanship. "Your accomodations are lavish. You've actually managed to seclude yourself from the city, which is not an easy feat. I don't think I can even smell it up here."

Tyrus smiled at the remark, intent on a glass globe containing a wraithlike substance, and then he rose from the table. He was taller than Annon, but only barely. There was no sign of pain in his expression, no stoop to his back. He looked hale and strong for a man past his prime.

The curtains by the window were velvet with threaded tassels that secured them to tall iron rings. The room would be quite dark if they were closed. Other than the brazier, there was no fireplace, but narrow vents in the ceiling above the room. A section of wall was pocked, as if something heavy had smashed into it, and ribbons of cracks ran through it. Annon had no idea what sort of work his uncle really did. Another door in the wall behind the desk probably led to his sleeping chamber. There were no gouge marks in it.

"You already know that I'm a terrible uncle," Tyrus said matter-of-factly. "I faced those limitations a very long time ago. You look well. Did you have any trouble along the way here? The taverns are ripe with tales from the kingdoms beyond. The dangers that walk the land..."

"There was more danger within the city than without," Annon said. He waited for Tyrus to explain. He did not want to appear overly anxious to hear Tyrus's news or too eager.

"What news in Wayland? Any new treaties signed?"

Annon shrugged. "I would not know."

"You do not keep abreast of politics in the King of Wayland's court then?"

"I am a Druidecht, Uncle. My place is the politics of nature. I can tell you about a beaver's dam that was disturbed by woodcutters. Does that interest you?"

"Not really."

Annon knew his uncle was testing him. He did not want to play games. He knew if he waited long enough, the truth would come out. He was not disappointed.

"Why not cut to the quick? I sent for you for two reasons, Annon. You barely know me, and that is my fault. But it's not that I don't have interest in you, lad. My…responsibilities in the tower are only getting heavier. I am not free to come and go as I would wish. My work keeps me confined to Kenatos."

He glanced down at the tabletop and then withdrew a thin golden circle with a cut in the middle—a hoop. He sighed. "I probably should have done this earlier, but it is too late for regrets." Tyrus looked at Annon fiercely, his expression no longer calculating. He looked deadly earnest. "You see, boy…you have a sister. I should have spoken of her before, but I did not. But now it is out in the open."

There was no way to prepare for such news, so it struck Annon in the pit of his stomach and nearly stole his voice. For a moment, he could not breathe. The words buzzed in his ears. He stepped forward, his eyes narrowing. "What?"

"I believe you heard and understood me."

Tyrus had always been his only relation. His parents were dead. He had been told that explicitly. The Plague had taken his father. Sadness had killed his mother. Emotions flooded inside his chest, but the chief of them was rage. Blood-scalding, fire-seething, implacable rage.

"Her name is Hettie."

"I cannot believe that you..."

"Let me finish, Annon."

"You tell me I have a sister as if you are commenting on the weather. For pity's sake, how do you think this makes me feel about you?"

Annon tried desperately to tame the anger roiling inside. A sister? How could that even be possible? Was it some sort of trick? Tyrus was the sort who manipulated others for his own ends. Reeder had warned him of that, but surely Reeder had not known. His loyalty was to Annon, not Tyrus. He would have told him if he had a sister.

"You are angry."

"Obviously that matters very little to you, or you would have told me earlier. This is outrageous. I'm not sure I should even believe you," Annon said, his voice nearly choking with rage and humiliation. "Surely, Uncle, you would have said something before now if it were true."

"A liar, am I?" Tyrus said, his eyes like flint. "Really, Annon, I told you before that you needed to master your temper. This will not do."

"How did you expect me to react?" Annon said, his voice shaking. The emotions spun and twisted him. He took a step forward, not sure what he would do.

A glass globe on the varnished desk suddenly lit with orange light. It was bright, like the sparks from a blacksmith's anvil. The light darted and bounced against the curve of the glass, toward Annon, as if it were a little bee stinging in rage.

Tyrus scowled with annoyance. "Be still," he muttered and fetched a dark velvet rag to cover the globe. "You are angry and rightly so. I owe you an explanation. I was attempting that when you began spitting at me." He glanced over some of the other globes, which also started to flicker awake with light. He whistled a low tone, and then began to warp it into a tune, a haunting yet soothing melody. He glanced at Annon and then scooped something up from the table.

Tyrus held up the golden hoop. "You are not the only one who has known a life of pain, Annon. I was raised in an orphanage here in Kenatos. My sister brought me here as an infant to earn wages scribing languages. My brother...to be honest, I would rather not even talk about him. I know about loneliness and unfulfilled hopes. I overcame them, and I have prospered here. You can even give me some credit in choosing your mentor. Now tame your feelings. Master yourself. We do not have much time, and you need to understand something. You told me that you know of beavers and woodcutters, but what do you know of the Romani?"

Annon struggled against his feelings, for he desperately still wanted to lash out at Tyrus. Sweat trickled down his ribs as he battled to tame himself. Irritation clung to his voice. "Everyone knows of the Romani. They run goods between kingdoms, except for Silvandom. They are worse than thieves."

"About their customs? Do you know what this is?"

"It is an earring. Romani wear them, the boys as well as the girls." Annon was impatient. He wanted to know about his sister, not the Romani. "Their ears are pierced at a young age, as babies, I believe. I've met several caravans through Wayland, though never trusted them. I was warned not to."

"You are correct. The Romani travel the lands and move goods from one place to another. They steal anything that has value. Give it a thought, Annon, but you are probably still too angry. What has the most value in a land routinely cursed with

Plague? Children. They are worth more than gold ducats. The Romani covet children. When they are stolen, they are marked in their ear by a single hoop. This they wear until they are eight, when they are first sold. The fee is for ten years."

Tyrus set down the hoop and waved his hands over several of the glass globes resting in intricate metal stands all over his desk. As his hand passed over them, some flared and flickered. Some dashed against the glass, as if trying to sting his hand. Some glowed brightly and remained lit.

His voice snagged Annon's attention back. "Then the Romani return and take back what was sold. They are sold again at eighteen. This is when their other ear is marked. Two hoops. They are sold again, ten years later. And again. And again. Each time, the price decreases until they are old. Each time, they earn another ring."

"It sounds like a miserable life," Annon said distastefully. "Do they marry?"

Tyrus nodded vigorously. "Absolutely. The Rikes of Seithrall would ban them from Kenatos if they did not. But the marriage only lasts until the term is done. If the husband refuses to pay again, they can be sold to another man."

"What if the child is a boy?"

"We are not speaking of the boys, Annon. We are speaking about the girls because you need to understand this to understand your sister. Hettie was stolen by the Romani when she was a babe. As you are almost eighteen yourself, so is she. You are twins but look nothing alike. It is time for her to be sold for her second hoop."

Annon shook his head, astounded. His emotions were simmering now, but he was still incredulous. "You are serious? She was stolen from you?"

"If I had a black ring like the Rikes wear, I would give it to you. Yes, she was stolen."

"And you are telling me that with all of your resources, you could not reclaim her? You have no small reputation in this city, Uncle."

"Which the Romani know. You do not understand them as well as you pretend."

"I did not pretend to know them. I'm only in shock that you could not hire an army or a band of mercenaries or something to reclaim her."

Tyrus waved his hand over an especially bright globe and a satisfied smile played across his mouth. Annon noticed the thin white scar on his lip. "I really am too busy for all this chatter. Let me be plain with you. She was stolen. You were not. When she was nearly eight, I did hire a Finder to help me track her down. Let's suffice it to say that they demanded a king's ransom for her. I refused to pay it. She was being sheltered, fed, cared for. I left. The Finder went back for her later. He paid for her out of his own purse. Not for me. I never asked him to, as they learned. She has lived with him in the woods, wandering near the lowlands of Alkire for the last ten years. She has become a Finder herself. And so she found me. She's here in the city."

Annon was amazed. He realized he was gripping the edge of Tyrus's table so hard his fingers hurt, and he slowly relaxed his muscles. He had met many Finders in Wayland. They were skilled in tracking, snaring, and hunting animals and occasionally, for the right price, people. "Here?" His heart suddenly panged with regret and longing. He had a sister?

"Not my tower, but here in the city. She is staying at the Bhikhu temple nearby, one that I occasionally squander ducats to support. Hettie can buy her freedom, you see. For one lump sum, she can purchase her freedom forever and no longer have to wear the earring. Of course, you understand that the sum will be outrageous. I am rather famous." He gave Annon a sidelong look. "Here is what I propose. I have no wish to see her sold as a wife or whatever someone may desire her for. But the price is set on one's ability to pay it. I cannot be involved in the deal or the price will be much higher."

"But you *are* involved," Annon said, frustrated. "They no doubt believe she is here. They will attempt to extort you again."

"As I told you, I am unwilling to settle the account myself. If I do not bid for her, then the price will be more reasonably set."

"You would have me do it?" Annon said, a sour smile on his mouth.

"How many ducats do you own, pray tell?" Tyrus chuffed to himself, wagging his finger over a globe as it continued to try and sting him with its spark-like light. "No, I was not thinking that at all. There is another way to buy her freedom. I know many things, being here in the tower. Many things that were whispered of in the past. There was another Paracelsus long ago, you know. A Cruithne, if you believe it, named Drosta. He was a good man. He left a great treasure in the mountains. The Romani learned of it and have been searching for it."

Again he paused, tending the globes one by one. His eyebrow arched as he looked at Annon.

"You know where it is?"

"I know a man who knows where it is," he replied cryptically. "And I know the key words that will open the door to it. The man is not in Kenatos, but lives in the east, in Havenrook. I have told your sister about him and encouraged her to seek Drosta's treasure to buy her freedom. Do not call me sentimental. You know I am not." He continued to look at the globes and methodically covered each with a velvet shroud. "As I said, she is staying at the temple orphanage, the Bhikhu temple. I have asked the master to send someone to protect her on her journey. I thought you might want to know this, as their journey will require a great deal of travel out of doors. A Druidecht would be useful, so I sent Reeder to find you before she leaves tomorrow."

Annon slid his finger along the smooth wood of the desk, staring at one of the little globes that was still uncovered. He reached his finger toward it, and the wisp of light responded immediately, throbbing into several shades of color: blue, then purple, and then lavender.

"What are these?" Annon asked, his finger nearly touching the glass. "They seem sentient."

"If you ask a Druidecht about his craft, he will say it is merely Druidecht and nothing more. Do you expect a Paracelsus to be any different? Please do not touch the glass. They are fragile things."

Annon was tempted to. He stared at the color and the comforting shade. Was it merely a bauble, some craft intended to delight a wealthy man's little girl? His finger nearly grazed it.

"Where is the Bhikhu temple?" Annon asked simply.

Tyrus gave him a knowing smile.

Annon frowned. He had the very real feeling that he was being manipulated. "You are withholding too much of the story from me. There is much more to this than you are saying."

Tyrus steepled his fingers over his mouth. "I can only reveal so much at this time. For your own sake. You will have to trust me. Maybe later I will be able to explain what you wish to know."

"Trust you? That is a bold request. How can I possibly trust you? Surely there is something else you can give me. At least tell me why you did not tell me before."

He shook his head. "I cannot. I have spent far too much time already. You do not understand the nature of my obligations and duties. I truly have very little time. You must trust me, Annon. Will you aid your sister?"

Annon stared at him as if he were mad. "You may be a terrible uncle, but I will not be a terrible brother. I will see her now."

"The highest possible stage in moral culture is to realize that we ought to control our thoughts. And no group does this better, in my opinion, than the Bhikhu. This order originated thousands of years ago and was the chief offering of the Vaettir to the establishment of Kenatos. It is said among the Bhikhu that the Vaettir can fly because their thoughts are so elevated. My observations, on the contrary, lead to a more prosaic conclusion. I have witnessed that their ability to float in the air is simply an act of respiration. They inhale and rise. They exhale and sink. It is a strange form of buoyancy that other races experience in bodies of water. Only Vaettir-born have this trait, and thus, the Vaettir make superior Bhikhu. I have been to the training yards and seen younglings race along the ground and then scamper up a wall as if it were not perpendicular to the ground. It is fascinating to observe. One may call their natural power 'magic.' In my experience, what is called magic is not contrary to nature, but only contrary to what we know about nature."

– Possidius Adeodat, Archivist of Kenatos

V

Paedrin saw the girl from the corner of his eye, smothered in shadows against the blazing noonday sun. She moved beneath the covered walk while he was in the middle of the training yard. He noticed the bounce of her hair and her tightly folded arms, and then he saw the gouged staff swinging at his eyes. Had he blinked at that moment, it would have broken his nose. Arching his spine, bending his knees, Paedrin leaned back as the staff whistled just over the tip of his nose. With so much backward momentum, he had no choice but follow it up with a flip, kicking out with his legs before landing on his feet in a low squat.

Another staff went over his head, and Paedrin lunged forward, striking with his fists, three times in rapid motion. The other Bhikhu crumpled and dropped the staff, which Paedrin snatched and spun around from one end. It clacked with another staff and soon the two were sweeping, striking, and parrying until Paedrin caught his opponent's fingers with an especially well-placed blow, making him yelp and drop his weapon. There she was again, walking down the aisle, arms folded, face intent on the ground, never once looking at the training yard. Her stride was quick and impatient.

Three more charged him the next moment, staves whirling dangerously in circles. It looked impressive to an outsider, but it was easy to disrupt as he jammed his staff into the wheeling wooden spokes. One strike to the chest and the fellow grimaced with pain. Another on his toe with a crunch that probably meant his toenail was cracked and would fall off in a few days. With the staff held before him, Paedrin disarmed the second and third attackers, a series of dizzying blows that were too fast to follow, let alone defend. Crack—crack—clatter. Another staff down.

Paedrin spun on his heel, bringing his weapon over his shoulder and dropping a silently approaching fourth opponent. The fifth and final Bhikhu charged him, face twisted with vengeance. Paedrin planted the end of his staff, took in his breath, and lifted himself up on the pole, swinging his body around it once, his foot clipping the last fighter in the temple, dropping him; Paedrin proceeded to swivel around the staff, coiling around the upper end like a lizard, balancing on it like a pennant of flesh. He made a perfect stance, shoulders back, legs locked, arm extended for balance, fingers raised up. He clung to the top of the staff, held his breath to keep his body floating, enjoying the feel of the sun on his neck and the sweat trickling down his back.

And not once—even once—did the girl bother to look his way and notice his triumph. Still concealed in the shadows, she hastily disappeared into the causeway of the temple and vanished.

He let out his breath and slid gracefully down the length of the staff.

"Did she look at you that time?" grumbled a voice as one eye peeped open from one of the fallen Bhikhu.

"Not even a glance," Paedrin said.

"I think you broke my toe," came another voice, outraged. "And she didn't even look?"

"Not once," Paedrin said, hoisting his arms on each side of the staff, like he was about to tote water barrels on each end. "Even if we were all wearing nothing but our smallclothes, she wouldn't have looked. She's *determined* not to."

Another of his brothers rose to a sitting position, shaking the dust from his dark hair. "I almost had you, Paedrin. What if I had broken your nose and knocked you flat?"

Paedrin smirked. "The day you can hit me, Sanchein, is the day I *will* drop my smallclothes and then walk into the girl training yard with nothing on. You are slow and heavy-footed."

"It is not our fault we were not born Vaettir." It was another of his friends, the tone sulky.

Paedrin grinned. "Well, we cannot *all* be wise, fast, and sleek as serpents. If you work really hard for the next year, I may let you sand the calluses off my heels."

"Where is your humility?" Sanchein said with a sniff.

"You just saw her go through those doors," Paedrin said, pointing the way with one end of the staff. "She is my humility. My bane. My mystery. Can you believe that she has been here for two days and I still do not know her name? No one does, except Master Shivu, and it would be the height of rudeness to ask him only out of pure curiosity." Paedrin spun the staff around, whipping it as fast as a scythe in circles on each side. He slammed the butt down on the flagstones and scowled. "There is something undeniably unfair about being tortured by a girl."

"Is she from Kenatos, do you think?" asked Beshop.

"No," said Sanchein.

"How do you know?"

"I just know."

"But how do you know?"

Paedrin hissed a low whistle to shut him up. It would go on for hours that way. He spun around again, slowly this time, full of restless energy. The staff was part of him, a tether, a kite string that kept him from floating away when he gathered and held his breath. He started rising again, slowly, gracefully, until he balanced on the end of the staff, his feet pointed toward the sky. He loved that feeling—the almost-flying feeling of being a Vaettir. He was the only one in the temple who was orphaned as a boy, unclaimed by any Vaettir family in the city. Peculiar, for certain, but Paedrin did not care. The temple was his home and his family. His lungs burned and he slowly exhaled, his body coming back down to earth.

He gripped the staff and stared at the door she had gone through. "That is enough," he said simply.

"What is enough?" Beshop asked, coming around.

"It is already turning black. Paedrin, you broke my toe," muttered Jaendro, still sitting on the flagstones. "Give me your hand, you sod! I need help standing!"

"What is enough?" Beshop pressed, wiping sweat from his forehead, looking at what Paedrin was looking at.

He gave Beshop the staff and started after the girl.

Who she was, Paedrin had no idea. She had appeared at the temple orphanage, wearing woodcutter's garb and keeping mostly to herself. How old was she? Paedrin guessed she was his age, or maybe slightly older. Twenty, perhaps. The curl and sneer of her lip made her seem older. As did the disdain with which she treated everyone and everything within the temple. She had dark hair cut past her shoulders, thick and heavy and slightly curled. She was Aeduan, he thought with a snort, nothing to be so proud of. Yet she walked with all the confidence of a Vaettir, as if she belonged to the orphanage as its overseer and not as a guest who could not afford lodging in the city beyond the walls. *That* was the only reason someone *chose* to sleep on the floor, on an uncomfortable mat, on hard flagstones, day after day.

Paedrin pulled open the doors and went into the momentary blindness of the deeply shadowed interior. The temple was a hodgepodge of structures, mostly one level tall with vaulted roofs, interconnecting to each other like the sluices they used to control water in the city.

From the roof, one could see a great deal of the city below—its serpentine maze of streets, squares, water fountains, and courtyards. From the roof, where Paedrin often went to be alone, he could see the vast lake in the distance and dream of the kingdoms and haunted wilderness beyond. The thought of Plague did not terrify him. He feared nothing except remaining trapped in the city his entire life, disciplining pickpockets and protecting the city from enemies of Kenatos. In his heart, he would rather be with his own people in Silvandom. But he owed the orphanage and the city his duty.

The dusty tiles met his sandals soundlessly as he maneuvered past columns and enormous urns. He listened and heard her voice, then changed his direction. He had heard her speak occasionally, and she spoke with a strong accent, a wild accent, as if she were from some unmannered country. Yet if that were so, why did she comport herself with the disdain of someone very wealthy? Was she in disguise, perhaps? That kindled Paedrin's curiosity even more. Out of favor with a wealthy father, a duke in Wayland? He could not help but let his imagination run wild.

He heard Master Shivu's voice next, a comforting but firm tone in it. He was resisting her request. He was patient about it, as he always was, but he was telling her no.

"I can pay," he heard her say. "When the job is done."

"We have little need for treasure, little one. It is contrary to our order to accept payment of any kind." He was excruciatingly patient. Paedrin did not understand this, considering how difficult little orphaned boys could be. "It is our duty to serve the races."

"But I am in need of a service for hire," the girl insisted. "It will not be a long journey. A fortnight or two. I need a protector."

Master Shivu came into view, his head bent thoughtfully, his wrinkled eyes warm with sympathy. His hair was a patchwork of silver and white stubble. "What protection do you need that these walls cannot provide?" He held his hand out, gesturing toward the structure around them. "If you are hunted, you are safe here. The Bhikhu will defend you. You are an orphan, as you said. There is work for you to do right here among us. There is no need to venture into the woods."

"But I do not *belong* here," she said, her voice betraying a hint of anger. "Nor am I safe here from my enemies. You do not understand. I turn eighteen soon."

Paedrin licked his lips, intrigued beyond calculation. If he lingered much longer, he would learn more about this girl. But it was rude to delay his approach. Even though he walked on cat's feet, she still heard him. Her expression shifted at once from sincere desperation to annoyance.

"Forgive me for disturbing you, Master," the girl said and started to go the other way, abandoning Master Shivu with a quick toss of her head.

It was in the moment Paedrin saw the subtle gleam in her right ear—the gold earring. Only one.

The pieces began to assemble in his mind.

"A word before you go, child," Shivu said, stalling her.

"Yes?"

"I would like you to meet your protector." Master Shivu opened his palm and gestured. "This is Paedrin."

"He's Vaettir," she said, sizing him up with cool eyes. The tone in her voice was insulting to him.

"I am," he answered, closing the gap between them. "And you are Romani, though you try to hide it. What is my assignment, Master Shivu? Protecting a special caravan?"

Her eyebrows arched. "I meant that you were Vaettir-born and that our people have a history. I do not see why he chose you."

"I chose Paedrin," Master Shivu said, "because he is the best our temple has to offer your uncle. He has been trained in all martial weapons as well as the subtle ways of hand and foot. He is nearly done with all of his philosophical training and will soon be introduced to the city as a defender. There is no one else I would trust more with your safety."

"Has he traveled beyond the city before?" she asked, her voice slightly mocking.

"I am right here," Paedrin said, not sure which emotion he wanted to subdue more—his excitement to be chosen or his animosity toward this girl. "No, I have not…"

"I guess this is the best I can expect then," she said, interrupting him. She nodded to him and then to Master Shivu and turned to leave.

Master Shivu waited until she disappeared through the archway leading to the female quarters.

"You should not lurk in shadows, Paedrin," Master Shivu said with no malice.

"Was I lurking?" Paedrin asked, smiling broadly to hide a grin. "I was trying to be respectful and not intrude on your conversation, Master."

"You were lurking, Paedrin." Master Shivu began to walk away, his colorful amber robes fluttering. Master Shivu was a Vaettir as well, so old his stubs of hair were white as snow instead of black. He had a flat nose and high cheekbones. "I should have told our guest that good manners or soft-spokenness is *not* one of your skills."

"Our guest is Romani," Paedrin said, keeping pace with him as they crossed the vast hall. "What do they know of good manners?"

"She is Romani, but she wears her hair long to cover the earring," he explained. "She wraps her spirit in many layers, burrowing deeper into her cocoon. She is safe here, but she does not believe she is safe anywhere. She does not trust. A sad existence, Paedrin. Life is about laughter; it is about believing what one does not see. Are you happy here, Paedrin?"

The young Bhikhu smiled. "I am, Master." He did his best impersonation of Master Shivu. "Felicity is produced not so much by great pieces of good fortune that seldom happen as by little advantages that occur every day."

Master Shivu laughed. "You mimic my tone very well. I enjoy your humor, Paedrin."

"I enjoy yours as well, Master. It must be difficult being a Romani. To have a family and yet be afraid of it. Has she run away then?"

"Hmmm? No, she is not fleeing her people or her traditions. She is trying to solve her problem in the way of the world. The way of Kenatos. With money." He rubbed his fingers together, as if stroking two coins. "She imagines herself to be captive to traditions and customs that were defined by her people. I told her she is already truly free. She does not need to buy her freedom from anyone regardless of her age. We are free, each of us. I am free to enjoy a cup of tea with some lemon juice and a taste of honey. Would you care to enjoy freedom with me?"

"I would," he said, chafing a bit, for he wanted to float up to the roof and let out a scream of triumph at the thought of leaving Kenatos. But it was rude saying no to Master Shivu.

"That would be pleasant. There is much we need to discuss. I have received a request from Tyrus Paracelsus. He has asked that I provide an escort to his niece. I have chosen you for this assignment, obviously."

Paedrin looked at his master with eager eyes. "I am honored, Master, that you chose me. I am only seventeen. I thought I was not permitted to leave the monastery until eighteen. You have always given me that as the answer when we discussed this before."

"That would normally be the case," Master Shivu said. "But this is special. Of all the students, you are the best equipped for such a journey. First, you have always longed to visit the world outside Kenatos. This may be your only opportunity. Second, you are Vaettir-born, which gives you abilities that will be useful in such a task. Finally, you are also the most accomplished Bhikhu student I have trained in many, many years. I think you are ready."

Paedrin flushed with pride. "As accomplished as Aboujaoude?"

"He was accomplished and humble. You, my son, are ambitious. And proud. And your feet smell strongly of dung, if I am being perfectly honest." There was a gleam in his eye that made Paedrin grin in response.

"Tell me more of this assignment, Master. I have heard of Tyrus of Kenatos. Tyrus Paracelsus, as he is called. He is an important patron of the temple. They say he was raised in an orphanage too, one run by the Rikes."

"I believe so," Master Shivu said. "That was long ago. He shares his great wealth with us, with this temple, to settle a debt he believes he owes us."

Paedrin smirked. "For a wise man, he is foolish. What debt could he owe us?"

Master Shivu smiled. "As you well know, there is no true debt. It is as with the girl; he believes he owes it. What was given was given freely. What was lost was lost freely. You must safeguard his niece. See her safely on her journey."

Paedrin wrinkled his brow. "Where are we going, Master? Not Silvandom, surely."

The bell attached to the outer doors rang, sending a shudder through the walls. The temple did not receive many visitors, so everyone would be wondering who it was.

Master Shivu turned and looked back at him, as if he were being especially dense. "That may be a messenger from Tyrus. You leave at dawn for Havenrook. It is the seat of Romani power." He reached out and rested his hand on Paedrin's shoulder. "It is a dangerous town, Paedrin. Even the road leading there through the woods is dangerous. Be careful. You are used to the laws and customs of Kenatos. They will not be the same there. You are used to the city and its shops, food, and mix of people and races. It will not be the same out there. Remember your training. Remember the ways of the Uddhava."

With a self-satisfied smile, Paedrin bowed to his master. "Thank you for choosing me. I will not disappoint you."

Master Shivu turned to the main doors as the bell sounded again. There was something in his eyes that Paedrin could not make out. It was a look that was almost anxious. "We do this as a favor to Tyrus Paracelsus to help secure a young woman's freedom. Not for any reward. Remember that, Paedrin."

"There is an occupation prevalent in nearly every kingdom called a 'Finder.' It is actually a shortened name from a Preachán word that is practically meaningless now, as the Preachán have adopted the Aeduan tongue as their own. A Finder is trained to 'find' what is lost—be it a person, an object that is stolen, or a safe path through the maze of the city. They even have a guild. Finders also exist in the wilderness, and their services are highly prized and well paid. It was said by one of the wise ancients that it is the very perfection of a man to find out his own imperfections. In a sense, that is what Finders do, but to others, not themselves. Even the tiniest impression of a boot heel can bring a criminal to justice or retrieve that which is lost. The most subtle and patient are the best Finders."

– Possidius Adeodat, Archivist of Kenatos

VI

ettie returned to her barren sleeping chamber and sat down on the reed mat, leaning back against the rough stone wall. Master Shivu had chosen a Vaettir to be her companion on the journey to Havenrook. It was a disaster in one sense, but a workable one. He was quick to speak and take offense. That made him a danger to himself and to her goal.

She rubbed her eyes, trying to clamp down her burgeoning resentment. The meeting with Tyrus had not gone as she expected. The stay at the temple had not either. There was so much to accomplish in so short a time. Her fingers strayed to her left earlobe, untouched by a pinprick or an earring. She had a fortnight to win her freedom. It almost seemed too much to hope for.

Biting her lip, she let her head rest back against the stone wall, staring up at the cobwebs and the dust in the corners. There were no windows, only open slats near the ceiling allowing the sunlight and breeze to enter unimpaired. She recalled seeing shutters on the exterior and thought how cold the temple would be during the winter. It was a life devoid of comforts. At least she had spent the last ten years in a cabin in the mountains of Alkire, always with plenty of wood to stay warm, providing she expended the effort to chop it.

A bell sounded from the outside, grabbing her attention instantly. Bells were harbingers of change in the city. She had been told that certain bells announced the arrival of Plague and that the city would be locked down as a result. This was a quiet bell, and she recognized it as belonging to the front gate. Was it Tyrus come to see her again? To provide the information he had withheld on how to open Drosta's treasure?

It was all such a riddle and a game. It frustrated her. Find a Preachán in Havenrook named Erasmus. He would know the location of the lost treasure. The key to securing it, in whatever form that took, would be given to her Bhikhu protector or to another individual he might enlist in the effort. He had assured her that she would leave on the morrow and she wondered whether the additional aid had arrived. Having the Bhikhu along would prove troublesome and likely aggravating. Adding another? She ran her fingers through her hair and sighed deeply.

Havenrook. Of all the kingdoms in the land, why did it have to be there?

It was not a long wait, but she did hear the sound of clapping sandals and the softer noise of sturdy walking boots. She listened closely, recognizing the footfall of Master Shivu. The other sound, she did not recognize. The step was too light to be Tyrus. One of his minions then, she thought.

The two stopped at her door; she heard a knock. She rose, tried to brush some of the travel dust from her pants, and opened the door, ready to dislike the person immediately. Most people hated Romani, and though she tried to obscure the fact that she was one, she could count on her uncle disclosing it.

As the door opened, she caught her breath.

Master Shivu, she recognized. But the young man next to him was her own age and bore a striking resemblance to her own reflection, especially his facial features. He was a little taller than her, his hair the true reddish hue that hers was when she did not dye it. He had some hair on his face, but definitely not a full beard. She saw the Druidecht talisman immediately.

"My name is Annon," he said, looking at her with an intensity in his eyes that startled her and a depth of emotion in his voice that struck her heart like an arrow bolt. "I am your brother, and I've come to help you."

She stared at him, completely shocked by his sudden appearance. What in all due glory was this? She could not speak. She stared, looking at his features.

He smiled kindly at her and held up his hands. She could see the calluses on his palms. "Our uncle said that you might not be convinced and suggested coming back to the tower; he will fetch a Rike to persuade you. But one look at you, and I know it is true. We look alike. Don't we? We are twins."

She realized her mouth was open. "Where...where are you from?" she asked, almost unable to string her thoughts together. Tyrus was a manipulative and secretive man, but this went beyond anything her imagination could have summoned.

"I was raised in Wayland," he answered. "My mentor was a man named Reeder. I did not learn that I had a sister until a short while ago. Tyrus summoned me to Kenatos two days ago. He told me of your situation and offered a way to free you." He took a step toward her. "I will help you. If you believe what I say."

Master Shivu had a strange smile on his face. He retreated slowly. "You will leave in the morning. I think it may be best if the two of you spoke a little while. I have known Tyrus Paracelsus for many years. There are always reasons for what he does."

Hettie did not doubt that for a single moment.

"Please," she offered, inviting him to enter. He did, glancing at the sparse accommodations with a look of simple pleasure. As a Druidecht he was probably used to sleeping on the forest floor.

"Do you believe what I told you?" Annon asked.

She smiled and tried not to look condescending. "We have a saying among my people. A loud voice can make even the truth sound foolish. I do not need a black ring to know when a man lies. But if you are my brother, then you possess a secret that is persecuted in these lands. Show it to me."

Annon looked at her knowingly. He did not say the words, but she could almost see them spoken in his eyes. A ripple of blue flames danced across his fingers.

Pyricanthas. Sericanthas. Thas.

She held up her own glowing hand, having thought the words as well, and touched her palm against his. She could feel the magic in his blood. Those with the fireblood were not persecuted among the Romani. They had made sure she was taught the Vaettir words at an appropriate age. That she possessed it only increased her value.

His arrival was unexpected. His arrival was almost a dagger thrust in her heart. How had Tyrus managed to keep this secret? What sort of man would do that?

She released her control of the flames, and they vanished from both of their hands.

"Please, sit," she said, gesturing to the reed mat. "We must talk. I need to know everything about you. My name is Hettie, if Tyrus did not tell you. What did he tell you about me?"

Annon seated himself cross-legged on the mat. She joined him, sitting opposite, leaning forward and giving him an eager look. A listening ear was usually all it took to get a man to start speaking. Silencing him, on the other hand, often took a great deal of work.

"That you are Romani, kidnapped at birth, and that you have your first earring. Since we are the same age, you are due for the next and wish to avoid it. He said you were trained as a Finder in Alkire by a man he knows. Despite his wealth and prominence, he refuses to bid for you himself." She saw his eyes narrow at that. Good. "He told me of an abandoned treasure in the mountains of Alkire. He gave me the key words that will open the treasure and implored me not to speak them to anyone until we have arrived there."

"It is no secret that is known to three," Hettie said. "It's another Romani saying. Go on."

"That is it. We seek Erasmus in Havenrook, and I was told he knows where the treasure is but not how to retrieve it."

"I see," Hettie answered. She wondered how delicately she should put it and decided to be bold. "For too long, Annon, I have been in debt. My entire life is a debt. I wish to be free of that debt forever. While I appreciate your help and that you are coming with us, I want to know how much of the treasure you want. If you come with me, you are entitled to a portion…"

Annon's hand grabbed hers. "Not a ducat or a pent. I am not like our uncle. A Druidecht has no need of money, really. Neither do the Bhikhu, I am told. I think Tyrus chose us to help you because we do it freely."

She shook her head warningly. "If a cat had a dowry, she would often be kissed. You say this now, Annon, but I do not know how sizeable this treasure is. I will give you a portion willingly. I just wish to agree right now as to what that is. We must have an understanding. I cannot be indebted to both you *and* the Bhikhu."

"Not a ducat or a pent. I will take none of it. You said you knew a man was lying. I am not like Tyrus. I am a Druidecht. I know the woodlands. I have abilities that can prevent us from facing certain dangers. And if the road gets hard, we both have the fire."

He was sincere. He was probably unwise not to request something from her. But she could not doubt his sense of integrity and commitment. It almost made her feel guilty because she had not been raised the same way. Such a contrast to her experience. It was like finding a butterfly in the middle of the sewers.

Hettie leaned forward and hugged him, shaking her head in disbelief at the unexpected source of help. A twin brother.

She felt his hand tentatively pat her back, as if the show of friendship had embarrassed him. She leaned back, gripping her boot cuffs and rocking slightly. "You grew up in Wayland then? Tell me more."

Annon was grateful for the fat candle that Master Shivu had brought hours before. It had burned down to a little pool of wax, which he and Hettie continued to coax further to provide light. Without being able to see the stars through the slats above, he did not know how close to dawn it was, but it did not matter. They had stayed up all night, talking.

From the dull light of the candle, he could see little edges of color in Hettie's hair that matched his own. When she turned her head and he could see the earring, part of him wanted to snap it off in anger.

"What would the Romani do if you just ran away?" he asked her softly. She was deft at getting him to answer her questions, and he noticed that she always replied in as few words as possible before turning things back to him. He could tell it was a way she protected herself. She drew the focus away from herself.

"There are stories," she said, staring down at her hands. "But they do not teach us what happens. I'm not sure how old you must be before you are trusted with that secret. They do not want me to know." She picked something from the reed mat and flicked it away with her finger. "But where do you hide from the Romani?" she asked, smiling sadly. "Silvandom? No Romani is welcome there. Boeotia? They would probably just as well kill me as help me. Where else does it leave?"

Annon nodded. "The Scourgelands it is."

She narrowed her gaze. "Are you mocking me?"

Annon shook his head. "No, I'm just reminded of something. My mentor warned me about coming to Kenatos. He said that Tyrus might try to persuade me to go to the Scourgelands. I was not expecting this adventure. Have you been to Havenrook?"

Hettie shrugged and made an obscure gesture. "Long ago, before I was sold. The caravans go back and forth through there. I was a child, so I do not know very much about the place. I have heard the road can be dangerous. Have you ever had to use...?" She wiggled her fingers.

Annon shook his head. "If the road goes through a forest, I should be able to help. I do not wish to use the flames if we can avoid it. I would try to talk our way past first."

She gave him an enigmatic look. He could tell she was cautious of her words and slow to reveal her opinions. There was something in her eyes—something that showed the depth of damage the lack of freedom had taken on her mind. Winning her trust would not be easy, even though they were siblings. But Annon was patient and felt that in time she would learn to open up to him more. He hoped so.

"You don't agree with my approach," he said simply.

"The least said, the soonest mended," she said.

"Which means?"

"It's often a man's mouth that broke his nose. We will see how good you are at talking, brother Annon."

A rooster crowed, and they both looked up at the slat on the roof, seeing the shift in the darkness that had come slowly and gradually. Hettie shook her head and chuckled softly to herself.

"What is so funny?" he asked her.

"Another Romani saying. I'm sorry, but I heard so many as a child, I cannot shake them loose from my head. It was a favorite of mine. A cock that crows too early gets a twisted neck."

Annon smiled at that one and rose, wincing at the stiffness in his legs and back. "I am ready to leave this city forever. You?"

She gave him a knowing look. "I have a feeling that we may not have seen the last of Tyrus."

"Many are frightened to travel the roads linking the great cities. There are stories that monsters roam the land, devouring travelers and leaving nothing but their bones. Others say that it is not monsters to fear, but bandits who prey on the weak. I have found in my journeys as a younger man that the road less traveled is often the safest."

– Possidius Adeodat, Archivist of Kenatos

VII

Paedrin stood motionless by the enormous metal doors of the temple, gripping a beaten-up staff with both hands; he waited. And waited. Dawn appeared as a flush in the sky, followed by cocks crowing and a flock of ravens heading east. He stood solidly, hands clenching the rugged wood, his stance firm and respectful. A bag with a single strap bulged against the small of his back, full of foodstuffs gathered from the kitchens, a small pot to boil water, two thin eating sticks, and a spoon carved from bossem wood. It also contained a few small pouches of spices, one of rice, and one of peppercorns. He brought no change of Bhikhu robes, and he wore sandals only because he knew he'd be crossing miles of mucky sewage before leaving Kenatos. After taking mental inventory of his bag for the fiftieth time, he waited. And waited more for his companions to arrive.

A creak from the inner door alerted him, but he did not glance quickly; he just shifted his eyes until he saw them approach from the doorway. Both were cloaked in the manner of the Druidecht, but he recognized the stiff, proud walk of the girl. Their heads were bent low in conversation. As they approached, Paedrin gave them a benign, incurious look, and nodded once. Their bleary eyes revealed that neither had slept that night.

Master Shivu was still abed, but he and Paedrin had traded quips and insults the night before. He nearly smirked at some of the more memorable ones, like the jest about using snails to train the other Bhikhu while Paedrin was away, as they would need something to fill in for his absence. But he dared not smile. Yet.

The footfalls approached, and the amber-haired Druidecht met his gaze. His skin was weathered by the sun, but he had a youthful look. Paedrin estimated that he could leave the Druidecht writhing on the ground in about the same amount of time it took to blink.

"Good morning. My name is Annon."

Paedrin gave him a respectful nod. "I am honored to join you." He looked at the girl. Her eyes were disdainful. He was expecting that. "It is nice to see you again." He stared at her, cocking his head slightly, waiting for her to speak.

She looked at him and said nothing.

"My name is Paedrin," he said to the Druidecht. He gave the girl a short glance.

Still nothing.

He almost smiled. She was a green nut, unwilling to open even a bit.

Annon noticed the exchange and stepped forward. "Have you been to Havenrook by chance, Paedrin?"

Paedrin's ears started to tingle with heat at her rejection, but he kept his composure. Before he could answer, she did.

"He's never left the temple, Annon." Her eyebrow arched at Paedrin. "He knows nothing beyond these walls. I know the way to Havenrook. And I can handle a blade as well as any man."

There it was. The barb, the derision—the withering contempt. It was just as he had expected. He had provoked her the day before, and she was holding a grudge.

He gave her an inconsequential shrug, a slight twitch to his left shoulder. "I have no doubts about your killing ability. The poison in your tongue alone would be suitable if we required *talking* someone to death."

Annon raised his eyebrows, and a smile broadened his face.

Paedrin wasn't finished. "But should we face something particularly lethal, I am certain your looks would stop it dead in its tracks. I feel so much safer being with you."

There it was in response, just as he suspected. She was sensitive about her looks. Best to poke there first. She could not control the sudden blush of heat in her cheeks, though her expression did not change. He had insulted her. How would she respond?

"The Vaettir I have known have always been gentlemen," she replied in a silky voice. "But you share only a portion of their blood, by the look of you. Perhaps you are more Aeduan than me?"

Paedrin kept his face impassive. She fought to draw blood; that much was certain. He attacked her beauty. She attacked his heritage. *Not easily flustered. Good. It was more fun that way.*

"I did not know the Romani were welcome in Silvandom," he answered. "Where else could you have met enough Vaettir to form such an opinion?"

"Indeed," she replied cryptically. She looked at Annon crossly. "We are wasting daylight. This journey should take a fortnight."

Annon looked amused. "I will not be sorry to leave Kenatos behind. I never liked it here. To Havenrook then."

Paedrin nodded, his eyes never leaving Hettie's. There were daggers in those eyes.

By the end of the day, they had crossed leagues of abandoned farmland and reached the fringe of the mountain forests of Alkire. Hawks swooped and soared overhead, and Paedrin longed to join them. He was tempted to suck in his breath and float upward, but he was saving that grace to impress Annon and Hettie later. His sandals dangled from the fabric belt. Walking the cobblestone streets of Kenatos had raised calluses on his feet, and the soft earth and prairie grasses were velvety in comparison. He was amazed at the various forms of life throughout the land—dazzling butterflies zigzagging in the air, curious rodents peeping from holes and gawking at them, and the buzz and drone of bees in their hives. Each was a fascination to Paedrin. The air was crisp and fresh, so different than the soot-filled skies over Kenatos. It was also so very quiet compared to Kenatos—unnervingly so. The huff of their breath as they walked, the chuff of Annon's and Hettie's boots. The constant murmur and roar of the city was long gone. Its absence was noticeable.

They set up camp within the shelter of the woods, Annon and Hettie both working side by side to put up a ring of stones and gather brushwood for a fire. Paedrin was at a loss for what to do, so he separated from them slightly and began practicing some of the complex forms he had learned in the Bhikhu temple. He did Five Animals and Five Elements along with Snapping Crane. Each was a series of intricate moves, which, if broken down into the parts, could be used to fight or subdue one man or many men. It was like a dance. A dangerous dance.

The crackle of flames alerted him that the fire was starting to take. He turned and saw Hettie was gone. Annon fed chips of wood into the growing fire.

"Where did she go?"

The Druidecht looked up from the fire, glanced around, and then continued the motion. "There is a warren of rabbits back the way we came. She is going to kill one for dinner."

Paedrin's stomach twisted. "I do not eat meat."

Annon shrugged. "I noticed some mushrooms and gathered them. There are also different forms of bark, depending on how hungry you are."

"I brought my own food," Paedrin said. "Shouldn't we be going with her?"

Annon looked up at him, curious. "Whatever for?"

"Your uncle wanted me to protect her."

"From wild rabbits?"

"I do not know these woods," Paedrin said, glancing around warily.

"Nothing will approach us unaware, Paedrin. I've seen to that already."

"What do you mean? This is a forest. Any form of creature may be lurking here."

"We share these woods with many kinds of creatures. Not just rabbits and foxes. They know we are here and have granted us safe passage. Should anything threaten us, we will be warned first. As I said, we have no need to worry."

Paedrin looked at him quizzically. "What you say makes no sense to me. I have been with you the entire time. What agreement could you have made?"

Annon smiled. "It is Druidecht, my friend. Just trust me. We will be safe here."

Paedrin was skeptical, but he did not let it show. He crouched down by the budding flames and waved his hand over the flicking tongues. "I know we go to Havenrook, but I know very little else. Can you tell me more about our journey?"

"There is no reason not to tell you. My sister is Romani and desires to buy her freedom. When she turns eighteen, she will be sold again. We seek a man named Erasmus in Havenrook who knows where a treasure is hidden. We must persuade him to help us find it."

Paedrin rubbed his chin thoughtfully. "This man—Erasmus—knows of a treasure. If he knows of it, why has he not claimed it for himself?"

Annon stared down at the fire and then up at Paedrin. "Only a Paracelsus can open the door to where the treasure is hidden. My uncle has given me knowledge that will open it. I expect Erasmus will desire a portion of the treasure as his reward for leading us to it. My aim is to negotiate the terms in our favor."

"Ah," Paedrin said. "You are skilled at negotiations then."

Annon shook his head. "I know very little about that craft. But the Druidecht are known for being the peacemakers within the kingdoms. I will merely help Hettie be sure the arrangement is fair."

Paedrin opened his food sack and rummaged through it for something to eat. "You have not been to Havenrook then either?"

Annon shook his head. "No. I was raised in the woods surrounding Wayland. What do you know about it?"

"I am surprised that your uncle is sending you to negotiate. Havenrook is the home of the Preachán. They are the shrewdest dealers throughout all the kingdoms. Remember the sort that tried to wheedle my staff from me when we were leaving? They wanted the charm around your neck. They always look for a gain with little effort. Personally, I despise them. They are dishonest and cruel. I am not certain they serve some use in this world other than generating copious amount of excrement. They are cunning and ruthless, which again surprises me why your uncle is sending us all into their trading city. I have heard there are no laws in that city. None at all."

Annon rubbed his mouth. "I did not know that."

Paedrin shrugged and tossed a decayed leaf into the hungry flames. "Your uncle did."

Hettie emerged from the woods, holding a dead rabbit by the ears. He flinched inside, seeing the dead thing gripped in her hand. It was a big one.

"Do you want to help me skin it, Paedrin?" she asked in a mocking tone.

"I do not eat meat," he said, his stomach churning with disgust.

"Feeling squeamish?" she asked, dangling the rabbit over him.

He could almost feel its fur against his cheek and resisted the urge to swat it away. Though he was a bit unnerved by the dead thing hovering near his face, he would never admit it. "No, I am merely annoyed by your smell. I had hoped that you would bathe before returning. Mint leaves help remove the stink, you know."

Her eyes narrowed slowly, but she did not stop her attack. "Isn't there some sort of prayer you Vaettir say over dead things?"

"I would be happy to teach you our prayers. Some piety would benefit you."

Paedrin saw Annon stifling a chuckle. Wisely, he kept poking the fire with a stick.

"I did make sure it was dead before I brought it," she said, lifting the rabbit slightly. "I wrung its neck, of course. I did not want you to have to see that."

"It does not shock me at all that you would do that with those hands."

She turned toward the fire, but the pelt brushed against his cheek. Again, he nearly jumped away and swatted it, but he knew she was looking for that reaction. He kept himself perfectly still. And he watched, moment to moment, as she gutted the beast, impaled it on a spit, and then cooked it over the fire. She glanced at him several times, looking for a reaction. He smiled at her and ate some day-old rice with his fingers.

Later that night, as Annon and Hettie slept, Paedrin lay awake, staring at the flickering coals of the fire. He was restless, anxious for the dawn to come. He was sick to his stomach at what he had seen Hettie do to the rabbit. It violated every ethic of the Bhikhu order. Part of him wanted to scream at her, but he would never give in to her taunts.

He stared at her form, the crumpled blanket covering her shoulder. Dark hair fanned over the cloak, which she had stuffed beneath her head as a pillow. Her back was to him, deliberately, and he watched the rise and fall of her breathing. Annon faced him, his eyes closed, his expression pained by his dreams. Paedrin stared at him for a moment, realizing how young they all were. A Druidecht, a Romani, and a Bhikhu on a journey to Havenrook to seek Erasmus. Something was impossibly wrong. There were details that Annon had offered which concerned him. There was much that concerned him.

He would not forget the sly look in Hettie's eyes as she mutilated the rabbit in front of him—and that he did not flinch while she did it. It was a look that said she was impressed by him. He was not sure if he even cared anymore.

"When the kingdoms banded together to create Kenatos, they minted new coins and forged common laws that all could agree to abide. While Kenatos has not authority over any other kingdom, its laws are inviolate within the city itself and the Bhikhu mete out the Arch-Rike's justice. For, you see, in the absence of justice, what is sovereignty but organized robbery?"

– Possidius Adeodat, Archivist of Kenatos

VIII

Waken, Druidecht! The Fear Liath comes!
It was just before midnight, and Annon awoke
to whispers in his mind, his heart surging with
terror. He blinked awake rapidly, sitting up, and listened to the
chittering voices in his mind. A spirit of great power and danger
stalked the woods, sending panic rippling through the denizens
of Mirrowen. The tiny spirits whispered its name—the *Fear
Liath*. It typically hunted high in the mountain passes of Alkire,
but it had sensed intruders in its lair and was hunting them.

Sweat gathered on Annon's brow as he waited, fearfully, for
the warning to flee. The spirits could not describe it, but their
kind were all helpless against its magic.

Paedrin was awake, staring at the embers of the fire. "Bad
dream?" Paedrin asked, looking at his expression.

"We are in danger," Annon said, tossing aside his blanket. He
rushed to Hettie to shake her shoulder, but his voice had already
roused her. As she rolled to her feet, he saw the dagger in her hand.

"What danger?" Paedrin asked, looking around. "An elk
passed near the camp not long ago, but other than that..."

"Hush!" Annon warned, trying to understand the spirits swarming around him. Mist began roiling through the trees. The spirits warned that the Fear Liath traveled in the mist.

Hettie glanced around the camp. She sheathed the dagger and drew her bow, fitting an arrow to the string. Paedrin looked at them both, perplexed.

It draws nearer!

Annon swallowed. He had never heard of a Fear Liath before, but its presence certainly terrified the lesser spirits in the mountains. He looked at Hettie and raised his hands, nodding to her. She saw the gesture, understood the meaning, and set down the bow.

Paedrin rose from the log and stood silently, eyes shut.

From the fog in the mountains came the silver silhouette of a wolf. It was a spirit creature, and Annon thought that he was the only one who would be able to see it.

Are you the Fear Liath? he challenged in his mind.

No—I am come to shield you, Druidecht. I am a Wolviren. My sisters surround your camp. It will not be able to smell your blood if you stay amidst us. These mountains are its lair. Be cautious.

Thank you, Annon said, bowing his head in relief.

He sat at the edge of the stone circle where their fire had burned out. "We are being protected now."

"What was it?" Hettie whispered, crouching near him.

"A bad dream," Paedrin drawled, sitting across from him. "There was nothing out there."

"It wasn't a nightmare," Annon said. "I was raised in the woods, Paedrin. You'll just have to trust me." He patted Hettie's arm. "I'm sorry I woke you. Try and get some sleep. We have guardians surrounding us."

Paedrin raised an eyebrow. His Bhikhu robes were dirty and seemed too colorful for drab woodlands. A flower out of place.

Annon had heard the Bhikhu were reverential, respectful, and rather naive—seeing all things as black or white, right or wrong, good or evil. They were unlike the Druidecht, who saw all the shades in between both extremes. However, Paedrin fit none of his assumptions about the Bhikhu or the Vaettir. He was proud, wary, and exceptionally funny. It was the humor that was completely unexpected.

Annon stared at him a moment. "Do you miss the city yet?" he asked.

Paedrin circled his legs and rocked back slightly. "Not at all. Ever since I was young, I wanted to roam the lands outside of Kenatos. I have heard the forests of Silvandom are legendary. Unfortunately for me, this trip to Havenrook is bound to be too short."

"I doubt the treasure we seek will be found in Havenrook," Hettie said, pulling up her knees and resting her chin on her arms. "We'll have to persuade Erasmus to help us."

"Do you think it will be enough?" Annon asked her softly. "To secure your freedom?"

Paedrin snorted and chuckled. "She is already free."

Hettie shot him a murderous look. "You know nothing about the Romani."

Annon intervened, touching her elbow. "Will it be enough?"

She sighed. "I hope so." She stared into the night, silent but seething.

Hettie was nothing like the Romani that Annon had known. She was intensely private and guarded, even with him, but they had spent the previous night getting to know each other and cobbling together insights from the scraps Tyrus had fed them. Neither had known about the other. Tyrus had visited Annon when he was nearly eight years old and taught him to control his anger and, by extension, his ability to summon fire with his hands. The Romani had taught Hettie. They had both been warned not to share the ability with others, for those who had the fireblood were hunted and killed. Tyrus himself had managed to conceal his from the world, despite his fame as a Paracelsus.

Hettie did not trust easily.

"What will you do with your freedom?" Annon asked her, wishing that Paedrin was asleep. He did not think she would be as open with him listening. He was watching them both surreptitiously.

"I'm not just a Romani," she said in a soft voice. "I was trained as a Finder. I could earn my own way." He sensed that behind her aloofness there was much more to her than that. He wanted to draw her out more. For her to confide in him.

The night before, as their conversation had gone on, Hettie began to open up more—just a little. If he had not been a good listener, he would have missed one comment of genuine warmth about the man who had purchased her from the Romani at age eight and taught her to be a Finder.

"Where is Evritt now?" he probed.

She shot him a look that was full of warning. She would not be as open in front of the Bhikhu. "Judging by the stars, the night is still young. Whose turn for the watch?"

He was disappointed she would not reveal more of herself that night. He resented Tyrus for keeping them both ignorant of each other, but his other feelings about his uncle were starting to change. How to describe them? Where he was accustomed to feeling hardness and bitterness when thinking about Tyrus, his feelings concerning Hettie were soft and mercurial. He wanted to protect her, to be certain that no man ever owned her again. The anger toward Tyrus began to shift, like a barrel jogged in a wagon, toward the Romani who had stolen her as a babe. He wondered why they had stolen her and not him.

"You both can sleep. I will keep watch." Paedrin's voice was slightly condescending. "I need very little sleep, actually."

Annon returned to his blanket and rolled over the other way, staring into the quiet woods, listening to the hum and chatter of spirits gradually calming from the near disaster. He felt the presence of the Wolviren around them, blanketing their camp with their magic. If only Paedrin realized that his errant thoughts could be heard by the spirits in the woods. You could never deceive a spirit because they could hear the whispers from your mind as easily as someone eavesdropping on a conversation. Annon was able to hear them in return because of the token he wore around his neck, and he was looking forward to meeting new varieties of spirits in his travels. Maybe Reeder was right. It was time for him to move on from forests of Wayland.

Closing his eyes, he drifted into sleep, thinking of his mentor and wondering at the trouble that was taking his friend to Silvandom.

Following the edge of the woods along the mountains, they finally reached a man-made road gouged into the forest that led to Havenrook. Before the road even came into view, Annon could tell they were approaching it. First, there were plenty of carrion birds. Second, fewer and fewer whispers from the spirits, which tended to avoid places where nature had been savaged deliberately.

The mountains of Alkire were impressive, thick with cedar and pine at the lower reaches and then snow-capped and silvered above the fringe of the woods. It would take several days to hike to the foothills of those mountains and probably weeks to cross them. They formed a boundary to the valley, and the continual snowpack created the rivers that fed the lake where Kenatos lay to the northwest. The mountains were stark and unyielding, wreathed in patches of man-made fog caused by forge-fires of the Cruithne. Ore was mined from the mountains and brought down to Kenatos by wagon and riverboat. It was rumored that the Cruithne's soot-colored skin was a result of generations of ore mining.

"There is the road," Hettie said, surprising everyone because she had rarely spoken during the journey. "We should reach Havenrook by nightfall if we hurry."

"Have we not been hurrying enough for you?" Paedrin quipped, giving her an impatient look.

She did not rise to the bait, and Annon saw a frown of disappointment flash on Paedrin's face.

The road was wide enough for three or four carts to go by at a time, which made sense because goods came to and from the city each day. The ruts were worn to dust and nothing grew in them at all; not even weeds could withstand the constant tromping of hooves, the crushing weight of wagon wheels, or the trod of people.

The three of them entered the lane and started toward the city at a strong walk, having finished a meal at midday a little earlier. There were signs nailed to trees, offers of cargo or passage. Trunks had been gouged for firewood or hacked at by bored mercenaries for no reason. There was not even a whisper of thought in the air from the spirits. The cruelty shown to the forest was an abomination to them. No wonder they had all fled. The desecration of the woods outraged Annon.

Garbage littered the fringe of the path—broken crates, frayed ropes, a few smashed barrels. All were abandoned, including several wagons, all of which were missing wheels. It was disgusting and brought out Annon's loathing. He felt unprotected, for there would be no spirits to draw upon for help. The woods of

Havenrook felt like the city of Kenatos—devoid of sentient life. His fingers tingled with heat after passing another rotting carcass of a wagon.

Glancing at Hettie, he noticed her scowling and wondered if she too were offended.

"What is it?" he asked in a low voice, drawing near her. He wondered if there were any Druidecht at all in the kingdom.

Seeing she had been observed, she gave a cynical smile. "Romani wagons," she answered, nodding toward a dilapidated set. "I am expecting we will cross paths with a caravan or two on our way."

That explained her reaction. "We can hide in the mess if we hear a wagon train coming."

She shrugged, eyes squinting as they continued to walk.

Annon's observation about the clutter being a place to hide turned out to be prophetic, as he realized shortly after. The road was not chisel-straight, but meandered around blind turns and hooks, as if the woodcutters had all been drunk while working. Or perhaps deliberately creating blind spots to waylay travelers.

As they rounded one corner, Annon noticed the Preachán immediately, sitting atop a broken-down wagon on the edge of the road. His boot dangled off the edge and started tapping against the plank. With a wicked-looking dagger, he fussed with something under his fingernail.

Annon, Hettie, and Paedrin stopped as soon as he came into view. He was a handsome fellow, with reddish-brown hair that was untamed. Though slight of build, he seemed bigger wearing a coat made of black leather with buckles and straps around the arms and shoulders. It was cured leather, not fancy leather. Leather meant to protect him. He wore black pants as well, with green and gold stitching along the leg, and a wide belt with an enormous buckle. There was another knife in his boot cuff. A small blade at his hip, as well as three more stuck in the wagon frame, within easy reach. A ruff of white at his throat displayed several jeweled necklaces, including a Druidecht talisman.

The Preachán glanced up at them and smiled. "Ho, there."

Paedrin swiveled his neck, as if loosening his muscles, and held still, gripping his walking staff in front of him. "Several in the woods on each side," he muttered to Annon. "Let me deal with them if you want to *chat* with the dagger collection ahead."

"Not yet," Annon said softly. He looked at the Preachán disinterestedly. "Ho, there."

The Preachán admired his long, sharp dagger deliberately, looking up and down its blade. "I can see that you are travelers bound for Havenrook." He had a quaint accent, one that Annon was unfamiliar with. "You are not from these parts. I take it as my duty to offer you my protection as you travel this road. There are dangerous sorts about, and I would not want you to come to any harm." He scraped his whiskers with the edge of his knife. "Three ducats would do as there are three of you."

Annon took offense at the tone and the trap. "There are three of us. And one of you."

The Preachán smiled appreciatively. "Yes. I noticed that. I am only the collector of the tithes, as the Rikes like to say in Kenatos. Three ducats is not an unreasonable value for the life of a person. I mean no disrespect. Perhaps I should demand more? But I was feeling generous this afternoon."

Annon saw Hettie glance at the woods, where he began to see the subtle shift of shadows hidden amidst the debris on each side. There was a gentle creak of wood.

"At least twenty," Paedrin muttered again, voice low. "Better to strike first than talk. I will…"

Annon used a hand gesture to quiet him, as if calming a horse. He looked back at the Preachán firmly, his voice rising with emotion. "Just to be clear, sir. Even if we had three ducats, you would not limit yourself to only those. You want us to show you where we keep our purses to save you the time searching our bodies. We appear as simple travelers and easy prey, and you know there are no caravans either coming or going to interfere with the murder. You do this every day."

The Preachán's eyebrows rose, as if pleasantly surprised. "Well, you can put it that way if you wish. In the end…"

Pyricanthas. Sericanthas. Thas.

Annon raised his hands and flames gushed from his body as he twisted and sent them rushing to the deadwood debris to the right. There was heat, light, and the crackling snap of raw flames exploding into wood. The debris of wagons and barrels and crates created a skyward blaze. Crowding trees were blasted by the heat and the flames began running up the trunks and catching the deadened branches afire.

Behind Annon, there was a twin explosion of flames, this one caused by Hettie as she followed his lead and turned the other piles into tinder. Screams filled the air along with the roar and groan of the fires. The Preachán sitting on the wagon rim fell backward in his shock and surprise, leaving the daggers stuck in the wood.

The feeling of loosing the flames was visceral and innately pleasurable. Annon could feel his blood singing with it. *More! Loose more!* They wanted to be freed, like some caged mountain cat bursting with savagery. He delighted in the power, in the taming of the fire, and he yearned in the deepest part of his soul to let it flow from him, engulfing the trees and rotting caravan ruins until nothing was left but cinders. Rebirth. That was what flames brought. A chance to be reborn.

Yet he knew the feelings were not telling the full truth. The longer he let the flames dance across his hands, the more they would begin to control him. The incomprehensible yearning of the fireblood was an illusion. It would fade in time and be replaced with self-loathing and guilt. He knew it, even though he did not feel it. Clenching his teeth, he tamed the fire within him and for a moment wondered if he had gone too far. It did not obey him at first. Slowly, so slowly, the impulse to unleash it began to ebb. Slowly, his mind forced it to obey. Flickering tongues of flame danced across his fingers and then guttered out.

Annon turned and saw Hettie, her eyes wide with frenzy, her hands still held open, flooding the woods with flames, sending it lancing out at the fleeing Preachán, streamers of liquid hate that hit them from behind and burst their clothes into flame. They were screaming and running.

"Hettie!" Annon called, grabbing her shoulder and pulling her off-balance.

The forest all around them was blazing with heat and billowing black plumes that arched skyward. The flames would rage and battle the rest of the forest. He could not let that happen.

"Hettie!" he called again, trying to get her eyes to focus. She blinked rapidly, unable to focus, a half-smile of pleasure on her mouth.

He smacked her hard. Pain was all it took. She shook her head, as if emerging from a dream, and the flames in her hands sputtered out. Her legs gave out, and she nearly collapsed, but he caught her.

Annon turned, glancing at Paedrin, and saw a look of shock and utter horror on his face. It was a look that said *what are you?*

Then Paedrin glanced over Annon's shoulder, and he was suddenly in the air, zooming like a raven and coming down on the Preachán who had threatened them, scrabbling down the road to escape the flames and the strangers who had unleashed it.

"Of all the races to have survived the great Plague, there is one feared more than any other because they, of all people, cannot be harmed by it. The race appears as Aeduan as any Waylander. They are often mistaken for Paracelsus because they can summon fire into their hands and use it to harm others. A Paracelsus can only do this through an implement of magic, such as a ring or a bracelet. Curiously, the majority of this race have red hair.

They are hated in Stonehollow. Though there are sparse records, I have learned that in the distant past, they used their immunity from the Plague to enrich themselves and their fellows. In places where the Plague destroyed entire villages, save their own kind, they inherited the wealth abandoned by their dead neighbors. They rose to thrones, principalities, and increased their dominion through deception and flattering words. In addition to calling fire into their hands, they are quick to learn and master skills, especially the skills of persuasion. This invoked jealousy, for men always distrust those wiser than themselves. And when it was eventually discovered that it was their 'fireblood' that made them immune to the Plague, the people of Stonehollow rose up against them when the seasons of Plague came. I watched this myself. A rumor of Plague came from the north. A rumor that turned out to be false. But a woman, red-haired and young, was dragged to a pillory in the center of town. They cut her with knives and collected her blood, which they brushed on the lintels of their homes. Many homes, they claimed, had been spared from the Plague in the past by so doing. Thus one death could save an entire village. The folk of Stonehollow do not consider this murder. No one would give me the name of this race. And no one with this blood willingly admits it."

– Possidius Adeodat, Archivist of Kenatos

IX

With flames devouring the woods and smoke billowing wildly, Annon motioned Hettie to join him as Paedrin hauled the trembling Preachán to his feet. The little man had paled as white as milk. He thrashed against Paedrin's grip for a moment before the Bhikhu gripped his hand, twisted his wrist, and suddenly he was helpless, his arm pinned behind his back.

Annon fingered the Druidecht talisman mixed with the necklaces around the man's neck. He gripped it and snapped the chain that held it, his anger still smoldering in his heart.

"I am worth more to you alive than dead," the Preachán pleaded. "There are others…wait…what I mean is that there are ducats. Many ducats. Casks of ducats…"

"I'm not interested in ducats," Annon said coldly.

"You may not, but the Romani girl might," he said with a tremor in his voice. "Eh, lass? Ducats aplenty. I can lead you there. I didn't notice the earring at first, forgive me. Had I known, I never would have presumed…"

"Yes, you would have," Hettie said, her look full of loathing. "Kill him now. He's of no use to us."

Annon saw the glint in Paedrin's eye, the sour expression of loathing. He remembered that they never willingly shed blood.

"How far is Havenrook?" Annon asked.

"A few leagues," he replied, trying to seem helpful. "I know a place you could stay..."

"Somehow I doubt we can trust your recommendations," Paedrin said. "Several leagues, you say?"

"Several. Maybe six? I forget. You will get there before nightfall if you hurry." He was panting, his eyes darting back and forth at their faces, trying to read in them any possible way to save his life.

Paedrin released his arm and shoved him hard, making him stumble and fall. As the Preachán turned and faced them, eyes dancing with worry, Paedrin swiveled his staff in a swishing circle and then jammed the butt into the tip of the man's toes with crushing force. There came from his mouth a howl of pain as he crumpled to the road in total agony.

"When we get there does not matter," Paedrin said, "so long as we get there before you. I suggest hobbling along quickly before the flames catch up with you." Giving a curt nod to Annon and Hettie, he said, "Let's go."

Crippling the man was a nice touch, Annon thought. Waves of heat from the flames pressed against their backs as they quickly left the scene of the ambush. The plumes of smoke would be seen as far away as Havenrook, in all likelihood. And it would halt traffic on the road until they were quenched. He did not care.

After they had left the lamed Preachán far behind, Paedrin suddenly whirled on them, his face flushed with anger. His voice was low and controlled, but his eyes were blazing. "What was that, back there?" he said sharply, pointing toward the road. "You started the forest burning! I thought you were a Druidecht, a protector of the woods."

Annon stared at him in surprise, and then he understood. To a man raised in a city, fire was a considerable threat and needed safeguards to control it. "Paedrin, you must learn to trust me. I am a Druidecht. I would never do anything to harm a forest."

The other opened his mouth in amazement. "You just set fire to it!"

"Fire is how a forest is reborn. There are certain trees that will only release their seeds during a firestorm. Oaks, for example, need fires to properly grow and to prevent being crowded out by weaker trees. This forest cannot even be properly called one. Green wood does not burn very well, Paedrin."

"There was no need to butcher those men, though."

Annon met his stare. "They are the butchers, Paedrin. They chose their kill unwisely this time."

The Bhikhu squeezed his eyes shut, as if choking off a retort and struggling to master himself. He opened his eyes slowly. "I was sent here to protect you both. Taking life should always be the final resort. The last option. I have been trained all of my life to fight. To maim. To hurt. To choke. To squeeze a man to within an *inch* of his life. But not to kill him. Not unless there is no other choice. That was not the case today. I was going to intervene. I tried to whisper it to you, but you would not hear it."

"I am sorry," Annon said.

The Bhikhu stopped, dazed.

"I should have warned you," Annon continued, mastering his temper. He understood the Bhikhu's feelings, while not agreeing with them himself. The sentiments were admirable. "I respect your beliefs. I respect the foundation of your order. But those men have no laws. They would have killed us without hesitation. I did not feel it right to ask you to do the same to them."

"The next time..." Paedrin said, his voice rising.

"Spare us a sermon," Hettie said, her voice full of disdain.

He rounded on her. "The next time we face trouble like that..."

"I will use my knife, or an arrow, or my hands if that will suffice," she answered hotly. "We are not at the temple anymore. This is the wide world. No one cares how you feel about it."

Annon watched Paedrin swallow, his eyes blazing with fury. "I was orphaned in Kenatos. I have seen every sort of man seek shelter in the temple. The wildest drunk to the sneakiest purse snatcher. I am not a child, and this is not my first experience with the wide world. Pain is a teacher. Pain is a harsh teacher. I have broken my fingers. I have broken my leg twice. My arm has been twisted out of its joint three times." He took a step closer to her, his face barely a breath from hers. "I am not afraid of hurting or bleeding or even dying. But when we come across trouble in the future, we will spare life. I insist on it. Or I will school you both as I have been schooled."

Hettie's eyes glittered like daggers. "You know nothing of pain," she said softly.

Annon put his hand on Paedrin's shoulder. "Very well, Paedrin. That is only fair. We startled you today. I did not wish to do that. In the future, you will get the first chance to make peace or finish things the Bhikhu way. If it works, well and good. If not, at least you know what we can do."

There was a hard line across Paedrin's mouth as he stared at Hettie. He glanced briefly at Annon, nodded once, and then stepped away from her, still scowling. "How is it that you both can summon fire from your hands? Is it magic your uncle gave you? I have seen rings and bracelets that contain special powers, but never something like what I saw you both do."

Annon glanced at Hettie and then looked back at him. "I have asked for your trust, and so I will trust you in return. It is something we were born with," he replied. "We may look like Aeduan, but there is something in our blood that gives us this power. It is called the fireblood. I have never used it like that before, and I normally would not have chosen to, but I have no Druidecht power in a place like this. In some kingdoms our race is persecuted. I will only use it as a final resort."

Paedrin looked at Hettie narrowly and then back at Annon. "It seems your sister went a little too far with it today. You had to strike her to get her to stop. I volunteer next time." He started back on the road at a brisk walk, never looking back at them.

Annon glanced at Hettie, trying to understand her. She stared at Paedrin with a look of defiance, her mouth twisted unpleasantly downward. Then she whispered, "Thank you, Annon. I nearly lost myself in the flames. The men hiding in the rubbish were not Preachán. They were Romani."

As she said the final word, her eyes burned with hatred.

"How many times have you used it?" Annon asked her, pulling her after him. "I was worried about you. The look in your eyes frightened me."

She nodded, casting her gaze down. "Me as well. I don't like to use it. It makes you want to use it again and again. There are stories of those who go mad."

"I know," Annon said, gripping her arm so that they could keep pace with each other. "I think you have used it more than I have. If we face danger like that again, let me act alone at first. Resist it, Hettie. Unless I need you."

Without arguing, she gazed into his eyes, a haunted expression in hers.

☙

To call Havenrook a town implied that there were borders and streets and houses. That was a better description of Kenatos. Instead, Havenrook was a stockyard adjacent to a slaughterhouse—all pens and sheds and braying animals, smoke, and reeking fumes. There were wagons loaded with various cargo; wiry Preachán men stood atop, shouting bids for each wagonload there. The words mixed with flashing hands, tapped noses, until a bell tolled signaling the end of the trade. A cart of lettuces was sold. A wagon loaded with apple barrels lumbered by. Pens of pigs and black-and-white cows filled every available space. The crowds were endless. By the cups of beer sloshing in nearly every available hand, Annon realized that the trades were probably turned over three or four times before dawn when the Romani caravans would start off on a new day.

As Hettie, Annon, and Paedrin entered the fray, looking for anything even remotely resembling an inn, a constant shove and jostle tensed Annon's patience into a thin wire again. Paedrin was the only Vaettir amidst the crowd of Aeduan and Preachán. Some looked at him in surprise, leered at him, and continued haggling over a cask of salted fish.

The smell of Havenrook was six degrees of dying. Goods were exchanged. Heavy chests loaded with ducats exchanged hands as well. The jarring noise of the callers, the snapping and whistling and goading of horseflesh had made him physically ill.

Paedrin slapped his palm down against a man's hand that was groping at his robes, then he quickly torqued one of his fingers and snapped it, making the man howl in pain. With a shove, he sent him sprawling away.

Annon looked at him in surprise.

"He touched me," Paedrin said with disgust. "Keep going. Any thoughts on where we will find your friend?"

Annon shook his head, but looked at the largest building that he could find. It was possibly an inn, but it seemed about ready to collapse under the weight of its beams. Miraculously, the crowd thinned around them after Paedrin had broken the man's finger. Pain was a teacher, indeed.

Hettie lifted her hood and covered her hair, keeping close to Annon. Her face was impassive, but he thought he could sense fear and loathing in her eyes. There was a steady stream of men and women coming from the doors of the enormous, misshapen building. Most emerged with tankards or mugs. As they drew nearer to the doors, Annon noticed a hulking Cruithne standing outside, soot-skinned and muscles bulging. With the thickening shadows, they had not seen him before.

"I thought the Cruithne hated the Preachán," Annon muttered to himself.

"Everyone has a price," Hettie answered. "And in Havenrook, everything is for sale."

The Cruithne scanned those coming and going, his eyes blue and dark like jewels. He noticed them and scowled.

Annon approached him directly. "Erasmus?"

He studied them a moment and then nodded toward the doors, letting them enter.

Inside was a huge gallery filled almost entirely with tables. Gathered around each one hung crowds of Preachán, most of them gesticulating wildly, shouting at men with small silver tokens who sat at the heads of the tables. At one table, they seemed to be trading a cargo of pears. At another table, they were trading for a girl with one Romani earring. Annon's stomach lurched when he saw the men bidding for her. At another table, they were betting on whether a caravan would arrive safely at its destination. At another, they were betting on the outcome of dice. The noise was deafening.

Hettie squeezed Annon's arm, and he turned to look at her. Her upper lip had a sheen of sweat. "He's looking at me."

Annon followed her gaze. Across the room, there was a cluster of chairs and a crowd of Romani men and women lounging amidst the chaos. In the center of the hive sat a tall man, darkly handsome, with Vaettir-like eyes and long jet-black hair. He was adorned with a bejeweled doublet and a gaudy black ring on his hand. Not just any ring, a ring of a Rike of Kenatos. There was something undeniably lazy about his slouch, but his slanted eyes belied the laziness—they were alert, probing everything happening in the room. He had taken notice of their entrance immediately.

He raised his hand to a gold hoop in his ear and massaged it. Hettie gasped.

"What is it?" Annon asked.

"He summons me," Hettie whispered with dread. "I must obey."

Annon tugged at her arm as she started away from them, stopping her. "You do not have to go," he murmured.

"You don't understand, Annon. That is Kiranrao. No one defies him. He has more ducats than the Arch-Rike. He can buy anyone or anything he wants. Believe me, I must go." She gave him a desperate look. "Find Erasmus. Quickly."

"Why is it that the Cruithne dwell in the mountain passes and the Preachán live amidst dying trees? Why do those in Stonehollow dwell amidst massive stones and Waylanders the open plains? Why an island kingdom? People are where they are because that is exactly where they really want to be—whether they will admit that or not."

– Possidius Adeodat, Archivist of Kenatos

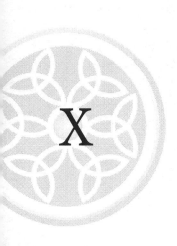

X

The din and howling commotion in that horrible room made Paedrin's thoughts seize up with icy blackness. The unmistakably raw demonstration of greed made his fists clench, his eyes narrow, and his breath seep from his body. As soon as they had entered, he had absorbed the scene in its fullness, every tinkling coin, every grunt of a bid, every gulp of ale or sour wine, and every horrid stinking breath from a hundred stinking Preachán. There in the periphery, like a king in court, sat the king of greed himself—a wretch known as Kiranrao. He had Vaettir blood. The fury congealing in Paedrin's chest made him forget every person in the room except for two.

He watched Hettie submit, drops of nervous sweat forming on her brow. Whether she knew him or not, she knew of him. Still wearing her mask of aloofness, she maneuvered through the crowd to him. Paedrin followed like her shadow.

As they threaded the knot of men and mugs and things for sale, Paedrin studied the Romani more closely. His doublet was fine, no doubt, but the rest of his garb was casual and ordinary.

The pants, for example, could have been any tradesman's. The shirt beneath the doublet, also black, was open at the throat though he wore a silken collar that would have made an excellent handle to choke him with. His boots were nicked and scuffed, not the polished black of the gentry. His hands were brown and large, fingernails immaculately trimmed. The black hair was combed back, part of it tethered in a braid and fashioned with a pin, and his teeth were white, barely visible past a wry smile as he studied Hettie.

The way he sat in his chair reminded Paedrin of a lounging alley cat. His arm draped around the back of another chair, lazily displaying the huge black beetle of a ring, flaunting for all to see what he had obtained from a Rike of Kenatos. No one could lie to Kiranrao, that much was certain. The ring detected any falsehood.

Hettie reached the cluster of Preachán and Romani thronging him. She stood at the outer edge, chin high, eyes haughty as she had always proven to be. It was then, when they were close, that Paedrin noticed the sword belted to Kiranrao's hip. He almost started when he looked directly at it and it wasn't there. A trick of the light? He looked away and noticed it again, hidden in the shadows of his dusky blue rider's cloak. It seemed to fade in and out of view, and Paedrin found himself blinking furiously, his mind starting to haze from staring at it too long, as happens to a child when gazing at the sun.

"What is it?" Hettie asked, arms folded, looking more put-out than defiant.

"I knew every Romani in Havenrook," Kiranrao said, his voice tinged with a Preachán accent. "Until today."

"Well, your reputation precedes you, Kiranrao," Hettie replied. "What is it?" she repeated. "What do you want?"

"A Finder," he replied, taking a sip from the cup near him. He swallowed slowly. "Are you for hire?"

"I'm on a job," Hettie answered evasively.

Paedrin watched an immaculate fingertip stroke the lip of the cup, causing a subtle squeal that could only be heard through the din because Paedrin was trying to hear it.

"How much will you earn?"

Hettie looked at him coldly. "Still being negotiated. I don't need another job yet."

"Whatever you are offered, I can offer more," he said. "I need a good Finder. Are you any good?" He fished inside his doublet pocket and withdrew an earring.

Hettie paled immediately. "I am not free to take on a new engagement right now," she muttered. "Maybe later."

"How old are you?" Kiranrao asked. His voice was mild, but there was an undercurrent in his tone, an implied meaning.

Hettie paused, her expression impassive. There was a tightness in her eyes, a fury as cold and ruthless as his own. "Young enough to wear only one."

Kiranrao played with the earring, turning it around between his fingers, letting the hoop twist. Hettie seemed to brace herself as if the earring was a threat. "You look older than your years then. I like them young. My Finders, that is."

Paedrin saw the expressions on the faces surrounding them. How they leered at Hettie hungrily, but no one would dare act against the one their leader had shown interest in. Like wolves desperate to hunt, but not daring to.

"It wouldn't be good for my reputation to abandon a customer before the mission is done. If I'm bored and need a job, I know where to find you."

"You do indeed, lass. You do indeed." He gave her a nod and again lifted the cup and drank from it. The earring disappeared back into his pocket.

Hettie turned abruptly and saw Paedrin standing behind her. Her eyes flashed with surprise, her lip trembling with barely controlled emotion. He smiled at her and waited for her to pass him, clipping his arm with her shoulder.

Paedrin watched her go and then turned his gaze back to Kiranrao.

"Yes?" the Romani said with amusement, his teeth all white.

"I fancy your sword," Paedrin said, catching another glimpse of the shadow thing out of the corner of his eye.

He was met by an amused smirk. "You have good eyes. I appreciate that. But I have no use of a Bhikhu in my dealings. Too much *conscience* isn't good for business."

"That suits me just as well," Paedrin replied. "Bhikhu don't work for hire anyway. Some people cannot be bought."

Kiranrao shrugged. "And what if I told you I owned the debt on the Bhikhu temple in Kenatos?"

"Then I would answer that it is in dire need of repairs and you have been negligent in your duties."

He got an eyebrow lift for the quip. It was worth it.

"Every bird relishes his own voice."

"Is that the best you can do?" Paedrin said mockingly. "I am just getting started."

He was met by a cold smile. But it was amused. Rarely did anyone stand up to this man, apparently. Cowards, all of them.

"Why are you in Havenrook, boy?"

"We needed some fresh country air to clear our lungs from the soot-filled skies of Kenatos. What clearer air is there to breathe than here?" He lowered his voice conspiratorially. "Does that ring hurt if I tell a lie? My mother was a fat Boeotian newt Finder and my father was a hob-nosed Preachán axle smith. Did it sting? A little?"

One of the Preachán started to shove his chair back, but Kiranrao raised just the tips of his fingers and the man stopped, his teeth clenched in rage.

"You are the world's biggest fool," Kiranrao said, almost in awe at the audacity.

"Perhaps," Paedrin replied with a shrug. "But I am also the best Bhikhu in the temple, save Shivu himself." He glanced down at the man's ring, cocking his head slightly as if listening for it to make a sound. He let his words hang in the air a moment, turned on his heel, and left without being dismissed.

"Do not turn your back on me," Kiranrao said.

Paedrin paused, but did not turn around. "You think a fancy sword will humble me? Use it then." He waited.

"The Bhikhu temple needs to learn a lesson in humility," the other man said softly.

"Really? And you teach courses in humility? I'm rather surprised. You don't wish to fight me? I will be on my way then."

He heard the chair legs squeal.

Paedrin was expecting a blade attack from behind. Perhaps a man pretending to be drunk who would stagger into him and let go with a poisoned needle or even just a fist. He was not expecting Hettie.

She dug her fingers into his forearm, her face nearly even with his, her voice a raw hiss of pure anger.

"What do you think you are doing?! Are you completely insane? Do you know where we are and what you just did?" There was a wild look in her eyes, the look of complete and abject terror. She wrestled against his arm, trying to tug him away from Kiranrao's table.

Paedrin glanced back at the Romani, offered a mocking smile, and then followed Hettie into the crush of bodies laying their bets at the various tables.

"Fortunes come and go and are as slippery as morning frost," Paedrin said. "I don't care how rich he is—his day will come sooner than later. There is more at work in this grand world than one man's will."

"You are an idiot," Hettie said in a low, menacing voice. "No, you are worse than an idiot. You are the droppings caked in the underside of an idiot's boot! Do you want to get us all killed, Bhikhu?"

Paedrin felt her fingers digging into his arm, but he ignored the pain as nothing more than an indifferent mosquito buzz.

"There was not a man at that table who I would fear to face or any five of them together. They are lazy, mostly drunk, and do not know the ways of the Bhikhu." He looked back at the table again, snorting with derision. Then he hooked his arm around Hettie's neck and pulled her suddenly close so that his lips pressed against the hair at her ear. "I'm drawing their attention to us and not to Annon. I think he's found Erasmus. Over in the far corner, but do not look. Let's give them a few more moments."

The startled look in her eyes pleased him. She shoved him away from herself, and he gave her an angry stare.

"That man has no right to treat you that way. They are all cowards, as you can see." He lifted his voice haughtily, glancing back defiantly at the table. He could see many of the Preachán nearby nudge away from him, as if expecting lightning to strike.

"This is not a game!" Hettie snarled, grabbing a fistful of his shirt. Her features had not softened, but her eyes had. She realized what he was doing. A distraction. A ruse. In a moment, she was playing along. "If I do not get that medicine, then all is wasted! You are only making it worse!"

"It is your own fault you need that medicine. If you would stop flashing your eyes at every man you see along the road, you may not need…"

"It was your fault we lost our way on the road. If you had not dropped the purse, we would not have needed to beg a ride. Flashing my eyes, you make me sick! It was better than walking here…"

"I saw how close you were sitting to the wagon master. Any closer and it would have been on his lap, and do not tell me you would not have fancied that."

"And here I thought that Bhikhu were immune to jealousy. I see that they failed to teach that at the temple. You are such a hypocrite."

"I am a hypocrite?"

"Yes! For all your fine talk of being truly free of obligations and misery, you are the most miserable man I have ever met. A girl wants a compliment, not sermons. Why did we even come here?"

Paedrin lowered his voice. "Keep it up." A little louder, he said, "This is your fault we need the root. And this is the only place it can be bought out of season." He glanced quickly at the table and found Annon sitting alone, watching them.

Paedrin scowled. "It is a waste of breath even speaking to you. You never listen."

"And your jealousy may have ruined all chance of getting it," she shot back in an equally lethal tone. "You never insult a Romani. Never! A grudge given is never yielded but with great interest."

Paedrin threw up his hands and started walking toward the table where Annon was waiting.

Why would Tyrus have sent them to a place like Havenrook? Annon had felt uncomfortable in the city of Kenatos. What he experienced in the Preachán homeland could not even be described. It was the very opposite of the Druidecht way, and because it was, he knew he was bereft of any of the skills he had learned.

He recognized immediately that survival would come by his wits more than his Druidecht lore. How to find Erasmus quickly? The answer came immediately to his mind, and he recognized it as soon as a half-sober Preachán accosted him.

"Six ducats for your talisman," the man insisted. "Seven."

Annon reached into a pouch tied to his belt and withdrew the talisman he had taken off the man earlier. He dangled it in front of the man's eyes, who promptly began fumbling in his pouch for coins, but Annon grabbed his shoulder.

"It's worth more than seven. We both know that. Tell me where Erasmus sits."

"You are a cheat!" the man complained. "Erasmus knows the price of everything."

"Why do you think I came to see him then? Hmm? Where does he sit?"

He knew the Preachán was going to lie to him, but he betrayed himself first because his eyes darted furtively to the northeast corner in the back.

"That's all I needed," Annon said, clapping him on the back. "Thank you." He tightened his fist around the talisman and plunged into the crowd. The northeast corner was not fully crowded, as most of the betting and dice-throwing was happening near the front. A few patrons sipped slowly from mugs and gathered around tables, playing strange games he had never seen before. Some involved stone pieces set on a wooden board. Others had black-and-white discs. Most of these Preachán dressed well and a few smoked pipes, causing an aroma to permeate the air.

Annon studied the tables quickly and settled on the one with only a single man seated there, his back to the wall, his face in front of the room. He noticed Annon's approach and muttered something under his breath. He had dark hair with wisps of gray and a prominent nose.

As Annon advanced, he leaned back languidly, folding his arms across his chest. "What business could possibly bring a Druidecht to Havenrook? Are ye here to buy some poetry, perhaps? I happen to own the finest collection outside Kenatos."

Annon sat across from him without an invitation. He leaned forward, resting his arms on the table and folding his hands. "I have come at the behest of Tyrus Paracelsus of Kenatos."

The man was startled. His look was suddenly grave. "Have ye?"

"He sent me to Havenrook to inquire of Erasmus."

The man revealed nothing in his look, only sternness. "Did he now." The tone of his voice indicated it was not a question.

Annon waited, staring at the man. He knew that silence had a way of torturing others into speaking. He won his gamble.

"My name is Dwyer," the Preachán said softly. "I can take you to Erasmus, but I must first know your business."

The Druidecht smiled. "Anyone who knows Tyrus Paracelsus knows he shares his business with no one. I will explain the matter with him directly."

"Is it just for yourself or does it include the other two you entered with? You've already caught the eye of Kiranrao, it seems. It is better to remain beneath his notice, if you understand me."

Annon gazed across the room at Kiranrao's table. He saw Paedrin and Hettie together, their faces animated in a heated exchange. He turned back. "When can we see Erasmus?"

"He left shortly before ye arrived. It gets too rowdy here at the Millpond after dusk. I'll meet ye behind the tavern. The mood is starting to shift. There may be a fight."

"I will gather my friends and meet you outside." He thought a moment about warning the man not to run, that the girl with him was a Finder, but he thought it best to say nothing and show him a little bit of trust. If he waited, good. If he did not, Hettie could use her skills to hunt him.

Dwyer slipped away from the table and Annon waited as Paedrin and Hettie continued their blistering tirade. Annon was sitting, somber and alone, when they reached his table. "We need to go," he said softly.

"Did you find Erasmus?" Paedrin asked after slamming his palms on the table petulantly. He gave a half-jerk motion with his head back at Hettie who approached rapidly.

"No, but a man who treats with him. He does little business here at the Millpond past dusk. He left before we arrived."

"How do you know the man isn't leading us into a trap?" Paedrin asked levelly, keeping his voice low. He gesticulated suddenly, stabbing his finger toward Kiranrao's table.

"I think we can trust him. He was a very different sort than the Preachán we have seen so far. Very cold and calculating. Not the kind who gushes and tries to sell you for a favor. He was surprised I even knew of Erasmus or how to find him here. When I mentioned my uncle, his countenance changed visibly. He'll meet us in the back right now and lead us to where he does business. I do not think it is safe to deal here. Follow me out the back."

Annon was glad he trusted Dwyer, for he was waiting just outside the rear doors of the tavern. He looked even more wary and distrustful, his arms folded across his chest as he waited in the alley for them.

"Tell me again why there are three of you," he said suspiciously as they approached. There was no greeting.

Annon motioned to him. "This is Dwyer."

Dwyer did not so much as shrug at them. "It is a long walk from Kenatos, lads, and before I take you to see Erasmus, I need to be clear the sort of business this is. Are you looking to wager with your uncle's money? Is that it?"

Annon shook his head. "It has nothing to do with a bet."

"Erasmus is not an easy man to negotiate with. He's as stubborn as they come because he knows what he knows. He doesn't suffer fools, and he doesn't barter. He asks a fair price. He'll not cheat you. But when he offers his price, he will expect it all. Not a pent less. He knows the value of things."

"That is understandable," Annon said. "What we seek is information, not a deal."

Dwyer shook his head impatiently. "Exactly. That is his business. Information. He remembers everything that anyone has ever said or written. Literally. I do not jest with ye, lads. For fun, he counts the mugs of ale and wine drunk in the Millpond each day as well as the number that are spilled. He gets his drinks for free because he tells the tavern master what to order and how much every moon cycle. He is never wrong, not that I have ever seen. He is uncanny, so they say. He is not like the crowd in the Millpond. He watches them, listens in, and feels what is going on in the room. He has the smell of it, you see. Drop a fistful of coins, and he can tell you how many ducats fell and whether they were silver or gold."

Paedrin folded his arms. "He sounds rather boring. When can we meet him?"

Dwyer looked annoyed. "He accepts few visitors."

"Take us to him, please." Annon stepped forward, asserting himself as their leader.

Dwyer gave them another appraising look, scowling when he glanced at Paedrin, and then motioned for them to follow him into one of the rough, ramshackle clusters of buildings inside the disordered hive. It was dusk when they left the Millpond and getting darker with each step. Paedrin seemed to watch each sleeping beggar or drunk who shuffled along the path. He was tense and tightly coiled, expecting violence from every side.

Their destination was at the northern edge of town, a small two-story dwelling, a shop with a living place above doors. There was a lamp lit above stairs, but no light in the shop below. The shop was closed and locked, but Dwyer withdrew a key and opened it. As they entered, the room was full of books and paper, bottles of ink, and soft, padded chairs. The carpet was dirty and well worn. The place was rather shabby overall. There was a desk, a counter, riddled with scraps of paper and ink blots. A small staircase went from the back of the room to the upstairs floor.

"What do you sell?" Paedrin asked, looking around at the books and quills but seeing no merchandise. He could not discern what the man's business was.

"Nothing," Dwyer said, affronted. "I have no need to sell. I made my fortune nearly twenty span of years ago, betting on the Plague. When Erasmus said it was coming, I took all that I owned and bet it at the Millpond. I live quite comfortably on what is left and translate poetry."

Paedrin stifled a chuckle with a feigned cough. "Poetry? Really?" For a stern man, he did not seem the type.

"You can be sure. I speak several languages and translate poetry from the original tongue into another. It is not as easy as you may think. Let me go upstairs and ask if he will see you."

He went to the staircase and took the steps two at a time. There were voices above, and promptly Dwyer returned. "He will make an exception for the three of ye, but only because there is a Druidecht among ye. He trusts those folk."

Annon felt a flush of gratitude.

Dwyer motioned for the stairs and then eased himself into one of the stuffed chairs, reaching for a book nearby and examining the binding and spine for a moment before blowing hard at the dust. Then he opened it.

Annon reached the stairs first and started up. Paedrin let Hettie go next and studied Dwyer for a moment longer. The lifestyle was not the ostentatious manner of one with wealth. He lived on the edge of town, in a ramshackle house. The brass lamp was soot-stained and had no frills. The stove was ordinary. The array of untidy books was a distraction to the eyes.

Paedrin followed Hettie up the stairs, watching Dwyer as long as he could, seeing no mark of nervousness or concern. They reached the top level, and Annon found the man pacing in the upper story.

There were books on the floor, stacks of them. Some were opened, others placed haphazardly. But what struck Annon immediately were Erasmus's eyes. Or more precisely, the fact that they did not appear to look the same direction at the same time. His dark hair was shortly cropped; he was wide about the shoulders and skinny about the ankles. He did not look like a man of great wealth. First, he was too young. Second, his shirt was homespun, and he wore no shoes, only tattered slippers. He glanced at them, rubbing his mouth nervously, pacing back and forth by the window.

"Are you Erasmus?" Annon asked formally.

There was a twitch in the muscles of the man's face, and he held up his hand, as if warning them to be quiet. "At so many paces per league, and then the walk from the Millpond to here. Yes, that must be it." His strange eyes stared at them, but not directly at them. One of his eyes was crooked.

"What is it?" Annon asked, his voice lined with doubt.

Erasmus went to the large window facing the street. He tapped his bottom lip with a long finger and then pointed out the window. "It is too dark now to see it, but there was a smudge on the horizon. From a fire. A large fire. Same direction as the road, so the fire must have started on the road. By the size of the smoke plume, it likely shut down the road. Which means goods will stop flowing and a lot of money will be lost and won tonight at the Millpond. It will delay the caravans ready to depart. It may ruin cargo." He clucked his tongue, muttering dazedly to himself. He glanced at them, his brow wrinkling. "I'm assuming it was you folk who caused the fires and did so deliberately. Very foolish." He clucked his tongue again, muttering to himself. "They will want you dead for sure. They murder for much less in this town. I imagine we do not have long before they track your path here."

"*The Preachán are a scheming race. They love those things which are precious, and they have an amazing gift for memory. I have once heard of a Preachán named Hollibust who could recite the name of every person living he had ever met. There are others, in Havenrook mind you, who have taken the power of the mind and exploited it to the point where they can read the minds of others.*"

– Possidius Adeodat, Archivist of Kenatos

XI

Paedrin looked at the cross-eyed Preachán with distrust. He did not bother to hide his expression. "What are you saying, Erasmus? That we were followed here?"

Erasmus fluttered his hands in annoyance. "No, no—don't be a fool, Bhikhu. I doubt anyone at the Millpond has noticed the closure of the road yet. Yet. But there was smoke, and smoke comes from fire; it is in the exact direction of the only road leading to Havenrook. And by the looks of you, you just arrived today. Which means you were on the road, which means you were attacked by the thieves on the road and defended yourselves, and if this brother and sister have the fireblood as Tyrus Paracelsus has, then it is likely and probable that you set fire to the road and will cause losses of profit and an interruption in the flow of trade." His hands stopped flapping. "Was I being clear enough for you, Bhikhu, or should I repeat several parts until you catch up? Wasted moments, wasted time. They will track you *here*, for undoubtedly you asked for me by name, and hence will bring whatever danger with you to my abode. Why have you come?"

Annon stepped forward, his expression taut. "We seek Drosta's lair."

"Impossible," Erasmus muttered, shaking his head.

"What is impossible?" Paedrin asked, unnerved by the man's flood of information and how he had assembled so much on such a casual greeting. It was as if he had thought about the situation for hours instead of just moments.

"Impossible. No, it is impossible. It cannot be done."

Annon looked back at Paedrin, confusion on his face.

Hettie stepped forward. "What do you mean, Erasmus?"

The man whirled and walked to the window, muttering beneath his breath. His broad shoulders hunched, as if he were suddenly under a tremendous burden. His breath came out in quick gasps. He counted on his fingers. "Even if Kiranrao doesn't know, he will. Forced march through the woods. Cruithne territory. Three-day walk. Two with horses, but risk losing shoes or laming half of them. Speed does not make up for the risk. Three days then."

Hettie shook her head. "You are not making sense."

He gave an abrupt hand gesture to forestall more questions. "Impossible. Kiranrao is the element I cannot account for or predict. Down too many branches this can go. I cannot provide a probable guess yet. Does Kiranrao know you are here?" He looked at them, but it was hard to tell which of them he was gazing at.

"You could say that," Paedrin answered.

"Impossible," he muttered. "We would make it to Drosta's, but not back again alive. I will not go. Be gone. I do not have a price. It is not worth my time. Be gone!"

Annon held out his hands. "I did not understand what you were referring to. Why should Kiranrao matter in this?"

Erasmus coughed as he chuckled. "He has sought the treasure at Drosta's lair for many years. There is a bounty for anyone who can lead him to it. He does not know that *I* know where it is."

Hettie looked confused. "What purpose would he have in gaining more wealth? Why would it even interest him?"

Erasmus looked up, as if suddenly confused. "Who says that Drosta's treasure has anything to do with wealth? There are a great many things in the world that no amount of coin will purchase. Drosta's treasure is not in coin."

Annon looked at Hettie and she looked back at him. "We were led to believe that it was," he said.

Erasmus chortled. "Led to believe. By Tyrus Paracelsus. Imagine that. I cannot believe that your uncle would want Drosta's treasure in that villain's hands. It was put there to safeguard it."

"What?" Paedrin asked, stepping forward warily. "The treasure was put there?"

"Of course, you silly sheep-brained Bhikhu. If you are going to hide something of enormous value from a Romani or the Preachán, you do not leave it in Havenrook. You put it in a fortress among the Cruithne. I know of it because Tyrus wanted to be sure that the safeguards could not be breached. He had me test the defenses. I could not break them. He was satisfied that it was safe."

"Do you know what Drosta's treasure is?" Annon asked. Paedrin could tell by the look on his face that he was genuinely worried now. Hettie looked flummoxed.

"No. Only *where* it is."

"You must take us there," Annon said. "My uncle knew we could trust you. That we could rely on you to…"

Erasmus quickly rushed to the window. "Torches in the street. They are already on the way here. You must go. Now!" He waved his arms and advanced on them, trying to shush them away. "Dwyer! Get up here! Our guests must leave."

"Please!" Hettie implored.

"What you ask is impossible. Even with a day's head start, we would be found out, and they would follow us to Drosta's lair. Even with horses, we would…"

"I know, I know," Annon said impatiently. "But we need your help, Erasmus. This is important."

"It is of no concern to me," Erasmus said, grabbing Annon by the fringe of his cloak and tugging him toward the stairs. "Dwyer! They must go! Out with them. Out!"

"But if you would…" Hettie said.

"They will be here in moments!" Erasmus said. "You do not have much time to escape out the back. We will delay your pursuers as much as we can. Return to Kenatos. Tell your uncle he was a fool for sending you here. Tell yourselves that you were fools for trusting him."

The sound of boots on the stairwell announced the arrival of Dwyer, who held a knobbed stick in his hand. "Out with ye, lads. Out with ye. Come on. Let's have no trouble."

Erasmus brushed his hands and turned back to Paedrin, who had not budged from his spot. "You too, Bhikhu. You have all caused enough trouble already." He reached for Paedrin's sleeve.

Paedrin was waiting for that. He intercepted the Preachán's hand and put his finger on one side of his hand and his thumb on his palm. With a quick twist, he had the Preachán in an armlock that completely halted him.

"I do not mean to harm you," Paedrin said. "If you do not move, it will not hurt. But you will listen and figure this out quickly. We do not have much time. Grab what you need and come with us, because if you do not, I will go back to the Millpond this evening and explain to Kiranrao that you know of Drosta's lair. What do you think he will do with you if he finds out you have known all along?"

The others froze in the stairwell. Dwyer's face hardened with rage.

Erasmus muttered softly. He said several things under his breath that they could not hear. Then he spoke up. "You are correct. That changes the situation entirely. Very black-hearted of you, Bhikhu, but wise considering the circumstances. Dwyer, fetch my cloak. I do hope one of you knows how to speak the Cruithne tongue. That will help us immensely." He gazed at their faces and saw the dumb shock there. "I see you do not." He let out a deep, exasperated sigh.

Dwyer stood by the rear door, cudgel still in hand. "I will give you as much time as I can. Make for the woods. The dark will help shield ye a bit, but not for long if they hire a Finder."

Paedrin glanced at Hettie and saw her face stiffen with disgust. Her eyes flicked once his way, but did not linger.

Erasmus pulled on some stiff wool socks and then stuffed his feet into a well-worn set of boots. "Dry feet. Never underestimate the value of dry feet," he muttered.

There was a loud hammering at the front door. Erasmus shrugged into his cloak and then motioned toward the woods visible beyond the next row of buildings. Annon and Hettie followed, but Paedrin stayed put.

Annon paused and looked at him meaningfully, his eyebrows lifted.

"I will join you shortly," Paedrin said, clenching his staff.

Annon and Hettie glanced at each other.

"Go on ahead. This won't take very long."

He did not wait for them to acknowledge his words and walked around the side of Erasmus's dwelling, watching the spatter of torchlight brighten from the front. The angry voices of a mob grew steadily louder.

Paedrin breathed in through his nose and out through his mouth, short, quick breaths to steady himself. He listened to the raucous voices and the shouts of anger and demand. He could barely make out Dwyer's voice, trying to turn the tide of anger. A stone or brick smashed into the front window. The shrill wail of voices grew louder. There was the sound of a door slamming and being bolted. But against such a mob, it was a flimsy defense. In a moment, the home would go up in a blaze, along with all the books of poetry and translations, a man's work for many years. It was unfair.

Paedrin inhaled, and as he started to float, he ran up the side of the structure so that he reached the apex before running out of breath. He flipped up onto the roof, still holding the staff in one hand, and crouched at the edge, looking down at the mob. There were easily thirty or more down there, some with torches, others with lanterns. They were all Preachán, and they were a ferocious mob, shouting threats and insults at the lone man inside. One man stuffed a rag into his bottle of spirits and set fire to the edge.

Paedrin stood up straight, adjusted his neck muscles, and then hurtled off the edge of the roof. Someone saw him jump, for fingers were suddenly in the air stabbing at him. He plummeted to the street like a stone, but just before landing, he hissed in his breath to soften the impact and managed to land on the man with the flaming bottle and crush him into the street.

Paedrin looked up, taking in the momentary shock on their faces. Then he spun the staff in a wide circle and set to work.

That they were drunk made it almost too easy, but it was still forty or so against one, and he saw the gleam of knife blades, swords, and chains with hooks. He struck hard and fast, smashing a man in the eye with one jab of the staff pole before reversing the stroke and hammering another on the top of his skull, likely shattering it—using just enough force so as to not make it lethal. He cracked ribs, maimed feet, and, for certain, dislocated shoulders and hips. The anger and fury of the crowd—or perhaps the promise of coin—made them exceptionally brave. It was a hive of bodies, all trying to get a snatch at his clothes, grip his staff, or trip him with a boot. But Paedrin dodged every attempt, striking with feet, hands, or staff in all directions at once, sending bodies backward.

They rallied, those that could, and tried to crush him with sheer numbers. Chain whips whistled in the air at him. He ducked and darted to keep them from striking him, but he recognized that there were still more coming, and others were drawn to the screaming. Sucking in a gulp of breath, he jumped up and rose above the mass of bodies, letting them crash into each other before exhaling sharply and landing down amidst the pile.

He was wickedly good with his staff, and he knew it. It was an extension of him, and he whirled it against daggers and rapiers alike, returning each stroke with a whack to the chin or cheek; he dropped men to the street as his weapon impacted between their legs. He did not stay in the same place but moved with the flow of bodies, sometimes going over them. Sometimes he met the charge head-on. Sweat slicked down his ribs and arms, but he knew his own body and knew he had the strength to continue the fight.

From the crowd emerged a new man, and he recognized him from Kiranrao's table. There was a subtle shift in the mood then others fell back, making way before the bearded fellow, his eyes molten with hate.

Paedrin studied his footing, his confident walk. No stumble with wine or drink. There was something in his hand that glowed like a firefly. As if he were holding on to a burning ember and it made his palm glow orange. It was a stone in the hilt of a dagger, and the blade was back near his wrist, underhanded.

The man moved impossibly fast. Suddenly he was right next to Paedrin, and the knife was slashing toward his ribs. Paedrin twisted hard to the right and clamped his elbow against the man's arm, pinning it against his body. He felt a razor line of heat flash across his skin.

Eyes widening with anger, Paedrin dropped the staff and sent his hooked fingers into the man's grimacing face. For a moment they wrestled against each other, each one trying to throw the other off balance. A boot went behind Paedrin's ankle, and he knew in another moment he would fall. Rather than fight it, he released his hold on the knife hand and rolled backward, over the man's shoulders, and grabbed his chin. He connected with the man's elbow and hurled the man off his feet, slamming him on the cobbled street with a bone-jarring crash.

A flash of pain went across Paedrin's side. Lights began to shimmer. He looked down at the man, his face contorted in agony, and he stomped hard on his forearm, enough to break the bones. He heard them snap. He twisted the dagger from his fingers and immediately the light from the gem winked out. It felt heavy suddenly, as if it weighed as much as a bag of gold.

The broken man did not scream. His face was contorted with rage. He reached in his belt for another blade and began hefting it. Paedrin stomped on his stomach next, watching the man's eyes bulge out. He had damaged him severely. It would take him months to recover.

The pain in Paedrin's side was getting unbearable, but he did not let it show on his face.

The two stared at each other, fixing the moment in their minds. It was the first time in his life Paedrin was tempted to kill. The look of hate on the man's face meant revenge. It meant he would stop at nothing to hunt Paedrin down for another chance. He knew if their positions were reversed, there would be no qualm on the other's part, and he would have buried the dagger to the hilt in Paedrin's chest.

But that is why I am a Bhikhu, he reminded himself. Even a life as miserable and wretched as this man's was too sacred to steal. It meant that Paedrin had to be better than him. Always. There could be no room for doubting that. Paedrin stared into the hateful eyes, unflinching, and gave him a subtle nod as he lay on the dirty street, unable to even stand up. Two broken arms. Some grave internal damage. It would stop him from following them.

No one faced him in the man's place. The wave had crashed with all its fury and might and was now slinking back to the place where it came from. Gripping the heavy iron weapon in one hand, Paedrin knelt and retrieved his nicked staff, and he walked away from Havenrook, knowing that if he ever ventured there again, he would die.

"I am always fascinated by the baubles and trinkets which are invented by the Paracelsus order. They know how to enchant weapons with special powers. They created the magic that gives light to the city. Their genius knows no boundaries. Even the Rikes use their magic to heal the sick or Plague-ridden. They say that each item must be carefully crafted. I do not understand the principles involved, but I have grown to appreciate the genius behind it."

– Possidius Adeodat, Archivist of Kenatos

XII

The fire was small and sheltered within a hollowed-out stump to help conceal the light. Annon winced as Hettie pulled back Paedrin's blood-stained shirt and exposed the gash. It was an awful wound, yet Paedrin sat like a stone, his face impassive. Several layers of skin and tissue that was white and purplish lay exposed. It made Annon ill to look at it.

Hettie shook her head slowly. "It's too deep for just a compress. We'll need to stitch it."

Paedrin shrugged one shoulder.

"It will hurt," Hettie said. "Do you want some ale for the pain?"

He looked at her coldly. "Do your worst, woman."

Annon noticed Erasmus pacing around the camp, looking at each stump and tree, counting off the paces between them, looking at each patch of ground, often testing it with the toe of his boot.

"Annon, what do you make of this?" Paedrin said to him, tossing the dagger he had claimed in Havenrook.

119

He caught it easily enough, then realized it was surprisingly heavy. "This is odd," Annon said. Immediately the stone in the hilt started to glow. That surprised him as well, and he brought it closer to the fire, where Hettie and Paedrin were.

"It did that in his hand," the Bhikhu said. "Right before he cut me."

Annon nodded, staring at the stone. He brought it closer to his face and thought he saw something inside, a little pulse of light. It was so tiny, yet it seemed to zigzag inside. It reminded him of Tyrus's tower in Kenatos, all those orbs with the light that Tyrus seemed to sooth.

The light grew brighter and the zigzagging more intense.

Does it understand my thoughts? Annon wondered. *Is it responding to my memories?*

The stone dimmed and then flashed again, even more violently. It was as if something were struggling inside the stone trying to speak to him.

He glanced at Hettie and saw her looking at it also, her eyes curious. Then she removed her travel pack and started rummaging in it for supplies to stitch Paedrin's wound.

"Not yet," Annon said, halting her. "Hold a moment."

He stared at the stone and saw that it was not a stone. It was a round orb of glass, no larger than a child's toy. It was connected to the blade through an intricate mesh of metal weaving.

"There is something curious about this," Annon said. It was a strange feeling, a familiar feeling.

"Why does it glow?" Paedrin asked.

"Because it is worth five thousand ducats," Erasmus said, glancing over at them. "It has some power within it. Power that makes it more useful than just a blade alone. It is the craft of the Paracelsus to make such things."

Annon turned the weapon over in his hand. The stone grew bright again, almost frantic. There was something about the weave of the metal in the hilt and how it formed an ornamental fashion around the stone.

"Five thousands ducats, you say?" Annon murmured. That was a lot of money in Kenatos or anywhere in the world. The light flashed almost pleadingly.

Erasmus stamped his boot on a spot of ground, probably after having inspected it a dozen times, and then slowly settled into the earth, wrapping the cloak about him protectively. "Five thousand. Maybe more, depending on the power."

Annon held the handle in the flat of his hand and stared at it hard.

Pyricanthas. Sericanthas. Thas.

He fed the flame with his anger, letting it bubble up within him. He focused it on the weave of metal, letting the flames dance over the swirls. He gripped it tightly in his hands until the metal became warmer and warmer, but it did not burn him. Still he fed the flames, letting it burn into the metal, softening it.

"Annon," Hettie warned, looking at his face.

He was in control of the power, but he noticed he had a smile on his face. It was a pleasurable feeling. He gritted his teeth and focused it more, focusing it on the band around the place where the stone was embedded. The metal began to hiss with smoke.

The hilt sizzled and the stone plopped to the ground, free from the metal encasing it. As soon as it touched the ground, it cracked with a loud snapping sound, and there was a blast of white-hot light.

The stone sang with joy.

Annon closed his eyes, flinching from the sudden explosion, but he heard it now as clearly as a song. A spirit voice.

Thank you! Many blessings on you, kind Master! Three centuries have I been trapped, but now I am free! Bless you, kind Master!

Annon opened his eyes, and he saw the spirit hovering in the air before him. It was as small as a butterfly, but instead of gossamer, its wings were crooked and spiny with thorns. Its tiny body was thick with thorns, like a desiccated rose branch. The creature bowed in homage to him, singing again in a tone so clear and beautiful it made his heart ache fiercely.

You set me free, kind Master. I am of the Briarlings. One of your companions is wounded by my hand. I shall heal him for you.

The spirit zipped over to Paedrin, who flinched and batted at it as it disappeared into the gash; he stiffened with surprise.

The cut was mended before their eyes.

Many tender thanks, kind Master! I go to Mirrowen at last. Farewell!

The light streaked through the woods and vanished.

"The cut is gone!" Hettie said, shocked.

Paedrin looked down and then at Annon. "Did you do that?"

Erasmus chuckled from beneath his cloak. "You have never seen Druidecht before, Bhikhu? I'm surprised."

Paedrin explored his skin, pinching the flesh and examining it closely. He moved his arms around in circles, testing them for movement. "Amazing."

"Even more amazing that he wasted five thousand ducats to heal you," Erasmus said dryly. "Whoever owned that blade will want you dead."

"He already does," Paedrin quipped.

Annon stared at the warped, mangled metal in his hand. "I did not heal you," he said softly, looking at the shattered object for what it was. A prison. A gloriously fancy one too. "There was a spirit trapped in the stone. I set it free. It chose to heal you because its power had wounded you."

Paedrin's eyebrows lowered. "A spirit? You mean the light?"

"You all saw it as light," Annon answered, fingering his talisman. "Only I could see it for what it was. It was trying to speak to me from inside the stone, but I could not hear it. The nature of its imprisonment prevented it. But it could sense my thoughts and tried its best to communicate with me."

In his mind, he thought about his uncle's desk and the dozens of orbs there. It filled his mind with unspeakable anger to think about what beings might be trapped there. More than Briarlings. There were many species of spirits. Trapped. Imprisoned. Unable to speak. It angered him.

"Annon," Hettie said warningly again, gripping his arm. His fingers were glowing.

"Thank you," he muttered, trying to master himself. "I was remembering my visit to my uncle a few days ago. Things are not as they seem."

Erasmus snorted.

Paedrin shot an annoyed look his way and then stood and pulled back on his robe, still stiff with blood. He wrapped his belt around it and adjusted it. "It would be wise, before we go any further, if we spoke more truthfully to each other about what is going on."

Annon looked up at him. "There has been no attempt to deceive you, Paedrin."

The Bhikhu waved his hand impatiently. "Not on your part. But it is clear to me, and I am no fool, that there is much your uncle should have told you and did not."

"Such as?" Hettie challenged.

Paedrin turned to her. "Let's start with your story. You are a Romani girl near the age to earn a second earring. That is a pretty significant custom among your people, as I understand things. I cannot say I know many Romani, but that is nothing to complain about. You were told of a location where a great treasure is buried that you might use to free yourself without implicating your uncle. Clearly…and I hope you are not as dense as Erasmus is…your uncle knew full well that Kiranrao has been looking for Drosta's lair. Maybe it is not the treasure we need but something that Kiranrao can provide."

Annon frowned and shook his head. "What are you saying, Paedrin?"

"It was no coincidence that we ended up in that place. We just disrupted trade on an enormous scale and made several thousand enemies, one of which is a man who can outbid Tyrus to determine your future." He looked pointedly at Hettie. "Maybe your uncle was intending you to buy your freedom with Kiranrao's coin?"

Hettie flushed darkly. "I do not want that man's help," she said venomously. "I am even regretting my uncle's interference in my problem. He told us nothing about what we would face. He sent us into the middle of Havenrook with very little information."

"Exactly my point!" Paedrin said, rounding. "What is truly going on here?"

"How am I supposed to know?" Hettie shot back. "I went asking for help, to find a way to *earn* my freedom. Part of me just wishes to march back to Kenatos, spit in my uncle's face, and have done with all this."

"Not a wise course of action," Erasmus offered with a smirk. "You have no idea how many ill things are caused by spittle."

"You are not in the least curious about what Drosta's treasure is and why Kiranrao wants it?"

"No, not really," Hettie answered petulantly. "I do not like being used."

"I do not fancy it either, but quitting now seems hardly the right approach."

Annon chewed on his thoughts, struggling with the dangling pieces. "Hold a moment," he said, raising his hand. He tapped his chin, struggling to remember. It was only a few nights ago, but so much had changed that he had nearly forgotten it.

Hettie's arms were folded defiantly, and Paedrin looked as if he were ready to continue arguing until dawn. Annon looked from one to the other.

"Please, sit down. I need your help to think this through."

Hettie came down next to him. "What is it? Do you remember something?"

Paedrin cocked his head curiously.

"My mentor came and saw me recently. He is a Druidecht, of course, and he gave me a warning. He warned me about visiting my uncle. He said that my uncle might try and persuade me to go north. Into the Scourgelands."

For a moment there was nothing but silence and the snap and hiss of the fire.

Annon stared into the darkened woods. "He warned me about trusting my uncle. That he has no care or feeling for anyone, even his own kin."

Paedrin stared at him hard. "That would have been helpful to know before leaving Kenatos."

Annon bit his lip, shaking his head slowly. "I was so startled to learn that I had a sister that I forgot all about the warning. Reeder told me that years ago Tyrus led a group into the Scourgelands. None of them survived. He was the only one who did." Annon tapped his palm. "I think that perhaps he did not tell us everything about his intentions for us."

Erasmus's voice floated toward them. "Tyrus Paracelsus takes counsel from no man or woman. He keeps his own counsel. As do I. From what you have said tonight, I think he is like a spider, catching many flies in the same web."

Hettie grabbed a stick and jammed it into the fire. "I hate this."

"Hate what? That we are being manipulated?" Annon asked, half smiling.

"But to what purpose?" Paedrin said. "What is there to fear in the Scourgelands?"

Erasmus sat up, the firelight playing off the grooves in his face. "That is just the thing, sheep-brains. The only man known to have ever survived that place is the one who has brought us all here by this fire tonight."

"It is not recorded when the Plague began. Every kingdom was ravaged and their populations decimated. Some races have ceased to exist. The remaining few banded together, united in a single cause—to preserve knowledge. Thus was the formation of Kenatos. It was created as the last bastion of knowledge. No one kingdom would rule it. All contributed to its survival by donating books and provisions and wealth. We do have records dating back to the founding of Kenatos. None describes when the Plague began. If we have learned anything, we have learned this: it is not the strongest of the races that survives, or the most intelligent. It is the one that is the most adaptable to change. Thus only the Aeduan race will survive the Plague. All others races will succumb to it."

– Possidius Adeodat, Archivist of Kenatos

XIII

nnon awoke from the dream, startled by the thoughts whispered into his mind from a pair of Jasmine spirits. They were night dwellers who only came out during the moonlight. As he blinked awake, he smelled their sweet aroma.

You are hunted, Druidecht. A band of Preachán, roaming the woods in the dark. There is a Vaettir among them. The leader. Be warned.

Annon swallowed the rising panic. *How far away?* He pushed the thought at them.

Far still. These woods are vast, and they fear being found out by the Cruithne. They hunt you, Druidecht. Be warned!

The two spirits flitted away, taking the smell with them. Annon rolled onto his stomach, nestled in the blanket for warmth, for there was a chill in the night and streamers of fog above the trees. He heard voices speaking in low tones and cocked his head slightly. It was Paedrin and Hettie. They sat side by side, their voices hushed to avoid waking anyone.

"But you are free," Paedrin said. "We cannot be bound by traditions invented by madmen for the purposes of enslaving others. These are traditions, Hettie. They are not binding."

"Traditions can be more binding than sturdy ropes," she answered. "You don't understand."

"You are right. I don't. I don't see why you cannot just walk away. There are places you could go—Kenatos for example—where the Romani will not be able to take you."

She snorted derisively. "You are a fool if you think Kenatos is safe from the Romani. They operate within the walls of the city through a guild, of sorts."

"How do you know that?"

"I've been told."

"Exactly my point. Fear feeds these sorts of traditions. They want you to believe that there is nowhere you can go. They use fear to keep you from thinking, from believing in yourself. You are free already. You do not need to pay a king's ransom to earn it. You are free now. Accept it."

She sighed. "It is not that simple, Bhikhu."

"Why not? Explain the complexity to me. It will be a long while until dawn yet. Tell me."

"I do not wish to wake the others." She turned and glanced toward where he was sleeping, but Annon shut his eyes and held still, listening to their banter.

"You don't want to discuss it because you know I'm right," he answered.

"You are arrogant."

"You are evasive. Explain this to me then. What will happen to you if you forsake the Romani and someone snaps that ridiculous earring off you? Hmm? What will they do to you?"

Annon opened his eyes and watched her lean her face against her arms, crossed over her knees.

"I don't know."

"What were you taught?"

"Nothing. Only that the punishment would be extreme. It was never something specific. Not like receiving lashes with a switch or punishment like that. Punished in other ways. It was always…vague."

Paedrin breathed out like a hiss. "And you were a child when you were told this?"

"Yes."

Paedrin let out a pent-up breath, a seething sound. "Truthfully?" It was quiet for a long moment. "There is no pain so awful as that of suspense. It is the cause of even the wise man's fear. Not knowing what will happen. It is more effective than any threat at binding someone's mind." He exhaled again, shaking his head. "To be so cursed as a child. You were bound with strong ropes indeed."

"I was taught the only way to freedom was to buy mine."

"Indeed. They bound you with cruel, vague threats and said the only key was coin. Do you understand me, Hettie? The key is in your mind. You need but turn the lock and free yourself."

"But if I am caught by a Romani…"

He made a dismissive gesture. "I know. So many possibilities. That is part of the trap." He pointed at her. "You were born free. You were abducted as a babe and purchased as a child. And because that is all you have known, you perpetuate the trap they have created for you." He tapped his forehead deliberately. "The lock and key are right here. Open them. I know that is asking much from a sullen Romani girl who gets lost in the woods. But truly, Hettie, you have little to lose."

"What if they kill me?" she asked, her voice barely a whisper.

He glanced at her sharply and snorted. "As if death would not be preferable to living as a slave-servant-wife for the next thirty to forty years?" He chuckled softly and shook his head. "I will, of course, strenuously object to any Romani who comes along and tries to kill you."

"How thoughtful of you," she replied sarcastically.

He shrugged deferentially. "I am all kindness, I know. So answer me this. Why has it taken you so many days to drop your sneering and behave?"

"It is the middle of the night, Paedrin. I am too tired for pretenses."

"So if I am ever to have a normal discussion with you, I must wait until midnight? How uncharitable."

"If you were not such a braggart and a spleen beetle, I might have talked to you before now."

"I have never bragged in my entire life!" he said archly.

She elbowed him in the ribs and then caught herself. "I'm sorry. Is that where you were wounded?"

"Good thing the magic healed me first or that would have hurt. You have quite a temper."

"Yes, but didn't you drone on about how pain is a teacher?"

Paedrin chuckled. "I could almost grow to like you. But I am afraid that your sulky disposition will forever ruin any chance of that happening."

"If you have nothing of intelligence to say, then I will get some sleep since you are supposed to be on watch now. You are a braggart, Bhikhu. I know I will always dislike you."

"I do not care about your good favor, Hettie. But sleep well, all the same. In the morning, we will be good enemies again."

Hettie crawled over to her bedroll that was near Annon's and slumped inside with a yawn. There was just enough light from the moon and stars to make out her face, her expression, as she rolled over and faced him.

"I'm sorry if we woke you," she whispered.

"I was sleeping soundly up until a short while ago. I'm glad we have him with us."

Paedrin's voice lifted slightly. "You should be."

Hettie scowled and shook her head. "Silence, braggart!" she hissed over her shoulder.

Annon thought about the others, prowling the woods for them. "It was not your talking that woke me. Some spirits told me that Kiranrao is hunting us. They did not name him but they said a Vaettir and a group of Preachán were roaming the woods following our trail. If they draw near, I will be warned again."

Hettie's expression hardened. "I will help conceal where we camped tonight. There are some things we can do to throw them off."

Annon smiled nervously. "Not that I doubt your skills, sister, but I imagine Kiranrao can afford a Finder himself. We may have to confront them. Like we did on the road to Havenrook."

Paedrin turned to look at them. "Only after they have killed me first. Save your magic. I'm not afraid of Kiranrao."

"You should be," Hettie said.

"And why is that?" Paedrin challenged. "No one speaks of him in Kenatos. No one even knows his name."

Hettie rolled over and looked at him. "Not now, Paedrin, but the Arch-Rike has offered a reward for his death so vast that even the Romani are tempted to betray him. He stole something from the Arch-Rike's palace and got away. Very few people have been able to do such a thing or fear the Arch-Rike too much to try. Kiranrao is dangerous and he is deadly."

"Which is why I'd prefer we stay ahead of him," Annon said. "Does he know about the fireblood?"

"Does he know that I have it?" she asked.

"That's not what I meant. Does he know that it exists?"

Hettie shrugged. "I am sure he keeps a vial of our blood with him at all times to ward off the Plague. Yes, I am fairly confident he knows about our race."

Paedrin leaned forward. "What exactly is your race? You never said in the woods before we reached Havenrook."

"There is nothing to tell," Annon replied. "We do not know what the race is called, only that it gives us the power of the fireblood. That power grows as we age, but also becomes more uncontrollable. We were taught the words to tame it and warned never to lose control of it."

"If anyone says those words, can it be controlled?" Paedrin asked.

Hettie shook her head. "No, it does not work like that. We say it in our minds before summoning the power. It helps us control it."

"But we run the risk of losing control," Annon said. "I would rather not use it at all. But if Kiranrao is hunting us, we may not have a choice."

"You always have a choice," Paedrin said. "If I hear them coming, I will wake you."

"If you all stop talking," Erasmus complained, "We will all be able to sleep. I told you this journey was impossible at the beginning. We may make it there before he catches us. But not away. I hold to my prediction."

Annon nestled down amidst his blanket. He stared at Hettie and saw her eyes gazing up at the stars.

"He is right about one thing, you know," Annon whispered.

"Paedrin or Erasmus?"

"Paedrin."

She rolled and looked at him, waiting for his explanation.

"You are already free."

Her lips pursed. "We will see, Annon. We will see."

He lay his head down, but it took a while before he fell back asleep. Hettie's warning about Kiranrao lodged in his throat.

"When the Plague strikes, it is different every time. In one generation, the sickness caused sores around the mouth and joints. In another, it caused a red, irritating rash. Each time it leaves a telltale sign of its devastating presence. White spores. Yellow skin. Red flux. When the Plague strikes a community, it ravages it quickly, leaving the majority dead. Some try and flee the Plague, which helps it spread to other cities and kingdoms. The change in symptoms has made it very difficult to cure. One thing is certain. When the Plague strikes, the people die."

– Possidius Adeodat, Archivist of Kenatos

XIV

The climb into the mountains of the Cruithne taxed their strength. Annon had been raised in the woods of Wayland, full of hardwoods like oak and walnut and crisscrossed with streams and brooks and wild berries. The higher they climbed, the more the mountains transformed the surroundings. Towering pine and cedar, rocky ledges, the occasional thunder of waterfalls. The footing was difficult, upward, with the taunting of jackdaws and blue jays. The strain on his legs and breathing revealed a weakness he had not experienced before. Paedrin did not seem troubled at all; neither did Hettie. But Erasmus wheezed and needed to rest constantly.

There was no trail to guide them, but Erasmus knew the way. He would often stop at a tree, feeling the rough bark for a sign of some sort, a memory from the past. He would nod and then point the right way. He seldom spoke, but he observed the woods continually and mumbled to himself.

After two days, the tension in Annon's mind had begun to ebb concerning their pursuers, but the peace ended abruptly with the whispers from several tree spirits clustered in a grove of pine that warned of danger behind them. Many spirits from Mirrowen traveled alongside birds, and Kiranrao's band had been spied earlier that day, following their trail closely.

When Annon announced this to the others, he was met with grave looks from Hettie, a dubious one from Paedrin, and a curt nod from Erasmus.

"We are still another day or two away from Drosta's lair," Erasmus said. "They have caught up with us faster than I expected. They may overtake us before sunset if we do not hurry."

"Why not wait for them in a place of our choosing?" Paedrin suggested, tapping his staff against his palm. "We have the high ground and the chance to surprise them."

Erasmus shook his head. "They outnumber us and I am sure they know about what we can do. We must go faster and reach the lair before them. We have only traveled during the day so far, so we should travel all night now. That improves the odds of outdistancing them...hmmm....a little."

"Only a little?" Annon asked.

"I have not changed my previous prediction, Annon, that it is nearly impossible. You see, there is a ravine with only one way in or out. We must get there and out before they catch us."

They pushed harder into the mountains and were not overtaken at nightfall. They were grateful for a waxing moon to offer light. It was an arduous trail and punished their legs and stamina, making the hours pass slowly. The stars shifted noticeably with the passing night. Still they went higher, and the landscape began to transform once more. The trees became more sparse, the scrub more barren. Jagged clefts of rock and boulders appeared next, creating tortuous trails that wound up and back. It was painful going, but eventually dawn greeted them, revealing a new world that the night had hidden from sight.

The waterfalls were even more majestic and imposing, giant clouds of water plumes exploding from ridges and crags, disappearing into a shroud of mist deep into canyons below. As they finally exited the woods, the caps of the mountains became visible at last, higher still and jabbing into the sky like knives. Towers and parapets were grafted into the snow-capped peaks, gushing an unending billow of sooty smoke.

Annon stopped and stared at the massive structures. He could not understand, for a moment, that hands had created them. There was a wall of mountains, and each mountain had twelve to fifteen towers crowning it, each tall and crafted with crenellations and crowned with pennants. The years it must have taken to craft so many. The city seemed older than the world. Bridges connected between some of the towers, and waterfalls tumbled from the upper reaches, mixing the water spray with the soot-smoke. Due to the height, there was perpetual snow, and the contrast between the white snow and the black towers was impressive.

"I have never seen such a thing," Annon whispered in amazement. "This is the seat of the Cruithne? This is Alkire? It is more massive than the island city."

Paedrin stopped short, hands on his hips, and whistled softly. "It makes the temples of Seithrall seem like a child's plaything. I never imagined such a place."

Erasmus, still wheezing, came up next to him. "The air…is thinner…up here. Harder to catch…your breath. Those fortresses have been built over centuries. Stonehollow built them."

"Why so high?" Annon asked, staring at the distant peaks and towers. "They are above the line of trees where it is too cold and rocky to grow. Where do they get wood for their fires?"

"Don't be an idiot," Erasmus said. "They do not use wood to burn for flame. They harvest blackrock. It burns hotter and longer. These mountains are thick with veins of it. They also harvest the waterfalls as well. They dam up the mountain lakes and use giant waterwheels to power their forges. See over there? See the dam?"

Annon did. Between two of the mountain peaks was an enormous wall, so massive it looked like the face of a cliff itself. Contained behind it was a mountain lake, so deep, blue, and rippling that it seemed a reflection of the sky. What life teemed in those waters? How cold it would be to learn the Druidecht lore of the high mountains.

Erasmus pointed to a squat mountain—one of the shortest. "Deep in the caverns, they find gems and precious stones, then shape and carve them. They sell these treasures to Kenatos. The rivers carry the goods downstream to Havenrook, and then they are boxed and loaded in barges or caravans."

Hettie shook her head. "But Kenatos is to the west of here. Why ship them south and then back up again? It doesn't make sense."

Erasmus turned and gave her a mocking smile. "Because the mountains to the west, between us and Kenatos, are cursed with beings of evil. No Cruithne will travel there. Or should I say, very *few* will travel there."

Paedrin frowned. "Which means that is where we are going."

Erasmus smiled. "Correct, sheep-brains. For once."

Annon remembered camping in the woods before reaching Havenrook and the warning he had received from the spirits. He shuddered, keeping his thoughts to himself. "How far is it?"

"We will make it there before sunset. But we need to rest a bit. We go down from here. My knees are not as young as they used to be." He stopped and stared at the vast range of mountains, at the fortresses and haze and waterfalls. He counted them softly, muttering as he went. "Hmmm. There are fewer waterfalls than last time. Interesting."

"What does that mean?" Hettie asked.

He smiled wisely. "Opportunity."

After resting, they started the treacherous descent into the canyon separating them from another vast mountain. The woods engulfed them again, full of trees and startled deer, foxes, and gray wolves. The air grew colder, and the daylight was dappled by a permanent haze hanging over the mountains.

Erasmus led the way, for each path and fork needed to be studied. Without his assistance, they would have been hopelessly lost. Annon kept close to him, listening for the warnings of spirits, uneasy because of the fearful aura surrounding them. The spirits were timid here. Some barely acknowledged his presence, and that concerned him even more.

"Drosta was a Cruithne, wasn't he?" Annon asked.

Erasmus muttered his response. "He was."

"And he lived so distant from the others of his race?"

"Obviously he valued his privacy. He was a Paracelsus. I'm sure you knew that."

Annon nodded. "Did the Plague take him?"

"No. I've heard said he was killed by a bear. Or something worse. A Finder discovered his bones searching for him. There were claw marks."

Annon swallowed, gazing into the gloom of the trail before them.

The afternoon began to wane, but it was difficult to judge how much daylight would be left. The canyon was steep and the footing rocky and loose at times. Sometimes the trailhead was so narrow that they could only pass one at a time. Brush scraped and scratched at them. The air was fragrant with the aromas of the woods, but there was a sourness in the smell, of things decayed and dying.

As they approached the bottom of the canyon, they were alerted to the sound of a waterfall, hidden in the trees ahead. The sound made Annon thirsty, and he suggested they refill their water there.

Erasmus stood and shrugged. "It cannot be that far."

"I will go," Annon offered. "Give me your water skins." He collected them all and started into the thin copse of woods, angling his way toward the sound. The ground was rocky and rose slightly. He huffed a bit, trying to quicken his step to get there and back. The woods ahead were full of haze from the waterfall. It did not sound like one of the mammoth ones they had seen, but it was sizable enough to be heard. As he drew nearer, an ominous feeling nagged at his stomach.

He was not that far from his companions. They were nearby. Surely there was nothing wrong in seeking water. He continued his pace, glancing cautiously as he went. There were no signs of animal life as he went.

How strange. This deep into the canyon, there should be many.

The rush of the waterfall beckoned from ahead. The water would be so cool and refreshing. It would taste so much better than the leathery flavor he was used to. The thought of it made his mouth water. He was tired and weary. Soaking his feet in the pool would be a relief.

As he advanced, the trees began shimmering in the mist. Even the sunlight was masked by the mist. There were no shadows.

Annon stopped short, hesitating. He yearned for the rush of water, to taste it and enjoy it. Why stop when he was so near? Would he return empty-handed to the others? Was he afraid of something?

Fear.

Annon felt its presence trickle down his back. He was afraid. His palms were sweaty and not from the arduous hike down into the canyon. A tremor went through his stomach, leaving a salty taste in his mouth. A shiver.

Fear.

It was foolish and irrational to fear a waterfall. Why hesitate? It would only be a moment and the flasks would be full. Then he would return to his companions and laugh at himself for being such a fool.

For being such a fool.

Annon swallowed. Why had he not sensed the presence of any spirits since arriving in the belly of the canyon? Always before, if there was danger, they warned a Druidecht of it. He alone could hear their thoughts. And he realized that he was hearing the thoughts of a spirit. Not the frantic whispers of a tree spirit or a thrush spirit. He was hearing the luring thoughts of something even more deadly and powerful.

It was the Fear Liath itself.

It recognized his change in attitude. His wavering indecision. A wave of dread struck him like a hammer to a post, driving his feet into the ground so that he could not move. It was paralyzing fear, wave after wave of dread and anguish. He could not move, only stare at the mesmerizing mists. That was its lair, of course.

Was it not a principle for hunters to watch places frequented by their prey? Treasure hunters seeking Drosta's lair were probably more frequent than rare. They were the Fear Liath's prey.

Annon tried to run, but he could not move. His mind clouded with terror. The Fear Liath was hidden within the falls. It was coming for him. It would kill him.

No!

He screamed the thought at it, trying to master himself. It was an emotion. There was nothing holding him back. He could move his limbs. He could breathe. He could run.

With that decision, his legs were unlocked.

Annon turned and ran, charging through the trees and away from the misty shroud that was thickening around him. He bounded over rocks, dodged past trees, and nearly wept with shame as he scrambled away from the deadly trap.

He launched himself over a rounded boulder and a creature scuttled from beneath him, a mass of thick dark fur. His heart went through spasms of terror and he darted away from it. A bear cub? A bear? It was large. He streaked away down the hill, gasping for breath, and saw a giant sloping boulder in front of him, one that tapered to a point at least a span high.

Unable to stop himself, he ran up the sloping edge until he reached the top. He gasped and panted, sweat blinding his eyes. It was behind him, in the mist. But somehow, it was not able to follow him that far. The mist crept down the hillside, slow as death. He could feel the presence of the Fear Liath, looming and angry at its escaped prey.

Annon shuddered, swallowing despite the parchment-like feel of his throat. He breathed in deep gulps, staring at the creeping mist. Slowly, slowly it descended. He licked his lips, staring at the unseen enemy, grateful he had managed to escape in time and horrified at how easily it had lured him away from the group.

He wiped his mouth on his sleeve, hunched over the peak of the rock, ready to leap down the other side if he saw anything move in the mist. He blinked once and saw a lone gray wolf, paused at the edge of the mist. The creature was staring at him, eyes silver.

He stared back at it, still drawing in each breath with relish. He recognized the spirit being.

The Wolviren padded away from the mist, weaving through the trees until it was gone.

Annon slowly detached himself from the shelter of the boulder. They did not have much time to find Drosta's lair and escape again. But he had a feeling it was very near. The Fear Liath's presence near it was no accident. His imagination could not fathom what type of treasure his uncle knew to be hidden there. What sort of power did it possess and why had it been hidden away for so long?

"*Each race and kingdom has certain specialties. Those from Stonehollow have earned their wealth carving living rock. When you venture into their lands, you are amazed at the enormous evidences of stone carving all around. The hills are littered with giant boulders and dark evergreen trees. Some families of Stonehollow helped lay the foundation stones for the first castles of Wayland. Building the island city of Kenatos was one of their shorter projects.*"

– Possidius Adeodat, Archivist of Kenatos

XV

Paedrin watched Annon emerge from the woods, ashen-faced and quivering. That he had seen something star-tling was no mistake. He looked rigid with fear.

"What is it?" Paedrin asked.

Hettie turned sharply, seeing her brother for the first time. "Annon?"

The Druidecht's voice was thick. "I nearly died." He gestured back toward the waterfall. "There is a creature hidden in the mist of the falls. This is its lair. We are in danger."

Erasmus's face scrunched, and he began flickering his fin-gers, counting.

"What was it?" Hettie asked, approaching Annon and put-ting her hand on his arm to steady him.

Paedrin was a little surprised at the show of tenderness. He squeezed the shaft of his staff, peering into the woods, alert now for danger. His ears reached out, listening for the sound of the creature.

"The spirits in the Alkire call it a Fear Liath. There are few spirits in this area. They are terrified of it. It moves at night."

Erasmus scratched his cheek. "In that case, we should not linger here. Better to get in and out of Drosta's lair before the sun sets. You said that your uncle gave you a key to enter?"

"Yes," Annon replied.

"Then we had better hope it still works. This way."

Erasmus took them down a scrabbling trail at the base of the ravine, one that meandered back and forth, with heavy, stunted trees clawing at their faces and arms as they walked. After passing a dense tangle, they arrived at Drosta's lair.

It did not require the Preachán's eyes to spot the place.

The clearing was wide and littered with abandoned campfires. Trees had been hacked down and used for fuel. Broken fragments of stone and branches littered the ground. Paedrin moved ahead quickly, for there was a dome-shaped rock in the center of the clearing. It was likely a boulder, probably up to his waist in height, and smoothed around the edges from the elements. All around it were broken hammers, pickaxes, shovels, and crowbars. The ground was pockmarked with indentations, but on quick observation, showed a layer of stone, of solid rock. A few scraggly bushes had sprouted up amidst the debris. The wood from the spade handles showed their age and sharp spurs jutted from the lengths.

Hettie wandered to the other side, searching the ground for signs of motion. Paedrin watched her from the corner of his eye as she bent low to the earth and touched broken fragments of rock. Her eyes flicked this way and that, studying the scene.

"It's the dome of rock," Erasmus said, sniffing loudly. "In case you hadn't figured it out, sheep-brains."

"No one has been here in some time," Hettie muttered. "These tools are well rusted. The wood has rotted. There are signs of at least five or six different camps that have stayed here." She rose and walked around the base of the dome. "They tried many different ways to pry the rock."

Erasmus hawked and spat. "It would require a steel beam and fulcrum to pry it loose. The beam would be too heavy for any horse or two horses, let alone making it safely down the trail. Twenty men might be able to lift one down here, over a matter of weeks. When Tyrus showed me this place, I told him that no one man would be able to open the dome." He jammed his walking stick into the solid ground. "No digging to the treasure either. As I said. You need a key to open it."

Paedrin rested his foot against the stone and pressed his full weight against it. It was unyielding.

Annon approached and rubbed his hand over the face of the stone. "Many have tried to move it."

"And failed," said Erasmus.

In Annon's mind, he could almost hear the ghosts of the dead. The air was thick with memories. A hammer lay nearby, pitted with rust. He grabbed it and hefted it. The handle held firm. The head did not wobble. He looked at it as a remnant of the efforts of many men. The hammer represented failure.

Paedrin straightened, watching the Druidecht.

Annon breathed out softly, then inhaled the dusty air. "Tyrus said that only a keyword will open the entrance. He taught it to me." He closed his eyes. "*Vickensatham. Restimos. Alloray morir.*"

It was the Vaettir tongue, and it surprised Paedrin that he knew it. Spoken a bit haltingly, but the words were correct. *Awaken from your sleep. Rise from the dust. Open the gateway to death.*

The domed rock shuddered. Annon and Paedrin stepped back as the enormous mass of stone separated from the earth, trailing dirt and flecks of debris. The boulder rose, hovering in the air, casting a shadow over the gaping circular hole now uncovered.

"Well, well," Erasmus muttered, smiling with chagrin. He approached and waved his hand beneath the stone, through the empty air. "I suppose that explains why it never opened for me."

Annon stared into the black depths, his eyes widening. "It will hover here for a time and then it will close. It will not open again until the next dawn."

"What is it?" Hettie asked, looking at his face. "You look worried."

Annon wiped his mouth, his eyes intent. "It is speaking to me."

"Another spirit?" Paedrin asked, scoffing.

"Yes. There is one trapped down there. I can hear it."

"What is it saying?" Hettie asked intensely.

Annon looked at her, his eyes widening. "It whispers that I must kill you all."

"*I have great respect for the cunning of the Paracelsus order. I was tempted to join it myself, but I lack the willpower it demands in addition to the physical capacities. Complete abstinence is easier than perfect moderation. While the Archivists record the lessons of the present to be useful to future generations, the Paracelsus order rediscovers the wisdom of the past to be used in the present. These are cunning men. They spend their time feasting on the runes and symbols that have long been forgotten, and they uncover various magics which are useful to mankind. There is a great deal of study regarding heat, power, energy, force, and the properties of various gemstones. They protect their craft with elegant and sophisticated traps. Some Paracelsus have been known to unlock secrets of power that they should not have. It is wise that the order is kept under the close scrutiny of the Arch-Rike of Kenatos.*"

– Possidius Adeodat, Archivist of Kenatos

XVI

P aedrin snorted. "A friendly spirit you've found. How touching. Well, I suppose we should get started." He approached the lip of the hole, peering down into darkness. He quickly sucked in some breath, feeling himself start to float like the stone itself. Then he stepped over the hole and slowly let his breath out, descending gradually, floating down like a speck of gossamer web.

There was a shaft of light coming from the gaping hole, revealing a depth to the chamber as he descended. It was a cave, nature-made, probably three times as tall as his full height. It expanded away in every direction, making the hole the apex of the chamber. Paedrin floated downward, searching the gloom for signs of disturbance. Much was hidden in the shadows. He was expecting a Paracelsus study, but there were no tables or flasks or cauldrons. No aging books. The floor was made from stone tiles, each one cut and fashioned into a grid-like surface. Beyond the dusty haze of light, he could see very little.

"Some torches would be helpful," he called up as his feet touched down on the ground.

As if in answer to his suggestion, three lights appeared in the chamber. There were three glass orbs mounted into the walls, and they sparked to life instantly, causing a reddish glare to fill the dark void. They were on opposite sides from one another, as if he stood in the midst of a triangle, with one in front and two in the rear behind him.

"Actually, there is light," Paedrin said, testing the sturdiness of the floor, for it had begun to tremble. He glanced around the room quickly, trying to adjust his vision. The floor trembled, shuddering, sending little pricks of worry into his stomach. He was as tense as a bowstring, listening, waiting, sensing each breath in his body, each rapid, fluttering heartbeat. The tremors increased.

Turning around quickly, he saw it.

It was a massive hulking shape, made from solid stone. It was easily half as tall as the chamber, vaguely man-shaped with huge, hammer-like arms and enormous trunk legs. It did not walk so much as shift its weight, and it was the shifting that caused the tremors in the floor. It came at him directly. No creature of speech, just a faceless mass of stone, shuddering the entire cave as it moved.

Paedrin did not wait to guess its intention. He darted to the creature's left and whipped his staff around as hard as he could, gripping one end with both hands to increase the force.

The staff collided with the creature, causing a loud whip-crack sound as the wood struck at its vague, leg-like structures. The power of his blow went all the way back up the shaft and jolted his arms. It was like striking a mountainside.

The creature shifted immediately toward him and continued its lumbering advance.

Paedrin came at it again, whistle-fast, striking it six times in moments. The staff clattered and clacked, but no amount of force he used could even slow the creature. A massive arm wheeled at him, and he ducked it easily, but it made his mouth dry thinking what would happen if it managed to catch him only once.

"Paedrin!" Hettie screamed.

"I am all right so far," he answered, moving around behind it again, drawing it away from the hole. "This creature is massive. It is slow, but very strong. I do not see any treasure here." The reddish glare of the light revealed nothing but walls.

"There is rope. Yes, over there!" Hettie said. "Get it. I'm going down there."

"Not yet," Paedrin said. "Let me see if I can find something further. I am faster than this thing." He raced around the perimeter of the cave, looking for any irregularity in the walls. There were four insets into the walls, little alcoves. He went from one to another. The final one, the fourth, he discovered not a door but a trapdoor handle. An iron ring set into the stone.

"Aha!" he shouted. "I found something!"

The creature lumbered at him again, and he had to escape to the other side of the room quickly. His heart pounded with excitement.

"What is it?" Annon called down.

"There is a trapdoor handle. It's fastened to a large slab of stone. I will try and lift it. Hold a moment. Do not come down here yet."

Paedrin watched the creature advance tirelessly at him and retreated, drawing it again to the far side of the chamber. It changed its speed suddenly, going faster. Paedrin ducked as the massive fist rushed past his head. He jumped away and then sprinted back to the trapdoor. He set down his staff and grabbed the handle tightly and pulled. His muscles groaned with pain. He felt it shift, barely. Clenching his teeth, he lowered himself down and pulled even more, trying to free the trapdoor lid. The creature was on him even faster now, swinging at him again.

Paedrin let go of the handle and rushed away again. He saw Hettie climbing hand over hand down a rope into the chamber.

"No, I said not yet!" Paedrin barked at her.

The rope suddenly snapped, sending her falling the rest of the way into the chamber.

Annon watched his sister fall. The jolt of seeing her there made his heart spasm with fear. The frayed end of the rope dangled near the lip of the opening.

"Hettie!" he yelled.

She shook her head, trying to move. Blood dribbled down from her forehead, pattering on the stone floor. The massive creature lumbered toward her, its speed increasing now as if each passing moment awoke its fluidity more.

The spirit voice whispering in his mind was cruel and taunting. *The Goule will kill her. It will kill the Vaettir. Claim me, Druidecht. Enter the cavern. I am trapped beneath a trapdoor. You sense me. You sense where I am. Use me, Druidecht. I will destroy your enemies. I will destroy the ones hunting you. Kill the Preachán first. He will betray you.*

It was almost impossible concentrating with its voice in his mind. Such a piece of magic should be hidden away. It was powerful—its presence as dark as the cavern below. Annon looked around quickly for another rope to lower himself down. Even though the others could not hear it, their minds would become infected by it just being down there.

Hettie raised her hands, her mouth muttering words in the Vaettir tongue, and the flames gushed from her hands, striking the stone beast full in the chest. Like a flood, the flames engulfed it, sending waves of heat to fill the room and brightening the walls.

Annon was terrified she would lose control of it again. He had to get down there to save her.

"Grab that rope!" he shouted to Erasmus. "Over there!" The Preachán was already there, grabbing the rope and joining him, quickly tying a knot around the stone where the other one had snapped.

The creature was on her before she realized it. The flames had done nothing to prevent its advance. A fist arced toward her head. Had Paedrin not arrived and shoved her away, it would have crushed her skull. The flames in her hands sputtered out.

There was a scorch mark in the center of its chest; the stone was livid. But despite the trailers of steam and hissing molten stone, it came on again, closing on the fallen Hettie with ruthlessness.

Paedrin struck at it from behind with his staff, harder and harder, trying to draw it back toward him. He yelled at it, but it was blind to him as Hettie scrambled to escape it. Paedrin struck it with all his power and watched in shock as his staff shattered against its broad shoulders, making his hands sting.

"Run!" Paedrin yelled at her.

Annon grabbed the rope, hoping it would hold. The voice was a murky drone in his mind. *I am here. Claim me, Druidecht. Claim my power. Drench me in blood that I might fulfill my power. Blood feeds me. Makes me stronger. You have the fireblood. I can sense it in you. I will obey it.*

With blood streaming down her face, Hettie rushed to the nearest wall and started along the edge away from the creature.

Annon landed in the middle of the room, his heart full of fear. He searched quickly for Hettie and Paedrin in the gloom.

"The trapdoor?" He could feel it in the stones, beckoning him. He did not know what form the treasure took, but he imagined it was something crafted by a Paracelsus. Something with a living spirit trapped inside. An evil spirit.

There is no evil. There is no wickedness. There are no laws. There is no blame. I am master over death. Take me, Druidecht. Take me from this prison. Use me.

"Over there!" Paedrin answered, pointing to the gap in the wall. Annon started toward it at the same time as Hettie.

Hettie stumbled over something on the floor and went down, landing with a crash. Paedrin sucked in his breath and vaulted into the air, rising like a bird and swooping over the top of the creature, before coming down hard next to her.

"Will you never listen to me!" he glowered at her, grabbing her around the waist and hauling her to her feet.

"Watch out!" she warned.

The fist of the Goule struck him on the shoulder with a sickening crunch.

Paedrin was flying again, but not because of his breathing. The wall of the cave rushed in, and he smashed against it, losing his sight for a moment in a sudden bloom of pain. Pain had never stopped him, though. Pain was a teacher. The creature was getting faster and faster.

"Both of you!" Paedrin said. "The trapdoor! It will only go for one of us at a time. The others need to open the trapdoor. Pull hard on the ring! I will face it."

He knew his arm would be useless pulling on the ring. He was the fastest of them all. The one most likely to avoid the creature as its speed increased. He rushed at it like a madman, coming up into the air and kicking at its head-like stump. The blows meant nothing to it. It surged at him again, massive fists swinging multiple times now as its speed increased.

Annon and Hettie rushed for the trapdoor and pulled frantically on the iron ring. Even their combined strength was not enough. The slab weighed more than they both could lift.

"Erasmus!" Paedrin roared. What if the treasure was already stolen? What if they were risking their lives for no end? Why had Tyrus sent them into a death trap?

Think! His mind was trapped in a fog of pain. His shoulder throbbed, but he shoved the thought of his pain aside. He had experienced worse at the temple. The creature was no being of flesh. It was a guardian. It protected the treasure. But surely there had to be a way to stop it? Physical force was obviously not enough. Flame did not hinder it. What else might?

Paedrin saw Erasmus climbing down a fresh rope, hand over hand. He hung from the knotted cord, studying the chamber quickly, his eyes darting this way and that.

"Help Annon and Hettie!" Paedrin said. "Maybe three is what it takes to lift it!"

A rock fist glanced off his temple. He flipped backward, putting more distance between himself and the creature. He was tiring. The relentless pursuit muddled his thinking.

"That's it!" Erasmus said triumphantly.

"Then get over there!" Paedrin roared.

"No, you have it wrong. The lights on the walls. The orbs. Touch them. Cover them with your hands or a cloak. Quickly, Bhikhu! Cover the one behind you!"

Paedrin thought the Preachán was daft. Cover the orb? But he remembered that the lights had illuminated the room as soon as he touched the ground. As fast as he could, he rushed to the nearest orb and smothered its light with his hands. He gritted his teeth, waiting for a crushing blow to come at him.

The room dimmed. The creature slowed and turned away from Paedrin, coming at Annon and Hettie.

"The other two!" Erasmus called. "Annon! Hettie! Cover the other two!"

Hettie rushed across the room and used her cloak to smother the second one. The creature had turned from her and started across the room, but its movements slowed as the light faded.

"The last one, Annon! Smother it!"

The Druidecht turned, watching the creature approach him ponderously. The chamber was nearly dark. "You do it, Erasmus. You cover it."

"Why?"

"Because the treasure is under the trapdoor. I can sense it. It will take over your mind if you touch it. Let me find a way to collect it without touching it."

Paedrin felt a hot surge of jealousy at Annon's words.

"I will take it," Hettie said. "The treasure belongs to me. You said you wanted no portion of it."

"This is a moment you must all trust me, friends," Annon said. "I can hear it fully right now. It is speaking to each of us. It wants us to fight each other to claim it. Although I can hear it, it does not control me. You must trust me. If we do not work together, this trap will kill us. Erasmus, the final orb."

The Preachán came the rest of the way down. As soon as his boots touched the floor, the creature shifted and started at him with slow, shuddering movements. Erasmus covered the final orb, plunging the chamber in darkness.

The creature stopped.

Paedrin breathed out, releasing the pent-up frustration and panic. He felt strange, his emotions jumbled. He wanted to kiss

Hettie. He wanted to kill Annon. He wanted to drown Erasmus in the waterfall. The feelings were violent and went against every aspect of Bhikhu precepts. He struggled with his feelings, trying to control his breathing.

"Annon?" Hettie whimpered. "I feel sick…"

Paedrin heard the grunt in the darkness, then a muffled voice muttering, "It is too heavy."

"Quickly, Druidecht," Erasmus said, his voice sounding pained.

Annon's voice rang out sharply. "Goule. Obey me. Open the trap door."

The creature shuddered again and slowly returned to the alcove. There was a grating, grinding noise as the lid was dragged away. A hiss emerged in the room. There was light in the alcove, and Paedrin saw Annon's face bathed in the silvery light. He stared at the dark space, his eyes wide with surprise. Then he reached inside his belt pouch, uncinched the drawstrings, and withdrew a set of sturdy gloves. After tugging them on, he reached gingerly into the pit.

The feelings intensified within Paedrin. Thoughts and images rushed through his mind that shocked him with their intensity and depravity. He trembled against the rush of feelings the images produced.

Annon lifted a silver dagger from the depths of the pit. There was a white stone embedded in the blade guard, one that glowed with a ghostlike light. Annon stared at it in awe and fear, his eyes widening with horror. Then slowly, deliberately, he withdrew a sheath from the pit and slid the blade inside.

The three glass orbs cracked, leaking a glowing reddish mist that dissipated, stealing the light slowly as the mist began to disperse.

There was a release of the emotions as the blade snicked inside the sheath. Its control vanished. The images in Paedrin's mind disappeared. He breathed a sigh of relief. Never before had thoughts such as those tormented him. He had not been able to control the surge of them.

The reddish glow was replaced by the blackness of the chamber. The only source of light was the gaping hole in the ceiling. It too dimmed. There was a shadow on the floor below—an obstruction in the light from the world above.

Kiranrao's voice descended into the gloom. "The day is fading. We are building a fire up here. Would you care to join us for a meal?"

"There is a Preachán saying I admire: If two friends ask you to judge a dispute, don't accept, because you will lose one friend; on the other hand, if two strangers come with the same request, accept because you will gain one friend."

– Possidius Adeodat, Archivist of Kenatos

XVII

Paedrin knew his shoulder blade was probably broken. His entire left side had the stinging tingles that made gripping anything with his left hand useless. He was weary from the action and concerned at the blood streaking down Hettie's face, at Annon's half-terrified expression holding the dagger, and Erasmus's sudden pallor. But never would a Bhikhu show his fear.

"I hope there are no onions," Paedrin said loudly, lifting his voice deliberately. "I cannot abide them. But to be honest, we are not hungry and would not wish to intrude rudely on your supper."

There was a chuckle. "We have enough provisions to starve you out of there," Kiranrao replied. "I'm not a fool, and we did not rest. We have trailed you all the way here and know you are tired, wounded, and in possession of Drosta's treasure. The treasure that Tyrus has successfully hidden from me these many years. I could as easily come down there and kill you all for it myself, but I'm rather lazy by nature as most Vaettir are. Besides, there is other information I want from you."

Paedrin looked at Annon and cocked his eyebrows. Annon shrugged, confused.

"What information?"

"Where is Tyrus Paracelsus expecting you?"

Again, Paedrin was confused. "Where is he expecting us?"

"Where were you going to meet him after this was finished? Where did he say he would be?"

Annon spoke up. "I mean no disrespect, but Tyrus was not planning on…"

"Don't waste my time, Druidecht. Please. I abhor it when people play themselves as fools. All of Kenatos is abuzz with the news. I do not rely on wagon trains for my information, surely you realize that. And I do not believe he is dead, or there would not be such a grand reward for information regarding his whereabouts. You were the last to have seen him before the explosion. Surely he told you where he was going?"

Even Hettie was perplexed. She pressed her sleeve against her forehead to stanch the bleeding. "Explosion?" she mouthed.

"Well?" Kiranrao said. "Obviously he sent you here for the blade. Yes, I know it is a blade. But to what purpose?"

Paedrin massaged his shoulder, and it throbbed with agony, nearly making him gasp. He stopped the effort at once. "What business is it of yours where we go and what we do?"

"All business is *my* business," he replied testily. "You want to be coy then. Very well. Girl. Finder. Come into the light."

Hettie stepped forward slowly, gazing up at the gaping hole in the ceiling.

His voice was full of disapproval. "You are Romani. Your assignment here is through. Come up here and tell me what this fuss is all about. You are Tyrus's niece. I know that to be true. You will not find a more wealthy bidder than I. Not even Tyrus himself, though he chooses not to bid for you. Come."

Paedrin stepped forward, moving until he was also in the light. He looked up at Kiranrao balefully. "She isn't yours."

They stared at each other, Vaettir to Vaettir. "A pity you are wounded, Bhikhu. It might have been interesting otherwise."

"I'm not the one cowering at the top of a cave. Come down and see how spent I am."

Hettie gave him a warning look, which he promptly ignored.

"You are Romani, girl. You *know* you must obey me."

Hettie gave them an imploring look. "My uncle sent us here for the treasure to buy my freedom."

Kiranrao chuckled and then laughed long and hard. "The most amazing part is that you actually believe it! Really? I am astounded." His voice fell serious. "Tyrus serves no man but himself. He used my services to steal that dagger from the Arch-Rike. He knew that I would want it, so he hid it in these forsaken mountains. Your coming to Havenrook was a personal insult to me delivered by yourselves. Instead of seeking my aid, he sent you to a brain-fevered Preachán. This is my lair. This is my country. You are intruders here. The dagger is already mine. You found it, fair enough, but I claim it as my own and challenge you for the right to it. Who will defend your claim on it? Hmmm? Who will bid for you, girl, when I state my intent? I own the dagger. I own you. The only piece of information I am interested in purchasing right now is Tyrus's whereabouts. I'll gladly spare your lives, save one. You can argue amongst yourselves as to which one of you must die. I don't care."

Paedrin's mouth went dry. His mind went through a flurry of thoughts. How many were up there with Kiranrao? A dozen? More? His staff was shattered on the floor. His arm was broken and useless. The other two could summon fire, so that would be of help, though the thought of killing them all was distasteful.

"You are bluffing," Paedrin said. "You are probably up there all alone."

Kiranrao sighed. "Now you have really insulted me. I think it is you who must die, Bhikhu. The girl is interesting. The Druidecht is bothersome, but at least he is respectfully silent. Erasmus, do you really want to die down in that Cruithnean stink hole? Girl, come closer. I will drop a rope down for you."

Paedrin scowled and took a step closer.

"No," Hettie said.

Paedrin stared at her in surprise.

"I was freeborn. I would rather die down here in the dark than be called Romani again. I belong to no man," she spat.

Kiranrao sighed deeply. "It will be dark soon. You will be hungry. And you will change your mind. I will not tolerate disobedience. You belong to me, girl. I claim you."

Paedrin saw her fingers begin to glow blue. "No," he warned.

Some dirt and pebbles tumbled over the edge as another man approached Kiranrao. Furtive whispers came from above.

"What do you mean?" Kiranrao snapped. "He hasn't returned from fetching water? Why should that…"

There was a roar.

It wasn't the roar of a bear or the snort of a wolf. It was a sound that penetrated to the deepest part of Paedrin's heart, a place where shadows bred monsters in the dark. It robbed reason. It stole confidence. Paedrin stood there, knees trembling, and wondered what could make such a sound as that.

Annon had given it a name. The Fear Liath.

The roar was followed by several moments of silence. But the silence was abruptly disturbed as trees and branches gave way to something enormous and strong. There was another roar, this one closer, more terrible. Cries of confusion came from above. There were the sounds of weapons being drawn. Bowstrings twanged. Then a grunt and the gasp of a man smashing into stones before collapsing. Screams followed, shrill and full of dread.

Annon stepped forward into the ring of light. *"Alloren morir,"* he said softly in the Vaettir tongue. The stone hovering over the gaping hole slammed shut, sealing them inside the darkness, blocking out the screams from above.

In the darkness, there was no time. There were faint breaths, ragged breathing. The orbs of light had winked out after the blade had been retrieved and sheathed. Even the creature that had attacked them, the Goule, was motionless. Whatever power that had charmed it was gone. The feeling of fear was ever present.

Annon knew he could summon light by his fingers, but he could not sustain it all night. "Are you all there?" he asked softly.

He heard all of their voices murmur in response.

"Paedrin, you are hurt the most. How is your shoulder?"

"If you want, I could twist your arm, and you would know the feeling. Broken, I think. I need to bind it so that it doesn't move." His voice grunted as he sat down. "But without any light, it will be difficult."

"I can help bind it," Hettie said.

"How is your head, sister?"

"Bleeding still. Nothing is broken, though. It is so dark. I dread this place."

Annon also sat down, tucking the sheathed blade in his belt. He dared not release it again. Even with it in the sheath, he was starting to hear it again. "We will do our best, even in the dark. There are no spirits here I can summon to help. The only spirit here is in this blade. It is a dark creation. What I do not understand is why Tyrus sent us to find it. Surely it is worth a treasure to Kiranrao, or he would not have hunted us. But a man like him with this. It would make him do awful things."

Erasmus's sigh echoed. "All is not as it seems, which is usually the case. If that boulder will not move again until dawn, we will be here for a while still. Better here than up there with that creature."

"I am not so certain we are better off," Annon whispered, again feeling the subtle urge to draw the dagger and kill them all in the darkness. He knew he would not sleep that night, knowing the others might be drawn to the weapon to try and take it from him. He doubted any of them would sleep.

The feeling in the chamber changed. Something had happened above. Was it dawn? Had the Fear Liath returned to the waterfall? Annon was bone weary and weak from the strain against his mind. As if awoken from a dream, he spoke the words again and the giant rock floated upward again, exposing the silvery-blue light of dawn.

There was a collective sigh of hope from the companions. They had lasted the night.

Paedrin stood beneath the open hole and inhaled deeply, floating effortlessly up to the opening and emerging from it. The signs of death were all about. Preachán bodies littered the debris field. But there was still some rope and he used it to pull the others out, using the floating stone for leverage and letting his bad arm rest.

One by one they emerged, dusty and pallid. Hettie began to crisscross the area, searching the ground for corpses and for signs.

"It was big," she muttered, pausing at the distinguishing tracks it left. Paedrin noticed the claw marks and quickly averted his eyes.

"What are you looking for?" he asked her. But as he asked the question, he already knew. They all knew the answer.

That they would not find Kiranrao's body amidst the corpses.

"There is much to be said about the Cruithne as a race. They are great experimenters. They study causes and effects. They are tall, in general, and robust, having great physical strength. Having spent thousands of years living among the volcanoes of Alkire, they are adept at trapping fumes and vapors, at learning which smells harbor danger and which can be curative. They have mastered the arts of the forge, creating new metals in their vast underground caves fed by living fires of blackrock. They excavate gemstones from the rock and shape them intricately. It is claimed that Cruithne have soot-colored skin because they dwell in a place full of smoke and ash. The pigment of one's skin has little to do with chimney smoke. It is said that their race originated in the great deserts beyond the mountains. That seems a more logical explanation of their pigmentation. Some even accuse the Cruithne of slowness due to their great size, but that is a common misperception. Cruithne are large and quick, giving them ample force against smaller men like the Preachán. They learned long ago that to survive the Plague, it would be wise to settle amidst the highest mountains, thus making it difficult for traders to reach them. Some in Havenrook believe that it was their meddling in the earth's depths that caused the Plague. A fool's rumor."

–Possidius Adeodat, Archivist of Kenatos

XVIII

The blade from Drosta's lair was a living thing. Annon had heard its whispers and felt the growing intensity of its compulsion to kill. It took every bit of self-control he mustered not to draw it again from its sheath. It would drive him mad. It would drive anyone mad eventually, but a Druidecht would be the most resilient. As they hiked down from the Alkire, he finally resorted to untying the talisman from around his neck. Only then did the whispers cease.

At darkfall he found himself staring into the flames of the fire, his body aching and sore from the strenuous hike through the downward maze of iron-hard rocks and evergreen. Hettie was slumped next to him, a makeshift bandage around her head. Boulders surrounded them, offering shelter from the wind. Paedrin's arm was bound tightly against his body, and he paced amidst the camp, staring at each of them in turn and searching the falling darkness for signs of Kiranrao or other pursuers. His staff was broken, but he held a fragment of it like a cudgel. Erasmus shook his head, his eyes bleary from lack of sleep.

Annon looked up, his mind a jumble of thoughts and ideas. "We are in danger in these mountains. One of us will need to be on watch all night long. The Fear Liath will start hunting us now that it is dark."

"Wonderful," Paedrin said, swishing the staff fragment violently. "We should keep walking and get free of the mountains tonight."

"Too dark and too far," Erasmus said. "Even you know that, sheep-brains. It took us several days just to climb in. Climbing out won't be any easier. The chances of our success are still abysmally low, unless it rains in the next day. And storms usually do not occur in these mountains this time of year."

"Do you think Kiranrao was lying?" Hettie said softly.

"About which part?" Paedrin said with a snort. "I don't hold much confidence in anything he told us."

"He has ways of knowing things," Hettie replied, bristling. "He has access…" She stopped, suddenly quiet.

"You don't understand," Paedrin said. "No doubt he is crafty. He would make a spider seem friendly. We cannot trust what he said because his intent was to misinform us and influence us into behaving irrationally."

"And you can judge his intent?" Erasmus said mockingly.

Paedrin chuckled to himself. "Are any of you familiar with the principles of the *Uddhava*?"

Annon stared at him blankly. "Is it a Vaettir word?"

"A Vaettir word but a Bhikhu philosophy."

"Which means no one could understand it unless he was both," Erasmus said.

"Which I am," Paedrin answered. He inhaled slowly, and they watched him begin to float in the air. He put his foot on the end of his broken staff and balanced himself with his free arm. He held the pose, drawing their eyes as he circled his hand fluidly in the air. Then he stepped forward and landed heavily on the ground, startling them.

"That was to be sure you were listening," he said seriously.

Hettie snorted and Annon smiled.

Paedrin walked as he spoke, gesticulating with his free arm for emphasis. "The Uddhava is one word that describes a myriad of explanations. A chain of things. Let me try and give you the color and shade of it. The principal element of the Uddhava is the act of observing. Observing is a form of power, a very subtle power. It changes behavior in others and oneself. You behave differently in front of a crowd than you do when you are alone. The observations of others cause you to change what you would ordinarily do. I will be crude to illustrate."

"As long as you are not disgusting as well," Hettie said archly.

He ignored her. "You have some dust in your nose. All right, perhaps it is more than dust. All alone, you would flick it away and be done with it. But in polite company, you do so surreptitiously. The fear of being observed has influenced your behavior. It is the same thing with criminals. If they believe someone is watching them, they do not commit their crime. In fact, it is typically best to distract the attention of the person you intend to rob so that they will not observe what is being stolen from them. Simple enough?"

Annon nodded. "So you are suggesting that Kiranrao was trying to distract us with his story about my uncle?"

Paedrin laughed. "Do not even try to apply Uddhava yet. I have not finished explaining it. Observation is the key element of it. It is more than mere looking. It is more than noticing. When we observe the world around us, we begin to notice that life is a current and we are caught up in the middle of it, but our actions change the course for others. Things act and react differently, depending on the forces that are used. The second element of

Uddhava is trying to intuitively understand why a person has done what they have done. What motivated them? It is not just the action itself, but the motive of that action."

Erasmus cackled. "And people are so transparent, are they? They love to deceive everyone, including themselves. You cannot judge my motives any more than you can determine the real reasons for your own."

Paedrin grinned and whipped the stick around, pointing it at Erasmus's nose. "If you all keep interrupting me, we will never make it to the end."

"Keep going," Annon said. "I am interested."

"This is starting to sound like a sermon," Hettie murmured.

"I will be quick, I promise. No moralizing. Once the intent is divined, the next two things come in rapid order. According to the Uddhava, you make a decision to test your conclusion for accuracy. Then you act on that decision. Your action then prompts the other person to do something. And it all begins again. You observe what they have done, see if it matches your intuition, make another decision about what to do, and then act on it."

He paused in front of the fire. The light reflected off his dark skin. "Every day, each one of us is dancing awkwardly to a rhythm of the Uddhava. Those who master it make the world dance to their tune." He scratched his scalp. "Let me be specific. You might think I was a fool to rush into Drosta's pit without studying it first for danger." He paused. "This is where you insult me, Hettie. Please...don't disappoint me."

His comment startled her and she said nothing.

"See! I just used it against you. I know your propensity for cutting remarks, and rather than letting you muster one, I forestalled you with my own. This is an example of the Uddhava. My actions were not without thought. I went into the cave first because, as you have already noticed, I can fly."

"It is more like floating," Erasmus muttered gravely.

"A choice of words," Paedrin said impatiently, batting away the comment with his staff. "I did not require a rope to leave there. I triggered the trap, which was my intent, to allow us all to learn what was down there and thus be better prepared for it. What you foolishly did," he added, whipping the stick around at Hettie, "was come down on a fraying rope after me. I did not anticipate you putting your life in jeopardy like that, but it helped draw the creature's attention two ways. It was clever to realize that shrouding the lights rendered it harmless. I did not figure that out. It required the collective action and reactions of all of us together to solve the riddle. Which, in my humble opinion, is the reason why Tyrus sent us there at the start. He has been using the principles of Uddhava against us from the beginning."

He was silent a moment and then slapped the staff against his palm. "Before we return to Kenatos, we must ponder his motives, make our decision, and then act. Kiranrao did the same thing. He fed us certain scraps of knowledge, though true or false they may be, in order to discern our reaction to them and thus learn more about our intentions."

He stopped speaking, triumphantly, and raised his eyebrow.

Hettie looked confused. "I'm not sure I even understood you, Bhikhu."

"Not surprising. You have always been a little slow."

"Hold the insults for now," she answered. "I want to be clear first. So the Uddhava is a strategy for manipulating others?"

Paedrin shook his head. "In an indirect way, maybe, but we all have our choices. It is the rhythm of life and governs our relationships with each other, whether verbal or physical. It applies to fighting. Let me demonstrate." He stepped around the fire and brought the staff in an exaggerated pose and slowly brought it down, as if to crack Annon's skull. The blow was ponderously slow, and Annon leaned to the side so that it passed harmlessly by.

"I did it slowly," Paedrin explained, "that you might understand. Let's try it again."

He stepped back and brought the staff down again, mimicking his earlier pose and attack. As Annon began to move aside, Paedrin suddenly whirled around, bringing the staff around horizontally, tapping Annon's cheek instead of crushing it.

"There. You suspected I was going to bash you on the head, so you reacted to it the way anyone might. But that was not my intent, to attack you the same way twice. My second move caught you off guard and would have incapacitated you. I did not *know* what you were going to do. I merely suspected. Now, imagine this playing out at full speed where you only have the blink of an eye to understand what I am doing, make a decision, and then act upon it. If you are right, you stop the attack. If you are wrong, you are unconscious."

Paedrin walked over to Erasmus. "The same principle applies to you." Erasmus flinched, holding up his hands wardingly.

"No, you fool, I'm not going to bash you in the head. Your wealth and success has come from understanding the motives of others, determining how they will react, and then betting on it accordingly. Rather than taking moments to see if you are right, your decisions may take months. A fire burning in the road. Caravans delayed in passing through. People losing money because cargo has spoiled. Those things may take time to play out, but they will play out. Others observe the loss of spoiled fruit. They can sell the next shipment for double. The faster they react, the more profits they make. It is the nature of Havenrook to use the Uddhava. And it is no coincidence that a Vaettir named Kiranrao is behind it."

Annon thought about what he had been told. What a perplexing way to look at the world. However, it did explain how attentive Paedrin was to their surroundings. It was as if he were constantly assessing dangers and forming plans. Like on the road to Havenrook, he had noticed the Preachán crouching amidst the wagons and suggested attacking them before being attacked. Having a Bhikhu as a companion was an advantage to anyone.

Annon prodded the fire with a stick. "Is that why the Bhikhu patrol the streets of Kenatos?"

Paedrin gave him a steady look and nodded. "Our presence alone is often enough to prevent crime. Not to mention that we have a certain reputation for inflicting pain on others. Pain is a teacher, as I have told you before. Most people fear it. We do not. We would never stop a child from touching a burning piece of wood. We would warn, but never prevent. Wisdom comes through listening to those with more experience. Only fools blunder through unnecessary pain."

"How is your shoulder feeling?" Hettie asked wryly.

He gave her a smirk. "It hurts. How is your skull? Thank the stars it was thick enough."

Erasmus whistled softly. "I am beginning to appreciate Tyrus's craftiness. I do not think he intended me to go back to Havenrook after guiding you to Drosta's lair. Since Kiranrao knew what was hidden there, he will slit my belly open to learn where you are taking it. It would probably be in my best interest to stay with you a while longer."

Paedrin crouched near the fire. Annon was amazed at his flexibility, how he could crouch so low while his heels were flat on the ground. His arm was tied to his body, but he still looked dangerous. He twirled the half-staff in his hand, slowly, thinking.

"Let us consider this together," he said. "I only know your uncle by reputation as one of the wealthiest men in Kenatos. A Paracelsus. That means he is a maker. His kind made the blade. May I see it?"

Annon shook his head. "No, it is a dangerous thing. It has great power over the mind."

Paedrin gave him a long look. "I am not a fool, Annon. Let me examine it. I was cut by a blade recently, if you remember. I appreciate the danger."

Annon withdrew it from his robe and felt the compulsion growing again. The blade did not want to be shown around. He felt a dark menace from it. Annon's fingers twitched. The surge of emotions was stifling, and he felt sweat pop out on his forehead. Hettie shrank from him, her eyes widening with fear. Erasmus squinted, his face suddenly ashen.

"Put it away," Paedrin whispered. His eyes were serious. "I could not control my thoughts looking at it, let alone risk handling it. Truly, it is an evil weapon. Put it away."

Annon obliged, hiding it in his belt, beneath his cloak. The blade went still again.

Paedrin cocked his head, scratching his forehead. "Why would your uncle send you for it? The pretext was buying your freedom." He nodded to Hettie. Her eyes were haunted. "What was his real motive?"

"Impossible to deduce," Erasmus said. "He reveals nothing of his plans. He is very guarded."

Paedrin frowned and shook his head. "The specific reason, perhaps. But we should not relax our thoughts because the riddle is difficult. First thought that comes to me. Did he expect we would be successful? Was it to test our craftiness or persistence? To see if we would quit?"

Annon thought a moment. "He gave us pieces of the riddle, but not the whole. He told us about Erasmus, who could lead us there. He gave me the words that would open the stone. So yes, I think he did want us to succeed."

"I hate being manipulated," Hettie said with an icy voice. "Why not tell us it was a blade and not a cask of ducats?"

"Another thought," Annon said, touching his lip. "Let us suppose that Kiranrao was not lying. That he truly is looking for Tyrus now. Maybe there was an explosion in the tower, that Tyrus is a hunted man. Perhaps he knew the danger was coming and wanted to send us far away?"

Paedrin nodded vigorously. "I like your thinking. It would be pretty easy to confirm whether or not Kiranrao was lying. We could even discover that without crossing the lake into the city. If the boatmen confirm it, then we know that there was an explosion. He obviously did not want us to know about the danger."

"That troubles me," Hettie said softly. "While I hate being manipulated, I would feel even worse if he did this to spare us. I do not want to owe him anything."

Annon put his arm around her. "He did not require anything from us. We seemed more like a nuisance to him anyway."

Hettie shook her head. "I'm worried about him."

Erasmus snorted. "Don't be a fool, girl. He is quite capable of defending himself. Even the Arch-Rike fears him."

At those words, Annon's eyes opened wide. "I'm a fool."

Paedrin looked curious. "What do you mean?"

He gritted his teeth and shook his head. "Maybe I am mistaken, but your words about the Uddhava make sense to me. How we are observed, and it triggers actions in others. When I came to Kenatos, I had to cross the gates. I told the Rike there that I was the nephew of Tyrus of Kenatos. I did not think of it until now, but the man started, surprised. He was shocked. Obviously his ring allowed him to know that I was not lying. He directed me to the Paracelsus Towers. No doubt I was followed." He turned to Hettie. "Did you mention who you were visiting?"

Hettie shook her head, her brow crinkling with worry. "Of course not. What business is it of theirs?"

"The explosion happened after we left. It may have happened the very next day. My mentor, Reeder, warned me about trusting Tyrus. That he was involved in some matter dealing with the Scourgelands. My visit may have started the cycle of the Uddhava."

Paedrin looked at him seriously. "No, it started before you arrived. It started when Hettie arrived in Kenatos, seeking her freedom. It may have started even earlier than that."

"What do you mean?" Hettie asked, her voice defensive. "You think that I caused this?"

"No," Paedrin answered, batting his hand at her. "When you were both infants."

"Oh," Hettie said. There was something in her voice, in her reaction. It made Paedrin pause. Was she hiding something? There was a growing pit of unease in Annon's stomach, and it had nothing to do with the blade hidden in his cloak. There were forces at work that baffled him. But it was as Paedrin had taught them. An unseen current was pulling them all along, bouncing and bumping them into each other. He needed to know where the current was taking them before he decided whether or not he wanted to swim with it or against it.

"We need to find Tyrus," Annon said resolutely.

Hettie touched his hand. Hers was warm. He glanced at her face and saw his concern mirrored in her eyes. Her look of defensiveness was gone now. It was probably his exhaustion and the effects of the weapon on his mind. Here they were together. A brother and sister, separated since birth. Was that even an accident?

"Then I suppose we will need a Finder," she said.

Somewhere in the deep darkness of the Alkire, a creature roared. It was then that Annon noticed the subtle mist snaking through the boulders.

"The wilderness is full of monsters, it is said. What men fear most is their unrealized expectations. A dark alley. A thief with a knife. A thousand regrets of what will never be. This is fear."

– Possidius Adeodat, Archivist of Kenatos

XIX

Achill descended on the little camp. Wispy tendrils of fog seeped slowly, bringing fear with the cold. Paedrin turned and stared at the darkness of the woods, gripping his shattered staff; he looked at the others. Annon felt his fingers tingle with heat, and he prepared to whisper the words that would summon the flames. Would such a being be immune to it? He hoped not.

Erasmus poked the ground with a stick, muttering to himself. "How many men did Kiranrao have? How many were slain? We saw the bodies. The chance for each of us surviving until daylight is bleak. Perhaps only two of us will. Those are bitter odds."

"Say nothing," Paedrin said, striding to the fringe of the firelight. "I hear something moving in the woods."

Hettie came to her feet at once, bringing out her hunter's bow and nocking an arrow. Her arms trembled.

"Be still!" Paedrin hissed. He stared into the woods, listening.

Another roar sounded, closer this time. The size of the creature, the noise it made terrified Annon. What were they facing?

What was it that hunted them? He thought about his talisman, stuffed in a pouch at his waist. It was useless to him unless he wore it around his neck. Had the spirits tried to warn him earlier? Or were they gibbering in fear as well?

There was a crunch and crash deep in the blackness, followed by a shower of branches.

The fire snapped and hissed as the mist curled around the stones hedging it in. A thick, silent fog came from the trees above, blotting out the stars.

"Do we run?" Annon whispered, his throat dry.

Paedrin held up his hand, his head cocked. "It's coming from below, not above. I hear it in the woods."

"I hear nothing," Hettie said, swinging the bow around and aiming it down.

Paedrin took a deep breath and exhaled it quickly. He turned to the others. "When it comes, I will slow it. You run as far and as fast as you can. Try to find shelter, a cave or something narrow where it may not fit."

"You are coming with us," Hettie insisted.

Paedrin shook his head. "Remember the Uddhava. Trust me, I will not be easy prey. I will make it hunt and chase me all night if necessary. I am faster than all of you. It improves the odds of our survival if I face it alone."

"No," Hettie said.

"Your injuries," Annon said, his stomach lurching. He respected the Bhikhu now. The thought of losing him was painful. "This is not fair to ask of you."

There was a half-smirk in response. "Of course it isn't fair. But I promised I would be your protector. My duty is not yet fulfilled, and I will face it. Get ready, it comes."

Even Annon could hear the approach from the south. Twigs and branches snapped and cracked. The crunch of vegetation was obvious now. Annon tried to swallow his fear, but he could not. In a moment, they would see it.

"Be ready," Paedrin said. "I will face it."

"There!" Hettie said, bringing up her bow and stretching it back.

"Hold!" Annon said, bringing his arm down over hers. The figure approaching was large, but not monstrous. The girth was enormous, or Annon would have thought it was Tyrus. A bushy, mottled, gray-and-black beard emerged from the cowl of a cloak.

Paedrin paused, weapon ready, scrutinizing the stranger.

The voice was deep, as deep as a barrel. "You do not have much time to determine whether to trust me. But I can lead you to safety this night if you choose to believe me. Either way, the Fear Liath comes. Make your decision."

Dark eyes appeared in the concealment of the cowl, which the stranger lowered, revealing a huge mane of gray-black hair. The mustache just below his nose was darker than the rest, as were his prominent eyebrows. But his swarthy skin and bulk showed him to be a Cruithne. And the talisman around his neck revealed he was also a Druidecht.

A gush of relief went through Annon's heart on seeing the token. "I trust him."

Hettie no longer resisted and released the tension in the bowstring.

"In a few more moments, your time to decide will be shattered by raking claws and the most horrible hide-stench you can imagine. You are in its lair still. I, for one, would prefer safety to debate. The choice is yours." He turned abruptly and started back down the mountainside at a solid pace, crushing the branches and debris as he walked.

Paedrin glanced at Annon in surprise.

"He is Druidecht," Annon said, grabbing Hettie by the arm.

Erasmus needed no convincing. "The odds of surviving until daybreak have just improved," he said.

Paedrin lingered amidst the campfire a moment, then followed them down the hillside. The mist continued to fall until it engulfed them all in a fetid-smelling cloud. A terrible roar sounded behind them, splitting the air with a shriek that went down into Annon's marrow. It was close behind them. Very close. There was a shuffling noise in the distance. The Fear Liath was tracking them.

The Cruithne increased his pace, each step announcing their location with thunder. If a small tree stood in the way, he simply went through it, snapping the trunk and causing it to crash awkwardly away. Redwoods towered over them, but the lower branches were lost in the thick gauze of milky white fog.

Annon nearly twisted his ankle on a root, and Hettie helped catch him before he fell. He wanted to keep turning around, but Paedrin scowled at him and gestured to keep his eyes on the Cruithne ahead. The shuffling noise grew louder, turning into a bark-like sound.

"This way," boomed the deep voice as he approached a lightning-struck redwood, one that had fallen and shattered so that only the tangle of exposed roots lay revealed. The thorny fingers of the roots made it seem like some enormous monster, but it was hollowed out by fire and created a small cave. It was not quite tall enough to stand in, but the Cruithne did not hesitate; he hunched forward and entered the cave-like entrance of the tree stump.

Hettie followed and Annon came up behind her. The Cruithne was breathing fast, but he stopped to rest along the curved structure of the cave. Erasmus joined them and chafed his hands for warmth. His breath came in puffs of smoke. Paedrin stood outside, staring into the maw of the tree. The mist trailed off his shoulders. He turned back and stared into the fog, at the sound of the approaching hulk.

The Cruithne watched him, saying nothing. "Stubborn one," he murmured softly.

Hettie nodded in agreement. "Paedrin!" she snapped. "Get in here!"

"It's a tree stump," he replied, not looking back.

"It is a gate to Mirrowen," the Cruithne whispered.

"What?" the Bhikhu said. "You speak in riddles."

"Trust us," Annon soothed. "There is shelter here. Come."

Paedrin hesitated a moment longer. Stubborn defiance seemed to make knots in his shoulders. His one arm was strapped to his side, but he still looked menacing, waiting for a battle. Waiting to test himself against his fears?

"Who are you?" Annon asked the Cruithne.

"My name is Drosta," he answered.

Paedrin whirled at that, his eyes wide with interest. He stepped into the cave-like opening, crouching so as not to brush his head against the root fingers. The chill of the mist began to dissipate. The fog started to fall apart.

There was a roar, a roar of helpless frustration and fury.

"The Fear Liath is blind to us now," the Cruithne said with a mocking smile. "That angers it."

"Why can't it find us?" Paedrin said, staring at the old man's face.

"You would not understand if I explained it. What was important is that I won your trust in as few words as possible. In desperate moments, scorching truth is needed, not convincing argument. We do not have long to speak. What I must say is crucially important. Listen for as long as you can."

Annon was about to interrupt, but the Cruithne held up his massive, thick hand. "You will be asleep in moments and will awake at sunrise in a different place. This is a gateway to Mirrowen, and you will suffer the effects to mortals. Remember as much as you can. A little learning, indeed, may be a dangerous thing, but the want of learning is a calamity to any people. That has been the failing of Kenatos. Not a lack of intelligence, but a lack of wisdom. My name was Drosta Paracelsus. And you have found my blade. I fashioned it. I made it. It is called the Iddawc."

He motioned for Annon to produce it. As he uncovered it from within his cloak, the Cruithne's face crumpled into a dark scowl. "It lives. It is a spirit weapon. There is a spirit hosted inside it, and Iddawc is its name. Knowing this, you can control it. There is only one being such as this in all of this world or Mirrowen. It was discovered by the Cruithne deep in the mines. I cannot tell you how many were killed before we learned what it was capable of doing. It was a Druidecht who warned us, but I was foolish. I knew it would be valuable to trap such a being. I devised a plan, and the Arch-Rike approved the price. I will not tell you the price, for it would be unseemly. We did not trap it; we helped it transform. It was my vanity, my pride. You see, power concedes nothing without a demand. It never did, and it never will."

As Drosta spoke, Annon felt his mind growing thick and foggy. He was weary. More weary than he had ever been in his life. Glancing to the side, he saw that Erasmus was already asleep, jaw open. Hettie's chin was bobbing as she struggled to stay awake.

Drosta grabbed Annon's shoulder and squeezed with his powerful fingers, digging in to invoke pain. "It concedes nothing! You are a Druidecht as well. The spirits have told me that you are faithful. You must listen to me. The Paracelsus in Kenatos are trapping spirits, binding them into service. The lamps of the city do not create smoke. They do not create heat. Their light is borrowed by spirits, who are enslaved for a season. The terms are odious to them. They are slaves! They are compelled to serve because they were captured. The Cruithne learned the craft. We created the Paracelsus order. Stay awake!"

Annon's eyes drooped shut and he blinked furiously. His arm throbbed with pain. But even that was beginning to subside.

"The weapon only serves one master at a time. It will *only* serve one. It will seek a powerful man and subvert him. When he is dead, it will seek out another. This is the Iddawc's hunger, its terrible power. It kills and has power over death. One cut from its blade severs the life's string. It was commissioned by the Arch-Rike as a weapon for his most feared protector, the Quiet Kishion, but it was never used as such. Tyrus of Kenatos arranged to have it stolen. To be hidden from the world without claiming more victims."

"Can it be destroyed?" Paedrin asked. He was down on one knee, gazing intently at the huge man.

"Never," he replied. "The Iddawc cannot be unmade. It will exist until its length of service has expired. That is well beyond my lifetime or even a dozen lifetimes. It was bound for ten generations. We are only in the second right now. It cannot be destroyed and must be hidden and safeguarded. It has no master but seeks one. I can hear it right now, and it disgusts me because even I crave it. I, who created this evil thing, in my foolish vanity I brought it into existence. A weapon to conquer death."

The final words were slurred and Annon felt his head bob. He struggled against the sinking oblivion of sleepiness. "Be wiser than I. Those of Kenatos are treacherous and claim to preserve knowledge. They preserve slavery, the slavery of beings that they cannot even see. What sympathy exists in a kingdom that enslaves others? When a civilization quietly submits to such a practice, you will have the exact measure of the injustice and wrong that will be imposed upon *them*. I have spent my days attempting to redress the damage that I inflicted on the spirits of Mirrowen." He gripped the talisman around his neck, tears bulging in his eyes. "They know my heart and they trust me. I was once their greatest adversary. Now I am like you. A humble Druidecht." He leaned forward, his voice husky with emotion. "Tyrus knows this truth as well. He and I are brothers in mind. We are likeminded. Remember this. It is easier to build strong children than to repair broken men. Forgive him for abandoning you. It cost him greatly. But there is so much at stake. So very much at stake."

Annon heard the mumbling bass of Drosta's words, felt the pain recede in his shoulder as he floated into the invisible threads of slumber. The horrors of the mountains faded. The chill night air was replaced with a comforting warmth. He thought he could smell flowers, not night jasmine but the heady scent of hyacinths and roses. There was a trickling of water, the soft lapping sounds carrying him away.

Remember.
Remember.
Remember.

"I once caught a young Rike tearing a page from an ancient book. I chastised
him severely and rebuked him for violating his sworn duty to preserve
knowledge. He said the page contained blasphemy and that it should be
destroyed by fire so as not to taint the minds of men in the future. After a
scolding and a thrashing, I told him that if the truth cannot bear the scrutiny
of candlelight, what will it do if exposed to the sun? He apologized profusely for
his error and swore he had only destroyed three such pages out of one hundred
books. The Arch-Rike assured me that he would be assigned to a stewardship
other than the Archives. The young make so many mistakes. They lack wisdom."

– Possidius Adeodat, Archivist of Kenatos

XX

S leep enveloped Annon like a shroud, burying him beneath layers of warm blackness. There were voices murmuring in the stillness, the faint whisper of the breeze rustling branches. The patter of rainfall, or was it a brook? Everything was hazy and tangled. But the sleep ended when a hand clutched his shoulder and jerked him hard.

"Annon!"

He was confused, snapping out of a forgotten dream and realizing that sunlight came in streamers through a copse of thin yew trees and half-blinded him. The smell was different, not the heady scent of pine and thin mountain air. Now, it was a lowland smell, thick with the pungent smells of grasses and weeds and brush.

"At last! Wake up, boy!"

He jolted, recognizing the sound of his uncle's voice. Twisting with a sudden desperateness, he whirled and beheld Tyrus kneeling over him. At first, he could not believe his own senses. His uncle, his face, his towering presence. Shock thundered inside him, and then he felt the first swells of anger.

"The sleep affects everyone differently. Your friends may awaken soon or not, but I needed to rouse you first." He gripped Annon's shoulder with a strong hand, clenching his tunic. "I may not have much time before the Arch-Rike's minion finds me again. Give me the blade you snatched from Drosta's lair. This entire area reeks of it, and the spirits are frightened of you. The blade Iddawc."

Annon struggled to sit up, but his uncle's hand kept him down. He was exceptionally strong. His fist was tighter than knots.

"What errand did you send us on, Uncle?" he asked, feeling every emotion fire up in hostility. "A treasure to buy Hettie's freedom? Was that even your intent?"

Tyrus rifled through Annon's cloak with his other hand and discovered the blade pouch fastened to his belt. He began untying the knot and Annon grabbed at his hands, trying to stop him. It was like trying to bend iron bars.

"I have precious little time to meddle with you," Tyrus warned with disapproval. "The one who hunts me would just as soon kill you with his fingers as waste a spare moment wrestling you. Come, boy! Stop fighting me. You are not wise or powerful enough to handle this blade."

"And you are?" Annon seethed, unsuccessful at stopping his uncle's fingers from snapping the cords of the pouch and claiming the weapon.

Tyrus rose, towering over the younger man like a boulder. It was then that Annon noticed the soot stains, the tattered hem of his uncle's cloak. The gash in his sleeve. His face was weather burned.

His uncle snorted. "I know far too much about this blade to ever be its master. It has no master but itself. But it *will* serve a useful purpose in the Scourgelands. I bid you farewell, nephew.

I will likely be dead before we cross paths again. Forgive me for being an unfit uncle if you can. Good-bye."

Annon surged to his feet, anger exploding in his heart. He shook with rage, his fingers tingling with unspent flames. Why was it that his uncle made him lose himself like this? After all they had been through, he wanted an explanation. He wanted the truth. To be dismissed as an errand boy galled him. "That is all? You abandon us here? Wherever *here* is?"

There was a grim look in Tyrus's eye. "Abandon you? It is what I am good at, after all. I come and I go when it suits me. You can have no faith in me. You do not trust me. Believe me, nephew, there is a murderer no doubt flying the aether as we speak to kill me. When he arrives, I must be gone or he may take his vengeance out on you. For your own safety, I must leave you."

"But why?" Annon demanded. "Have I not earned at least that? Why did you send us there? Why did you deceive us? What about Hettie's freedom?"

Tyrus arched an eyebrow. He took a step forward, his gaze menacing. "Think, boy! Use those scraps of brains. I turn the question back on you. Why did you not insist on knowing more? Why were you satisfied to go knowing so very little? Why did you assume I would tell you all when you took no thought to even ask me?" He pointed to the woods, at nothing. "Well? Why did you not ask?"

Annon gritted his teeth together, but he would not back down. He stepped closer. "Because I did not think you would tell me, Uncle."

"A fair statement. A fool's answer, though. If you only knew the danger...the real danger that just being near me presents to you." He swallowed a muttering oath. "Let me be candid with you, Annon. I have nothing left to lose. I have lost all except my wits and my will. I believe the Scourgelands is the source of the changing Plague which has decimated the races. It comes in different disguises, but it is still the same Plague. The answer to stopping it is hidden within the Scourgelands. You will not understand this, but I will say it anyway. Some treachery happened long ago. A promise made by a Paracelsus, I believe, but none have ever recorded the memory of what the affront was. I have spent my life piecing together all the clues. I know how to end the Plague. And the Arch-Rike of Kenatos will stop at nothing to prevent me from doing so."

His eyes blazed. "We have different opinions, he and I. Were I to stop the Plague, he would lose all his power and authority. The last time I attempted this was before you were born. Everyone who went with me into the Scourgelands died. So you see, my young friend, my dear nephew, that you are far better off never having known me or what I am going to do. For your sakes, I bid you both farewell."

"Uncle."

It was Hettie. She had risen where she had lain, pretending to be asleep. Her eyes were dark with concern. Her arms were folded defiantly across her chest. "How can we help you?"

He looked at her in surprise. "You are fledglings. All of you. The last group I brought into the Scourgelands were tested and trained. They were the best of their generation. They perished in the nightmares that roam inside."

"Answer my question, Uncle," Hettie demanded.

Annon struggled to control his anger. He did not want to help his uncle. He wanted to lash out at him with hateful words and erase the memory of him from his mind. But he could not. Tyrus's words buzzed inside his head like a hive of angry bees. He remembered Reeder's warning about the Scourgelands. He could almost imagine his friend's worried expression.

Annon's voice was raw. "Do you seek us to join you?"

Tyrus shook his head angrily. "Yours was a good question, Hettie. They typically are. Annon, you are too concerned about trying to understand *my* motives. You miss something obvious. If I am capable of deceiving the Rikes of Kenatos and their beetle-black rings, then I can surely dupe someone as foolish as you. Annon, you will never understand my motives until you understand me. You will not understand me until you understand what motivates me. And you will not understand that without seeking to do my will. In other words, you must trust me. Remember, I told you that in my tower."

"Did Kiranrao speak the truth?" Hettie asked. "Was there an explosion?"

Tyrus nodded. "One of my latest projects for the Arch-Rike was inventing ways of releasing power in a blast. They are volatile spirits and they are bound for one reason and one purpose. You saw them on my desk when you both visited me. They were designed to help the masons of Stonehollow crack boulders. I am sure the Arch-Rike plans to use them to destroy castle walls. When he sent his man to kill me, I used a device I made to travel far away and triggered the room to explode, hoping it would kill him. It did not, but it destroyed my tower. I am still being hunted."

Annon stared at him. "Did my arrival to the city cause this?"

Tyrus smiled grimly. "Yes, but you did it unwittingly. I protected you both the best I could."

"I have no love of Kenatos or the Arch-Rike," Hettie said. "How can I help?"

"I applaud your question. Was it sincerely given?"

She nodded, arms folded. Her shoulders seemed to scrunch, as if she were tightening into knots inside, awaiting a blow.

"There is a prince in Silvandom. A Vaettir-lord named Prince Aransetis. He has agreed to journey with me into the

Scourgelands. There was something he had commissioned from me that will help him survive. I did not have time to retrieve it before the explosion in my tower. You must go to Kenatos and find it. Bring it to Prince Aran. That is how you can help me."

"What is it?" Hettie asked.

"A small leather pouch. A sturdy pouch. There are three jewels inside. They are uncut stones, not polished gems. Raw stones. There are spirits trapped in each one, bound to serve the Vaettir. Only a Vaettir can handle them and use them."

Hettie swallowed. "Where is the bag?"

Tyrus smiled grimly. "I wish that I knew. It was in my study when it exploded. It would not have been destroyed; the magic is too powerful, and those gems were fashioned inside a volcano. It may be in the rubble. I do not know. But if you could find the stones and bring them to Silvandom, that would help me."

Annon glanced and noticed that Paedrin was standing next to Hettie, watching them carefully. "What of me, Tyrus? Are you still in need of my service?"

Tyrus shook his head. "A Bhikhu is always very useful. But you would need to seek your master's approval to serve me further. Your obligation to me is fulfilled. I am an outlaw now in Kenatos. You are sworn to uphold its laws."

Paedrin nodded. He was silent for a moment. "Is that how Aboujaoude died? In the Scourgelands? He was a very famous Bhikhu, but he died before I was born."

Tyrus stared hard at the young Vaettir. "He did indeed. What you do not understand is that you have been protecting his twins. Hettie and Annon are his offspring." A look shadowed Tyrus's face. The emotion vanished as fast as it appeared. "He believed in my cause, Paedrin. He gave his life for it. He knew all my motives, and he did it anyway."

Annon swallowed hard, suddenly parched and desperate for a drink, as if water would somehow slake his fury. What was this? His father had been a Bhikhu? Then why had Annon not been raised in the temple orphanage like Paedrin? Why had he been sent to the woods in Wayland?

"What of me, Uncle?" Annon asked.

"You seek to help me as well? Or to challenge me further?"

"I do not trust you. Not yet. But like Hettie I have no love for the Arch-Rike and I am enraged at the plight of the imprisoned spirits in the city. I suspected spirit magic, but I had no idea until Drosta told us."

"That is fair. Seek your friend Reeder. He is in the woods of Silvandom, I believe. Seek his counsel. More importantly, seek an answer that I need. The Arch-Rike has a secret temple outside of the city. I do not know where it is, but it is called Basilides. It protects an oracle that the Arch-Rike uses to divine the future. There is a connection there to the spirits of Mirrowen, a pool or a grove of some kind. The Arch-Rike uses it as a source of his power. If it truly exists, then it can tell us how much time we have before the Plague will strike. That is knowledge that I desperately need. It is knowledge that the Arch-Rike undoubtedly has, which is why he moves against me so viciously. Seek Reeder. Seek the oracle. Seek the answer to my question. That would help me."

Tyrus looked down at Erasmus, who had also joined the group. "A question for you, Master Erasmus."

"Yes?"

"What are my odds of surviving an encounter with a Kishion?"

"Which one?"

"You know the one. The one the Arch-Rike was training to use the blade Iddawc."

Erasmus rubbed his mouth. "With the weapon in his hand, not even you could beat him. I think the Arch-Rike planned it that way."

Tyrus nodded sagely. "I am counting on it anyway."

There was a rumble of thunder, though no clouds mottled the sky. It was a bubbling, spurting noise. Annon glanced up at the sky through the screen of branches and yew leaves, seeing something flash.

A man stood behind Tyrus, perhaps a dozen paces off. A cowl covered most of his face. He stood resolutely, appearing from nowhere. He wore a woodsman's garb, dull browns and grays with leather bracers buckled across his forearms. A scar ran from his lower lip down across the side of his chin.

Tyrus withdrew a cylindrical object studded with gemstones from his belt. It was the size of a baton, made of brass or gold, and thick around the middle with caps on each end. He stared at each of them, smiled tiredly, and suddenly he was gone.

"I rarely speak of the Kishion, the Arch-Rike's personal bodyguards. They administer the city's justice on those convicted of heinous crimes, such as murder, rape, and treason. Only Bhikhu and Finders are chosen to be Kishion and are given extensive training in survival, diplomacy, and poison. They are unswervingly loyal to the Arch-Rike and to the ideals of Kenatos. They are few in number, perhaps less than fifty. There is one who is feared above the others. He is never seen at state functions or even in the presence of the Arch-Rike. He is always in the background, fulfilling the greatest service to protect the city. He is reverentially spoken of as the Quiet Kishion. They say, and this is purely speculation, that he cannot be killed."

– Possidius Adeodat, Archivist of Kenatos

XXI

Erasmus's breath whistled in a rushed gasp. He dropped to his knees and showed his hands. "This is the Kishion!" he hissed.

Annon turned and faced the intruder. "He is gone," Annon said curtly, his stomach clenching with fear. "You are too late." His mind raced quickly, but he remembered the words. *Pyricanthas. Sericanthas. Thas.*

"Where did he go?" the Kishion asked softly, his voice deep and full of menace. He started toward them.

"Hold there," Annon warned, raising his hands with his fingers shimmering with blue streaks. But the Kishion did not flinch. He came resolutely, closing the gap between them.

"I will do this," Paedrin said, bringing his broken staff around in a whirl. He shouldered past Annon and Hettie and faced the Kishion first. "Greetings, brother. Perhaps we should talk before…"

The Kishion did not slow. It was impossible to determine who attacked first. It was as if two crossbows released in the same instant. The staff end whished around toward the Kishion's head, met nothing but air, and the two were suddenly enmeshed in a struggle of arms and legs. Paedrin's damaged arm was still bound to his side, giving him a decided disadvantage in the match.

Annon scrabbled backward, nearly tripping over Erasmus, who watched the battle rage with wide eyes, muttering under his breath. He did not move.

The blows exchanged were dizzying. Paedrin's feet snapped out, trying to clip the Kishion's head, but the other man was impossibly fast, dodging the hail of blows with studied preciseness. The staff came down again and was caught by the Kishion, who yanked it out of Paedrin's grip and flung it aside. He stepped in fast, landing two blows into the Bhikhu's ribs that would have felled another man.

Paedrin grunted and was suddenly floating. The Kishion grappled with him as he rose and cuffed him on the side of the head, expelling his breath. He sank like a stone. Landing awkwardly, his face contorted with anger, Paedrin struck with his palm first, right at the Kishion's face, directly at his nose to smash it.

The blow never landed.

There was a loud snapping sound that Annon realized with horror was Paedrin's arm bone. The Kishion had crossed his arms in front of him, blocking the blow toward his face, but his forearm bracers caught Paedrin's extended arm in a vulnerable spot, and the bone had broken.

Hettie gasped.

Paedrin's scream shattered the air in the grove. The Kishion used the arm further to draw him in, delivering a vicious blow to his temple, and he went silent as he collapsed to the forest floor.

Annon and Hettie had retreated and stopped as the Kishion turned on them next. Annon raised his hands and focused his rage, his shock, and all the antipathy he had toward his uncle and unleashed it on the Kishion. Searing pain went through his fingers as he channeled the magic at the intruder, sending out a bloom of bright blue flames in a surging mass of writhing fire. It slammed into the Kishion with the force of a storm's fury. He was lost in the searing blue for a moment and then reappeared suddenly, stepping through the fire as if it were a harmless mist. His boot struck Annon squarely in the stomach, knocking the air from his lungs and sending him backward into a tree, making sparks dance in his eyes.

Hettie was on him like a cat, twin daggers in her hands as she launched at him from the side. He met her attack squarely, stepping inside the first sweep of the knife; he caught her wrist. In a movement as fast as a blink, the dagger fell to the earth and she was wrenched around, arm twisted behind her back, hand bent at an excruciating angle.

Annon coughed and wheezed, trying to clear his vision. The Kishion continued to tame Hettie, sending the other dagger flying, and then his arm wrapped around her neck, stopping her from breathing. Her eyes went wild with fear, her mouth gaping open as she struggled in vain to breathe.

"Where did he go?" The Kishion turned to Annon for the answer and spoke with a whispering voice as Hettie's legs thrashed and flailed.

Annon knew she had moments left to live. The Kishion would continue to choke her and see if Annon would watch her die. Then he would come at Annon again and torture the answer out of him. Either way, he would tell it. Perhaps they would all die.

This was the man hunting his uncle. This was the one he had fled to avoid facing. The Quiet Kishion, the Arch-Rike's personal protector. He knew the man would likely have a ring, one of the cursed black rings of Seithrall. But he also knew his uncle. His uncle, who was wiser than other men. He had given Annon information to reveal, knowing he might be taken.

"Silvandom," Annon answered pleadingly. "Please, do not kill her."

The Kishion's eyes were blue. The cowl had dropped back. There were other scars on his face, as if some beast had ravaged him with its claws. His hair was a shock of dark, his cheekbones high and cut like stones. He stared at Annon with pure indifference. Life had no value to him. Not even his own. Annon could see it in his dead blue eyes.

The Kishion released Hettie and let her drop to the ground. He rose and approached Annon forcefully.

"Where in Silvandom?"

Annon licked his lips, knowing he was facing a deadly snake that could destroy him with one bite. His heart shuddered in his chest with fear.

"Prince Aran. I do not know where he is, other than Silvandom."

"He has the dagger. The blade. Iddawc."

It wasn't a question.

Annon nodded.

The Kishion glanced at Annon coldly and then walked back to where Paedrin lay unconscious on the earth. Erasmus knelt still, hands up and staring meekly at the Kishion, who ignored him. He crouched down by Paedrin, gripped him by his shirt, and said in a clear voice, "Kenatos."

There was a flash of blinding light, a murmuring spatter of thunder, and they were both gone when their vision cleared.

Purple bruises decorated Hettie's neck. Her expression was twisted into a sour frown, one hand holding her injured wrist. "So that was a Kishion," she muttered. "Even the Romani fear them."

Annon examined her neck, tilting her jaw to one side. "Where else does it hurt?"

"My wrist, mostly. It hurts, but I do not think he broke it. I feared he did at first; it hurt that much."

Annon nodded, rubbing his stomach. "The flame did not touch him."

She gave him a pointed look. "Obviously, or uncle would have used it to kill him."

He sighed. "I did not think of that."

Erasmus shook his head and whistled. "You are both lucky to be alive. Few defy a Kishion and survive. They are absolutely loyal to the Arch-Rike. They do his bidding and no other's. This one was sent to kill your uncle. He rarely speaks. The Quiet Kishion. They say he is cursed in a way that no magic will harm him."

Annon took her arm and examined her wrist. She flinched when he touched it, but he stared at the wound. Now that he no longer wore the blade Iddawc, he put his talisman back on. The forest was alive with chattering from the spirits who had witnessed the scene of violence. Many were sympathetic.

Is there a sylph near? he asked, projecting his thoughts. *We are injured.*

Hettie's scowl furrowed deeper. "Why did he take Paedrin?"

Erasmus sighed. "The Bhikhu are also loyal to the Rikes. I would deduce they will get what information they can from him and then send him back to the temple. I do not know how he travels or by what means, but we can judge the following. Either he could only take one person with him...presumably he meant to take your uncle's corpse. Or he did not consider us a sufficient threat to bother with."

"Not yet anyway," Hettie said through ground teeth. "It hurts, Annon."

"Be still," he said, hearing a reply to his thoughts. A timid spirit approached, though he could not see it. Annon closed his eyes and focused his thoughts, feeding them with intense gratitude. The sylph responded to his emotion, hovering in the air between him and Hettie.

"Close your eyes," Annon whispered.

He could feel the warmth of the magic seep through him and into her skin, threading through the muscles and tendons and bone. Hettie started to flinch, but Annon held her still. There was a gentle pulse of heat and then the creature was gone.

Annon opened his eyes. The bruises on her neck and arms were gone as well. She looked at him in awe and stretched out her arm, twisting her wrist as if it were completely healed.

"How did you do that?" she whispered. "Was it a prayer?"

"In a way," he answered, smiling. "It is a bit complicated, but the magic is part of the Druidecht lore. I invited a spirit to heal you. It agreed. I could not force it to do so. But it had compassion on you and our situation and decided to help us." He turned and gazed at Erasmus. "One of the things I learned before we fell asleep in the tree. I have not had time to mention it. Drosta spoke to me. He is a Druidecht now. He isn't a Paracelsus any longer. He said the entire city of Kenatos is enslaving spirits."

"I don't understand," Hettie said. "I fell asleep so quickly. I was so afraid and then suddenly I could not keep my eyes open. I heard him speaking, but I could not understand him."

"He told us that the Arch-Rike and his kind are trapping spirits in Kenatos. They are binding them into service. Into slavery. You remember the lights in the city? When the darkness comes, all of the city starts to glow? Those are trapped spirits. The Arch-Rike has been trapping them and using them. The blade we found in Drosta's lair. It contains an ancient spirit called the Iddawc. Knowing its name can give you power over it, but it seeks to subvert strong men into killing. It was forged to kill those like Uncle Tyrus."

"Then why did he send us to find it?" Hettie asked, frustration on her face.

"He means to use it in the Scourgelands. Obviously it is a powerful magic. Perhaps powerful enough to survive the dangers there."

"Then why not get it himself?" Hettie asked.

Erasmus clucked his tongue. "Never presume to understand his thinking. That way lies madness. It seems he has work for us to do. If he knows of a way to end the Plague…if he has finally discovered the solution to that riddle, it is worth more than every ducat in Havenrook. An event like that would topple the Arch-Rike."

"I don't care about the Arch-Rike," Hettie said. "It is that Kishion I would see humbled. It was unfair of him to cripple Paedrin like that. Now both of his arms are broken."

Annon looked at her dark expression. "Will you go to Kenatos and seek the jewels Tyrus asked you for?"

She nodded gruffly. "I am a Finder, after all. And a Romani. It would not surprise me if the rubble was searched for treasures. There are thieves aplenty in that city. Any one worth his *carnotha* would have searched the grounds or bribed a guard for trinkets found." She sighed. "Only I have nothing to barter for it, so I may have to steal it back."

Annon felt a huge pang of worry for her. They had not known each other long, but the surge of protective feelings swelling in his heart startled him. As he had watched the Kishion strangle her, he would have done anything to stop it. He gripped her shoulder and then pulled her close.

"I was so worried when he was choking you," he whispered, squeezing her. He knew that her life had been spared because he spoke. He would not have done any differently. Her hair brushed against his face, and he felt her arm offer a timid hug in reply.

"Thank you for saving me," she said. She pulled away, but only enough to look in his eyes. "You are not what I expected, Annon Waylander." She reached down and took his hand, squeezing it. "I wish you knew the truth...I wish we had *known* the truth about each other."

"I would have come for you," he promised. "I would have searched every Romani caravan until I found you." He fingered the single hoop in her ear. "I would tear this off you right now..."

"Don't," she flinched, shaking her head. "You don't know the Romani. If I help Tyrus, perhaps I will earn my freedom. We've made an enemy of Kiranrao, but he still wants that blade. He won't stop until he gets it. He is relentless."

Annon could see the danger his uncle had warned them about. The most powerful men in the kingdoms were his enemies. But apparently, he had allies as well. He sighed. "I don't want you to leave," he said, rubbing her arm affectionately. "We have been through so much together already. I worry about you. Don't use the fireblood unless you absolutely must. Please."

She leaned up and kissed his cheek. "Only if I must. Our paths lead to Silvandom. You to your mentor. Mine to the Vaettir prince." She paused, glancing down, her expression suddenly cloudy. "This is harder than I thought it would be."

"Saying farewell?"

She hesitated and then nodded. There was something in her eyes. He had noticed it before.

"Erasmus and I will meet you in Silvandom then. If you need anything, Hettie, seek out a Druidecht. Tell them I am your brother and they will offer you aid. I wish…I wish I could help you, but the city is not a place where my knowledge will be useful."

She smiled in response and mussed up his hair. "I have taken care of myself for a long time. You are the one who was raised innocently. I do not begrudge you that, Annon."

"I wish that I had been sent in your place," he said, meaning it. His heart ached for her.

The look she gave him was full of pain. "I will look for you in Silvandom when I find the jewels, brother. For your wisdom and knowledge, Master Erasmus, I thank you. Will it rain before I reach Kenatos, do you think?"

Erasmus folded his arms. "Too early in the season. Or were you teasing me?"

She smirked at him and gave Annon a final hug good-bye.

He almost asked her if she would seek Paedrin in the Bhikhu temple as well. But he already suspected the answer to that question.

"In every great city, with all its gleaming walls and massive libraries, with all the shimmering fountains and sculptured gardens, there is a superfluity of dung that must be carted out. In our world, the Romani fill that role. Granted, they do cart all manner of substances through this Plague-ridden world. There are ducats enough to bring bushels of wheat or baskets of figs. But they also cart the seedier stuff. They traffic vice. They traffic slavery. Nothing pains my heart more than to hear that a child has been abducted from Kenatos. I abhor them all and their glittering earrings. Never trust a Romani. That is the only rule one needs to know about them."

– Possidius Adeodat, Archivist of Kenatos

XXII

There was a Romani saying that came often to Hettie's mind: *He who pays the piper calls the tune.* She had learned it as a child, over and over again. And she had heard it more recently when Kiranrao arrived at Evritt's cabin in the woods. That day had shattered her peace and left her desperate.

A mass of swirling guilt consumed her as she hurried north along the plains toward Kenatos. It was like clutching knives into her bosom, each one a lie told to preserve the illusion. Her entire life was a lie. Even in her best days, she could barely discern truth from tale. Lying was important. Deception was crucial. If one believed in them enough, not even the Arch-Rike's ring could unmask them. Her mind had been subverted as a child—a drip and drop of lies and deceits woven into a fabric that smothered her. Yes, the best lies were half-truths. Just enough honesty to flavor the falsehood. Yes, she was very good at flavoring her words.

She was miserable as she walked. Events had almost spun completely out of control. She had been so close to capturing the blade. Somehow, the Druidecht spell that had vaulted them away from the Alkire into the lowland plains had taken time to wear off. With that, her plan to steal the dagger from Annon and then flee had been ruined. Instead, Tyrus had arrived and claimed it. Tyrus! Her cursed, scheming uncle had spoiled the opportunity for her. How she hated him!

Her fingers tingled with heat and she forced the emotions down. She walked swiftly, trying to cover as much ground as she could. Kiranrao would be furious, of course. Not in a blustery way, but in a deadly calm way. She knew that not even a Fear Liath could kill him. Its arrival had ruined the first opportunity to steal the dagger. But she knew he was alive and that he would seek her out again, demanding the tune once more. Betray her uncle and steal the blade.

Hettie hated herself the most. She had played her part too well and had earned the trust of Annon and Paedrin. They were such fools. Such simpletons. They knew not the ways of the Romani or the Preachán. A thousand deceits spun around them like gnats, yet the lies were totally invisible. It amazed her how people could be so blind. She even thought she might have Tyrus fooled, though Kiranrao had warned her never to assume that. Tyrus was cunning. He saw through every trap.

She clenched her jaw in fury, summoning all of her despair and self-hatred into a bubbling cauldron of feelings. Annon was so naive. Paedrin was clever, but he was also a fool. She clamped the feelings down with brutal willpower, slamming the lid on the cauldron and wrapping it with chains. This was her life. This was the way of the Romani. Deceive the world into giving you what you wanted.

What did she want? Freedom. But she knew that she would never get it. She had lied to Paedrin during their midnight conversation. She had said she did not know how the Romani controlled their women. It was a half-truth. No one had told her, specifically. But when she was five she had seen it happen. Romani were excellent poisoners. They knew the properties of every plant with deadly or harmful aspects. Some poisons killed quickly. Some made you blind. But the worst by far was monkshood. It made you wish you were dead before it killed you.

She had seen a young woman be disobedient and then watched as her food was tainted with monkshood. Being so young herself, she did not realize it until after the meal when the girl had started retching violently and was unable to control her bowels. She screamed for help. She pleaded her repentance. Still, they just stared at her coldly, letting her experience the full effects of the poison. When she was almost dead, she was given the antidote. Seeing that had shocked Hettie at how merciless they had been to someone ten years older than her.

So Hettie had grown up knowing that even if she ran away from her fate, a Romani would poison her with monkshood and let her die. She would not know who it was. She could not know when. There were so many subtle ways the poison could be added to her food. Too many to consider. Freedom was something she wanted more than anything else. And Kiranrao had promised it to her in return for her help. Of course that was a lie as well. But it was better than the prospect of being bartered off as a wife.

She kicked a stray scrub away as she walked, scanning the sky as thunderheads threatened in the north. She was not cold, not at the pace she was keeping. Her heart pounded with the rhythm of her walking. The breeze was scented with wildflowers. She still waited for the sour smell of the city, which would be the first indication she was getting close to Kenatos.

In her mind, she thought over the events of her current plight. Evritt had indeed purchased her when she was eight. Kiranrao had allowed the sale, of course. He more than suspected that Tyrus's hand was behind the purchase, even if it could not be proved. Rather than force the issue of her theft then, Kiranrao would force it later. Everyone knew that Tyrus was one of the wealthiest men in Kenatos. Yet he was miserly and rarely parted with ducats for anything except for purchasing his equipment and exotic spirits. The Romani whispered that he had even paid an enormous sum for a monstrous oak tree to be excavated and brought inside the city walls to the Paracelsus Tower because he fancied the shade. It was dead and rotting now, but the rumor was famous amongst the Romani. If he would pay that much for a tree, how much would he pay for a niece?

Kiranrao had told her before Evritt had taken her away that he would visit her again and demand an accounting of any inter-actions with Tyrus. In the nearly ten years since that time, her uncle had not visited her once. Her entire life was given over to training to be a Finder. It was a handy skill for any Romani to learn, and she had enjoyed the years living away from the trav-eling caravans that used wagons and steeds to transport goods throughout a land riddled by Plague.

He had warned her to stay in good health and take pains to keep herself physically attractive. All Romani girls were expected to be beautiful and cold. The more mysterious and alluring, the higher the value to prospective buyers. She had dyed her unfashion-ably red hair and made it a brown instead, disguising the trait that might have revealed her fireblood. Her lifestyle in the woods had kept her fit and trim, and she wore her clothing tight deliberately. Other Finders sought out Evritt, not so much for his wisdom and experience but for a glimpse of his Romani-girl, Hettie. Some of the younger men had tried to win her eye. But her instructions from Kiranrao were plain. She was to be Tyrus's undoing. She would be the one to trick him into revealing the blade's hiding place.

She understood fully well that Evritt's life was at stake if she did not comply with Kiranrao's plans. He did not threaten the old man, but it was implied as surely as water freezing into ice during winter. He coached her in what to say, what to reveal, and what not to reveal. Just enough truth to flavor the stew. Not to ask for his money but for a way to prove herself worthy of his trust. She was furious with herself for even caring. What had her uncle ever done for her?

Tyrus had seemed genuinely pleased to see her, willing to help. Was it because he, as a man, simply could not resist helping a beautiful girl who had come to him for assistance? Kiranrao had warned her not to be fooled. Tyrus was not an emotional man. Yet he had seemed so convincing. He had summoned a Druidecht boy and claimed him to be her brother. They were as unlike as syrup and milk, yet there was a blood connection between them. She had felt it in Annon's presence, just as she did in her uncle's. They were family. Despite the lies, that mattered.

She had not expected to be sent to Havenrook to look for Drosta's treasure. It was the last place she wanted to go, to be surrounded by Preachán and Romani and the hive of deceit. She suspected Kiranrao was startled to see her so soon as well, which was why he had summoned her to his table. The conversation they had with their hands masked completely the conversation they employed with their voices. Even their words had multiple meanings, meant to confuse and deceive Annon and Paedrin while giving Kiranrao the useful information he needed.

She warned him about the deaths on the road, of course, and the trouble that would come. She had told Paedrin and Annon that the men hiding in the trees were Romani and had exaggerated her hatred to add conviction to her ruse, but, of course, she never would have willingly killed a Romani man. She knew they were all Preachán and their lives were worth little more than the money they gambled with. She had given the Preachán on the wagon a subtle hand sign to see if he would let them pass, but he had either not noticed it or was stupid enough he didn't care.

Hettie sighed deeply. Paedrin and all his chatter and talk. His entire outlook on life was almost comical. Just walk away from the Romani. The imprisonment was only in her mind. She wanted to believe him. But how could she expect him to understand that defying them would mean she would never have a moment's peace the rest of her life? Every crust of bread, every swallow of wine could contain monkshood. Just enough to kill her and anyone else eating with her. She would spend her days in mortal suspense, wondering which dish would be her last.

If it was freedom she truly wanted, only Kiranrao could ensure it. And he wanted the blade Iddawc. All of his thoughts were bent toward locating it and claiming it as his own. The most powerful weapon forged by a Paracelsus. A weapon that would not lose its power in a thousand years. Kiranrao did not want it in the hands of a Kishion. He wanted it for himself.

She wondered if she should stop by the temple and see how Paedrin was faring when she arrived. Her uncle's task to find the bag would be ridiculously simple. All she needed to do was show her *carnotha*, ask the right question, and all of Kiranrao's resources would be put to her use. If someone had found it already, they would be able to trace it and give it to her. If not, every thief in the city would be scrambling for a chance to do Kiranrao a favor. All she needed to do was wait the appropriate amount of time, to make the discovery *seem* convincing, and then travel to Silvandom with the missing stones.

Her uncle had given her the clue to finding him again. That alone would be worth a sizable fortune from Kiranrao. And the assignment to bring the bag of stones would give her a reasonable excuse to approach him again, to win his trust.

There was a strain in her heart as the kettle of emotions rattled again, surging with the force of shame and guilt. She refused to let the contents leak out. It was a vicious world. Every day, people were murdered for nothing more precious than a fistful of ducats. The more ducats, the better the chance of surviving the next bout of Plague.

She wondered if that was the real reason Kiranrao wanted her near him so much. She had the fireblood. It was said that those with it could never be harmed by the Plague. Was there some distant connection between her ancestors and the origins of the Scourgelands? Some riddle remaining with no one living who knew the answer to it?

Hettie rubbed her forehead, smelling the first hint of fetid air. She would reach the lakeshore before midnight. Good. It meant a warm bed to sleep in unless she went to the temple again and slept on a pallet on the floor. The sound of Paedrin's arm breaking made her stomach clench in revulsion. His injury would hamper him for many months. Perhaps she should bid him good-bye.

It was a strange compulsion, actually, and she wondered at it. Why should she care a bushel of figs about saying good-bye to Paedrin? He was a haughty, arrogant Bhikhu who had less sense than a sheep. Why bother? It nagged at her that he had saved her life amid the dangers of Drosta's lair. Of course, she had gone down there in the hopes to steal the blade while he fought the creature. But when she was struck by it, he had come to save her.

She bit her lip. What a foolish boy he was. He had no idea at all that she was using him to her own ends. Most males were blinded by beauty. Start off angry and contemptuous. Treat them with apathy and revulsion. Then slowly dribble out a compliment or favor them with an occasional smile. They would become your servants for life. It was the way of the world. For certain, it was the way of the Romani.

What harm would it do, though, to stop by the temple and see him? She did not care for him. She did not care for anyone, even her brother.

A part of her had died, she realized, when she saw her *father* poison her *sister* over an act of disobedience. Maybe that part of her was still dead. But for some reason, she wanted to see Paedrin again. It was a foolish thought. She had probably derived a small flicker of pleasure arguing with him. That was probably it. She decided not to see him. It would be better for him, after all, to never see her again. She was rather sure that Kiranrao would kill him if they ever crossed paths again.

"A wise leader, a past King of Wayland actually, wrote this in his personal history at the end of his very successful reign. I found his advice in the Archives and think it some of the wisest advice ever written: 'Be courteous to all, but intimate with few, and let those few be well tried before you give them your confidence.'"

– Possidius Adeodat, Archivist of Kenatos

XXIII

ost of the main streets of Kenatos were named. There were major thoroughfares that connected the different regions of town inhabited by the different races: Aeduan, Preachán, Vaettir, and Cruithne. But the streets themselves were a blend of the different cultures. The higher elevations of the city were dedicated to the founders of Kenatos; this area included the Paracelsus Towers and the Temple of Seithrall. The temple was the largest structure in the entire city, occupying the entire upper heights—a fortress hewn out of stone carried from Stonehollow and ferried across the lake. It had taken nearly a generation in its construction. Hettie had heard it whispered that Kiranrao was the only man ever to have plundered the fortress.

Keeping her sights on the enormous structure, she wove through the streets leading to Gracesteeple Gate and entered it. Rubbish littered the streets and beggar children approached her instantly, but with a subtle hand sign, they dispersed. The sun had already set and the lights were aglow in the streets, spewing no fumes or smoke and casting the stone with a silvery hue. Only the main streets were lit at night; Hettie marked her way down a side alley that was surrounded in shadows. The smell of offal was oppressive, and she wrinkled her nose. She found one street further in littered with the homeless, hunkered beneath tattered blankets. A few moaned at her passing, but she ignored them. At the final crossroads, she turned to the right and saw a candle in the window of a shop. It was the solitary shop on the street.

Hettie approached it cautiously and then rapped firmly on the door in a sequence she had learned. She waited a few moments, then knocked again. The lock turned, and a burly young man opened the door. His face was pockmarked and his chin full of wispy tufts. His hair was a dirty brown, though his eyes were a stunning hazel. He looked at her warily; he opened the door wider and let her in without a word when she showed her *carnotha*.

The smell of bird droppings choked the air and the sound of dozens of different species filled the room with exotic sounds. A woman waddled between the cages, stuffing little crusts between the haphazard bars. Her hair was obviously dyed, and her clothes too tight-fitting for one of her girth. A silver cane was gripped tightly in her left hand, helping to steady her as she maneuvered between the vast cages filled with rainbow-hued parakeets, canaries, finches, and warblemoss. Little playful finches ducked and bobbed their heads and sang in trilling tunes at her as she entered.

The young man shut the door behind her and bolted it.

"Thank you," Hettie said. He shrugged, finding his way back to an overstuffed couch that was split at the seams and spilling its stuffing.

"Yes, and here is your dinner, little Apathy. And yours too, Vengeance. My, aren't we hungry tonight. Craven and Meek, you are lovely. Tsk, tsk. Don't be rude. Yes, I know. I know. She is weeping next door again. Curse her. Always weeping and chanting spells. Look at you, Glutton. If there was ever a parrot which lived up to its name, it is you. You should be more like Meek. And now we have Precious and Sated. There you are, my lovelies." She reached into a pouch belted to her waist and stuffed another cracker into the slot between the bars. The birds pecked at each other, and the woman clucked her tongue at them.

"How are you, Mondargiss?" Hettie said, running her fingers down the firm metal bars of a cage. The finches trilled at her and bobbed their heads furiously, looking for crumbs or seeds from her.

"Well enough, child. Well enough," she said disdainfully. She cooed at more of the birds. "Pretty Vespers. I like you the best. What a lovely song you have for me. If only..." She stopped, scowling, and stamped her cane on the ground. "Cim! She is weeping again! Can you not hear her? I am all fury with the sound of it." She stamped her cane again. "Cim! Go next door and bid her be quiet!"

Cim stared at the woman, his eyes full of loathing, and did nothing but wait. In a moment, Mondargiss straightened, her eyes shifting from cage to cage as if she could not remember where she left off. "Pout, did you get a cracker? I do not believe so. I can't remember. Here is another one. You are not as fat as Glutton, so maybe it will be all right if you had more. And look at you, little Cheer. How quaint."

Hettie let the reek of bird scat wash over her and she sighed, waiting for the ritual to be over. She did not advance deeper into the room until invited. It took quite a while, for Mondargiss was thorough. When she had visited the last cage with a compliment, she turned at last to Hettie. Her eyes narrowed.

"You returned sooner than I suspected. Did you fail, girl?" She started wobbling toward her, face painted as if she were ready to perform on the stage. A dribble of smoke-colored sweat trickled down her cheek.

"I did not fail," Hettie replied coldly. "There is a new assignment from Kiranrao."

"Ahh, you failed then. Pretty thing. He will forgive you your blunder. You are too pretty to be cast aside. Too young. Only one ring in your ear? Poor lass. Would that we could trade places." She parted her honey-dyed hair and revealed six gleaming rings in her own ear. "What I would not give to be useful again. Useful and young."

Hettie stared at her with contempt. She had been a beauty once. Now it was a husk, an illusion. "You are useful to Kiranrao, which is why he bids me seek your help. I need information, Mondargiss."

A wicked smile played on the older woman's lips. "Of course you do, child. What do you seek?"

"There was an explosion in the Paracelsus Tower recently. The tower of Tyrus Paracelsus. You know of it?"

Mondargiss slowly closed the gap between them, shuffling forward lamely. Her eyes were dark and cunning. "We felt it explode. It shook the entire city. Windows shattered. Glass on the floor. My little doves were so upset by it. I knew Kiranrao would wish to know of it. I sent my swiftest little one."

There was a flapping of wings and then a dove flew in from the window, landing in a dovecote above.

"Cim!" she shrieked, but the young man was already moving, climbing up a rickety ladder until he reached the dovecote. He fussed with the bird a bit and then brought down a tiny slip, which he handed to Mondargiss.

The woman craned her neck and studied the small scrawlings. She chuckled gleefully. "An ill wind from the east. An ill wind from the west. An ill wind from the north. My, what a

storm that will brew. Yes, my darling, what is it that you need?"
She reached forward and flicked some of Hettie's hair teasingly.

"Tyrus left something behind, likely in the rubble. It is a
sturdy leather bag with three unfinished stones. Not cut gems,
but likely polished. It would not have been destroyed."

Mondargiss shook her head knowingly. "Little stones, you
say. Little uncut gems. There were weapons found. Spirit-touched
blades. Arrowheads survived, but the shafts did not. They are
selling for many ducats and being stolen away to Havenrook
for bidding. But you know that I cannot go near the Paracelsus
Towers, my dear. Not myself."

Hettie bridled with impatience, but kept her temper. The
woman's eyes were always cruel. "Surely I did not believe you
were scavenging the rubble, Mondargiss."

"Not even when I was younger. Any number of boys would
have gladly searched the rubble at my command. But they will
search for me again. Cim! See to it. If someone has captured the
stones, bring them to me, or bring me word of who has them."

The young man rose from the dilapidated couch and
shrugged. Hettie stopped him before he passed her.

"How long will it take you?" she asked him softly.

His eyes gleamed. "Dunno," he said with a shrug.

"Thank you, Cim," she said, flashing him a quicksilver smile.
His face remained impassive as he went to the door and unbolted
it. He disappeared into the street beyond.

"You think you are so clever," Mondargiss said with a sneer.
"He is impervious to any woman. I could name him the king of
stone. He feels nothing. He cares for nothing. For no one."

Hettie felt her eyes tighten, but she managed to keep herself
aloof. "What is Kiranrao training him for then? A Kishion?"

Mondargiss smiled wickedly. "I will not betray his secrets.
You know that. I was his favorite once. You are so young. So pretty,

but you are Romani. We understand each other, girl. Someday, you will be like me. You will ache at the thought of being useful again." Her free hand tightened into a fist and crushed against her heart. "I was a singer once. I graced the stage, and I sang for princes and dukes and the wealthiest of Kenatos. My voice could transfix a man. I had many admirers back then. As do you, child, as do you. I did not want flowers. I asked for birds, birds of every kind. Someday, sooner than you wish, you will find that age has left you bereft of usefulness. And then maybe *you* will tend my menagerie and wait for scraps of paper!"

She started, head cocked, listening. Her face contorted with rage. "She is sobbing again! I hate it! I loathe the sound of it. I can hear her in the upper floor, next door. I will give you a thousand ducats, child. Go there and kill her. Stop her from weeping. Oh, how it torments me. A thousand ducats to kill her. Cim won't do it. He says no one lives next door anymore. He is just too lazy. Too lazy. A thousand ducats. Will you do it?"

Hettie stared at the old woman, revulsion overpowering her. "I will return in three days. Kiranrao will pay for the pouch. He will pay handsomely for it. I must go."

"Do not leave me alone, child," Mondargiss pleaded, grabbing her by the hem of her cloak. "I cannot bear to hear the sobs when I am alone. The birds are too quiet. We must wake them. Then I will not hear her anymore. Help me rouse them."

"Three days' time," Hettie said, shaking off her grip.

"Do not leave me!" she shrieked. "I was once the greatest singer in all Kenatos and Silvandom! I was famous once. The world demanded my music, and I demanded my riches. Even the Arch-Rike fancied me. Even he! I sang for him in private audience. I moved him to tears. If you had seen me, you would not scorn me now. Look at me, child! You will be here someday. You will wear this crown of thorns. You will not look so fine forever. Do not leave me! Cim! Cim! Bolt the door! Cim!"

Hettie shut the door solidly behind her, shivering with disgust and horror. Six rings in her ears. Six rings. The smell of bird droppings nearly made her retch in the street. Her first night in Kenatos, she had come to see Mondargiss. A Finder did not belong in such a muck-filled abode. She would not end up as Mondargiss. She promised herself that she would not.

But where would she stay for three days? Where could she rest and learn more about the explosion in the Paracelsus Towers?

She roamed away from the rank alleys and wandered north along the main roads higher within the city. Even though it was after sunset, the streets were crowded and full of trade. It was more active than she had seen in the past, as if a certain giddiness swelled the air. Pausing to eat a meat pie, she watched the ebb and flow of oil-skinned Cruithne moving through the crowd. The sight of Bhikhu robes caused her to start, but she did not recognize the man, nor was he a Vaettir. She did remember, briefly, Paedrin's little lesson about the Uddhava and how just the presence of a Bhikhu could alter someone's actions.

Hettie finished the pie and started through the streets, watching the spectacle of the city float past her. It was too noisy. She needed a respite from the crowds. Passing into a new quarter, she started up a steep climb of steps that brought her up to the next level. The din and noise of the crowds faded behind. There were plenty of lights atop metal poles on each side of the steps.

As she neared the top, she realized where her legs had taken her. The Bhikhu temple was before her, gates closed. What good would it do to see him again? She fussed and fumed with herself, standing awkwardly in the shadows, wondering what madness had driven her. Perhaps the dung from the birds had deranged her mind.

It was getting late. Any number of inns or taverns could provide a night's rest. But for some reason, she had felt particularly safe asleep on a pallet in the temple. It was her uncle's suggestion.

Her legs began moving again toward the doors, and she exhaled softly, chiding herself. She reached the gate and pulled the taut cord fastened to the bell. It clanged ominously. There were no lights from the temple. The Bhikhu typically did not linger after their meals but retired to their cells to meditate and think righteous thoughts, no doubt. She hugged herself, waiting patiently. The sound of slapping sandals came from the other side of the large door.

The crossbar lifted and the door opened inward, revealing Master Shivu. He saw her standing alone in the doorway and his smile suddenly wavered, replaced by a frown.

"You are alone," he said softly, barely masking the throb of concern in his voice.

Hettie nodded. "I came to see how Paedrin was doing. If he was healing…?" She let the words die on her tongue. It was obvious by the expression on Master Shivu's face that Paedrin was not at the temple.

"Come inside," Master Shivu said, holding the door open. "You must tell me what you know. I have not seen Paedrin since he left with you and your brother."

A cold lump of fear solidified inside Hettie's stomach.

"*Will we ever comprehend the Plague? I think not. Some things are not meant to be understood. They must only be endured.*"

– *Possidius Adeodat, Archivist of Kenatos*

XXIV

The tea was uncomfortably hot, making Hettie wince. A single fat candle caused a sparse glow in Master Shivu's chamber. The temple had the semblance of a crypt. A plate was offered to her with some cold rice, a few dates, and some dried fruit and cheese. She accepted the humble fare and ate it gratefully, though without appetite.

"When I first saw you, I feared he was dead," Shivu said, his brow furrowing. "You say he was alive?"

Hettie nodded. "We were ambushed by a Kishion several days south of here."

Master Shivu wrinkled his nose. "What cause would a Kishion have of interfering with your return journey?"

"My uncle found us. I believe it was tracking him some way. Paedrin was already injured from our journey into the mountains, but he tried to defend us and was thrown down; his arm was broken cruelly. He and the Kishion disappeared through some form of magic, but the Kishion said the word 'Kenatos' before he left, so I assumed he was brought back to the city, that I would find him here."

Shivu shook his head. "I must speak to the Arch-Rike."

A pulse of alarm ran through Hettie at the words. "Tell me what happened to my uncle after we left. I have only just heard word that there was some destruction at the tower. Do you know what happened?"

Master Shivu folded his fingers above his mouth. "Your uncle was declared a traitor to Kenatos, child. There are accusations that he was plotting with our enemies to overthrow the city."

Hettie exhaled deeply. What else would a Bhikhu master believe? She hesitated a moment before replying. The truth was a careful balancing act. "I have no knowledge of such a thing. The treasure he sent us to find was gone. There was evidence all around the entrance that others had been there long before we arrived. I think he was sending us far away to protect us from harm." She sighed deeply. "If the Arch-Rike wants my uncle, he may want me as well. I should be going."

Shivu gave her a wan smile. "I will not send you to the Rikes, child. You are under my protection. Even the Arch-Rike himself has no authority within these walls. He relies on the Bhikhu to keep the peace. May I assume you are here in peace?"

Hettie nodded. "I only came because I thought Paedrin was here." She bit her lip. "It would relieve me greatly to know that he was safe."

"I am sure that if he was wounded, as you say, the Arch-Rike is tending to his injuries as we speak. I will send word in the morning and see what I can learn. You look tired. Why don't you rest for the night?"

"Thank you," Hettie said, trying to hide her smile. These Bhikhu were so easy to manipulate that it almost wasn't fair. But still, there was a part of her, deep down, that nagged her. Why wouldn't the Arch-Rike have sent word that Paedrin was back in the city? She was certain she was imagining the trouble.

Borrowing worry where there was none. He would show up, smug and confident and boasting of his duel with the Kishion. That was just his way. She was sure of it.

☘

A day passed. Then two. Hettie stalked the temple grounds, lingering for word. A runner had been sent to the Arch-Rike and returned with word that the master of Kenatos was dealing with pressing matters of state and had not found the time to reply yet. There was a trade interruption from Havenrook, and shipments of grain and fruit were delayed and spoiling, causing prices in the city to bob on the rising tide. He would inquire about the missing Bhikhu, he promised, and send word in a day or two.

After two days, Hettie was impatient and started off on her own again, seeking after the ruins of the Paracelsus Tower herself. Approaching it from the west, she saw it was clearly a work of immense power or magic. The tower where she had last met her uncle was gone, with only loose fragments of broken stone showing the remains. She was in awe at the power involved in such a manifestation. The tower had been a massive stone bulwark, suspended high in the air. All that remained was a warped iron stairwell protruding from one of the four corners, a little nub displaying to witness what had been there before.

"By degrees the castles are built," Hettie whispered, staring at it as she approached. "How fast they fall." Bricks littered the street all around. The front windows of shops were being repaired. In some, blankets had been nailed over to cover the void. Broken crockery and pit-marks covered the homes and shops facing the tower proper.

There were many people milling around, but most were repairing the damage with plaster and cobbled stone. She ventured into the main gate, which was open, and found the interior courtyard full of workmen and wheelbarrows, carting off broken fragments of stone to be reused elsewhere. There were a few taskmasters at hand, but they were primarily ordering low-paid folk doing the work. Hettie studied the ruins of the tower and saw a steady stream of men venturing in and out, carrying bricks in their arms.

There was a giant dead oak tree in the middle of the court-yard. Amazingly, none of the branches had fallen as a result of the explosion. Nor had fire touched its bark. She stopped, staring at it curiously.

How peculiar, she thought. She began walking the perimeter of the oak, beneath the veil of branches, and saw not a single brick or stone beneath the boughs. There were bricks littered elsewhere, but none directly beneath it. The branches were bare of leaves, which would not have been the case normally due to the season. But as she scrutinized it, she did see a few scattered branches with foliage, and some with clumps of lush mistletoe. The presence of the mistletoe meant the tree was still alive, if barely.

She followed around the perimeter of the oak, wondering at its age and how it came to be in the center of the Paracelsus Tower. Had it been tended or had her uncle purchased it and moved it, as the rumors stated had happened. Some workers rested under its paltry shade and shared a flask between them. She walked around to the other side and found no one there; she slowly approached the trunk.

The bark was rough and craggy, like an ancient woman's skin. The branches seemed to be sagging, as if they had been defeated long ago. As she approached, she felt something stir inside of her, a warm, buzzing feeling. It was difficult to describe. It was a little like drinking sweet wine, and it made her slightly dizzy. She approached warily, reaching out until she touched the bark with her fingers. It was brittle, making it easy to pry loose a chunk with her fingers.

She gazed up the length of the trunk until the branches began mushrooming away from the base. The majesty of the oak tree had always impressed her. Oak was great to burn and produced a solid, satisfying flame. Acorns could be made into food. It was interesting that there was no debris beneath the canopy. Not even a desiccated leaf.

The feeling came over her again. It was a warm feeling, like a lingering kiss. It made her shiver involuntarily. Her breath started up. What was happening to her? Why was the tree making her so dizzy? She started to back away from it nervously, unsure at the flood and surge of emotions conflicting within her. There was something eerily comforting about the tree, and she was not used to that feeling. It was a dangerous feeling. It threatened her with tears.

She turned and was about to walk away when she heard it whisper her name.

"Hettie."

Her breath caught in her throat. Was it her imagination? There was a presence behind her. She knew it. She could feel it.

Whirling, Hettie turned to face it.

The spinning motion disoriented her, nearly making her stumble. There was no one there. She blinked with surprise.

A leather pouch nestled in the earth at the base of the tree. It had not been there before.

Her heart thudded in her chest. Fear snaked inside her skin. Kneeling by the trunk, she reached for the leather pouch. It was thick and slightly heavy, but it felt empty. As she touched it, she felt hard objects encased within the leather. Her lips were suddenly dry. Opening the drawstrings, she peeked inside at the smooth, uncut stones.

There was a nagging sensation in her mind, as if she were missing something obvious. Why was the bag sitting at the base of the tree? Had it been there all along? Had she seen it while circling the tree and that was what had brought her closer? She could not remember. Someone had whispered her name and then she had found the bag. How did the tree know it was her?

She stared at its ancient boughs, feeling overwhelmed and small. Deftly she stuffed the bag into her tunic belt and retreated from the branches. There were two workers, idling with their flask, staring at her. One raised it toward her, inviting her over. Men were always the same, especially when drunk.

She gave them a cold, disdainful look and then left the Paracelsus Tower, walking briskly away, going as fast as she dared. Her heart raced. There was something so odd and strange about the experience. Something crucial, but she could not remember it. She continued down into the lower realm of the city and ventured back toward the Bhikhu temple. She would hide the stones there for now. It would be safer than if she were caught with them. Anxiety throbbed in her stomach. Something was wrong. Something was missing. She wanted to run, to sprint.

When she saw the Bhikhu temple, she nearly wept with relief. The door was open, so she entered and hurried inside, walking past the training yard where she had first seen Paedrin practicing with his fellows. The memory was sharp and acrid in her mind. It was painful as well. Where was he? Had the Arch-Rike provided information about his whereabouts yet?

Hettie went to her chamber and silently knelt on the pallet, removing the small leather bag and testing the drawstrings again. Her fingers were trembling. She did not know why.

Tilting the bag, she emptied the stones into her palm. They were cold, ice cold. It was uncomfortable. The stones were blue with milky white streaks through each one. They each looked unique; they were not a matching set. She stared at them a moment, feeling the cold burn her palm, and then she dumped them back into the leather bag and rubbed her hand against the side of her leg.

A shadow fluttered in the corner of the cell.

Kiranrao leaned against the far wall, his eyes gazing into hers quizzically. "My, my, you *are* resourceful. There is an old Romani saying. There are three creatures beyond ruling. A mule, a pig, and a woman. Is it still true?"

Hettie's heart nearly failed her. She was shocked to see him in the heart of Kenatos, in a city where he could be arrested and killed on sight. He had earned the Arch-Rike's contempt many times over.

She responded to his quip with one of her own. "I don't know. Is the saying true that a man who owns a cow can always find a woman to milk her?"

Kiranrao smiled pleasantly. "Well said, little dove. Well said." His expression hardened. "I think it is past time that we had a talk about your loyalties."

"One often hears of Seithrall as a religion. It may be called that, for thus has it evolved. But the term itself, as I have come to read in the Archives, is more likely a mistranslation. The earliest reference I have seen was written by the first Arch-Rike of Kenatos, Catuvolcis, who said that in order to survive, the populace must be held under the thrall of faith. Over the centuries, these words have been rewritten and copied inaccurately through laziness on the Archivists' part. I abhor such errors. Some versions show that he claimed 'the thrall of fate.' Both Vaettir words—saith and seith—are one letter apart but have vastly different meanings. They are loosely translated as faith and fate. In our day, the Rikes have become less of a religion and more of a political faction. Their order was originally created because it was believed that the Plague was attracted by the thoughts of the populace. That is blatantly absurd. But centuries ago, the Rikes roamed the city, speaking platitudes to help reduce panic and instill confidence that those who lived in Kenatos would survive. Whether by faith or fate it makes little difference. It is now clear, and the Paracelsus would affirm it, that the Plague is transmitted through bad air. Thoughts have nothing whatsoever to do with it."

– Possidius Adeodat, Archivist of Kenatos

XXV

It was a prison, and Paedrin was trapped. The dimensions of his confinement were narrow enough that he could plant his palms against each wall. It was tall enough to stand, but too narrow to sleep stretched out. The door was made of tall metal rungs fastened into a mesh, the hinges capped in steel. A tiny privy hole was in the far corner; it smelt badly. There was no light of any kind.

When he awoke in the dank, shadowless cell, he did not remember his own name at first. Slowly the memories returned, flitting through his mind like butterflies. He stretched out his arm tentatively, expecting excruciating pain—but the injury was healed. So was his damaged shoulder. He had no recollection of his healing. He did not remember being placed in the cell.

Food arrived once a day, a watery gruel made of millet, the portion tasteless and not enough to strengthen a man. He was weak with hunger and thirst. Lights appeared in the hallway, so painfully bright he had to shield his face while the clomp of boots arrived, delivering the thin gruel, and then retreated. Then the darkness prevailed again and spots danced in front of his eyes.

The cell was too small to practice any of his Bhikhu fighting forms. It was too small to do nearly anything but sit cross-legged and meditate. That worked well for a while, but soon he was chafing because of the inaction. How long had he been trapped there? Why had they not sent anyone to interrogate him? There was no way of counting time. No stars swirling overhead. No rise and fall of moon and sun. The world was a void, and he was trapped inside it.

Maddening. The solitude was absolutely maddening. The air was stale and rank. He could hear no other prisoners, not even the scuttle of rats. He was completely isolated and alone. Being raised in the temple, he had always been surrounded by others. There was no one to talk to, and so he did not speak at all. All his life he had sparred with his fists and feet and tongue. He wanted an enemy to fight, even the Kishion.

How long would they keep him? How long had it been? Sleeping and dozing came fitfully. At least in his dreams there was sunlight and grass. When he awakened, he was met by the horror of the void. He wanted to scream. But maybe that was what they were expecting. Maybe they were trying to break him.

Paedrin exhaled slowly, beginning another round of meditation. His strength was failing. Hunger ravaged his gut. But still there was only darkness, and in the darkness and loneliness lay madness. He felt it there in the cell, crouched in the corner by the stink hole. Gibbering madness.

The flash of light startled him. He shielded his eyes with his forearm; he was used to the searing light by now. He gritted his teeth to avoid seeming too anxious for the gruel. There was the sound of boots on the floor, but it was a different sound. It was firmer. It had a clipping sound. A metal torch was fastened to a wall bracket. Silence.

Paedrin tried to look at the light, but it was too bright. His eyes throbbed in pain, but he forced them to remain open, to adjust to the searing pain that stabbed him. There was a shape beyond the bars. A man.

"Who are you?" Paedrin croaked. His voice was hardly a whisper.

"My name is Band-Imas. I am the Arch-Rike of Kenatos."

Paedrin flinched at the sound, the delicious sound of a human voice. He craved it desperately. Part of his mind warned him that he should not trust this man. The Bhikhu served the Rikes of Kenatos. He should not have been allowed to languish in a cell.

"Why am I here?"

"Paedrin."

The sound of his own name startled him. He tried to stare past the glare at the man who was slowly coming into focus. A haze of frosty hair glittered on his scalp, little stubble that did not grow. Eyes that were so gray they were nearly white, except for the twin black pupils. He wore a magnificent robe and the jeweled stole of his office. A velvet doublet festooned with gold buttons and red stitching showed beneath the fur-lined robe.

"Yes?" Paedrin whispered.

"That is your name, is it not? Paedrin? From the Bhikhu temple?"

"Yes."

A deep exhale came from the Arch-Rike's throat. "I am sorry then. If you were a Bhikhu from Silvandom, then my ring would have warned me of the lie. When dealing with Tyrus, one must always be on his guard. I am sorry he ensnared you in his treasonous plot. There will be a trial soon, my young friend. Your life will most likely be forfeit."

Paedrin tried to wet his lips, but he had no moisture in his mouth. "And what treason do you suspect me of? I was sent by my master on the mission. Surely you are not implying he is imprisoned as well?"

"There is much we can discuss, Paedrin." His voice was patient, yet there was an edge to it. A man used to being obeyed and never mocked. He twisted a large garnet ring from his finger, the stone ink black. "I am sure you recognize the fashion of this ring. It is imbued with a spirit that prevents any falsehood from being spoken or one uttered in its wearer's presence." He offered Paedrin the ring.

He looked warily at the Arch-Rike but slowly extended his hand and reached for the ring. He had seen it come off of the Arch-Rike's hand. The weight of it in his palm surprised him. He slid it on his finger.

"Tyrus of Kenatos is a traitor to Kenatos," the Arch-Rike said. "He seeks to overthrow the religion of Seithrall. He conspires with the enemies of the city to do his bidding. He is a most dangerous man, Paedrin. He sent you to recover an artifact that was commissioned and paid for but never delivered. It was stolen. He was behind the theft. That weapon is very dangerous. Did he tell you what it does?"

Paedrin felt the compulsion to tell the truth. Drosta had told them, not Tyrus. He mastered his tongue. "He did not."

"Let me explain it then. It is a most marvelous blade. There is only one of its kind. There can only be one of its kind. The spirit that powers it is stronger than death. It holds the very power over death. You are young. You do not understand the nature of the Plague and how death destroys knowledge. This city was created to preserve knowledge. The blade is a tool. Whoever it kills, it will preserve their memories and experiences and trap them inside the hilt to be used by the bearer of the blade. You must understand this, Paedrin. I cannot lie in the presence of the ring. That blade is the key to our survival. When the Plague comes again, and it will, for I have foreseen it, then those who are afflicted will be relieved of their suffering and their memories preserved. Think of it! Even were the Plague to strike me, my essence, my knowledge, my wisdom would be preserved for the next Arch-Rike to benefit from."

Paedrin felt sick inside. "What gives you the right to claim their memories?" he asked. "Are all of their secrets laid bare?"

"Yes," the Arch-Rike answered, his eyes glittering with passion. "Their secret thoughts. Their secret treasons. Our rings cannot force a man to divulge the truth. The blade can. It was fashioned at great expense. It was meant to preserve knowledge."

Paedrin scowled. "It would also make a great temptation to murder."

"Yes. Yes, I agree with you. It requires great wisdom to direct its power. I do not wish to hold it myself, only to direct its wise use."

Slowly Paedrin rose from his crouch. "What gives you the right? Why should you be allowed to dole out death?"

The Arch-Rike smiled, a thin-lipped, cold smile. "Because each time the Plague grows more fierce. Each time more lives are lost. Only through wisdom and unity will we survive. The Cruithne will die in Alkire. The Preachán will perish in Havenrook. The Vaettir will be dead. Even the barbarians of Boeotia will perish. All civilization will come crashing to an end, except for this city. I have foreseen it, Paedrin. Before the end comes, we must harvest the wisest from all cultures and preserve their knowledge. If you were the last of the Bhikhu, I would order you cut down to preserve the priceless knowledge that you hold."

He paused, smiling wryly. "But you are not the last Bhikhu. You are merely a pawn in a game of power played between Tyrus of Kenatos and myself. He would send us back into the abyss of ignorance by freeing all of the serving spirits. Yes, I said *serving*. He and others claim they are slaves. They serve us. They are not our slaves. Every one of them will be set free when their commitment is fulfilled. They are preserving us, Paedrin. They will help us survive the coming onslaught. And Tyrus seeks to hasten it. Tyrus aids our enemies and undermines our ability to save as many souls as we can."

Paedrin shook his head, hearing the Arch-Rike's words but unable to understand what he meant. "By this ring, I can see that you believe you are telling the truth. But certainly there can be two opinions on this matter. Locking me in this cell is hardly befitting one who has been trained to *serve* Kenatos."

"Of course you will continue to serve Kenatos. But you must die first."

Paedrin shook his head. "How can I serve Kenatos when I am dead?"

"You will serve me best as a Kishion. They are dead as to things of this world. They do not marry. They do not have children. They have no past. They have no future. You will accept blame of your role in the theft of the blade Iddawc, and you will be hung for the crime. But of course a Vaettir cannot die by hanging, so long as he has breath. You will survive and you will be reborn. I have great need of you, Paedrin. You must serve Kenatos still."

Paedrin felt a sheen of sweat appear on his back and trickle down. He thought of his master. He thought of Hettie. He thought of the man with the ravaged face who had broken his arm.

"I will not," he answered. "I would rather die by hanging."

"Or remain here in the dark for the rest of your life?" the Arch-Rike said with a small smile. "Come, Paedrin. You will serve me. Twist the black gemstone on the ring."

An overpowering compulsion rushed inside his body. Unable to stop himself, he turned the gemstone on the ring. The stone detached itself.

"Give it to me."

Paedrin tried to stop his arms from moving, but he could not. The compulsion was incredibly powerful, going directly through his arms and fingers. He reached through the bars and handed the stone to the Arch-Rike, who fastened it to a jeweled necklace around his neck. There were matching ink-black stones inset into gold.

"With this necklace," the Arch-Rike said, "I control all of you. You are my servants. You will forget your name. You will remember being born in the darkness. You will say what I wish you to say. You will do what I wish you to do. Is that clear, Paedrin?"

The feeling was total and utter hopelessness. Every instinct screamed at him to resist, to defy the Arch-Rike. But somehow part of him was taken away when the stone left the ring. Some spirit magic was at work now. It crushed him.

"Yes, my lord," he whispered in a choked voice.

"The Romani girl was snooping around the Paracelsus Tower today. What was she looking for?"

Again his tongue loosened without the ability to stop. "Tyrus sent her for spirit magic that he had left behind. A leather bag with three uncut gems." *Stop it! Stop speaking!* he screamed at himself. The realization of his helplessness struck him with horror.

The Arch-Rike's brow wrinkled. "Peculiar. We discovered no such artifacts when we searched the debris. Well, we will have a chance to speak with her tomorrow. She is at the Bhikhu temple, you see. When Master Shivu comes to see you in the morning, I will send a Kishion to fetch her. She is Romani, after all, and Romani are forbidden to enter the city. One cannot trust them, you see." The glint of his smile revealed his triumph.

Reaching for the torch, the Arch-Rike gave Paedrin one last look before retrieving it. "You realize that removing the ring will kill you. I am certain you are clever enough to consider that, but just to be sure." He walked back down the hallway, plunging him into blackness.

"I was once at a banquet with the Arch-Rike and some intimate associates. For all his vast wealth and lavish accommodations, he exercises the most amazing self-control I have ever seen. I saw him eat no meat, only natural things like apples and cucumbers and the like. He refused any attempt to refill his wine goblet. Some say he is overly suspicious of poison and that is why he eats so little. I propose that he will not take any substance into him that might addle his thoughts or control his emotions."

– Possidius Adeodat, Archivist of Kenatos

XXVI

When Paedrin was a child, he had broken a bone for the first time climbing a tall dresser. He had managed to pull out the drawers to act as rungs and thought it was a brilliant idea until the entire structure came down on top of him and smashed his leg. He was five years old. Paedrin remembered the brace, the tight bandages, and the crutches that allowed him to hobble around. Mostly, he remembered the pain, especially at night. While there were leaves he could have chewed on to remedy it, he was given nothing. Pain was a teacher. It was cruel at times.

The pain in the night was the worst tormentor. It was easy to be brave in the daylight. But at night, with his leg throbbing and swollen, it was easy to succumb to tears. In the blackness of the Arch-Rike's prison, it was tempting to do the same. There was no one else to hear him cry. No one would tease him about it later. He almost did succumb, for never had he been so discouraged. He was going to become a Kishion. He would be bound to the Arch-Rike's ring for the rest of his life.

He missed Annon at that moment. Perhaps some tidbit of Druidecht lore was needed. He did not believe the ring was poisoned in some way. It was likely bound with a spirit. Annon had freed a spirit from the blade and it had healed him as a result. Was there a way to free the spirit in the ring? Maybe it would require him losing his finger. He would gladly make that exchange. But certainly the ring would try to prevent him from cutting it loose or kill him in the attempt.

He hunkered in the darkness, victim to despair. The absence of light. The persistence of hunger. How many days had it been? There was no way of knowing.

A sound came in the distance, and he wondered if it were food. The thought of tasteless sludge did not arouse his passions. Light appeared in the distance, and he covered his eyes, knowing it would hurt. It did. There were several sounds of boots, but in addition, the clap of sandals.

Paedrin leaned forward, shielding his eyes. The pain of the light stabbed and hurt, but he forced his eyes to focus, to adjust. Was it? Could it be? He grabbed the bars and pulled himself closer, wincing with pain at the light.

Fingers wrapped over his.

"Paedrin," Master Shivu whispered.

The feelings in his heart. The voice in his ears. It nearly unmanned him with tears. He squinted, seeing only the shadow of the face kneeling before him.

"Paedrin?"

An immediate compulsion seized him. He began to sob mournfully and tap his forehead against the bars. "I am so sorry, Master. I am so sorry. Forgive me!"

"Hush, Paedrin. You must listen to me. You must listen to my words."

"It is my fault. The Arch-Rike is just. I betrayed Kenatos. I was too proud. Too ambitious. I will be executed, Master. I will bring shame to the Bhikhu temple."

"Paedrin, I know. I know. The Arch-Rike told me of the plot. He explained what must be done. Listen to me, boy. Listen to my words."

Paedrin heaved some strangled sobs, unable to control his emotions or his words. He stared at Master Shivu, at the patchwork gray stubble on his head. He saw the tender look in his eyes, not accusatory but full of sympathy. He saw love and forgiveness there. A man who had invested all of his life patiently teaching the Bhikhu way. He loved this man. He was going to resist the Arch-Rike's will. He would resist it all of his life until he found a way to be free.

"Yes, my Master," he whispered, clenching his jaw and refusing to speak. His body shook and trembled as he fought the feelings that smothered him.

"This is for the good of the city," Master Shivu said pityingly. "You were not alive when the last Plague came. You do not understand the terror that overcomes people when they all fear they will die. The savagery. Be grateful that you are spared it."

Paedrin nodded, his heart shuddering with sadness and firmness. His Master did not know that he was not going to die. Rather, he would live a life worse than death.

Master Shivu clung to his hands between the bars, gripping him fiercely. His nails bit into Paedrin's skin. "I never spoke of this to you before. The Bhikhu temple is a shadow of another temple. A replica and a poor one. The original Shatalin temple was hidden in the mountains. It did not fall from the Plague. Only Vaettir studied there. Only Vaettir could reach its heights. I came from that temple, when I was a boy. I left with a small band of others who sought to escape its fate."

Paedrin shook his head, confused. He had never known this before. It made no sense to him. He presumed the original Bhikhu temple was in the woods of Silvandom, not in the mountains.

"There was one among us. A student who bested the masters. He was ambitious. He was fast. Faster than anyone else. He corrupted the temple with his pride. You must understand, Paedrin. He was powerful. Not just in the Bhikhu way but in his words. In his speech. There was a weapon in the temple. A sword. Only the most virtuous of men ever sought to use its power and only to defend the temple from attack. This Bhikhu, Cruw Reon, sought the Sword of Winds to use it to conquer other kingdoms. To place himself at the heights of power. He took the sword from its casing. He drew it from its sheath."

Paedrin held his breath, staring into his master's eyes.

Master Shivu bowed his head. "He went blind. He could no longer see. Forever. The Shatalin temple fell that day. He would never give up the sword. And he could never learn how to cure his blindness, for the answer was written in the Book of Shatalin and smuggled away by my master. I have the book now and the secret to Cruw Reon's blindness. But the sword and the book cannot be rejoined. The book cannot leave Kenatos, for it is in the archives. The sword will never leave the temple. If only someone had acted before Cruw Reon's madness. If only his ambition had been thwarted earlier. The fate of so many would be different to this day."

He felt Master Shivu's grip as hard as stone on his hands. "You are proud, Paedrin. You are ambitious, like Cruw Reon. What we do now is for your best good. To prevent another tragedy. You must die so that the tradition and honor of the Bhikhu shall endure and be restored. You are no longer my pupil. You are no longer bound to the Bhikhu!"

Paedrin stared in shock. Master Shivu rose and stared down at him. His face was hard and tugged with a scowl. His eyes— there was something in his eyes. A look that transcended any specific meaning. He stared at Paedrin coolly and nodded once.

"Do what must be done," Master Shivu told the Arch-Rike. "I have said my piece. If he must die, as you say, then I wash my hands of him."

Paedrin's heart threatened to shatter into a thousand shards. But there was something in Master Shivu's eyes. There was something in his expression. Some silent words unsaid. His mind twisted and contorted to divine the meaning, but he could not make sense of it. Was he truly, now, abandoned and alone?

"It is a pity," the Arch-Rike said, nodding gravely. He turned to leave. "He was certainly one with great promise."

Paedrin stared at them, watching his master walk slowly down the hall, fading into the blackness until an iron-lidded door slammed shut, plunging him back into night. He knelt by the bars, unmoving, scraping his fingernail along the smooth bars. His breath came in short, heavy gasps. Why had Master Shivu said what he said? He had not asked him any questions about his betrayal. He had shown little sympathy. Why? There was none of their usual banter. Instead, there was connection through fingers and eyes. Two of the senses acting in unison. A third, the voice, was not.

A wave of fear and loathing came over him. His mind felt like a bowl of mush. He could not think clearly. He could not understand properly. He rubbed his eyes with his hand and, when he finished, spots danced in the blackness for a few moments and then vanished. Except for one. A small blue spot was moving along the roof of the hallway outside in the corridor. It approached slowly, coming forward like a serpent in a sinuous movement.

Paedrin stared at it, wondering if his imagination were totally rattled now. It was on the ceiling, drawing nearer to his cell. He waited, staring in awe as it approached, and then suddenly there was a rush of air and the light thump of two boots landing just outside his cell.

The blue light grew brighter until it revealed a face.

Kiranrao.

"Our conscience is our worst accuser. I once heard a great man from the Theater in Kenatos expound on this subject. I rarely visit such popular entertainments, but his words are worth writing down. Upon common theaters, he said, the applause of the audience is of more importance to the actor than his own approbation. But upon the stage of life, while conscience claps, let the world hiss."

– Possidius Adeodat, Archivist of Kenatos

XXVII

Hettie waited in the dense brush against the wall of the Arch-Rike's palace on the top of the island of Kenatos. She had crouched for hours by a stream, waiting to kill a deer with a single shot, but never had she waited more nervously or anxiously than at this moment. The hair on the back of her neck was prickling with gooseflesh, and every sound made her start and examine for its source.

She was dressed head to foot in dark leathers, every article bound tightly to prevent even the tiniest noise. Blades were strapped to her boots, her thighs, her belt. She gripped a short-bow in her hand, and a brace of arrows was fixed to the small of her back, each shaft fitted snugly in a compartment to prevent them from shifting.

The dawn brought the warbling of birds, which made it difficult to hear anything else. She waited, as still as she could be, slowly rubbing her hands together. In her mind, she rehearsed the story that Kiranrao had explained to her. She had summoned him to Kenatos to help free her friend when she learned he was in the Arch-Rike's custody and not in the temple. She was worried about him and his injuries, especially since he had sustained them as a result of trying to save her life in Drosta's trap. If he had not been wounded already, the fight with the Kishion may not have been so one-sided.

That was right. Those were the words. She struggled to put some feeling to them, to make them seem genuine. To make her eyes not betray her. But the truth was that she *was* worried about him. The waiting was torture.

Suddenly there were bells tolling. Great enormous bells shuddered from the spires of the Arch-Rike's palace. Hettie froze. That was the signal Kiranrao had warned her about. They were the alarms of the city, and they meant that all traffic into and out of Kenatos would halt until the bells sounded again. There was no explanation given, only the sound of the bells. Every boat in the slip would need to stay at anchor. Boats that had not docked yet would be stranded and forced to return to the outer network of piers.

The clanging noise frightened a group of starlings into flight, and Hettie watched them flee, oblivious to the Arch-Rike's orders to the contrary.

The bells meant that Kiranrao had been discovered. That did not necessarily mean that his plan had failed. She rubbed her palms together briskly, staring up at the wall and then down the sharp slope into the grounds. They were not sculpted gardens, for the terrain was too craggy for that. The parks were on the other side of the palace, facing the majority of the citizens of Kenatos. In the rear of the palace were thick brush and dwarf pines and other rugged plants that could survive with little water and no attention.

Sounds came to her, and she quickly ducked lower into the brush and tried to identify them. Lower down from the wall approached a retinue of guards with several black hounds on leashes. They were still a way off, but they were sniffing and look-ing for a scent or a trail. She frowned, knowing that the beasts would eventually find her scent. Her stomach began flip-flopping violently. How many men? A dozen? She counted them quickly. They were all soldiers except one. The one with the biggest hound was a Rike of Seithrall.

Two men landed right behind her and Hettie nearly screamed.

In that instant, she swung around with her bow; Kiranrao caught the stock before she could follow the movement with an arrow. As Kiranrao and Paedrin had struck the ground, they had dropped to a low crouch to allow the brush to hide them.

"Were you worried I was captured?" Kiranrao asked play-fully, his eyes searching her face. Then he looked at her sugges-tively. "Finder garb suits her well. Doesn't it, Bhikhu?"

She saw Paedrin gawking at her and almost favored him with a smile. But they were far from danger. "There are soldiers over there, searching for tracks. Ssshh!"

Paedrin's eyes were bloodshot and his chin covered with recent growth. He looked haggard and spent, but his eyes fas-tened to hers with a desperation she had never seen before.

"Your shoulder?" she asked, nodding toward it.

"Healed," Kiranrao answered for him. "He is not prone to much talk since I rescued him. Notice the ring on his hand? It looks like a wedding band, does it not?"

Hettie had not noticed it and cursed herself for spending so much time absorbing the look on his face. Paedrin held up his hand for her to see it. It was an ugly thing, made of iron with silver symbols carved into it. His eyes were haunted.

"What is it?" Hettie whispered.

Kiranrao gave her a snort. "He's more to be pitied than laughed at now. It's a Kishion ring. The lad is wedded to the Arch-Rike now. Still happy I saved him for you?" He held out his hand. "Payment due. Give me the stones."

Hettie hated deceiving Paedrin like this. She gritted her teeth. "He is no use to us if he has not his own will!"

"Let Tyrus unscramble his brains then. I want the stones to trade him for the blade. My service is performed. Hand me the stones, girl."

Hettie took the pouch from her belt and untied it, then flung them at him roughly. "Take it!" she snapped angrily.

Kiranrao nodded his head with a broad smile. "He still hasn't spoken a word. The silent are often guilty. I will draw away these fools and then meet you at the boulders by the shore." He clapped Paedrin on the back. "Go with her, boy. She will lead you away." He rose slightly and stared down at the soldiers at the base of the hill. "A windy day is the wrong one for thatching. Time to fly!" He broke away from the brush at a sprint, making plenty of noise to draw the attention of the dogs and the men.

"Look! Up there! There he goes!"

The soldiers let out a shout and started at a run, letting the dogs loose to begin the chase. One of them held a horn to his lips and blew hard on it, sending a strong sound into the morning air, but nothing compared to the clanging of the bells earlier.

Hettie still nestled in the brush with Paedrin. She took his hand, the one with the ring, and gently squeezed it. She gave him a wry look. "No insults yet? Why dark leathers don't look so subtle at dawn? Why I look like I haven't slept all night, since I haven't? Do you need some help or is your mind truly gone?"

His other hand closed on top of hers. "It is difficult...for me... to speak. The Arch-Rike is controlling...trying to control...me."

She looked him firmly in the eye. "You will have to do better than that, Paedrin. It wasn't even funny."

There was a sudden tic, a twitch in the corner of his mouth. "I thought I had you for a moment. What gave me away?"

She smirked. "Aside from the fact that Kiranrao brought you here alive? What kind of grease is it on your finger? I noticed it when you held up your hand. Is that tallow?"

Paedrin smiled and held up his hand again. "Linseed, I think. Smells like it, anyway. It helps disrupt the connection, apparently. Glad Kiranrao had some fat with him. You would never find any fat on me."

Hettie nodded. "That's a little better. You aren't angry with me for hiring him to save you?"

Paedrin chuckled. "I offered to kiss his little toes in payment, but he said you had worked something out between the two of you. Your uncle will take it amiss for giving him the stones."

"If there was ever a man who could outsmart Kiranrao…"

"Other than myself?" Paedrin added, offering her a cocked smile.

"Well, first we must outsmart the Arch-Rike. The ports all closed, as you know, when the bells tolled. But I also told you before that the Romani do not need the ports to get into the city. Follow me, outlaw."

Hettie stayed low to keep the bushes as a screen and started off in the opposite direction than the one that Kiranrao took. Paedrin kept pace behind her. She was relieved to hear the sound of his breathing. Even though they were far from being out of danger, his presence soothed her worries. There was no doubt getting away from the island would require some conflict. She had seen him fight. She even respected him for it.

They reached the end of the wall before it turned, and the scrub ended abruptly. Leaving cover would be a problem, but there were trees farther down that would hide them from anyone patrolling the upper walls. She waited, listening.

Paedrin's breath was in her ear. "Why delay?"

"Hush. Listening for the sound of footfalls on the wall above us. Do you hear any?"

He paused, craning his neck. He shook his head. Together they started down the slope, staying low to the ground to keep from losing their footing. Hettie caught herself on exposed roots and used them as handholds to maneuver down the steep slope. When they were near the end, there was the sound of barking, and suddenly a black hound leaped from the woods and rushed at them, followed by several soldiers.

"The horn!" Hettie warned. "Don't let them use it!"

Paedrin sprang from the edge of the slope and soared into the air. She flattened herself as he sailed over her gracefully, as if he were nothing more than a leaf suspended by the breeze. The Vaettir awed her with their innate ability to float and hover depending on how they controlled their breath. He went past the rushing hound and then suddenly came straight down, landing in a kneeling crouch. He looked up at the advancing soldiers and shot out at them like an arrow loosed from a bow.

Hettie brought up her weapon and sent an arrow into the dog's flanks, piercing its rear leg. It yelped and howled with pain, spinning in the dirt as it struggled to free itself from the arrow.

As Hettie slid the rest of the way down the hillside, Paedrin was in the midst of the soldiers, his hands and feet moving everywhere at once. They all had weapons, but none of them came close to touching him. One man raised a horn to his mouth and Hettie pulled free another arrow to silence him.

Paedrin blocked her shot as he vaulted upward and landed with a foot to the man's forehead. The horn tumbled to the ground, and Paedrin brought his heel down on it, crushing the end. Dropping down, he landed his fist into the man's temple, and he was out cold.

Six men were dispatched in moments.

Hettie approached, looking sidelong at the whimpering hound.

Paedrin cocked his head at her. "You didn't kill the dog."

She gave him a lazy smile. "Are you criticizing my aim?"

"Well, it would have been preferred if you had wrestled it into submission," he answered. "Or bit its ear. But you probably aren't an expert in wrestling beasts. Only skinning them."

She gave him an arched look. "Bit its ear? Paedrin…" She shook her head.

He stood straight and tall, his Bhikhu tunic rumpled and stained from their long journey. His eyes were glittering with intensity. It made her pause a moment.

"I am only just getting back my sense of humor," he said. "I have never felt so alive and free as I do at this moment. When you feel as if the rest of your life is going to be plunged into shadows, it makes you willing to risk it all over one thing. Let's find your uncle. I want to go with him into the Scourgelands. I even think I know a way that I can help."

With such a look of pure intensity and honesty on his face, Hettie nearly told him the truth. That moment of pure certainty was something she wanted for herself. He looked so convinced, so self-assured that she desperately wanted to believe in him. That he wanted to seek out her uncle as well, played right into Kiranrao's hands.

She almost told him.

Instead, she reached out her hand and bid him take it. It was cruel. It would deceive his feelings. But she needed him, if only to remind herself that her freedom was worth anything.

"I abhor the Druidecht taboo of documenting their beliefs and practices.
They are said to learn by heart a great number of verses; the course of
training takes up to twenty years. They regard it as unlawful to commit
these to writing. That practice they seem to me to have adopted for two
reasons. First, because they do not desire their doctrines to be divulged
among the mass of the people. Second, they suppose that a dependence
on writing would relax their diligence in learning. I contradict them. It is
quite possible that errors have been introduced into their learning and have
been further expanded each generation. Let us tenderly and kindly cherish
all means of knowledge. Let us dare to read, think, speak, and write."

– Possidius Adeodat, Archivist of Kenatos

XXVIII

The woods of Silvandom were legendary, and Annon approached them with trepidation. Most forests began to increase in thickness at a distance, tree after tree clustering together until they formed a massive net of limbs and roots. As Annon and Erasmus approached Silvandom, they passed the fertile plains without seeing another tree until suddenly a wall of them emerged after the crest of a hill. They stared down at the massive expanse of forest, stretching as far as the eye could see in either direction. The guardian trees were enormous, with long, bare trunks that reached skyward and were crowned in huge green swaths of leaves and branches.

"Well," Erasmus huffed, staring down at the vast woodlands. "By degrees the castles are built. I have never seen such a place in my life. All that straight wood is worth a fortune."

Annon smirked at the comment, glancing at his companion. "Except the Vaettir do not sell it."

Erasmus waved his hand. "Only makes it worth more."

"Life is worth more than ducats, Erasmus."

It was the Preachán's turn to give him a shrewd smile. "I assure you, master Druidecht, that is not true. Many wars are hazarded on the arithmetic that a life is worth less than thirty ducats. Maybe twenty-five."

Annon sighed and started down the slope.

Erasmus followed, mumbling softly to himself. "Considering the vastness of those woods, the likelihood of finding your friend Reeder will be considerably narrow. At a rate of two furlongs a day..."

"Do not strain your mind, Erasmus," Annon said, slightly annoyed at his constant predictions. "I will find him or he will find me much faster than you think."

"And how will that be achieved?"

"The same way I knew where the ford was in the river we crossed two days ago. The same way I have provided us with sufficient food. It is Druidecht lore. And while my uncle may think that a spirit only has value when it is trapped in a gem..." He trailed off, giving Erasmus a hard stare. "I do not."

Before long, they had crossed the long grass. Annon let his palms glide over the feathery tips of grass and downy weeds. He inhaled the sweet scent in the air, watching the towering trees sway gently ahead. It was a vision of beauty and grace. Overhead a hawk swooped. Annon watched its seamless plunge.

As they approached the huge shroud of trees, Annon felt the spirits immediately. Their tiny voices chittered to him, recognizing his talisman and position, and came to him in a swarm. For a moment he was confused at the rush and chatter, coming from tiny butterflies and gnats that rushed and whirled around him. They were solicitous, anxious to seek his will and assist him. He was treated with high honor.

Welcome, Druidecht. May we serve you?

I saw him first. Be silent. I will guide and lead you, kind sir.

What good would you be to him? I am the fastest. Shall I carry a message for you?

Never had he encountered such a swarm of spirits in Wayland or the mountains of Alkire. They were friendly, eager, and nearly jostled each other to get this attention.

Be silent, foolish ones. He is weary from his journey.

At the rebuke, the tittering vanished away, cowed into respect by a being of greater power. Annon felt the presence immediately and a sense of thrill at being singled out. It approached him in the form of a mountain cat, lithe and sleek and sinuous. Its tail lashed lazily.

Erasmus clutched his arm. "Annon," he hissed. "Do you see it?"

The creature approached on padded steps, a soft, purring growl in her throat. *You travel far, Druidecht.*

Annon inclined his head as it approached. He saw Erasmus trembling. *What may I call you, wise spirit?* Annon entreated in his mind.

I am Nizeera. I am a guardian of Canton Vaud.

Annon smiled in pleasure. Canton Vaud was the seat of the Druidecht hierarchy. It was much like a king's court and traveled from land to land, settling disputes and arbitrating between the spirits of Mirrowen and those in the mortal world.

I was unaware that Canton Vaud was in Silvandom. Is the matter truly as grave as that?

The huge cat purred and nuzzled against his arm. It slowly slinked around behind them, pausing to sniff disinterestedly at Erasmus, who stiffened and began twitching uncontrollably.

He is frightened. I like that. The matter is severe. Do you seek to aid in the matter?

Annon reached out to Nizeera in his mind. *I seek Reeder.*

The coarse fur bristled slightly then fell flat. It finished circling Erasmus, emitting a low growl intended to frighten him more. The long whiskers stroked against the Preachán's wrist, and he issued a shiver of breath.

"Druidecht?" Erasmus whispered hoarsely.

Nizeera turned back to Annon, fixing him with her gleaming eyes. *He stinks of the city, of ale and wine and coin. I do not trust him, but I trust you, Druidecht. You are of the fireblood. I smell it in your hands. I am bound to obey you.* The great cat lowered its head respectfully, shocking Annon.

No one serves me, Annon thought. *You are not bound to me.*

Do not mock my oath, Nizeera said with a growl. *It was not given lightly.*

He felt its offense rising hard and fast, its eyes glittering, the air chilling suddenly. He nodded in acquiescence, and that seemed to satisfy her.

Lead on, Nizeera.

The great cat turned on its haunches and padded away into the woods of Silvandom, its tail lashing playfully.

Erasmus's voice was just a faint whisper. "I thought…it was going to eat us."

Annon looked at him and smiled. "It wasn't tempted by you, Erasmus. You stink. She is our guide in Silvandom."

Erasmus gave him a blank look. "You mean it wants us to follow it?"

Annon ignored the question and started off after Nizeera.

Canton Vaud.

Annon had been told about it, but he had never expected to visit it before he was twice his current age. It was comprised of

Druidechts from every land and every race. They were the wisest of men and women, those who had earned their talismans and other gifts from the spirits, and they roamed the lands seeking to arbitrate troubles.

As Annon and Erasmus approached Canton Vaud, the young Druidecht stared in awe at the large tents, some elaborate in size and fashion. There were large brackets full of smoking incense attached to wooden poles, giving the air a sweet and musty scent. Spirits enjoyed smells and tastes as well as music, and there could be heard across the pavilions the airs of song and instruments. Zigzagging lights streamed through the air, the physical presence of spirits communing with the Druidecht of Canton Vaud. There was an urgent, anxious feeling in the air. The spirits were whispering about dangers in the forests. Of threats and ax blades and the smoking torches that harmed their kind. The snippets of thought and fear surprised Annon.

"This is a sight," Erasmus muttered, staring at the colorful pavilions, the taut ropes, the scurrying of animals and birds and other enchanted beings like Nizeera. The big cat padded through the throng, never once looking back at them.

"This is the seat of the Druidecht," Annon explained in a low voice, growing more anxious himself as he heard the thought whispers. "They never stay in one kingdom for long."

"Who are the leaders?"

Annon rubbed his mouth. "Only the wisest are chosen. There are thirteen. I have never met any."

A flicker of light suddenly appeared in front of them, buzzing as it approached and hovered in front of Erasmus. Annon could hear its chittering voice as it studied him, commenting on his smell and his queer eye.

Erasmus froze, staring in confusion. "Is this really a huge bumblebee? What does it want?"

"It appears that way to you. It is merely curious. Walk on."

"How can I walk on when it is likely to sting me?"

"It is a sylph. It will not hurt you. It is just curious."

Annon continued the walk and Erasmus tried to shoo the spirit away before following. Nizeera finally padded up to a small pavilion and turned, eyes gleaming. Her tail lashed.

Quickly Annon advanced, for he recognized the voice coming from within the pavilion. It was Reeder.

The sound of his friend's voice brought a rush of emotion to Annon's heart. He could not contain a fierce smile as he ducked at the entryway of the pavilion. There was Reeder on a small stuffed bench, a large flagon in one hand and his finger pointed at a gray-haired man across from him.

"But what reason do they have? Why the insistence? It is not common for the Boeotians to behave in such a way."

The older Druidecht had a thick mane of gray hair and was large of frame, with a crooked smile and a deep voice. "There is no way of telling except…" He paused, seeing Annon in the doorway.

"Forgive me," Annon apologized. "I was looking for my friend."

Reeder started when he heard Annon's voice and sloshed some wine on his wrist. "There he stands! Look at you, lad!" His expression was amazed, thunderstruck. Hastily setting down the flagon, he rose and grabbed Annon by the shoulders, his face full of worry and concern. "Yet here you stand. When I heard about the damage in the Paracelsus Tower, I was filled with dread because of you."

Annon looked at him quizzically. "Why?"

He stepped back, giving him an appraising look. "By the spirits, though you do look older. Much trouble you have had these many weeks. But you are not a boy, you are a man grown.

Sunburned too, if only a little. I feared that when you met your uncle, there was anger between the two of you. I should not have worried. Was I right? Did he try and persuade you to enter the Scourgelands?"

Annon was not sure what to say, especially with the shrewd eyes of the gray-haired Druidecht on him.

"I am lapse in my manners," Reeder said. He turned to the other man. "This is Palmanter, one of the Thirteen."

Annon stared at him, his voice vanishing.

"You are Annon of Wayland," the man said with a shrewd smile. "I know of you." He extended a meaty hand that Annon shook. There was a ring on his finger made of silver or white gold.

The startled feeling and expression on the older Druidecht's face made Annon feel like blushing. "I am honored you know of me."

"Reeder says you are full of promise, and I trust his judgment. Have you come to aid us? Who is your friend?"

Annon turned and saw Erasmus hesitating at the threshold. Several spirits hovered around, tormenting him. He tried to flick them away gently. Nizeera purred.

"Erasmus of Havenrook," Annon replied. "A companion."

"Havenrook?" Reeder said distastefully.

"There is much to tell and much to explain," Annon said. "I came seeking your advice, Reeder."

Palmanter gave them both a quizzical look. "I will leave you then." To Reeder he said, "You will depart in the morning then?"

"Yes. A fair night of sleep will help these old bones. Not that I object to sleeping in the woods, but I am not as young as I used to be. I will depart on the morrow."

Palmanter nodded. "Well enough. Seek me out before you leave. The Thirteen take counsel tonight."

Reeder perked up. "Regarding the Boeotian matter?"

He shook his head. "No." He gave Annon a probing look. "Regarding Tyrus Paracelsus. He arrived days ago seeking asylum at Canton Vaud."

Annon swallowed, unable to control the sudden surge of emotion that rose in him after hearing his uncle's name.

Reeder knew Annon well, especially his expressions. His face softened, and he patted Annon on the shoulder. "You need some wine. And bread. The soup is not as tasty as Dame Nestra's, but it will give you a moment to silence your seething." He motioned Annon to the rug and then beckoned for Erasmus to enter. "Come in. You have the look of a Preachán, if ever I saw one. A little tall. You could almost pass for Aeduan except for the nose and the queer eye."

Erasmus entered the tent and Reeder offered him the chair where Palmanter had sat. In short order, food was arranged, and they set about eating as the sun sank beyond the towering trees and blanketed the woods in darkness. An oil lamp was lit by Reeder before he took again his cushioned seat and started back in on his dinner.

"My uncle is here?" Annon asked softly, thinking himself the world's greatest fool. Tyrus had told them to seek him in Silvandom, but he had misled them deliberately regarding his destination. Annon was angry with himself for not seeing it sooner. The counsel to seek his friend Reeder for advice had allowed him to play right into his uncle's hands. It was the Uddhava all over again, and he was sick with fury because of it.

Reeder shrugged complacently. "The Thirteen do not typically discuss their business with me directly. I think your presence startled Palmanter, and so he let it drop to see what impact it had on you. I am as certain as wheat that you will shortly become a topic of conversation among them. That can be good or bad, depending on how feelings go."

Annon took a bite from a slice of bread. He chewed it absently, not even tasting it. Erasmus dipped his into the bowl of soup and ravenously ate. He glanced around for more and Reeder motioned toward the bread plate.

The older Druidecht looked at Annon thoughtfully as he ate. "So you came here seeking me and wound up finding your uncle as well. You did go to Kenatos?"

Annon nodded, wondering how much he should say. Should he tell Reeder about the blade Iddawc? About the Arch-Rike? About the Kishion who had come? Should he say anything about Drosta and his warning? How much did Reeder already know? *Be wise*, he warned himself. *Do not reveal too much, even to your friend.*

"You are pensive," Reeder said softly.

"Much has happened since I left Wayland," Annon replied. "Tell me of your troubles, though. What is happening in Silvandom that you came to help? Troubles with the Boeotians?"

Reeder nodded. "You could say that. And I do. They began encroaching on the woods of Silvandom. They are killing trees."

Annon frowned. "For profit?"

"No, they do not seek to trade the wood, or to build with it. They seek to burn it."

"For fuel then?"

Reeder shook his head. "What do you know of the Boeotians, Annon?"

"Very little. The other kingdoms consider them barbarians. They have no seat of power. No cities. They roam the north just below the fringes of the Scourgelands. They rarely settle but for hunting. They share an enmity with Kenatos and routinely wage war with her. I did not know they liked to burn wood. But are there not many trees in their country?"

Reeder nodded pensively. "You are mostly right. The Boeotians have a leader who they call the Empress. She does not treat with anyone and they guard and protect her. But the various tribes are fractious, and they do enjoy warring amongst themselves when they are not warring against Kenatos. But let us go to the crux of the matter." He glanced over at Erasmus, who was nodding off with sleepiness. "There are blankets over there. Sleep, friend."

Erasmus yawned uncontrollably and set down his cup. He went over to the pile of blankets and lay down. Reeder stared at him. A spirit full of gossamer threads flittered into the tent and delicately kissed Erasmus's eyes. His breath came in and out heavily. He was asleep.

Annon looked at Reeder in confusion.

"What I have to tell you is Druidecht lore," Reeder said. His eyes were deadly serious. "It should not be spoken of, even to your uncle. Do you swear it?"

"I swear it," Annon replied promptly. He took Erasmus's chair and pulled it closer to Reeder's stool. "Tell me."

Reeder glanced at the tent door as Nizeera slowly padded inside, eyes wide and glassy. She stroked against Annon's leg before settling down on the blankets near him, tail flicking this way and that.

"How well do you know your forest lore?" Reeder asked. "You know of sylphlings. You know of hamadrods and cepints. You know all the spirit life in Wayland. It varies depending on the location. Depending on the menace, you might say. As you can see, there is much spirit life in Silvandom. This is their last bastion of safety.

"In the mountains of Alkire, they are caught and trapped and bound into service. In the forests of Wayland, where you and

I are from, they struggle against the local woodcutters and hunters who do not bother to understand their ways. It leads the poor folk to some harm at times. Of all the spirit life you have learned about, have you ever heard of the spirits that guard the trees? Tell me what you know of the Dryads."

Annon stared at him in confusion. "I know nothing. I do not even know that name."

Reeder nodded, smiling as if he had not expected Annon to know the secret. "Good. It is not usually part of the Druidecht lore we teach at your age. For good reason, for which you must trust me, young as you are. As I said, they are spirits. They are very rare, Annon. Hidden. Even for spirits, they are quite vulnerable. Dryads are only female. They live inside the trees that they protect, but not in a way that you would understand. Their trees hold the knowledge of the portals to Mirrowen.

"There is very little that is known about the Dryads, the guardians of the Ways. There is a reason for that. You see, it is their defense. They protect the knowledge stored in their trees in a special way. When someone approaches, they appear before the intruder suddenly. They are said to be very beautiful. But no one can remember what they look like, for they steal your memories. Look at them once, and you forget what it is you came to do. There is no magic that can prevent this from happening. That is why it is only *said* that they are beautiful. They do not allow those who have seen them to remember, so they can protect their trees from harm. A Dryad can preserve a tree and live for a thousand years. There are a lot of memories in their trees, many secrets."

Reeder licked his lips, keeping his voice low, "Now for the Boeotians' purpose. The Boeotians are not coming into Silvandom to harvest firewood. They hunt the Dryads and destroy their trees. How do they know of them? How do they know which trees to cut down?" He gave a big shrug. "This is Druidecht lore, and we do not share it. But they have a way to know which tree belongs to a Dryad. And they come to hew it down with axes and then burn it."

A chill went down Annon's spine. As Reeder spoke, a memory stirred to life in his mind. A twisted, aging oak in the courtyard within the Paracelsus Towers. An old, desiccated tree. Unusually placed in such a vast throng of humanity.

Annon swallowed, his stomach fluttering with the memory and its implications. "Is there a certain kind of tree the Dryads choose, Reeder?" He felt he already knew the answer. But it was confirmed from Reeder's lips.

"The oak, my boy. The mighty oak is their home."

The hour was late, and Erasmus continued to quietly snore on the stack of blankets in the corner of the pavilion. Annon waved away another offer to fill his cup with wine. His head throbbed dully and his stomach was queasy with information and the lateness of the hour. Reeder finished off his cup with a mighty swallow and wiped his mouth with his arm.

"Thank you for trusting me with all that has happened to you," Reeder said, for Annon had changed his mind about revealing all to his mentor. He shook his head in disbelief. "You are caught in a snare, to be sure. The more you wriggle, the tighter the noose."

"But what should I do?" Annon said, trying to quell the evil feeling. "Should I believe what Drosta told me? What my uncle told me? What the Arch-Rike believes? What the order has trained me to believe? My mind is tangled in knots right now! I do not know which to unravel first."

Reeder held up his hand, shaking his head. "Lad, it comes down to who is telling the truth. That is the state of the matter. Truth is knowledge. Things are or they are not. You and I are here. We are sitting and sharing wine in Canton Vaud. One may say you are in Havenrook. One may say you are in Alkire. One may say you still hide in Kenatos, but that is not the truth. You are here." He leaned forward. "The trouble with truth is that people are unwilling to be convinced that they have been deceived. It impugns their judgment. It stains their character. People love themselves above all."

Reeder sighed deeply, staring at the slow-burning wick of the oil lamp. "They hate truth for the sake of whatever it is that they love in its place. When truth benefits them, they love it. When it rebukes them, they hate it. They love truth when it reveals itself and hate it when it reveals *them*." He shook his head wearily, his countenance falling. "As one of the Thirteen once told me, 'Thus, thus, truly thus: a mind so blind and sick, so base and ill-mannered, desires to lie hidden, but does not wish that anything should be hidden from it.' And yet the opposite is what happens, does it not? Yet even so," he said with a sad chuckle, "for all its wretchedness, the mind still prefers to delight in truth rather than in known falsehoods. Lies never satisfy us, Annon. They do not satisfy our internal hunger for truth."

His gaze pierced Annon. "I cannot tell you whether your uncle's story is true. I lack the knowledge. In the morning, I go to defend a corner of Silvandom where the Thirteen say a Dryad is hidden. Come with me. They live for hundreds of years. She may have the knowledge you seek. Your uncle told you to find the oracle Basilides. Perhaps the Dryad knows where the oracle may be found and whether your uncle tells the truth." His eyes narrowed. "Or not."

The suggestion startled Annon. His eyes were getting drowsy, but he sat up and stared at his mentor, his friend. "Go with you?"

"I would enjoy the companionship. Most of the raids are happening in the northern borders of Silvandom via the mountain passes. I seek to safeguard the western edge. If there is trouble, we will send for others to assist. That is, if you will join me."

Annon thought it over quickly. What he had been told about Dryads fascinated him immensely. There was something about them, some connection to his uncle that he had not revealed to Reeder. The oak in the Paracelsus Towers. That was not a coincidence. Did his uncle know the tree likely contained a Dryad? Had he anticipated the distrust Annon would have? Likely so. If the mysteries of his uncle could be revealed in a manner that would satisfy a Druidecht, he would be more likely to believe his uncle's version of events.

"I see you hesitate," Reeder said. "I will not push you. My older bones are ready for a blanket. Decide in the morning if you wish to accompany me."

Annon shook his head. "It is not that, Reeder. I think it would be useful if I did join you. I was only mulling what you told me."

Reeder reached for a blanket and wrapped himself in the warm folds. "Think as long as you like. Only spare the oil lamp and blow out the flame ere you sleep."

Annon was beginning to think that truth was like the knowledge of Mirrowen. There was evidence of it all around. Only most people did not bother to notice it. They were so set in their minds as to what existed and what didn't that they left no room to explore the possibility that they shared the world with the spirits of Mirrowen. That both worlds existed simultaneously. That it was even possible to connect them.

"I will go with you," Annon promised, giving his friend a smile.

From the corner of his eye, he saw Nizeera's tail lashing. He felt her thoughts graze against his mind smugly.

Yes. Yes, you will.

He looked at her in confusion, seeing the gleaming reflection of the lamplight in her eyes.

Why do you stay with us? he asked her.

Because of my oath to you, she replied.

And why did you swear an oath to me?

There was a long pause. A shiver began from the base of his spine, welling up until he shuddered.

I did not swear the oath to you, mortal. I swore it to your mother. A Druidecht with the fireblood. Like you. Her tail began lashing back and forth. It reminded him of a serpent.

"*Some say the greatest evil is physical pain. The Bhikhu reject this notion, of course. I reject it as well. Wounds of the heart run more deeply and cannot be treated with salves and herbs.*"

– Possidius Adeodat, Archivist of Kenatos

XXIX

The woods were dark and lonely in the morning light. A thin haze crept amidst the trees, blanketing the morning with a veil of fog. Annon and Reeder walked side by side, enjoying the brisk air and the chance to be together again. Annon's emotions were tangled and conflicted. He thought about his uncle. He thought about Erasmus. More importantly, he wondered if he had lost his senses completely. Why was he doing this? Why was he even involved? Why had he bothered to listen to Reeder in the first place?

Amidst his tangled emotions was a sense of dread. He was worried about Hettie. What was she doing? Where was she? Was she safe? There were too many questions to answer. More than anything else, he wanted answers. He did not want explanations or excuses. He wanted to *know* the truth. He wanted certainty before he chose.

The spirits of Silvandom heard his troubled thoughts. There were many in the forest. They were aware of him, listening to his troubled feelings, his conflicting thoughts. He felt their presence all around him like gossamer butterflies, attracted to his intensely personal feeling of doom.

"You're deep in thought," said Reeder. "I was a little surprised you chose to come with me this morning."

"I hope to find answers," said Annon. "Is that so strange?"

Reeder chuckled. He pointed into the mist. "There are always answers. Some we do not like. Some we are not ready for. But looking for them is good all the same."

It was difficult judging when dawn had actually broken. The mist blocked the rising sun, causing the light to gradually grow. Annon was not sure of the moment when he realized that it was day, but the details around him grew sharper. The lush green trees, the dewy grass, the chittering of insects. Before he knew it, he realized it was dawn. Somehow it just happened.

"How far is it?" asked Annon. "How long will it take us to get there?"

"It will take most of the day," answered Reeder. "The place we are going is on the far, far fringe of the woods. If we are lucky, we should get there before dusk." Reeder pointed to a shimmering spiderweb. "Do you see that?"

"What kind of spirit is it?" asked Annon.

"I don't know, but isn't it beautiful? There's so much about these woods I'm still learning. I miss Wayland. Of course I do. There are many different kinds of life here in Silvandom. There are creatures I've never even dreamed of." He sighed. Then he gave Annon an arch look. "The most dangerous spirits, they say, are up north. In the Scourgelands. That even to look at one is to die."

"Do you think I trust my uncle that much?"

"It is your feelings I distrust more. You've always been an angry lad, Annon. It makes me worry about you."

The trees surrounding them changed from slender giants to red maples that swayed gently with the breeze. The smell of the forest was mesmerizing. There were plants that Annon had never seen before. Trailing behind them was the big cat Nizeera. Annon had almost forgotten about her, so quiet did she move. They walked for a long time in silence, watching the colors of the forest shift as they entered a new domain populated with different plants and spirits.

A burst of light suddenly exploded in front of them. It was a spirit, frantic and throbbing tense feelings of urgency. It hung in the air, buzzing in front of their faces like a hummingbird.

Come, Druidecht! You are needed! Come with haste! Haste! Follow me!

Reeder held up his hand, trying to calm the frantic creature. "What is it, friend? Tell us."

The spirit zoomed away through the woods, leaving a shimmering trail of dust. They could hear its frantic screech as it raced back the way it came, the dust-motes of magic starting to descend like hoarfrost from the air. Annon and Reeder looked at each other and then plunged into the woods after it, caught up in the emotion it had summoned inside of them.

They ran as best they could. Annon was younger and more healthy, but he stayed near his friend and followed the disappearing trail left in the spirit's wake. Annon's heart pounded with the exertion of their pace, but the creature's emotions compelled them forward. It was a warning of the imminent death of another creature, another spirit.

"Do you see that?" Annon asked, pointing ahead. A flurry of activity was going on up ahead in the trees. Spirits dashed this way and that, leaving streamers of magic as they raced and circled the scene. Sparks exploded in small puffs as spirit magic attacked violently. There were noises, voices thick with a guttural language. And then there was the unmistakable sound of an ax biting into bark.

"Boeotians!" Reeder gasped, both from surprise and lack of air. He staggered to rest, catching himself on a tree. "How can they be this far into the woods?"

Annon realized that the shape of the woods had suddenly changed, going from tall proud red maples to twisted oaks. It was the dense array of knotted branches that blocked the full scene, but Annon could see enough as a giant of a man stood next to an ancient oak; his muscles rippled. He took another hard swing, blasting away fragments of wood.

There were others present as well, waving smoky torches in the air. The smell of smoke had not drifted far before another attack of spirits came amidst it and exploded in little puffs. Annon realized that the spirits were dying from the smoke.

"No!" Reeder said, staring at the scene in bafflement. Then his face flooded with anger and he charged forward. "No! Noooo!"

Save us, Druidecht! Save the tree!

Annon stared at the intruders in horror. They were a race he had never seen before. Tall and corded with muscles, yet their skin was mottled with protruding veins, giving them an almost purplish cast. They wore only loincloths and high hide boots. Each man carried a weapon in one hand and a cluster of burning sticks in the other. Annon did not know what kind of wood they held, but the smoke was obviously anathema to the spirits of Mirrowen, who fell as soon as they came in contact with the haze.

The giant man had a huge double-sided ax, and he took another powerful swing, spraying the glen with fragments of wooden splinters.

"No!" Reeder roared. "This is forbidden! These are not your woods! You must go!"

Reeder clutched his talisman in one hand and sucked in his breath. Annon felt the strength of his summoning. He could feel it jet past him, a wash of feelings that went into the surrounding woods for leagues. He was summoning the woodland animals to help. Foxes and wolves, bears and serpents. Hawks and falcons. All who felt the summons would be called to the Druidecht's service. But he needed time. It would take time for the allies to arrive.

"Be gone, Druidecht!" The man with the ax had a hoarse, gravelly voice. "We will burn this tree! Atu! Banvenek!" He brought the ax back for another mighty swing.

Reeder's face twisted with rage. "You do not know what you do!" he sputtered. There was a frenzy as the spirits redoubled their attacks, plunging at the tight cluster of men with determination, despite their falling numbers. A fierce wind began to rake through the woods. The air was suddenly full of howling and commotion.

"Atu!"

Annon saw the spear too late.

It struck Reeder full in the chest. He was a big man himself. The blow would have toppled another. Reeder stood, staring in shock at the huge shaft protruding from his skin. The jettison of magic imploded. His knees buckled. Reeder collapsed onto the forest floor, toppled like a tree himself. A mesh of scrub cushioned him.

The pain and rage that blasted inside of Annon was nothing he had experienced before. There was no way to describe it, even to himself. Part of him literally exploded. His friend. His mentor. Someone who was more a father to him than anyone else in all the kingdoms lay dead or dying.

There was a smirk on the leader's face. A ruthless smirk. The death of a man meant nothing to him. It was a face hardened and callused by death. His eyes passed over Annon, barely giving him another look or thought. He hefted the ax back for another swing.

Never in Annon's life had he been so tempted. His instincts did not tell him to run. That would have been the wise thing to do. Instead, he promised himself he would kill every single one of them or die trying.

Pyricanthas. Sericanthas. Thas.

Flames gushed from his fingertips, racing across the gap of woods until they smashed into the man with the ax. The Boeotian. The murderer. Annon watched his skin blacken but not blister. For a moment it seemed as if he were protected even from fire. He turned in shock and surprise, face wild with pain and panic. The flames suddenly engulfed him and he disappeared in a plume of ash. The heavy ax blade thumped to the forest floor, the handle consumed.

Annon did not wait a single moment. He charged into the grove of oaks, heading straight for the other Boeotians. His rage was insurmountable. He doubted if he would ever be calm for the rest of his life. The injustice and cruelty of these men defied his reason. There were more, and he sent the flames rushing into them, sending it streaking into their midst. Cries of terror sounded in the grove as they struggled to dodge the deadly fire.

Nizeera screamed and charged into the glen, teeth and claws savagely raking the men holding spears and axes. *We fight together, Druidecht. We must save the tree.*

A spear ripped into his arm, lancing his skin as it went past him. He did not feel the pain. Another one hefted a spear, bringing it back to throw; Annon extended his palm and a spray of flames blasted him into dust. He did not know how many there were.

Movement to his left.

He ducked around a tree and listened as the spear struck the trunk. It would have killed him had he not moved a fraction faster. He emerged from the other side of the tree and sent flames into three men at once. The feelings sapped all sense of will and restraint. The bubbling emotions they caused were euphoric and delightful. He was giddy inside, with his friend dead nearby. How could that be? How was it even possible to be consumed with such happiness when he should be crying?

How many men were left? How many killers?

More over here. He heard Nizeera's shrieking warning and saw her dart between trees, swiping and clawing at them.

Annon shoved away from the protection of the trunk and came after them again, seeing several trying to hide from him behind stunted oaks. Flames spewed from his hands, engulfing the trees with crackling flames. This was dangerous. He did not want to burn down the entire forest. But he could not stop himself. He did not want to stop himself. Something had seized control of his mind. Some dark vapor prevented him from thinking. It commanded him to lash out at those who had desecrated the woods.

Cries of pain came from those he caught. He heard the crunch of boots to his right and turned just as the ax edge whistled toward his head. Annon ducked reflexively, feeling no fear, and brought up his hands to the man's face. Suddenly a knee connected with his stomach and he felt his air vanish. The Boeotian continued the swoop of the ax and brought it up and around, coming down to split open Annon's skull.

Nizeera launched at him, leaping over Annon's crumpling body, and caught the Boeotian with claws in his face and chest as her weight slammed him down. The catlike scream made Annon shudder.

Scrambling back to his feet, struggling to maintain the fire pulsing in his fingertips, Annon stared as the other Boeotians ran off into the woods.

He gulped in air, trying to breathe. Nizeera finished off the man and turned to look at him, eyes gleaming with satisfaction.

They are coming.

Annon nodded, unable to speak. *How many?*

She cocked her head.

Spirits thronged him, coming from all sides at once. Many were cheering and grateful, but others were frantic as well.

They come, Druidecht! More mortals come! Do not abandon us! Do not abandon her!

He breathed heavily, glancing back at the sinewy form of the oak tree, split wide with fleshy bark. The broken ax lay at its base. The tree was defenseless. The tree would be butchered and killed. A Dryad tree. He knew it was so. He could feel memories emanating from its ancient hull.

Stand strong. Do not fear them. Nizeera's eyes bored into his. *We will take them together. You and I. We fight together.*

Gritting his teeth, Annon straightened. He was just beginning to feel the razor of pain in his shoulder. The emotions of elation began to crumble. He needed to tame the fireblood. He could not let it run wild again. He would control it better; he would burn the men and not destroy the woods. *I fear nothing,* he thought to Nizeera.

The hummingbird spirit zoomed into the grove, flittering in front of his face. *He comes before them! He comes to challenge you!*

Annon's mind raced. *Who comes? Who is it?*

The spirit wailed with terror. *One of the Black.*

"When Kenatos was founded on the island in the lake, all races and peoples were invited to send representatives of their culture, traditions, and knowledge to dwell in harmony and thus preserve their way of life. Too many races had been decimated. Too many crafts and knowledge had been lost. Of all who remained, only the Boeotians refused. In fact, when they learned of the founding of Kenatos, they vowed to destroy it. For centuries, they attacked the island by boat. Some tried to make an earthen bridge to connect to the city. Each attack was repelled. Each ambassador sent to negotiate with the Boeotians was killed. Only the Druidecht can safely pass into their borders unharmed. They are a wild and savage race. It is said that they are ruled by an Empress, much as a beehive has a single queen. Their savagery and violence know no bounds. Kenatos would have failed if the races had not banded together to protect her infancy. A common danger unites even the bitterest enemies."

– Possidius Adeodat, Archivist of Kenatos

XXX

T he very mention of the Black Druidecht made Annon shudder. As with all creatures, so it was with the spirits of Mirrowen. There were helpful spirits who cooperated with the races or mostly just left them alone. But there were other spirits, the dark and the foul, that frightened and sought to destroy. Beings like the Iddawc. They looked at the world as a plaything. The Druidecht opposed such and had learned from the spirits ways to protect against them. But some Druidecht—only a few—joined forces with them.

Sweat beaded on Annon's brow. He glanced back at the scarred oak tree, wondering whether the damage caused to the trunk was enough to kill it. His fingers tingled with heat and anticipation from using the fireblood again. He had almost lost himself in it.

Courage, Nizeera whispered to him.

Annon steeled himself, swallowing his fears, and drew deep within himself. This was his charge as a Druidecht—to protect the denizens of Mirrowen who were helpless. And as Reeder had told him the night before, no creature was more helpless than a Dryad.

A sylph flitted to him. *You are injured. Let me heal you.*

Heal my friend, if he lives, Annon pleaded.

He is dead, Druidecht. He is already dead. The wound was mortal.

A quivering sob threatened to ruin him. Tears stung his eyes, but he refused to let them fall. Reeder. His friend. A blinding rage enveloped him. He had always heard that the Druidecht were welcome in any land, even Boeotia. How could they have slain him so mercilessly? The anger gave him strength and helped steal the tears from his eyes. He would mourn Reeder later. He would mourn him the rest of his life.

Glancing over, Annon saw his friend still lying where he had fallen. Reeder's face was waxy and pale.

Annon turned away, breathed deeply, trying to calm his pounding heart, to focus on the task at hand. He could not face Reeder's death yet. It would undo him. He felt the healing touch of the sylph as it restored him, binding the wound at his shoulder and restoring his strength. Other spirits came and blessed him as well, kissing his forehead to give him clear thoughts. One touched his heart to bolster courage. They swarmed him with magic, and he realized that once the other Boeotians arrived with their sticks and smoke, he would be on his own.

It did not take them long to arrive.

Annon heard them before he saw them. Battle screams filled the air, a strange singsong mesh of voices set at discordant rhythms that made his courage shrivel. How many were there? A hundred? The wails grew louder, and soon the first of the Boeotians appeared, rushing through the woods with spears and axes, holding smoking sticks in their hands, the vapors warding off the spirits.

As soon as he was visible to them, their fervor and pitch increased even more, and he saw the wild look of rage in their eyes as they converged on him. His hands went cold with terror and his stomach lurched. He wanted to be sick. He wanted to run. He struggled to master himself. One spear thrust was all it would take to end his life. Annon realized he was going to die. He would never see Hettie again. Her face flashed in his mind, spurring pangs of sadness.

The spirits of the woods seemed to recognize his faltering feelings. They surged into the midst of the Boeotians, exploding with puffs of magic as they tried to stall the advance, to protect the ancient Dryad tree at all costs. He watched them vanish out of existence, popping with dazzling colors. Why was his own life any more significant than theirs? Should he not also give his best, even if it meant his life?

Reeder had.

Pyricanthas. Sericanthas. Thas.

Annon fed his anger as his hands turned blue, wreathed in flames. He saw a Boeotian rear back with a spear and hurl it straight at him. Everything seemed to slow around him. He could sense every breath, every flash of his eyelids, the prickle of gooseflesh on his arms. The blessing of the spirits heightened every sense. He twisted sideways and leaned, feeling the spear streak by him. Annon countered, raising his hands. Fire swirled from his palms in spheres and struck the Boeotian, slamming into him and engulfing him only, not the trees near him.

Nizeera screamed and launched herself at the oncoming mass of men. She was all teeth and claws, ripping and savaging into their midst like some whirlwind. Annon let loose a curtain of flames to try and block the advance. The trees around the area caught fire, mixing gold with the blue. Branches shattered. A windstorm swept into the woods, fanning the flames and causing smoke to billow and blind them. He made it far enough back, hopefully creating a break between the trees to preserve the Dryad's oak.

Annon saw them flanking him on both sides, trying to get near him and the tree. Gritting his teeth, he lashed out at them with the fireblood, drawing a circle of fire around his position. Spears whistled at him, but he felt them coming and ducked. Several struck the massive oak, burying into her craggy bark. Each one caused a spurt of anger and hatred inside him. He unleashed fire in return, blasting away the intruders one by one.

Giddiness. The overwhelming feeling of giddiness made him nearly start laughing. Was he in control of himself? Had he loosed the madness his uncle had warned him of? Pain struck his leg as a spear glanced him. He felt the skin rip and blood begin flowing down his leg. A hulking Boeotian charged him with an ax. Annon joined his hands together and sent a mass of fire into him, turning him into ash.

He could not see Nizeera through all the smoke, but he could hear her screams and the sound of dying. There was a chunking sound as an ax bit into the tree again. A Boeotian had managed to breach the circle of fire and had struck again at the tree. Annon turned abruptly and destroyed him. How many were there? How long would he last before exhaustion consumed him?

Smoke and fire flooded the woods. He could see shimmering streaks of spirits through the gloom, coming to aid in the battle. The cries of the Boeotians did not fade. More were coming. An impossible number. Annon staggered back into the tree, gasping for breath, trying to keep the fire in his hands burning. As soon as he touched the bark, he felt a presence. It was like a sigh, a breath in his ear.

Nizeera padded to his side, tail lashing restlessly. He saw the cuts and singed fur.

Courage, she whispered to him again.

Annon nodded, unable to speak. He was so thirsty, desperate for a drink of water. A shape moved in the smoke and Nizeera growled.

Pushing himself from the trunk, Annon advanced, bringing up his hands. Blue flame rippled across his fingertips.

He noticed the same effect from the man approaching him. Blue flames danced from his as well.

His Boeotian name was Tasvir Virk. He no longer remembered the name he was given as a boy in Stonehollow. After earning his talisman, he had chosen to enter the Boeotian lands and be a Druidecht among them. The Boeotians respected and feared the fireblood in his veins and he found himself almost revered as a deity. He lacked the physical size of their race, but he was strong and hard and had learned to survive. He would be strong enough to survive the Scourgelands, they told him. His power was truly greater than any who had come before.

Only later did he realize they were using him.

Tasvir Virk had entered the Scourgelands alone, believing he was strong enough to survive the horrors there. He was wrong. The woods destroyed him. But not before he learned one of its secrets. There were Dryad trees in the woods. Ancient trees. Older than the world. They befuddled intruders, turning them back again to face the horrors inside when they tried to flee. The horrors that had caused his madness.

Tasvir Virk stumbled out of the woods and vowed to destroy the trees. He consorted with the evil spirits of the hinterlands to learn about the Dryad trees and they taught him to see patterns and how to discern which trees contained them. They taught him how smoke from a rowan tree was lethal to lesser spirits. The fact that he had survived the Scourgelands cowed the tribe to his authority. If anyone crossed him, he had them sacrificed on a stone altar. His anger needed to be appeased. He had survived the Scourgelands.

His authority and power slowly spread into the other tribes until it happened. There were rumors that one from Kenatos had also survived the Scourgelands. Perhaps he was now the greatest man of all. Word of his legend spread through the Boeotians. He was Tyrus of Kenatos. Tyrus Paracelsus. A man loyal to Silvandom and its rulers.

Tasvir knew that he was possibly the only man who might be able to unite all the tribes against the Empress and against him. He needed to die.

Now that all the Dryad trees in Boeotia were destroyed, he turned next to Silvandom. He would conquer the lands one by one, razing the trees until they were extinct.

Now one of his hunting parties had encountered a bearded man in Silvandom with the fireblood protecting a Dryad tree. It was time for Tyrus of Kenatos to die.

The man was older than Annon, maybe three times his age. A shock of gray hair tinted with red was equally telling. His face was mottled with blood veins, the same as he had seen among the Boeotians. His skin was hard and leathery. He had been a handsome man once, but the livid scars and purplish veins gave him a frightening look. The man was dressed in black robes with a talisman around his neck. He was tall and gaunt, his lips pallid.

"Druidecht," the man whispered in a raspy voice. He frowned, his eyes narrowing. "You have fought well and bravely. It will be a pity to kill you."

"Who are you?" Annon said warily as the two began circling each other.

"I am the reaper of life. I am the bane of the Plague. I am the heart of the Scourgelands. I am Tasvir Virk." A faint smile tugged at his mouth.

I will kill him, Nizeera growled.

No, he will destroy you!

He saw her bunch her muscles to leap at him, but the man's eyes went black and he raised his hands, unleashing a plume of blue fire at Nizeera. He jumped in front of her, colliding with it. Annon felt it wash over him, warm as bathwater, but not burning.

I will fight him. You take the others.

"Ah! So you too have the fireblood! Excellent! Excellent!" He started to cackle deliciously. "Atu! Atu vast! Atu vast!"

The gaunt man rushed forward and grabbed Annon's wrists.

Though he was bone-thin, his grip was like iron. Boeotians rushed through the smoke, closing in around them, around the tree. Nizeera screamed and launched herself at the foremost, claws raking. The gaunt man laughed with madness, his eyes blazing. A horrible stench came from his lips. He wrestled Annon, keeping him from defending the tree. Annon struggled against him, trying to break free. He was amazed at the Black Druidecht's strength.

The sound of an ax chopping into the trunk. Another blow and then another. Annon struggled to free himself, but his captor was maddened. He howled with laughter.

"Atu vast! Atu vast! Tolx Enas! We will destroy her, Druidecht. This tree and each and every one like her. Including the tree in the Paracelsus Towers. The last tree. The last one! They will all die! That is how the Scourgelands will fail. They must all be killed!"

Annon shoved and pushed, trying to free himself. The gaunt man would not let go. Another blow against the tree. Then another.

"The fireblood brings madness," Annon shouted. "You were a Druidecht once, sworn to protect beings like her!"

"I am a Druidecht!" he shouted, wrenching Annon around. "I am of the Black. They steal our memories, boy. She subverts you. Let me destroy her!"

Annon's mind raced frantically. Nizeera was attacking as many as she could. The ax blows continued. Annon whirled around, trying to throw the gaunt man off balance. He was bigger than the other man, weighed more. His wrists throbbed with pain at the clenching fingers. The Boeotian faced him, ax chopping furiously at the bark, exposing the depths of the gash. It was a huge scar on the tree, growing like a stain.

Annon waited until the man pulled back to start another swing. Then with all his strength, he shoved the Black Druidecht backward into the path of the blade.

There was a gush of blood, the spray blinding Annon momentarily. The grip on his wrists went slack as the Black Druid suddenly fled, screaming in agony. Annon saw the severed arm on the ground at his feet. He raised his hands again. *Pyricanthas. Sericanthas. Thas.*

The blast of fire consumed the Boeotian with the ax.

Whirling, Annon found himself surrounded. He unleashed a controlled firestorm in the grove, sending it out in wave after wave. His heart pounded. His ears rang. He was losing himself in the magic. He was vanishing. A blow struck his side. Another against his leg.

A sharp spasm of pain brought him down on one knee. Spots danced in front of his eyes. He was going to die. He had failed. Uttering a groan, he drew from his depths once again, sending another sheet of flames fanning out in front of the tree. Crookedly, he tried to rise, but his leg would not permit it and he fell backward, striking the base of the ancient oak. He felt his life draining away. The flames in his fingers dissipated. He was defenseless. A single blow would finish him.

His vision was speckled with tiny fireflies. Nizeera screamed in rage and pain. His chin began to dip against his chest. He had tried his best. He had done what he could, fulfilling his Druidecht vows to preserve and defend.

Forcing his eyelids open, he saw the Boeotians advancing on him, spear tips pointed. Several had huge axes.

And that was when the Bhikhu began to fall from the sky.

They were all Vaettir-born, like Paedrin. Over a dozen slammed into the earth, crashing through the smoke and haze of fire. They held swords and staves, whips and javelins. The Boeotians charged them in a clash of bodies. Annon felt a sliver of hope. Just a shard. The weapons whirled and clacked, fists and feet and skin smacking and shoving.

Annon closed his eyes, feeling himself floating. It was a peaceful feeling. It was dying. He knew it. Somehow, it was familiar.

Heal him, whispered a voice. A woman's voice. The most beautiful voice he had ever heard. Just a whisper. Just a breath of air. But it was the most lovely sound he had ever heard.

It came from the tree.

"We do not understand the Boeotians' hatred of us. We do not understand why they invade our lands. With gratitude, we thank the brave ones of Silvandom who form the primary defense against their intrusions. Such opposite philosophies. One race kills. The other preserves. Even the combined might of all the kingdoms could not destroy Boeotia. Yet the combined strength holds the Empress at bay."

– Possidius Adeodat, Archivist of Kenatos

XXXI

P aedrin crouched so near to Hettie that he could smell her skin. She definitely needed a bath. He nearly commented on that fact when Kiranrao appeared on the other side of her, turning from smoke to solid in an instant. The air tingled with magic every time he did that, and it was starting to annoy the Bhikhu.

Hettie smoothed the hair away from her ear so she could hear him better.

"They are not far," he whispered. "Be silent and wait. They have a Finder with them."

"We have a Finder with us as well," Paedrin reminded him.

"Well and good, Bhikhu. But if you have a clear shot, Hettie, kill him."

Paedrin planted his hand on her arm as they skulked on the low, sparsely wooded hill.

She shook off his hand. "The Bhikhu is squeamish about such things." She gave him a scolding look. "I can hobble him, though."

Kiranrao sighed, shaking his head. "There's a fool born every moment, and every one of them lives! If you had been raised in a decent orphanage, lad, you would have learned to outgrow this conscience of yours."

"If it makes you feel any better, I might consent to see you strangled and not intervene," Paedrin said.

"Quiet. Here they come!"

All three flattened themselves against the slope of the hill, carefully wrapped in the dark side of the bluff. The night had fallen already, but there was a broad moon in the sky giving off ample light.

There was the sound of marching and the snuffling of hounds. A swinging lantern caused a bobbing plume of light to crest the hill. They were low enough that it could not find them. For a moment all three quit breathing. Paedrin was aware of how close Hettie was to him, and it made him scowl for being distracted. There was something musky in her scent, an earthy smell like grass, sweat, and trampled wildflowers. He swallowed, trying to master his thoughts again, to count the various sounds and try to imagine how many soldiers from Kenatos were hunting them.

They passed the hillock, heading east. Soon the hounds were barking and the men began to jog. Around the far side of the hill, the one with the lantern became visible. Only one lantern. How foolish they were. In the dark they would not find anyone, even with those hounds.

Paedrin began counting the soldiers as they appeared.

"How many?" Kiranrao whispered.

"Thirty men," Hettie answered, slowly rising. "No horses. I'm surprised."

"There are thirty-two," Kiranrao said, smiling at her condescendingly. "The Rikes walk more quietly. There they are. Do you see them?" The black robes made them difficult to see.

"Thirty-two," Hettie answered calmly. "Why the Rikes?"

Kiranrao touched his lips with a finger. "To communicate back to Kenatos. This is not the only group that hunts us, I imagine. They are only following our trail to Havenrook."

"Which is why we double-backed and now head west," Paedrin said, bristling with impatience. "They may miss our trail in the dark, thinking us bound east. When they realize it, we are already gone. It is the Uddhava."

Kiranrao nodded as if it were an accomplishment. "It is. The Bhikhu are not the only ones who use it."

"You flatter us."

"I did not intend to."

"Quiet, both of you," Hettie snapped. "It worries me that they found our shore trail as quickly as they did. I had hoped for a longer lead. I did not think they would catch up to us after only a day."

"The Arch-Rike can afford the best Finders, my love. Better than you. We lead them on a merry chase. But they will not stay far behind us."

"Then we should be going," she said impatiently, starting to stand.

Kiranrao tugged her back down rudely. "Caution says wait. They may not all have traveled in a mass. Patience."

Paedrin wanted to break his arm. He wanted to stab Kiranrao's eyes with his fingers, chop his throat to make him choke, and slam him face-first into the nearest tree trunk. He watched covertly as Hettie rubbed her wrist. Pain was a teacher. Kiranrao was overdue a lesson himself.

In the dark stillness, they waited. The line of soldiers had long vanished into the night. Still they waited. Then two more men, walking side by side, could be heard; they hastened to join the others. Had they left the hilltop, they would have been exposed in the plains.

Kiranrao tapped his nose, smiling smugly.

Paedrin gritted his teeth, admiring the man's keen senses but also hating him at the same time. When the final two had passed, the three rose from their hiding place and continued westward, toward Silvandom.

Kiranrao vanished into a shadowy mist, leaving the two of them alone again. For all they knew, he could have been walking right next to them. He had some sort of magic imbued in his sword that gave him the abilities beyond ordinary men.

"Explain to me again why he is with us," Paedrin said in a low voice. "I know you said it before, but every time he opens his mouth, I seem to forget it."

"He wants the blade, Paedrin. He will barter with my uncle for it. The stones for the blade."

"But *you* found the stones. He would not have been able to get them on his own, by what you told me. It was as if the tree gave them to you."

"There is a Romani saying, Paedrin. Let your bargain suit your purpose."

He sighed. "And that means?"

"When he found me at the temple, I was going to lose the stones anyway. A man like him can just take what he wants. So I made a bargain with him to free you, in exchange for the stones, knowing that he would try and bargain with Tyrus for the blade. Of the two, I think Tyrus is far more clever."

"How did you know he would accept your bargain?"

She gave him a wrinkled-brow look that reminded him of a disdainful cat. "You can be such a fool, Paedrin."

"Yes, I know. But humor me anyway."

"He relishes a challenge. He is the only man known to have stolen from the Arch-Rike's palace and lived to boast of the deed.

Stealing a prisoner from the dungeon is just the sort of thing that appeals to him. Romani love a challenge. They thrive on risk."

"It probably didn't hurt that he knows how much I loathe him. That made the risk all the sweeter."

Hettie nodded. "He is always trying to gain leverage over someone. A way to turn them to his will. Once he could see that I cared…" She clamped her mouth shut, frowning fiercely at the word that had slipped from her mouth.

Paedrin's heart shuddered at the slip. He wasn't sure how to take it, and the silence became awkward and fraught with energy. Well, it should not surprise him that she cared. He had saved her life, after all. Their long talks had been something he had enjoyed much himself. He cared for her, with no doubt. Probably much more than she did him, but he would never have admitted it openly like that.

"Well, I am grateful that you did rescue me," he said, coughing into his fist. He showed her the Kishion ring. "I hope your uncle can find a way to remove this. I would not want to use goose grease on it every day. But better than the alternative of having no control over myself."

She said nothing, and an icy silence fell between them.

The wind was mild that night. They walked firmly, keeping a strong pace to pass the time. To the south, light glimmered on a hill, many leagues away.

"Is that a town?" Paedrin wondered.

"Minon," Hettie replied. "It is a border village between Kenatos and Wayland. A walled place where shipments are protected. We are approaching the road."

"Have you ever been…?"

The sound of baying hounds trumpeted in the distance behind them.

Hettie frowned. "They found our trail too quickly. I hid our tracks very well. The only thing that would have made it better was to kill a skunk to completely mask our scent."

The sound of horns filled the air next.

"Persistent," Paedrin said.

"They are calling to Minon to box us in. We should probably run. If we can clear the other side of the road, it will get easier. How did they find us so quickly?"

Paedrin frowned and started to jog. "Maybe they can track my ring?"

Hettie shook her head. "If that were so, they would not have missed us at the hill."

"Their Finder must be better than you thought."

Hettie was quiet a moment. "But how can they track us? Is someone following us? Can you see?"

Paedrin looked back the way they came and could not see anyone in the distance. Not even the lantern was visible yet. A shape flittered past his vision up above, startling him. Looking up, he realized the sky was circling with birds.

"What sort of bird flies at night?" he asked aloud. "I thought only bats did."

Hettie looked up and let out a sharp breath. "Owls! Of course, I should have thought of that. They can track us better at night than during the day. Owls have great vision in the dark. We are being followed from above."

Just then a snapping sound struck nearby, the small rumbling sound of thunder. They recognized it immediately, for the same sound preceded the Kishion's arrival. Paedrin grabbed Hettie's arm and pulled her to a halt.

Three men appeared.

They were Aeduan, by the look of them. Each wore a black jacket buttoned down the front with a small white ruff at the collar. Each also wore an intricate gold chain around his neck with a multifaceted gem embedded in a medallion. White ruffles appeared at their wrists too.

"Paracelsus," Hettie said.

The three men said nothing, but as one they touched the medallions and a streak of red light shone from each, connecting the three medallions in a triangle of light, trapping the two of them inside.

Paedrin rushed toward the nearest one. As he approached, he felt a rush of air shove him backward. The air in front of the man was hot and jarring, forming some sort of force that prevented him from approaching the man. His ears rang with pain, and he backed away. The pain lessened.

"We have you caged, Bhikhu," one of them said. He had a short gray beard, cropped close to his jawline. He motioned for the other two with his free hand. "Close ranks."

The other two Paracelsus each took a step forward, shrinking the size of the triangle.

Hettie whipped out her bow and quickly nocked an arrow.

"Hettie, no!" Paedrin warned.

She loosed the shaft at the lead man. The arrow raced toward him, only to be repelled right back at her. She managed to sidestep it in time, but the three men continued to close on them.

Paedrin felt the force looming, pushing at him from three sides. If they got too near, he knew he would be immobilized. Being captured again by the Arch-Rike was not something he intended to let happen.

He took a forceful stride forward, sucking in his breath. His body lifted in the air, soaring up past the streaks of red light. The cage, he discovered, did not have a top.

"Stop him! Use the ring charms!"

As Paedrin hovered in the air a moment, he watched a blade emerge from the leader's chest as Kiranrao appeared in smoke-like coalescence. The look on the man's face was contorted with agony as he slumped to his knees and then pitched forward.

The streams of red light winked out.

Paedrin exhaled and landed with a thud. He vaulted at the nearest Paracelsus, watching the man's sudden panicked eyes as he brought up a ring and aimed the crystal at Paedrin's chest. The Bhikhu did a forward roll as a blast of white energy emerged from the ring, zooming over him. Rolling up, he caught the man's outstretched arm, jerking it up and high so that the ring blasted its white light into the sky. He struck sensitive parts of the man's underarm and ribs, and then crippled him with a blow to his kneecap.

The man's face was ravaged with suffering, and the only sound he could make was a guttural moan.

He turned, watching as Kiranrao stalked the final Paracelsus, who struck at him with his ring. The blasts of white light missed him. The Romani moved closer and closer, teasing at him with the tip of his blade. Then he whirled around and threw his sword, the blade impaling the Paracelsus and knocking him down. The Paracelsus's body convulsed, and he withdrew a cylinder from his cloak. He seemed to touch the end of it before he vanished, disappearing into the night.

As Paedrin turned, he found Hettie near the empty clothes of the first Paracelsus, taking the jewelry up and stuffing them in her pack. The one Paedrin had disarmed was writhing in the long grass.

"Take his magic," Kiranrao said. "It will help shield you from his kind in the future." A wicked grin twisted his mouth. "You must be worth more to the Arch-Rike than I thought. Or maybe it is me that he wants so badly."

Paedrin stared at him, feeling nothing but anger and loathing in his heart. How quickly he had dispatched the other two. There was no lesson in death. These men had studied their craft for decades. Their knowledge was now lost forever. It was a pitiful waste of existence.

"Do not *kill* when we can only harm," Paedrin said in a low voice. "It should be the final resort."

"Spare me your sentiments, Bhikhu."

"Spare me your callousness, Romani." He shook his head. "I will not travel with you. I will not go a step farther with you. We part ways this instant unless you swear you will not kill."

Kiranrao looked at him in disbelief. "I swear to no man. I owe you nothing, Bhikhu."

"Then find Tyrus Paracelsus on your own."

"Paedrin," Hettie said, her voice low with warning. "You cannot expect a Romani to..."

"Keep his word? I had not thought of that. Even if you did swear it, I could not believe it." He stepped away from the fallen Paracelsus and began circling Kiranrao to the left.

Kiranrao began circling to the right, hand still clutching the sword hilt.

"You wish to fight me?" Kiranrao said in a low voice. He sounded amused.

"Maybe we are brothers," Paedrin replied sardonically, feeling his entire body focus and harden. "Separated from birth and raised in two different orphanages. Are you my brother? Are you truly Vaettir-born? You mock everything we stand for."

"Every bird relishes his own voice."

It was the sound of the hounds that interrupted them.

"There are enemies enough surrounding us!" Hettie said sharply. "Please! For pity sake, will both of you be silent!"

Kiranrao stopped circling. His eyes filled with menace. "You are an insignificant whelp. I value no life but my own. If you wish to school me in pain, trust me when I say that it is you who will be the learner. You are not even a second-order Bhikhu. You know nothing. I come and go as I choose. I do as I please. It is through my mercy that you are even here." He paused, smiling again. "Is that clear, lad? Or do I kill you now?"

"The King of Wayland controls a vast breadth of land that is used to farm the wheat and grain that is shipped to other kingdoms. Each of the main farms is governed by a Duke. Each Duke is required by the king to provide riders to patrol the borders of Wayland and prevent other kingdoms from stealing crops or herds. These mounted soldiers roam the frontier and are called Outriders. It is understood that the laws of Wayland do not apply to these Outriders. When I travel to Wayland, I always bring a purse with sufficient ducats so that I may go my way in peace."

– Possidius Adeodat, Archivist of Kenatos

XXXII

There were many things Paedrin wanted to say. An equal number of gibes and threats bubbled up into his mouth. But it was the look of horror on Hettie's face that stayed his hands. It was a look of abject terror, a look that said she knew what Kiranrao could do to a man. He felt slightly dizzy, as if he had stopped at the edge of a precipice with a foot poised to take another step.

Patience. Wisdom. Know your enemy. Learn his weaknesses.

He could almost hear Master Shivu clucking his tongue at his foolishness.

Kiranrao cocked his eyebrow.

"The hounds," Paedrin said. "They are chasing us now."

"Take the boy on ahead," Kiranrao said to Hettie. "Leave those who follow to me."

Hettie reached tentatively for Paedrin's sleeve. She tugged him away from Kiranrao, and he allowed himself to be led, his skin clammy, his stomach clenching with fear.

Hettie pulled him into a brisk walk and left the scene behind. Paedrin glanced back, noticing Kiranrao approach the wounded

Paracelsus. He turned his gaze, unable to watch the murder. The barking of the hounds and the braying of the horns muffled it.

It was not far from the scene before Hettie began scolding him. "You are the world's biggest fool, Paedrin Bhikhu. The biggest. I warned you about him. I told you that he is dangerous. If I pointed to a rattlesnake in a field, you'd probably tease it with a stick."

Paedrin almost enjoyed the shrill sound of her voice. His stomach knotted with dread, recognizing he had come very close to dying that night. His honor and overconfidence had blinded him to mortal danger.

"How do you know him?" Paedrin asked huskily, trying to get the taste of fear out of his mouth.

"Every Romani knows of him," Hettie said impatiently. "There are stories about him that would blister your ears. He is known among all of my people. I heard stories about him as a child. I never thought I would meet him, though." She glanced back worriedly into the darkness. "We must run."

"Tell me one," Paedrin asked.

"What?"

"Tell me one of the stories."

"We should really start running."

He could hear the sound of the approaching soldiers. "Just one story. Please."

"Very well, but only one. He was a young man, caught thieving in Kenatos, they say. He was held in a cell and warned the guards that he would kill them all if they tried to hang him. Of course they laughed and spat at him. Some said it would be difficult to hang a Vaettir-born; they promised to tie a sack of stones around his ankles to keep him from floating. He warned them again that each man would die if they tried to hang him.

"The day came. He was marched to the gallows. A crowd gathered in the streets to watch him die. There were jeers and mocking shouts. His hands were tied with ropes behind his back. A cord was knotted around his ankles. They were just about to put the noose around his neck when suddenly the hangman himself had been hanged. The trapdoor was sprung and two more were bashed against the edges, falling in. The crowd panicked. By the time the Bhikhu arrived to restore the peace, all twelve of the officers were dangling from the gallows." She gave him a serious look. "That is the man you insulted in Havenrook. And again tonight. Now run!"

They ran as fast as the wind. Hettie easily kept up with him, and he deliberately tried to outrun her. This was her terrain, and he could tell she had spent many a night sleeping under the stars. The sound of the horns burst through the air behind them. Torches appeared from the way ahead. They were mounted on horseback.

"Outriders!" Hettie called. "Waylander army!"

Paedrin did not slow his stride. He was running from himself, it felt. Running from the past. His heart hammered in his chest like a blacksmith's hammer against an anvil. Sweat streaked down his body, freeing him, loosening his muscles.

"Paedrin!" Hettie warned, starting to lose him in his sprint. "They have crossbows! We should try to go around them!"

He ignored her, running straight for them. His legs pounded into the meadow grass. He saw the horses begin to converge from the road. He made no attempt to hide his approach.

"Hold there!" someone warned, thrusting the torch forward. "Hold!"

Paedrin ran even faster, rushing toward the leader, rushing straight at them.

"Shoot him!"

He watched the crossbows lower. He saw the light of the torches spatter their faces.

"Paedrin!"

The Outriders shot at him from five sides.

He sucked in his breath instantly and rose into the air, taking flight like some eagle above a lake. The bolts all hissed and zoomed beneath him as he rose higher and higher, moving forward. His momentum carried him to them quickly, and he would have sailed over their heads, except for a sudden exhale of breath that brought him straight down on the leader and toppled him from the saddle.

It was chaos.

Horses whinnied and shrieked. Men were half-blinded by their own torch fire. He struck man and beast in a frenzy, causing mayhem with every blow. He darted between the horses, running and gasping to gain height, rising up enough to kick an Outrider in the face, toppling him from the saddle. He moved haphazardly between them, changing his focus of attack from one moment to the next. Every fallen man received a sharp blow to the neck or ribs, hard enough to crack the bones. Paedrin whirled around as two tried to trample him with their steeds. He jumped straight up, sucking in his breath, and allowed the beasts to collide with each other. He floated down and struck both men in the noses simultaneously.

The fight thrilled him. He struck each man down deliberately, aiming to injure but not to kill. He broke arms. He dislocated shoulders. He took some pity on the beasts but did not refuse to yank at their bridles or jerk the bits to cause them pain and make them rear back violently, throwing the riders from their backs.

There was commotion all around him, riderless horses tearing into the plains in a panic. Men groaned and thrashed. Each torch had fallen and began to gutter out, for the grass was too damp to burn.

"Come, Bhikhu!" Hettie said, appearing out of the darkness on a big roan. The beast trotted up and she reached out her hand to him.

He looked around at the fallen Outriders.

"Yes, I'm impressed," she snapped. "Take my hand!"

He sucked in his breath one last time, allowing her to pull him up and straddle behind her.

"Hold me tightly, fool. We ride hard for Silvandom. If the furies are not chasing us yet, they certainly will be by dawn!"

The roan stallion was well lathered. Hettie had driven it mercilessly throughout the night and hard the next day. It was a big beast, and he was surprised at her skill in handling it. They rested it periodically, but the ride was hard and fast. In the distance, they could see the Outriders pacing them, closing the distance slowly but inevitably. It could not be otherwise, for their beast had two riders and the others did not. Thankfully Hettie had grabbed for the strongest animal, not the lightest.

They were hungry, but they had neither food nor time to forage. Every stream provided an opportunity to drink, but they were not plentiful. There was an enormous savanna on all sides. Mountains loomed to the southwest, several days off. Each hill brought another stretch of interminable plains. No cover. No woods. It was a race against the Outriders, and Paedrin realized they were losing.

As dusk started to fall and his stomach reminded him of their lack of meals that day, he noticed plumes of soot in the air.

"A village?" he asked, pointing.

"Good eyes," she said. "I've been looking for that sign. We crossed many leagues today. But I had hoped to be within sight of it before nightfall. That is Fowlrox. It is the gateway city to Stonehollow."

"Each kingdom has a gateway city then. Like Minon that we saw last night?"

"Yes. They are the furthest border city belonging to the kingdom, and they hold the wares for shipment to Kenatos. Stonehollow is where the stone is quarried and carried to the city. They also sell timber, wine, and oxen. Heavy things that make for slow caravans."

"We haven't seen any oxen yet. We've met no one."

"That is because the road is over there. See it? It is the shortest distance between Fowlrox and the docks. It is well worn, and there are traders day and night because the cargo is so heavy."

"Have you ever been to Stonehollow, Hettie?"

She shook her head. "No. I might have as a child, but I do not remember it. The Romani work all of the roads. Everywhere there is a shipment to be made. We know the best routes. Of course, it helps when you are quite ruthless." She glanced back at him, deliberately brushing her hair into his face. He was sure it was deliberate.

"So we are riding to Fowlrox then?"

"No, to Silvandom, which is to the northwest. But we must make our pursuers believe we are escaping their lands so they will stop following us further. There is a river to cross, but there are bridges in Fowlrox. Our stallion is too spent to be able to swim it. We'll sell him in the city and cross the river."

"I have a better idea. We wait until nightfall and then leave the horse and cross the river alone."

"The river is wide, Paedrin."

"You can't swim?"

"Of course I can swim. But what is the purpose of swimming when there is a bridge?"

He could not believe she did not see it. "Because I have noticed in Kenatos that there are always people on a bridge. People who are watching to see who crosses it. People who will sell information about us. If we truly do not want the Arch-Rike knowing our destination, then we should deprive him of the opportunity to find out."

She gave him a serious look.

"Our horse is exhausted. They are closing the distance and will try even harder to overtake us before we get to the city. If all they overtake is a bone-weary nag, they will have no idea where we went from there. It is the Uddhava. We will have a better sleep tonight knowing that they do not know where we are. And besides, I'm hungry."

"Hungry enough to eat a rabbit? I see one over there. I could probably get it from here."

"I'm almost tempted to eat the nag. But no. Let's cross the river tonight and try and rest on the other side. If our nag can't swim it, neither can theirs."

"What bothers me is that it actually sounds like a good idea. I must be too tired. You rarely make so much sense."

"I'll try not to make it into a habit. Ride hard. Let's see if this plan actually works."

She gave him an approving nod and a smile that pleased him more than any compliment could have.

"It would amaze you how many maps occupy shelves in the Archives. For each kingdom, there are maps dating back centuries. I am always melancholy after reviewing them. When those ancient cartographers had put ink to the quill, you see, those cities and towns were alive and full of husbands and wives, sons and daughters, parents and families. One may as well scrape the ink off with a knife blade now. Entire cities have succumbed to the Plague. Small towns are lost forever, and only the Romani brave the ruins in search of ducats or other treasures. Each generation it seems to strike. In the end, I wonder if there will be but one map remaining. An island kingdom called Kenatos."

– Possidius Adeodat, Archivist of Kenatos

XXXIII

It was a grace among the Vaettir to be able to control their breath. That grace made it particularly useful when crossing bodies of water, for rarely did a Vaettir sink unless he chose to. Paedrin's ability could not extend to Hettie, but he carried her bow, quiver, and pack and transported them across the wide, sluggish river while she set out with strong strokes to reach the other side. The river felt wider than it looked, as is often the case, and he found her drifting downstream despite her stamina. He reached the other side first, which was only natural since he could walk across the lapping waters as if they were merely puddles, and after depositing her gear, he went back to help her, even though he knew she would refuse.

"It is not much farther," he coaxed, watching her strength flagging as she swam. The bank was a bit farther off, but he stayed near her, in case she floundered. He could see the determination in her eyes, though, and knew she would never ask for help.

It was dark and cold by the time she reached the far bank, so exhausted she could not speak. Lying on the sandy bed, she gasped for breath and lay still. Her clothes were soaked through and her hair drenched.

"You smell better," he offered with a smile. Her glare was vengeful.

He crouched near her, almost able to hear the pounding of her heart except for the ragged breathing. After several moments of rest, the smell struck him. Wood smoke, from a fire.

"Do you smell that?" he asked.

She lifted herself a little, rolling over a bit and resting on her arm. Then she nodded. "It is nearby."

"Though we could use the warmth, we should probably go farther upstream. I'll fetch your things."

She agreed and stood, clutching herself and trembling with the chill of the water and the night air.

Paedrin went to the bushes where he had stashed her gear. It was no longer there. He stopped, confused, and the smoke shape coalesced near him, almost making him flinch.

"I put her things by the fire," Kiranrao said. "It is in the woods a little ways, a cave of sorts to hide the light. Over in the trees that way." He pointed with a gloved hand.

Paedrin did not like being surprised, but he kept control of his expression. "Thank you."

"Gratitude? What a surprise. Let me see your hand. Is the goose grease still there?"

Paedrin had not given the ring much thought, and looked down at his hand. It felt only like cool steel. "It has not bothered me since we left the city."

"With some spirit magic, there is no distance." He removed a small tub from a pouch at his waist and opened it for Paedrin. "Another layer of grease will not hurt. You must keep it from touching your skin. Foolish of you to put it on, Bhikhu. May cost you your finger in the end." The last was said with a smirk.

"I had hoped we lost you by now," Paedrin remarked coldly as he applied more of the salve to his ring finger. "But we do not always get our wish. You followed us then?"

Kiranrao nodded and said nothing more. "I travel faster than you do. There is other business to attend to. Romani caravans to gain news from. The Arch-Rike hunts us still, but we are quickly passing beyond his reach. There is a comfortable caravan wagon not far from here where I will sleep tonight. Enjoy your cave, and I will see you in the morning. We enter Silvandom together. Brother."

Paedrin nodded reluctantly and turned to find Hettie approaching. She was shivering uncontrollably.

Kiranrao gave Hettie a mock bow. "Even a tin knocker shines on a dirty door. At least you are clean now. Get her warm any way you choose. But remember that she *belongs* to me."

Paedrin glowered and said nothing.

"Praise the ford when you have crossed it," Hettie said through chattering teeth. "And I have...with no Vaettir trickery."

"I will drink to that," Kiranrao said, smiling. Then he vanished.

Paedrin stood for a moment, savoring his displeasure. He would kill that man someday. Or be killed by him. One of the two outcomes was becoming more and more inevitable. Though in all truth, he would prefer seeing him maimed beyond recognition. Alive enough to breathe and little else.

"You are freezing," Paedrin said, motioning her to follow him.

"I'm glad you noticed," she said mockingly. "Where is the fire?"

"This way."

He led her into the tangle of trees and into a gulch. The glow of the fire could finally be seen then, reflecting off the trickle of a stream in the gulch's belly. He breathed himself down the embankment and then reached up, helping her jump down. The cave was little more than a sloughing of earth that had collapsed long ago during a rainstorm. Trees sheltered the area on all sides and provided cover for sound as well as shielding the light from the fire. Kiranrao had chosen the place well.

Hettie hurried forward and crouched by the small tongues of heat. She bathed her hands directly into the flames and they did not burn her. Her face showed the first signs of relish.

The inlet was small but it could fit both of them, sitting close together. He joined her next to the fire, savoring the light as much as the heat. She twisted a clump of hair and quickly began drying it. He watched her, fascinated.

"Quit staring," she said, not looking at him. "Would you fetch my blanket?"

Behind them, he found her pack and opened the buckles. He withdrew the blanket and spread it over her shoulders.

"Not yet, fool," she said sharply. "I want to warm it by the fire first while my clothes dry, otherwise I'll be sleeping in a wet blanket tonight." She sighed deeply. "I am hungry but too tired to hunt. It was a hard swim."

"You did well," he offered.

"I wasn't looking for praise."

"Can I say anything and *not* offend you? I have often wondered that."

"Your silence least offends me," she said. "I am in no mood to banter tonight. I am exhausted and cold."

"You have always been cold," he pointed out. "But I understand the exhaustion part." He was curious about something and decided to venture further. "I notice that you and Kiranrao trade Romani sayings. They are clever. Like the one you used about fording the stream. You have more, I presume? Teach me."

She gave him a quizzical look.

He wanted to understand Kiranrao better. He wanted to understand her better. Little sayings and catchphrases were common in every culture. But he wanted to understand his enemy better. To understand the way his mind worked. What better way than to study from his traditions? It would also help him understand Hettie as well.

"I really am tired," Hettie said sullenly.

"Only a few then. I won't keep you up long."

She sighed, which he took as surrender.

"There are so many," she said. "Hundreds, probably. It is a point of Romani pride to be able to speak a saying that the other person does not already know. If that happens, you nod your head in deference. Since I have spent the last ten years training as a Finder, I do not know all the latest sayings. But some have been handed down for generations."

"Like?"

"Patience cures many an old complaint. Patience is a plaster for all sores. I think every kingdom has its own version of that one."

"Indeed. Pain is a teacher. But the best teacher is wisdom. Wisdom is learning from the pain of others."

She looked at him in surprise and then gave him a slight nod. "Well said."

"Thank you."

"There are others that can sound strange to a foreigner. Do not mistake a goat's beard for a fine stallion's tail. Do not build the sty until the litter comes."

"Or count chickens before they hatch."

"Exactly. As honest as a cat when the meat is out of reach. A little dog can start a hare, but it takes a big one to catch it. A nod is as good as a wink to a blind donkey."

Paedrin smiled and leaned backward. "So many are about animals. One would think the Romani are farmers."

"We were all farmers long ago," she replied.

"Are there any that talk about enemies?" Paedrin asked, and she nodded emphatically.

"The Romani forgive their great men when they are safely buried. Speak well of your friend, of your enemy say nothing."

"Ahh," Paedrin said, smiling, savoring the wisdom in the words. "Yes. That is true."

Hettie rubbed her arms, more slowly this time. He could see little trailers of steam rising from the cloth.

"Can I fetch you anything to eat?" he asked her. "Mushrooms? Slugs? Bark?"

"Sharing your meals again?" she replied with a wicked smile. It was the smile that tore into him the most. So rarely bestowed, so much the more valuable. "Thank you, but no. I am tired, as I said before. If you would take the first watch…"

"I will," he answered. "One more question. Are there any sayings about…secrets?"

The question startled her. He suspected it might. There was something in her eyes in that moment, something that warned him. Exhaustion had a way of producing true sentiments.

She was quiet a moment and then stared into the fire. Her voice was distant, almost a whisper. "It is no secret that is known to three. Never tell your secret even to a fence." Her voice fell even lower. "A secret is a weapon and a friend."

That was it. That was the one she valued the most. He could hear it in her voice. He had used the Uddhava against her and managed to get her to reveal part of herself to him. She stared at the fire, her eyes focusing on the flames, as if she dared not look at him. He could almost feel the emotions roiling inside of her. She was struggling with her feelings. Without knowing her as he did, it would not have been noticeable. But there was a little bulge in the corner of her jaw. A clench of muscle. Her gaze was so intense at the flames. She was mastering herself. She was almost failing.

Good.

"Thank you, Hettie. Get some sleep. Do you think we will reach Silvandom tomorrow?"

She nodded absently. Then taking her warm blanket, she nestled near the fire. Her cheeks were flushed. She stared at the flames, as if drawing in their heat through her eyes.

Tell me what is troubling you, he nearly whispered. *Trust me, Hettie. You can trust me.*

She said nothing. Soon her eyelids were growing heavy. A few moments more, and she was asleep. He studied her face. He longed to stroke her hair. He swallowed the pang, mustering his will to save him from his feelings.

How many times had Master Shivu taught him? To be prepared for his life's journey as a Bhikhu, he needed to purify his thoughts and feelings. *You have the power to decide, deliberately and intentionally, what thoughts you allow in your mind and what emotions you feel in your heart.* By patient and persistent practice, he knew he could gradually gain control over his harmful emotions. The discipline and effort involved would be worthwhile, for it would bring greater harmony internally—in his own mind—and externally, in his relations with others.

He sighed deeply. In the temple, in the confines of the training yard, the lessons were so easily accepted. But since leaving Kenatos, he had experienced stronger emotions than he had ever imagined existed inside him. Hatred of Kiranrao. Jealousy of Annon. Even desire for Hettie. He recognized these as base emotions. They needed to be controlled.

Staring at her sleeping would not help him gain control of his emotions. Instead, he stared at the ring on his finger. The markings on it were intricate. It was a work of great craftsmanship. It was a prison. He despised it. He was willing to lose his finger if Tyrus could not find a way to remove it.

You realize that removing the ring will kill you. I am certain you are clever enough to consider that, but just to be sure.

The whisper in his mind was so real. He could hear the Arch-Rike's voice as fresh as it had been in that horrible, stench-filled cell.

Of course you can hear me, Paedrin.

His eyes widened. Was he going mad?

Not mad. Naive. Believe me, boy, a little salve cannot save you from my influence. I let you go. You are my servant. I let you escape. You will become a Kishion, and you will serve me. No, do not try to stand up. Stay where you are. You will say nothing. You will speak nothing of this discovery to anyone. I bind your tongue. Here are your instructions. When you reach Silvandom, you must take the dagger from Tyrus. You must kill him with it. And then you must hand it to me. Is that perfectly clear to you? Those are my orders. I will prevent the blade from destroying your mind.

Paedrin felt the terrible compulsion overwhelm him. It thundered in his mind and screamed at him in a long, desperate howl.

You are my pawn. You are my creation. Tyrus must be stopped. It is better that one man should perish than a kingdom. He will unleash the Plague on us all. More virulent. More devastating. He must be stopped, Paedrin. You will stop him. Your first killing will bind the ring to you forever. It cannot be undone.

He felt as if his mind would melt with heat.

Kill Tyrus.

"Unfortunately in our world, ignorance more frequently begets confidence than knowledge does. You see, it is those who know little, and not those who know much, who assert that certain problems will never be solved by reason, study, and practice. Patience is the companion of wisdom."

– Possidius Adeodat, Archivist of Kenatos

XXXIV

There was so much pain that Annon welcomed death. He sank into its folds, embracing the weightless submission. His senses became acute. He stared down at his own body, collapsed against the base of the damaged oak tree, and saw blood trickling down his fingers. It was an odd feeling, staring at himself. And then he saw the spirits swarm.

He almost resisted, afraid of the agony awaiting him, but as he felt himself thrust back into his body, his eyes blinked wide, and he felt air fill inside his chest. Tingles of pleasure shuddered through the core of his being. He stared at the craggy bark of the oak, blinking furiously, unable to speak.

"He's still alive!" one of the Bhikhu said in surprise. "Khiara! This one lives! Hurry!"

Annon tried to push himself up, but his legs and arms were void of energy. He wobbled and nearly collapsed when a Vaettir woman caught hold of him.

She had long black hair, a sharp contrast to the short black stubble of the men nearby. Her eyes were angled and her skin dark. She did not wear Bhikhu robes, though. Her shirt and pants were the color of saffron with wide sleeves and colorful embroidery on the hem and edges. She wore a charm around her neck that first made him think of a talisman, except it was made of bone or shell. She touched the side of his face to steady him and gazed deeply into his eyes. Then she closed her eyes, and he felt a surge of power come from her body and infuse him with strength and vitality. The weakness melted away.

Annon trembled. His emotions became giddy with excitement and energy. He felt as if he could run for leagues without tiring. Her touch summoned a gush of warmth that suffused throughout him.

Her eyes opened. Her expression turned sad, her mouth drooping. "I am sorry I could not save your companion. Sooner, I may have. But his spirit form has passed beyond to the other world. He would not be called back."

A stab of anguish struck Annon like a blade. "I know. He was already dead."

As the girl nodded, Annon felt the sobs finally break loose. He knelt as he wept, ashamed to be seen like this, but unable to withstand the painful emotions engulfing him. Memories of Reeder flooded his mind. Sharing a moment with Dame Nestra and her stew. The warning about visiting Tyrus. He clutched his head and tried to control the choking feeling in his throat.

The girl remained with him in his grief. Her hand touched his shoulder and she squeezed it. "We pass through sorrow. We remember the good. He is not gone forever, just from our sight. In another world, they greet him and bid him welcome as we bid him good-bye. This is death."

She removed her hand from his face and stood. The Boeotians were retreating, fleeing through the smoke. Many writhed in pain on the forest floor, their bones broken by the efficient brutality of the Bhikhu who had come to help.

"You are not a Bhikhu," Annon said in a broken voice, wiping his eyes on his sleeve.

"I am a Shaliah. A healer. A keeper. A penitent." She gazed at him sorrowfully and bowed her head. "I did little to aid you. She saved you. Do you...remember?"

Annon saw the subtle flick of her eyes toward the tree.

He struggled to remember. It was only a voice. He remembered her voice.

"Yes."

The Vaettir girl nodded slowly. "That is rare, Druidecht. My name is Khiara Shaliah." She bowed her head to him in respect and responded to the call of a Bhikhu who had been slashed by a Boeotian ax.

She is wise, Nizeera said, butting his arm with her nose. *You may see Reeder again. In Mirrowen.* Her fur was made whole and her teeth were sharp and almost grinning. *You fought well, Druidecht. You showed courage.*

Annon's mind was in a fog of despair, and he did not want to accept the compliment. Smoke from the fires that he had started diffused in the air. The stench was acrid. He lingered by the tree, stroking Nizeera's ears, hearing the shrill voices of the spirits thank him for rescuing the Dryad tree. Little flitting streaks of light zoomed past him. He felt their emotions, the joy mixed with sorrow. They had lost many of their own as well.

He slowly stood and walked around the craggy trunk to the spot where the axes had ripped into it. His stomach lurched at the damage. The wood was pale as splintered bone. The cuts were jagged and crisscrossed. It would have taken more time to fell the tree. But the damage was severe.

Annon nearly wept again. He stared at the gaping hole and then down at the dismembered arm. Would the Black Druid survive his injury? Would a spirit heal him? Sinking to his knees, Annon stared at the pale hand. He had seen flames from those fingers and knew the man had the fireblood. His derangement had come from losing himself in it. His actions were certainly that of a man who had lost his mind. He had called himself the Reaper. The Plague. Gibberish. Or was it? He dreaded the thought of meeting him again and shuddered with fear.

He was unsure how long he knelt by the tree. Other Druidechts arrived, including Palmanter. His expression was hard. His eyes full of emotion. He crouched down next to Annon, running his meaty hand across the bark of the oak.

"You saved her," he said in a deep voice.

Annon nodded listlessly. He was so miserable and tired. So much confusion. So many threads in his life had gone askew. Reeder was dead. Part of him refused to accept it. He felt a tide of emotions welling within him, but he shoved it aside.

"Reeder's body is being taken to Canton Vaud. The Vaettir wish to pay him their respects before we return him to the soil. You will wish to do that as well. It helps with the pain. Every creature must die, Annon. Even a friend." His big hand rested on Annon's shoulder.

Annon looked at him, burying his emotions deep. He nodded. "I will come with you."

The other shook his head. "No, you must stay here. You must stay by the tree. When a Dryad's life is saved, they must offer a boon. It is yours alone to claim. Wait for her to appear. She will not with so many here. The Bhikhu will chase off the Boeotians. We will establish a defense around this part of the forest. But you must not leave this place without her boon." His eyes crinkled. "It is rare, Annon. Very rare."

Annon licked his lips. "What is the boon?"

"I do not know. It is never spoken of. Nor should you tell anyone what it is. Perhaps revealing it negates it. But do not leave this place until you receive it."

Annon nodded and hunkered down at the base of the oak. He wondered how long it would take for the smoke to clear.

Palmanter rose and moved away from Annon. He looked at smoldering branches and then back at Annon. He said nothing. But his eyes revealed much.

The Dryad came at dusk.

Annon sat cross-legged with his back to the tree, gently stroking Nizeera's fur. The sun was fading between the interlocking branches of the woods, offering faint pinpricks of light to stab his eyes as he watched it shrink. Grateful spirits had brought him berries, seeds, and mushrooms to eat. He waited patiently, wondering how long it would take.

There was a crackle in the dead leaves behind him. It was unmistakable. His nerves warned him to turn and prepare to defend himself, but his instincts warned him not to move. Another step. Then another.

Hair on the back of his neck began to rise. He could hear the breath. Another snapping twig, just behind him. Nizeera's tail was perfectly still. He waited, wondering what would happen. Would she speak? His heart hammered in his chest. Conflicting emotions whirled inside of him.

"Well met, Druidecht," she said. "Do not look at me, or you will forget."

Annon recognized her voice. It caused a tight pain deep in the center of his heart. "You speak my language?"

"Of course. It would be difficult talking to you if I spoke in another tongue. Perhaps you would prefer it?" Her voice sounded teasing. "What is your name?"

"Annon."

"How quick you are to give it up. I am Neodesha. You saved my tree. I owe you a boon."

"I am sorry I did not come sooner. Will your tree survive the damage?"

He could hear her moving behind him, coming to the edge of his vision. He turned his head the other way.

"You are determined not to look at me."

"You told me not to."

"I warned you what would happen if you did. It is only fair, after all. You are young for a Druidecht. They keep the younger ones away from us." He felt fingers graze his hair.

Annon closed his eyes. It would be easier that way.

"Closing your eyes! What an idea. Now I can move anywhere I want." He heard the twigs snap again as she passed in front of him. He could feel her presence, the warmth emanating from her. It was maddening hearing her voice but not knowing what she looked like. A craving filled his insides. The curiosity was extreme and intense.

Annon kept one hand on Nizeera's fur, digging his fingers into it. He tried to concentrate on the feel of the fur.

"Do you want to look at me?" she whispered in his ear. He startled, but kept his head down, his eyes squeezed shut. Sweat had gathered on his brow and beneath his arms. The feelings were maddening.

"What kind of creature is a Dryad?" Annon asked, his voice suddenly, embarrassingly hoarse.

"I'm a creature, am I? No, foolish boy, you know nothing at all. I am Aeduan, like you."

Annon was confused. "How can that be?"

"I was born of a mother. I was raised in these woods long before the Vaettir came here. I am bound to this tree. But I am very little different than you, other than the magic that my binding allows me. We are very weak, Annon." Her fingers grazed his chin, but he swerved his head the other way, refusing to open his eyes. "But our magic is powerful."

"I know," he muttered, beginning to tremble at the influence she was having on him.

"No, you have not even begun to feel it yet. It will get worse before it gets better. But you are doing well, Druidecht. Very few have made it this long."

The compulsion to look at her was nearly overpowering. It was a monster inside of him. He could feel it roaring and snarling. A drop of sweat began to sting his eyes. He brushed it away and found his entire face wet.

"You see," she went on, moving around him again, her voice tantalizing in the twilight. "Only those who try to resist know how strong we are. A Druidecht who gives in right away simply does not know what it would have been like later. You will be stronger as a result. Even if you do not make it. I am impressed already."

"Why do you torture me?" Annon asked. He dug his fingers into Nizeera and felt her twitch with pain.

"I am not torturing you. You are torturing yourself. Why do you do it?"

"Because I seek a boon."

"What boon do you seek?"

He hesitated.

"What do you seek?"

"What can you give?" Annon asked, turning the question on her.

"Very good. Ask questions instead of giving answers. Do you know why most seek me?"

"No. Tell me, Neodesha." Saying her name made his tongue burn.

"You spoke my name."

Annon was startled. There was something in the way she said it. He felt the strength of the magic begin to release him. He almost looked at her at that moment. There was something in her voice that demanded he look.

"Tell me!" he pleaded.

"I must, for you spoke my name. That is the boon. I gave you my name. You can bind me with it. You can free me from this tree with it. That is the boon."

"Do you want to be freed from the tree?" Annon asked, his mind racing. He was confused. Terribly confused.

"No! But you have the power to if you choose. Men are selfish by nature. They want to possess things. To possess people. You could force me to go with you, even if I did not wish to go. That is the boon. That is the power you have over me. But if you look at me, you will forget my name. You will forget this even happened. Do you see it now, Annon? As long as you do not look at me, you hold power over me. As soon as you look at me, I hold power over you. I *want* you to look at me, Annon."

"No," he replied, steeling himself. "I need you to answer me, Neodesha. I need you to tell me the truth. Do you know my uncle, Tyrus of Kenatos?"

"Yes and no."

"What does that mean? I asked you to speak the truth!"

"I know Tyrus of Kenatos. I also know that he is not your uncle."

The words struck him like another blow. He nearly opened his eyes in amazement. He struggled with the surging fury that awakened inside of him.

"I thought…"

He felt her finger on his lips. "You are so young, Annon. But I respect the strength that brought you here. You saved my tree. Not one man in a thousand who was not a Vaettir would have done that willingly. They would have fled from certain death. You faced my enemies and you destroyed them and saved me. Because you did that, I will trust you. I am going to kiss you, Annon. That is what men seek me for. The kiss of a Dryad brings wisdom. It will help you to remember that which you have forgotten. It will prevent me from stealing your memories when you look at me. I speak the truth, for you commanded it of me. I do not do this for most mortals. But I trust you, Annon. I trust you will not harm me with this knowledge."

He started to breathe heavily. He felt her kneel in front of him. He began to panic.

"Will it harm me?" he asked.

"Yes. But not in the way that you think. Memories can be very painful. The pain lessens in time as we forget. Except for you. You will remember everything. Every word ever spoken to you. Every slight you have suffered. Every joy, every thrill. Your memory will be perfect. And thus you will gain great wisdom."

He was about to tell her he wanted to think on it. He was opening his mouth to say the words when he felt her lips press against his. The sensation of her mouth, the smell of her skin lasted a moment, but he felt his mind awakening. It was as if he had been asleep his whole life. Scales began to fall from his thoughts, allowing in bursting rays of light. His entire life was before him.

"Look at me," she said softly.

Annon opened his eyes.

"What's the benefit of dragging up sufferings that are over, of being unhappy now just because you were then? There is good in doing this. We must not flinch when we look at the past. We must strive to learn from our mistakes. So we must learn to bear and endure. The sorrow will one day prove to be for your good."

– Possidius Adeodat, Archivist of Kenatos

XXXV

The face that Annon saw was young—a girl not even his own age. Her hair was the color of wheat and her eyes such a pale blue-green that they were almost ivory. She smiled at him, almost timidly, and he noticed that she wore a rich green wool gown. There was an embroidered pattern on the thin wrist cuff that extended up the side of her arms. She could have been any damsel in Wayland by the look of her.

He was startled and supposed it showed on his face, for her expression turned impish seeing his reaction.

"And what were you expecting, Annon? A gown made of oak leaves or moss? Twigs in my hair? Claws instead of fingers?" Her smile was mischievous. "I am Aeduan, just as I told you. But I have lived for several thousand years."

Annon stared at her in surprise. "How is that possible?"

She smiled demurely. "There is a tree in Mirrowen, Druidecht. One taste of its fruit grants eternal life. I have bitten its fruit as part of my binding. I was sixteen. That is the age one becomes a Dryad, you see. That is the age we are reborn."

Her pale eyes were transfixing.

Annon cleared his throat. "So I am immune to your magic now?"

She nodded intently, pleased. "Rarely do I get to speak to another Aeduan. To learn about the world and how it has changed. Many have misperceptions about my kind. Everything I tell you, you will remember. You will come back here again, Annon. We are connected now, you and I. You will tell me about your world. I will tell you about mine."

She knelt in front of him, so close he could feel the heat radiating from her. She looked eager to talk to him.

"The damage to your tree," Annon said. "It did not harm you?"

She shook her head. "The tree is injured. But I am not. We are not connected that way. I do not feel her pain. She does not feel mine. What we share is much deeper." Her voice fell lower. "We share memories. She is the receptacle. I am the engraver. You would not understand how it works, but I will try and explain it. I can take a man's memories and implant them into the tree. What he no longer remembers, I hold safe. We are the guardians of great secrets, Annon. The past long forgotten. Yet the spirit magic that makes this work is very vulnerable. As you saw, I could not defend the tree from deliberate attack. I can only rely on others to protect me. Had you not come, I would not have died. I cannot die. But those memories would have been lost forever and I would have been trapped in Mirrowen with no way to return to the mortal world. This is my home, after all."

Annon shook his head in amazement. "And you say you are thousands of years old? You were here before the founding of Kenatos?"

"Certainly. It is young compared to me. But there are Dryads even older than I. There are groves even more ancient." She gave him a meaningful look.

He swallowed. "The Scourgelands."

She flinched at the word. "That is not what we call it, Annon. Something happened there. Something long ago. A taint. An injustice. I am only a child compared to those Dryads. But they no longer speak to their sisters. They hide away. Something was done to injure them. A betrayal. That is what Tyrus seeks. That is the knowledge he is after. He is a protector of Dryads."

It came to Annon's mind immediately. "There is an oak tree in the middle of the Paracelsus Towers in Kenatos."

Neodesha smiled at him and twisted her fingers together. "She is a Dryad tree. One who was doomed to die because of her proximity to that city. He saved her."

"The tree looked dead to me," Annon said.

"Oaks are very resilient. It would surprise you. Was there a clump of mistletoe in the branches?"

He remembered it perfectly though he only recalled seeing it once. His memory was astonishingly clear. "Yes."

"That is one of the ways you can tell. The mistletoe is a sign of our presence. In some kingdoms, it is a tradition during the winter festivals to kiss beneath a sprig of mistletoe." Her smile was offset by a dimple. "The tradition was created by the Druidecht, of course, who alone know the truth of it."

Annon shifted uneasily, uncomfortable from the intensity of her gaze. There was a power in it still. "And by looking at a person, you can take their memories."

She nodded. "Tell me of your world," she said, shaking his knee. "What kingdom do you come from?"

He shrugged, feeling awkward. "I am an orphan, but I was raised by the Druidecht in Wayland. Reeder was my...my mentor." He felt the crushing weight of the loss suddenly, so powerful and violent that tears stung his eyes.

"Your memories are powerful," she said comfortingly. "They will be from now on. They will burden you, it is true, but they will also serve you. You will remember things that others have forgotten. Tell me of Wayland. Where is it?"

"Several days south of here," Annon said, struggling to control his feelings. He brushed his eyes on the back of his hand, amazed to see tears glistening on his skin. "The kingdom is sparsely populated due to the Plague. Small villages here and there, spread far from each other. Farms mostly. They grow much of the food that feeds the other kingdoms."

"And how do they treat the spirits of Mirrowen?"

"They are mostly ignorant of them. Unwittingly, they destroy their lairs and homes. The Druidecht try to teach them, but they are more interested in the price of wheat." He reached out and touched her hair, surprising himself. He jerked his hand back.

She smiled. "It's the magic, Annon. Keep talking. It will help you if you keep talking."

He wanted to. The look she gave him was so eager, he could not resist. He told her about his childhood. He explained his feelings of abandonment by Tyrus and how he had thrown himself into Druidecht lore. He revealed the fireblood and asked if she knew about it. She shook her head and implored him to keep talking. So he did. He explained the summons of Tyrus to Kenatos, the quest for Drosta's lair. Even meeting Drosta himself and the encounter with the Kishion. He held nothing back. It was a relief to talk about it to someone. To purge the emotions and confusion he had been carrying for so long.

It was midnight by the time he finished.

The air was cold, but her presence warmed him. They sat so close their knees often touched. As he finished his story, she nodded in understanding and covered his hand with hers.

"There," she said. "Speaking our troubles to another lessens them. Some seek me to purge their memories. They do not wish to know my name, only to speak of their troubles and thus pass them to me. When they leave, they have forgotten that portion of their lives. Some say too much and forget who they even are when they leave. They abandon a wife or children because they no longer wish to be bound by the connection or feel the hurt that comes with it. But those kinds of men leave weaker, not stronger. They feel an ache that they cannot salve. Part of them is missing. Part of them is left at the tree."

Annon felt the softness of her hand. He looked in her eyes and nodded slowly. "I do not wish to be rid of my memories. You were speaking the truth to me, though? I will not forget that this happened when I leave?"

"Will you?" she asked teasingly. Then she rested her hands in her lap and sat straight. "Now, Annon. You have recounted your troubles. Use your new gift of wisdom and begin to solve them. You likely have harbored some ill-formed notions about yourself and others. Start with your sister."

Annon exhaled slowly. He brought her face to his mind. Almost in a moment, everything she had ever said flashed through his mind. He frowned, for a feeling of dread had begun to squirm inside his stomach.

"Why do you grimace?"

Annon stared at her. "I have a bad feeling about her."

Neodesha gave him a knowing smile. "Why?"

He thought more. Fragments and pieces began to slide together in his mind. "Because she is Romani. She is not trying to buy her freedom. She was sent by the Romani, likely Kiranrao, to steal the blade...the dagger I told you of." His neck prickled with anger and resentment.

Her lips pursed slightly. "Do not be too harsh in your judgment of her, Annon. If you were raised in that life, you would have done the same. But I have the feeling you are right. She is trapped in a hunter's snare. Remember that an animal will often kill itself faster trying to escape. What it needs is another creature to free it from its bondage. That is the way with most traps."

Annon felt the wisdom in her words. "Paedrin is who he always claimed to be. I do not know where the Kishion took him. But I feel he can be trusted."

She wrinkled her nose and nodded in agreement. "Bhikhu are rarely duplicitous. It is easier to speak the truth all the time than to try and remember the lies told now and again. Paedrin can be trusted."

"Erasmus. I do not know him very well."

"Tyrus trusted him with your safety. Whether you trust Erasmus depends on how much you trust Tyrus. The same with Drosta."

"But Drosta is a Druidecht."

"But he was a Paracelsus first. Strange how people yearn to become holy only after years of depravity." She smiled knowingly. "Give me chastity and continence, but not yet."

Annon chuckled softly. "So true."

"Believe me, many a young Finder have hunted the woods in vain to glimpse a Dryad. And it was not wisdom they sought. My kind tend not to aid Finders until they are well seasoned in years and more desirous of imparting memories and conversation. Consider it a compliment that I have trusted you with my very life. With my name, you could force me to do many things I would detest."

Annon shuddered. "I would never…"

She touched his arm. "I know."

He sighed heavily. "I suppose I must think now on my uncle. Or the man I believed to be my uncle." He rubbed his lower lip thoughtfully, awash in the conflicting miasma of emotions. "I do not recall him ever telling me he was my uncle."

"Go farther back," she coaxed. "What is your earliest memory of him?"

He explored his memories even farther. Most were new to him. Brief flashes of feelings and intense loneliness. He suffered under the weight of a child's pain. Memories were blurry, especially further back. If he went further, would he even remember his birth?

She touched his wrist. "Please understand, Annon. The strength of my magic is related to memories. We have memories to keep specific people in our thoughts. Our emotions bind the memories to us. Emotions like love, loyalty, or gratitude are strongest. The stronger the emotion, the more vivid and influential the memory. As you seek your greatest pains, you will find the memories that contain the greatest wisdom."

It was as if saying the words made it true. He remembered a woman. He remembered her face—the claw marks on her face. The wounds that had barely healed. He was young—a babe, if that. A year old? Certainly less than two. He remembered her face and the fierce love he had for her. But then she was hurting him. She was making him cry. She was shaking him. He was frightened, terrified. There was shouting and screaming. He did not understand the words because he was still too young to comprehend language. But he understood the emotions and knew the woman was his mother. She was hurting him. She was shaking him. And there was Tyrus—younger but just as imposing. His face also scarred by claw marks. Tyrus had taken him, pulled him up into his huge chest and shielded him. There were blue flames, orange flames spitting at them both. His child's heart was in a terror. He clutched at Tyrus for protection and safety. He loved his mother, but she frightened him.

They abandoned a stone hut and went into a storm. Tyrus covered him with his cloak. There were screams of rage. The home was burning. The roof was ablaze. Screams of pain. Screams of madness. Tyrus was cooing to him, trying to blot out the sound. Annon was wailing hysterically. He was lost in the moment, in the nightmare. The rain was freezing. He was hungry, cold, abandoned.

There was a horse. Tyrus mounted it, clutching the baby in his arm. Smothered in the wet smell of wool, Annon struggled and whimpered until he cried himself to sleep.

When Annon awoke, he found his head in Neodesha's lap, her fingers gently stroking his hair. She blotted his tear stains on her embroidered sleeve. Her look was tender.

He looked up at her, his emotions nearly too fragile to speak.

"We are bound together, you and I," she said. "I experienced your memories as you relived them." She smiled sadly, continuing to stroke his hair. "I do not think Tyrus of Kenatos means you harm. He felt and feels a certain degree of responsibility for you. The past makes that abundantly clear. Your mother had the fireblood. She was mad. Do not judge him harshly, Annon." Her fingertip traced the edge of his lip. "Wisdom helps us understand that we are not alone in this great world. The sufferings of others cause us to suffer too. We are all bound. More so than we realize." She looked him firmly in the eye. "I believe it is time you faced the man you've known as your uncle. I do not think it coincidence that he is in Canton Vaud right now. Waiting for you."

Nizeera began to purr. *She is right. It is no accident. We face him together, you and I.*

"I read this in a volume written a thousand years ago, 'Tears at times have the weight of speech.' They do indeed."

– Possidius Adeodat, Archivist of Kenatos

XXXVI

Annon would never forget her face.

The Dryad's kiss had altered him permanently. It was unsettling to realize that his memories were so sharp he could cut himself on them. Insignificant details from his past flitted through his mind as he walked back to Canton Vaud. Nizeera padded silently next to him, subdued by the experience that nearly cost them their lives.

You have powerful allies, Druidecht. And powerful enemies. Be cautious.

It was dawn again when he reached the camp, the night having passed in sullen silence. He was fatigued, weary from the march, but he first sought Reeder's tent to see if Erasmus was still there. He was not.

He asked for directions to the Thirteen and was pointed toward a series of grand pavilions. Thin trailers of mist crept amidst the awakening Druidecht. Small dashes of light displayed the presence of the morning spirits, some carrying gossip. He was approached by several, some bowing in respect before flitting on. Nizeera's tail began to swish again. He thought he heard the faint murmur of her purring.

As Annon approached the grand pavilions, he caught sight of Palmanter emerging from the folds. Several spirits attended him, and he nodded his head to them and offered a few words in response. Gazing around the camp, his eyes fell on Annon. He seemed surprised.

"It happened that quickly?" he asked in a low voice after approaching. "You met the Dryad?"

Annon nodded. "I must speak with my uncle."

Palmanter pursed his lips. "I thought you might. Your Preachán friend is with him." He put his meaty hand on Annon's shoulder. "He sought asylum here, lad, but we cannot grant it. He bears something of great evil. A blade that speaks to the mind. We cannot permit it to remain longer in Canton Vaud. There are many Druidecht suffering from its effects. Will you leave with him?"

Annon stared at the older man. He was not sure of the answer. Palmanter sensed his hesitation. His eyes narrowed. "Be wary, Annon. There are stories about your uncle. Be careful."

"I will."

Palmanter gestured to another pavilion, a smaller one. Several Bhikhu guarded it.

"He is your prisoner?" Annon demanded.

The older man shook his head. "They are there to protect him from the Kishion. At his request."

Wise of him, Nizeera thought.

Annon stroked Nizeera's head and then walked over to the small tent. He could hear voices inside. The Bhikhu stared at him, studying his features, and then nodded; they opened the flap.

Tyrus was inside, sharing a morning meal with Erasmus. Both were seated on large cushions, eating a variety of gathered fruit.

"I estimated you would arrive this morning," Erasmus said smugly to Annon. "I should have wagered a few ducats on the outcome. Your uncle offered that you would breakfast in the city of Silvandom and not here. I was a fool not to take the wager."

Tyrus looked up at Annon. "Have you eaten yet?"

Annon shook his head. His jaw muscles felt as hard as iron. He kept his emotions in check and stared at Tyrus's face for any sign of resemblance. There were the tiny scars, as if claws had ravaged his face long ago.

"There is a place in Silvandom," Tyrus said. "A bridge on the outskirts of the city proper. Not many know of it because it connects to the city amidst the mountains at a higher elevation. A waterfall is nearby. It's impressive. There are shops on the bridge. A place for weary travelers to rest before entering the city. A place to eat. It is called Shearwater."

Tyrus rose to his full height. He withdrew the long cylindrical object that Annon had last seen him holding. Holding it in his fist, he extended his arm toward Annon.

"If we had made that wager this would be cheating," Erasmus said as he gobbled another piece of fruit and hurriedly stood. He rested his hand on Tyrus's arm.

Annon stared at the jeweled object. There were stones set into cunningly worked gold. The stones sparkled in the lamp-light. The device was extended to him—an offer. An invitation.

"You are not my uncle," Annon said, unwilling to move. His anger started to rekindle. He shoved it back violently.

"I know," Tyrus answered simply. "Come with me. Learn the truth. I promised you in my tower that you would."

Annon hesitated. A part of him whispered a warning. Another part of him was too curious to resist. This was the invitation to learn Tyrus's secrets. He knew it would only be offered once. He had to make a decision. One choice was to stay at

Canton Vaud and learn more of the Druidecht ways. The other was to accompany Tyrus and eventually face the Scourgelands.

He reached out and gripped the open end of the cylinder.

"Have a hold on your cat," Tyrus said, a pleased glint in his eye. As Annon grabbed the ruff of Nizeera's neck, he heard the angelic song of spirits shudder as the device made everything go black.

In a moment, the blink of an eye, they were leagues away. The air was frigid and sharp. It smelled of fir trees and juniper. The land was choked with snow. They stood on a stone bridge, wide enough for a single wagon to cross. On the other side was a stone house with works of timber for a roof and faded red tiles. The roof had a curious slant to the corners, which were pointed like an ox's horns. Instead of a straight edge, it sagged, creating little dips and sways that gave it a distinguished appearance. There were three levels to the building—a large main section of house and then two narrower levels forming a second and third floor, each with their own slanted rooflines and pointed corners.

The strange house was built into the rock itself, and it was difficult to see where the walls began and the mountainside ended. The air was frightfully cold, and Annon hugged himself immediately.

"Look," Tyrus said, pointing at the edge of the bridge down into a lush valley below.

Annon stared in amazement. The valley was teardrop shaped and full of majestic trees and enormous stone structures, each with the same shape and design of the home ahead of them—only grander and more impressive. The structures below existed with the trees and were shaped and defined in open spaces. It seemed that no tree had been felled to clear the way, but that the structures had been built amidst the trees deliberately.

Erasmus whistled. "Silvandom. It is too beautiful to describe. The timber here is worth a fortune."

"Many poets have tried to describe it," Tyrus said. "And many Romani have tried to steal it. It's protected by the mountains on all sides. Only a few narrow passes lead into the valley. See the cliff edges? This valley was carved by ice thousands of years ago. Giant walls of ice strong enough to split stone. See that bald rock face over there? The other half is there, on the opposite side."

Annon saw it and was skeptical. How could ice have carved such a thing? The cliffs on each side were full of waterfalls, emptying into rivers and streams in the valley below. It was an idyllic place. No wonder the Vaettir had claimed it.

"That is the Shearwater," Tyrus said. "We can rest and eat there and then journey to the city later. You have questions, I am sure. Hopefully they are good ones."

Tyrus took them to the stone house on the far side of the bridge. He paused on the entryway, staring up at a blotchy stain on the wood frame at the top of the door. Annon wondered about the stain, noticing Tyrus's slight pause on observing it. He rapped firmly on the door and then pushed it open.

Inside was a tiny Vaettir woman, her hair well silvered; she walked with an obvious shuffle caused by age and pain. She looked at Tyrus and smiled a beaming smile and began to prattle off in the Vaettir tongue. Tyrus answered fluently, much to Annon's surprise. He made some requests and then motioned toward a table and benches. The old woman nodded in reply and limped to the kitchen. No one else was in the room.

Tyrus seated himself at the table, planting his elbows on the pocked wood, and motioned for Annon to sit across from him.

Nizeera wandered over to a large hearth and settled down on the warm stone.

Erasmus prowled around the common room, silently counting the number of seats and tables. Annon knew he would be lost in his guessing for a while. He sat down opposite Tyrus, unsure of what even to say. Then a thought came to him.

"My mother's name was Merinda," Annon said softly, remembering it suddenly. "I only heard you say it once. She was not your sister."

Tyrus shook his head. "No."

Annon felt weary. The emotions of the night were still thrumming beneath the surface. "You led me to believe she was. I grew up believing I was your nephew. Why did you deceive me?"

"Why do you think?" Tyrus asked, raising an eyebrow.

"You promised me answers."

"You must earn them. You were kissed by a Dryad, Annon. I see it in your countenance. You have new gifts of insight and wisdom. Use them. Open your mind to the possibilities. Trust what your heart tells you. You already know the answer. You cannot be lazy with me. Think."

Annon rubbed the rounded edge of the table. It was a light, stained wood. Easily twenty men could sit around it. "You protected me from my mother. She was sick. She used the magic without controlling it. You took me away from her to protect me. But I have no recollection of my sister. Why is that?"

Tyrus nodded slowly. "You would not. She was stolen nearly at birth by a Romani midwife who did not realize there were twins. Neither did I. I did not have the knowledge I needed at the time. I could have saved Hettie and lost you to death in the birthing process. Or save your life and lose Hettie to the Romani. It was a terrible choice." His face was like flint. "But I chose to save you and lose her. The story I told to the locals was that Merinda was my sister. Which is one of the reasons the Romani kidnapped Hettie in order to blackmail me."

"Surely you did not lack for ducats," Annon said tightly.

"Not ducats," he answered. "Freedom."

"I do not understand."

"No. Of course you do not. It took me years to understand that I was a prisoner in Kenatos. Granted, it was a gilded cage. But a cage still. Whenever I tested the limits of my freedom, I felt the bonds around me cinch tighter. Allow me to explain, Annon. I must tell someone, for the Arch-Rike is determined to kill me. I know too much. I pass this knowledge on to you in case I am murdered. Someone else needs to understand the pieces. I have chosen you."

Annon nodded. His heart throbbed with curiosity. He leaned forward on the bench. Part of him was cautious. Tyrus had deliberately deceived him. He needed to judge for himself whether he was told the truth or not.

"It is my life's work to banish the Plague, Annon. I chose that calling as a young man. I have lived to see its devastation twice. The suffering is unimaginable. I cannot even begin to explain. There is a great principle you must understand. If you study the lives of the great men and women from any age, you begin to discern a pattern. There are famous individuals, like Band-Imas, the Arch-Rike of Kenatos who built the great temple of learning, but greatness is never achieved alone. One person cannot change the world. I learned this from him as a child. He surrounded himself by others more talented than himself. He united them in a cause—a cause so important they gave their very lives to attain it. The preservation of knowledge. Kenatos. A principle and a doom."

Tyrus breathed out softly, rubbing his palm across the table-top. "To fulfill my desire of banishing the Plague, I assembled my own followers. We were united to a single cause. I studied every account. I began to interview anyone who had traveled into the borders of the Scourgelands. There were stories aplenty. I needed facts. Facts are stubborn things, you will discover. I took with me the brightest minds. The fiercest warriors. The most gifted Bhikhu in a generation—your father. I assembled these and sought the blessing of the Arch-Rike. He granted it, and we ventured north and entered the Scourgelands, determined to conquer whatever lay ahead." His expression began to harden into stone. His eyes were haunted.

"We were destroyed."

Tyrus stared down at the tabletop, looking at his thumbs. "I would have died myself. I should have died. Your mother saved my life. She was grievously wounded. We were attacked by the creatures that guard the Scourgelands from intruders. She unleashed the magic in her blood to save us and lost her mind as a result. I promised to see her safely home and allow her unborn child a chance at life. The only way we escaped was her revelation to me of the Druidecht secret of the Dryads. They guard the Scourgelands. They are what went wrong. The missing piece of information that ties it all together."

Annon swallowed, excited. His pulse quickened. "I learned this last night. The Dryad I spoke to told me. Something happened there. What did she call it? A taint. An injustice. She said that the Dryads there are vengeful. Something was done to injure them. A betrayal."

Tyrus nodded. "Exactly. It is lost to human memory. But it is written in the trees in those cursed woods. Another Dryad could read what is written there. Another Dryad could learn the truth. I have my suspicions, but you need facts. Let me hasten to provide them." Tyrus leaned forward, his face intense. "While I was in hiding, caring for your mother, I pondered what went wrong. I did not have your insight then. I wish I had it earlier, but experience is the thing that you get just after the time when you need it most. It was in a little stone hovel when I realized we had walked into a trap. We had hardly grazed the outer defenses of the woods before we were so violently attacked and repelled. I kept asking myself how they had known we were coming? How had they assembled so quickly? I could not see it then, but it came to me."

A thought struck Annon forcefully. "The Arch-Rike."

Tyrus smiled broadly. "Truly you are wiser than I was at your age. Exactly. He had given us his blessing. Blithely sending us away to our deaths. Some secrets must remain hidden at all costs. Whatever travesty or injustice occurred in the Scourgelands, it is clear to me now that the Rikes of Kenatos seek to continue it. I had a choice to make. I knew that if I did not return to Kenatos, the Arch-Rike would suspect that I had discovered his treachery. So I voluntarily went back into my prison after you were born and left you to live with the Druidecht in Wayland. I returned and admitted my failure to the Arch-Rike. I told him I had barely escaped with my life and had been healing and regaining my strength. This was true, of course. Just not the whole truth. I gave him just enough. He never knew Merinda was with child. I did not want him to know about you."

Annon pursed his lips. "Why did you come to me as a child?"

"You know the answer already. Why even ask it?"

"You knew I had the fireblood and that it would destroy me if I did not learn to tame it."

Tyrus gave him an approving nod. "Then I went back into my prison so that I could continue my work. I know as a child you wished I could call for you. That I would claim you. But I could not, Annon. I needed knowledge that could only be found in Kenatos. I learned everything I could about the Dryads. I even had a tree brought to the tower. I became obsessed with understanding them. I needed to know their powers and their abilities. There are no detailed records, since the Druidecht refuse to document their knowledge, but there are clues. Even a few stories about them in the archives. I realized that in order to learn the truth, I would need to bring a Dryad into the Scourgelands. A Dryad that was not bound to a specific tree."

"What?" Annon asked, his mind racing. "You are going too fast!"

"Hush," Tyrus said, holding up his hand. The old woman emerged from the kitchen with trays of cheeses, nuts, and figs. Tyrus thanked her politely and asked for something else. She nodded and retreated back into the kitchen.

Tyrus leaned even closer to Annon. "I still do not know what the injustice was. I could only imagine it was a betrayal of some kind. I needed wisdom. I needed knowledge that I could not have any other way. I had studied and studied. I wrung every drop of truth I could find. But I could not put the pieces together. And so I sought for a Dryad's kiss myself. I did not know it at the time, but I had rescued the tree because it was the last of its kind, existing on the road to Kenatos. All of its sister trees had been cut down. It would fall to the woodcutter's ax. I had it moved into the city at great expense. There were many who thought me quite eccentric. But I moved it and planted it in the courtyard of the Paracelsus Towers. I waited by the tree. She visited me. I did not look. I knew it would not be wise to do so. I learned her name, just as you did last night at another tree. And she gave me a kiss, which allowed it all to make sense. That is when I realized the truth. That is when I realized what I needed to do."

"The Arch-Rike is a man of great personal integrity and honor. It is a position, to be sure, but also a legacy that goes back many centuries. How does one become the Arch-Rike of Kenatos? A king of Wayland is born to rule. The Vaettir chose their princes of those with the most compassion and humility. The Preachán follow he who controls the most ducats and influence. But the Arch-Rike must be a leader of men. He must have vision and the ability to express that vision in words. He must set a high moral standard that others gladly follow. He is chosen in a conclave by the Rikes of Seithrall. The decision is always unanimous."

– Possidius Adeodat, Archivist of Kenatos

XXXVII

Annon's mouth was dry. The food sat untouched on the tray before him. "Yes?"

Erasmus sauntered over and began swiping dried figs from the tray. "You sired a Dryad," he said between mouthfuls. "Didn't you?"

A tortured, painful smile hovered on Tyrus's face. "I did. She is my greatest secret. She is the key to solving the riddle. She is everything. And she has no idea who she is."

Annon stared at him, aghast. "You forced the tree Dryad to…"

Tyrus's expression hardened like flint. "No, Annon. I did not force her. You know more about Dryad lore than most Druidecht do. Your soul revolts against the idea, doesn't it? To take a defenseless creature, one who has trusted you with her name, and to abuse that trust. Only a twisted man would do that. I think that something along those lines happened up in the Scourgelands. Those oaks are ancient beyond any reckoning. They have long memories. They hate us. It is clear. There was a wrong done. A betrayal. I seek to mend it. To correct it. I explained my theory to the Dryad. I explained what I intended to do. Only a Dryad not bound to a tree could enter the Scourgelands. Only a Dryad could bind to those trees and learn the mystery. She agreed willingly."

Erasmus took a piece of cheese and ate it slowly. "Under the Arch-Rike's very nose. He would be furious, Tyrus. You are brilliant."

Tyrus shook his head. "No. I am determined. I relied on others far wiser than myself. Drosta, for one. He knew the truth about the gilded prison of Kenatos. He managed to escape it as well. I am bound to that tree in the Paracelsus Towers just as she is bound to me. The Dryads have a ceremony for when it is time to reproduce their kind. They choose their mates. I was chosen. In our culture, when a man and woman marry, they wear a ring on their finger as a symbol of their union. When a Dryad chooses a mortal, she wears a bracelet around her ankle until the man is dead. It is an ancient custom. She does not choose a man very often. Only when she senses a need to reproduce her kind. The Dryad in the tower is my wife. I never forced her. Annon—what you need to understand is that I do have a daughter."

Annon nodded slowly. He understood that each kingdom had its own tradition of marriage. It was even so among the Druidecht. Why should the immortals be any different?

"Where is she?" Annon asked.

"Stonehollow. That is where my family came from. It is where those of the fireblood came from. Our people, Annon. I knew that I would not be able to seek her out and teach her what she needed to know. I entrusted her to people who would protect her and teach her at the right time. She was to be raised an orphan. She is sixteen. She is the age when she must choose whether or not to bond with a tree. The stones I sent Hettie after are the way she will be found. She should have a necklace with a blue stone embedded in it. The other stones will be drawn to it. That is the only way I can find her."

Erasmus sat on the bench, playing with an apricot. "Stonehollow is almost beyond the Arch-Rike's reach. They are wary people and slow to trust outsiders. A wise location."

"Thank you," Tyrus said. He then reached across the table and rested his hand on Annon's. The gesture was remarkably tender. "I cannot tell you how it relieves me to share this burden with someone else. If the Kishion had killed me, the secret would have been lost for another generation or two. The Plague will come again. This may be the chance to stop it. I know you have hated and despised me, Annon. I have not been a good father or a good uncle. I accepted this when I decided to enter the prison of Kenatos. To be honest, you were the one who first gave me an idea of the solution."

Annon was startled. "What do you mean? How could I have possibly done that? We have hardly ever met."

"I know. But you marked me deeply, Annon. I once heard a Rike say something that described the experience I had at your birth. It was spoken at the marriage ceremony he conducted for two love-struck fools who were poor enough to be truly pitied. He said this after commissioning them to start a family without delay. Parents—be they Vaettir, Cruithne, or Aeduan—realize that the most powerful combination of emotions in the world is not called out by any grand celestial event, nor is it found in archives or histories. The most powerful combination of emotions is caused merely by a parent gazing down upon a sleeping child."

Tyrus paused, his voice thickening. "I cannot tell you the anguish and torture it was to let Hettie be stolen by that Romani midwife. I hated myself for not predicting it. I helped you enter this world and was the first to hold you. Your father was a good man. He trusted me. He lost his life because of me. As I watched you sleep for the first time, curled near your mother's breast, I felt a surge of emotions that were completely alien to me. It was that experience which helped me understand that I needed to be willing to sacrifice something important in order to repair the damage of the Plague. A child would be required. A Dryad child to bond with a tree in the Scourgelands and learn the truth about the past. How could I ask that sacrifice of anyone else other than myself? How could I expect a mother to suppress her feelings if I was not willing to? You see it all now, Annon. You see my secret. You know my plan. The Arch-Rike realizes I am up to some mischief. He has no idea what. By telling you both what I have, I increase the odds of my success."

Erasmus rubbed his mouth. "Along with our likely demise," he muttered. He sighed heavily. "You could have warned us, Tyrus."

The Paracelsus smiled smugly. "I did when we first met, old friend. But you wanted to make a difference in this world. You have ambitions of making it a more just and equitable place. Not to mention this would be the greatest political upset in a thousand years."

Annon stared at the platter of food and realized how famished he was. Tyrus watched him begin to devour the meal. He looked calm and peaceful. The frantic edge in his eyes had been replaced by a look he could almost call tender.

"So what do I even call you?" Annon asked at last, unsure of his own feelings. "You are partly my uncle. Partly my father. Partly a total stranger to my family. What are you to me?"

"You may call me whatever you like. There is more to family than just blood. Is there anything else you would know of me?"

Annon thought a moment. "My mother. What became of her?"

Tyrus pursed his lips. "When I returned to the stone hovel later, I learned of her death. Her madness made her unleash the flames in their full power. The roof burned and collapsed. The fire could not harm her. A wooden beam did. The villagers were unnerved that her skin was not burned after the blaze ended. They realized she had the fireblood. When I came back, they tried to kill me."

It sickened Annon to hear it. "You always warned me to tame my anger."

Tyrus smiled weakly.

"What is your plan then? Where do we go from here?"

Erasmus stood and began pacing again, looking around the room. He quickly counted on his fingers. He held up his hand to preclude either of them from talking. "Silvandom," he announced triumphantly. "You told Hettie to meet you in Silvandom at the prince's manor. She was to fetch the blue stones from Kenatos that will find your daughter. Given how long it would take to walk there, fetch the stones, and return, she could be arriving as early as today." He beamed triumphantly.

Tyrus nodded. "She arrived last night with Paedrin. They were brought under escort to the prince's manor where they slept. As soon as you are both done eating, we will join them. I will tell them the truth as well. Paedrin's master was one of my allies in Kenatos, but he never knew the whole truth. The Arch-Rike will be working against us. He will marshal all of his power to try and stop us."

Erasmus looked thoughtful. "A formidable enemy."

"So am I," Tyrus replied, rising from the table.

"Men go abroad to gaze at the enormity of mountains, the huge waves of the sea, the long courses of the rivers, the vastness of the ocean, the circular motions of the stars, but they never stop to gaze at themselves. While this is true of most men, it is least true of the Vaettir. They examine their own hearts and motives as the Preachán examine the aspects of a trade."

– Possidius Adeodat, Archivist of Kenatos

XXXVIII

Hettie walked between Paedrin and Kiranrao. She did this to keep them from killing each other. Her stomach was in knots, her feelings anxious and fretful. She had almost told him the truth around the fire. She had almost revealed her secret. That it had nearly bubbled out of her lips frightened her. How had he managed to get past her defenses? Kiranrao would poison her with monkshood if he knew.

They entered the monstrous woods of Silvandom early in the day. Hettie had known forests all her life, but these woods were different than anything she had seen. The trees had unnaturally slender trunks that shot straight up in the air with flowery green vegetation above. Tightly bound together, the trees formed a massive maze that met the travelers with an almost uniform consistency. With the sun shielded by the leaves, it was almost impossible to determine which direction they were going.

The foliage was lush and smelled sweet and fragrant. Small pools could be seen at various points along the way, with floating flowers and clouds of gnats. They marched in a northwesterly direction, as best as she could tell. It was several leagues into the woods before they encountered anyone. A Bhikhu floated down from the upper regions of the trees and halted in front of them.

He was middle-aged, his dark skin chapped and his skull completely bald. A drooping mustache adorned his lip. His robes were similar to Paedrin's but more weather-worn and fraying.

"An unusual greeting," he said in a rich voice, sizing each of them up individually. "Two Vaettir and an Aeduan girl. Are you lost in the woods?"

Hettie did not wait for her companions to speak. "We are guests of Prince Aransetis of Silvandom. He is expecting us."

The Bhikhu gave her a stern look as if she had done something to offend him. He looked at Paedrin and Kiranrao searchingly.

Paedrin nodded. "She speaks true."

"I do not doubt her honesty," the man replied. "Only you do not seem the kind who would be seeking the prince. Are you selling something?" He started to move, gliding around to their right, watching Kiranrao all the while.

It was the Uddhava, Hettie realized. He was distrustful of them. Whether it was their clothes and appearance, she could not tell. Kiranrao did not move, but she could sense him poised, ready to strike.

"No," Hettie said, stepping forward. "We bear a gift to the prince from Kenatos. He will be expecting us."

"Indeed," the Bhikhu said warily. "Then I will escort you.

Hettie saw a sheen of sweat on Paedrin's brow. He looked wary also, as taut as a rope.

"Thank you," Hettie said. "We will follow the way."

The Bhikhu directed them into the woods until they reached a dirt path carved into the trees. Once they reached it, the journey progressed much quicker. It was a well-worn path with no scrub or weeds disturbing the carefully tamped earth. The wind caused the enormous trees to bend and wave, bringing out a shushing sound as the greenery embraced.

Their guide led them in silence. Occasionally Hettie saw the branches bend and drift as shadowy shapes bounded across their tops. She realized that the road was meant for visitors and that the Vaettir did not use it themselves. It amazed her. She wondered how long the Bhikhu had watched them before presenting himself.

The road began to climb and the journey became more difficult. The forest floor started to slope and dip with undulations, and large boulders began to appear in the forest. Some were carved with symbols. Others had faces. Occasionally there were small huts built off the road, made of thatch and the strange narrow trunks.

Hettie glanced at Paedrin. She expected him to be fascinated by his homeland. His people had come from Silvandom originally. She was surprised that he looked so tense, so ill at ease. Something was troubling him greatly. She could see it burning in his eyes. He caught her eye and looked away, ashamed.

With Kiranrao and the other Bhikhu there, she knew she would not have the means of talking to him privately. His obvious discomfort made her worry.

The road began a tortuous pace upward, weaving between large boulders and crevices. Her legs began to burn with the climb, but she did not want to seem weak. Birds chirped and watched them. Once she even heard the scree of a hawk, but she could not see it. The road ascended up the twisty path of a mountainside. They were climbing higher now, emerging from the green-hued stretch of forest. It was after midday and Hettie was starving. The Bhikhu offered them nothing. He just continued at a punishing pace, just hard enough to make her work at it. She knew she was holding them all back. The others would have been able to make it to Silvandom by then if not for her. She resented the feeling.

As Hettie looked backward, she saw the clouds of green leaves behind her, creating the illusion of rich green grass, undulating in the breeze. From that vantage, she saw other Vaettir crossing the forest. They had not encountered another soul along the way. Now she could see why.

The road climbed mercilessly higher, and she found herself soaked in sweat, trying to keep up. She drank from her flask, but the water was starting to run out. Still she pressed on, angered by the enigmatic guide who refused to speak to them. Kiranrao said nothing as well. Some insects had taken a special interest in him, especially some rather large dragonflies. But he did not swat them away. It was against the Vaettir way to injure any creature unjustly. She had learned that from Paedrin.

The steep climb changed the scenery dramatically. The higher elevations did not allow the thin, pole-like trees to grow. She saw cedar and pine and even some redwoods. The road was no longer made of hard-packed dirt. The sun tilted in the sky, making her see spots. She shook her head, trying to clear it. Paedrin touched her arm, looking at her in concern. She jerked her elbow away from him, furious suddenly.

Ahead, the road began to widen and opened into a scene of transcendent beauty. A dazzling waterfall thundered from the crevice of a mountain on the left, sending tendrils of never-ending water cascading down the side. There were interconnecting bridges and gorges, mounted into chasms that defied belief. Then she noticed the peak-roofed buildings that sloped and pointed gracefully. They were made of stone and timber. Chimney smoke trickled into the air, giving it a faint musty scent. She was breathing hard, wiping the sweat from her lip on her arm. The view was breathtaking. The structures each looked unique and perhaps a thousand years old. It felt as if the farther she walked, the more they had gone into the past.

"A little farther," the Bhikhu said, looking at her with a shrewd smile. "I think you will make it."

They crossed fourteen bridges and steps cut into the mountains. More and more homes and structures could be seen. Her stomach was ravenous with hunger. But she would not stop to eat if the men did not. Her pride demanded she keep up.

After the fifteenth bridge and an agonizingly painful set of steps going down, they passed another chasm that opened up into a valley.

Hettie stared at in shock and felt tears sting her eyes.

Never in her life had she imagined such a place of beauty could exist.

Silvandom.

It was nearly sunset when they reached the prince's estate on the eastern outskirts of Silvandom. The Bhikhu who had guided them nodded in farewell and left without a word, floating into the air and off to another destination. A destination he would reach much faster this time.

They were met by a Vaettir woman who was perhaps a little older than she or Paedrin. She was pretty, in a very subdued way. She had long jet-black hair that was perfectly straight. She did not wear Bhikhu robes, but did appear to be in some form of ceremonial dress.

"Welcome to Silvandom," she said perfectly in their language. "My cousin, Prince Aran, will join you shortly. He asked me to offer hospitality. My name is Khiara Shaliah."

The word seemed to interest Kiranrao. "A healer?"

She nodded meekly. The estate was not what Hettie expected. In Wayland or Stonehollow, the rich had opulent palaces, but that was not the fashion in Silvandom. It was an open-air estate and made of stone. The buildings were interconnected by bridges and garden paths. The setting was private and secluded, not as bustling as the deeper center of the city proper had been.

With the light fading outside, Hettie found the interior lit with a few candles and oil lamps, giving it a natural darkness. Incense burned in the air, flavoring each breath.

Khiara led them to a chamber with a low table and cushions. There were no chairs. She motioned for the table. "There are bowls, spoons, and eating sticks. Many years ago, this house sacrificed much to save the citizens of Silvandom. In return, the home is blessed with food. Think of what you would eat and it will appear inside the bowl. You may eat your fill. There are no servants here. The prince delights to serve his guests personally, but he has asked me to on his behalf as he is currently busy. He will join you shortly."

Hettie approached one of the cushions and seated herself gratefully. Her legs and back were exhausted. She watched Paedrin seat himself and stare at the bowl in front of him. It filled with steaming rice with small seeds and he looked surprised. Taking two long sticks from the table, he lifted the bowl and began shoveling the hot rice in his mouth. Kiranrao knelt on the cushion, formally, and his bowl filled with a dark, steaming soup.

She thought of stew she had made with Evritt. He had taught her how to cook it just the way he liked it. Her bowl filled instantly. Raising it to her nose, she inhaled the fragrance. The smell made her mouth water. Taking the cropped spoon from the table, she ladled some into her mouth and was amazed that it tasted so delicious. It was like eating a memory. She could see his wizened eyes. She could almost hear his words. Evritt's life was in her hands. If she betrayed Kiranrao, she knew he would be poisoned too. The feeling made the soup taste bitter.

Khiara watched them begin their meal. She let them eat for several moments and then sat on a nearby cushion herself. "You walked a great distance today. There is shelter here to sleep and rest. Tyrus said we could expect two of you." Her eyes went to Kiranrao. "I did not know we would receive a third."

"Luck comes in threes," he replied, his voice devoid of emotion.

"That is so. Tyrus passed through here recently. He went to Canton Vaud, the seat of the Druidecht hierarchy. They are here in Silvandom now."

Hettie squirmed in her pillow. "Is it far?"

"He will come here," she answered. "Many years ago, he came here as a child to wait out the Plague. His sister's blood is on the lintel of the great house. No one who was here died of the Plague that year. None have died since. He is greatly esteemed in this house. My cousin esteems him the most." Her eyes brightened for a moment as she seemed to look over their shoulders at someone else.

"I do," said a stern voice. Hettie turned and saw the man enter. He was Vaettir-born, but had not shorn his hair to nubs like a Bhikhu. What struck her immediately were his clothes. He wore a dark black tunic with a high collar, marking him as a Rike of Seithrall.

She flinched, her hand straying to the knife at her belt.

"The Vaettir escaped a terrible Plague by crossing the great waters in mighty ships. They were granted land in the west by the seashore. They were given the land that was once occupied by a race previously destroyed. Just as the Cruithne crossed great deserts and inhabited the mountains of Alkire, the Vaettir claimed the forests known as Silvandom. There is very little need for shipbuilding now, as the great races continue to converge in the hopes of surviving the future devastations to come."

– Possidius Adeodat, Archivist of Kenatos

XXXIX

"My name is Aransetis," the man said, his voice deep and slightly hushed. He was stern but not unfriendly. "You are my humble guests." He entered the room and inclined his head to each of them. "Forgive my appearance if I have startled you. You have traveled long and are weary. In your eyes, I represent those who have hunted you. But I do not serve the Arch-Rike or his minions. This jerkin helps to remind me of our cause. One only knows his enemy when he has worn his shirt, as they say. Welcome to Silvandom. Welcome to the mastermind."

Paedrin stood and bowed in respect. Hettie had not released her grip on the knife hilt. Her instincts were at war. Kiranrao looked unimpressed, and he gazed at their host with an air of indifference.

Hettie glanced back at the girl, Khiara. Her eyes were aglow, her expression softening as she stared at Prince Aran. It was as obvious as the moon at night that she had feelings for him. Hettie scorned her blatant adoration.

"Please, you must have questions," the prince said. He walked to the head of the table and seated himself in a graceful move. "Let me answer what I can."

"Where did you get your outfit?" Kiranrao asked, his voice slightly smug.

"I had it made. And you are?"

"Kiranrao. Do you know of me?"

The prince's expression was stern. "Your reputation extends to these woods. You will find no Romani here except for the two of you." He extended his hand, palm up. "I believe you have my stones."

Kiranrao's eyebrow twitched. He said nothing.

"They will not serve you, Kiranrao. They are powerless in your hands."

Hettie felt the tension increase between the two men. Paedrin leaned forward—just slightly. His gaze shifted between them.

"What do they do?" Kiranrao asked at last, his voice disinterested.

"They will find someone who is lost. It is easy to lose one's way in the Scourgelands. The trees there are ancient."

"Trees?" Kiranrao asked with a half-chuckle.

"Ancient ones. As old as the world. The stones, please." His palm did not waver.

Kiranrao stared at him silently. He did not move.

Hettie felt uneasy. She knew Kiranrao was sizing him up. He was examining him for weaknesses. She was not sure what she had expected. A pampered Vaettir lord who was soft and simple? This one surprised her in every possible way. He had none of Paedrin's bravado. His eyes were deadly earnest. He had the look of a Bhikhu who had killed.

"You are a guest in this house," Khiara said, her voice serious. "It is the only thing that shelters you in this land. Though you are Vaettir-born, you are not familiar with our ways. The prince has been lenient thus far. Do not try his patience."

"Do not try *my* patience," Kiranrao warned softly.

"The stones," the prince repeated firmly.

Hettie's hands began to tremble. There would be violence here. There would be blood spilled. She sent a pleading look at Paedrin, but his eyes were fastened to the prince's. The air in the room was oppressive and heavy. Even the incense smelled too strong.

Kiranrao flung a small leather bag onto the outstretched palm. It was tossed too hard and would have bounced, but the prince's fingers closed like talons, seizing it.

He opened the drawstrings and emptied the stones into his palm.

The feeling in the room began to shift. The tension ebbed.

Each stone was a mottled blue color, unpolished, uncut. They could have been river pebbles, except for the streaks of green and white that marked them. The prince stared down at the three, his gaze firm and hard. The stones began to glow. Satisfied, he stuffed them back into the pouch.

"You didn't trust me?" Kiranrao said with a smirk.

"It's for her own good that the cat purrs."

Hettie was startled, for that was a Romani saying. It was not a commonly known one. She nodded to him in deference. Kiranrao did not, but she saw his countenance darken.

"You said welcome to the mastermind," Paedrin said, speaking at last. "Where did you get that word?"

The prince did not smile, but his expression softened slightly. "The Arch-Rike taught it to Tyrus. Tyrus taught it to me. We are a mastermind. All of us. Some who use the word consider a single person. A force behind a single idea." He shook his head gravely. "They sadly misunderstand. The formation of Kenatos was a mastermind. The congregation of thieves in Havenrook is a mastermind. When individuals choose to align themselves for a common goal—that is a mastermind. Before you were born, Bhikhu, Tyrus led a mastermind into the Scourgelands to defeat the Plague. We are preparing now to go back and finish what was started. We..."

Kiranrao looked perplexed. "I have no part of this..."

The prince gave him a withering look for interrupting him.

"You are warned," Khiara said softly.

Kiranrao's face flushed with emotion. He said nothing, but Hettie could see the fury roiling in his eyes.

"You have all been summoned to join this great mastermind," Prince Aran continued. "Those in Kenatos would call it a conspiracy. But I say to you that it is a rebellion against death. When Tyrus came to me, he was bleeding and nearly dead—defeated from his last attempt. I swore on the honor of my house that I would be ready to join him the second time. I was too young back then. I have been training since that day to join the cause and usher in an era where the Plague cannot kiss another child with death. You are here for this purpose. Tyrus chose you. All of you. Yes, even you, Kiranrao. You are all needed in this task. We may fail. We may die. But he is coming to tell us his plan. He is coming to explain his purpose. Come back to this place at dawn. Then, your questions will all be answered."

Prince Aransetis rose. Khiara rose as well, her eyes still adoring. He nodded to them again, each in turn, and left the spacious room. Khiara followed, speaking softly to him, and then returned. "Rooms are in the hall outside, one for each of you. There are mats to sleep on in the corner. Rest yourselves, for you are weary. There is a chamber for bathing beyond. We will join you in the morning."

She left, sliding the door shut behind her.

Kiranrao stood slowly, exhaling. "I nearly killed him."

Paedrin snorted, earning a withering stare himself. "Not likely. I have never been in the presence of a Chin-Na master before. Until tonight."

"I am not afraid of a Bhikhu," Kiranrao said contemptuously.

"He is not a Bhikhu," Paedrin replied. "Chin-Na is different. A Vaettir floats and flies. One who practices Chin-Na is heavy. They become part of the earth and its energy. Hitting one is like hitting a boulder. They are fast and strong. One punch can stop a man from breathing. They can kill by robbing one's breath."

Hettie gazed at him intently. "I thought the Vaettir do not kill."

"I think this one does," Paedrin replied ominously.

Hettie could not sleep. The mat was terribly uncomfortable and the lingering smell of the incense was alien and unfamiliar. Everything about the room and structure was different than what she was used to. It was a different culture. It was a different lifestyle. It was the closest thing to feeling safe she had ever experienced in her life.

In the wilds beyond Silvandom, the Romani were everywhere. But here, in this kingdom, they were unwelcome. That meant she did not have to worry that someone would slip monkshood into her food and murder her. For the first time in her life, she began to experience the possibility that she might actually free herself from her Romani bondage. Not through paying an outlandish bribe. But by living in a place where the Romani were not welcome. If she aided her uncle in his quest, if she truly joined the mastermind, would she gain the privilege of living in Silvandom?

She was awestruck by the beauty of the land, the forested hills, and the amazing cleanliness of the city. The air did not reek as it did in Havenrook. The people were civil and respectful, if a bit odd too. But she would gladly accept their traditions and customs if it gave her a chance to live her life and choose her own future. She wondered if Paedrin would want to stay as well. Going back to Kenatos would not be possible for him.

Unable to sleep and restless with anticipation for Tyrus's arrival, she rose from the mat and padded softly to Paedrin's room. She needed to talk to someone. Her feelings were nearly bursting inside her. She slid open the door to his chamber and found it empty. The mat looked undisturbed.

Hettie retraced the path back to the main room where they had eaten the night before. The sky in the windows was beginning to brighten with the dawn. Outside, she began to hear the chirping of birds. She gazed in the room and almost withdrew, but she saw something flash in the corner of her eye and turned, gazing into the corner. There was Paedrin, hunched over, rocking slowly. He looked as if he were in great pain.

Rushing to his side, Hettie found him wet with sweat. He was huddled on the floor, arms clasped around his middle.

"Paedrin!" she gasped. He stiffened and looked at her, his eyes wild with panic. She touched his shoulder.

Calmness began to settle over him, as if her touch were magic somehow. The quivering muscles began to ease. His breathing slowed. She watched, transfixed by the metamorphosis. The strange look in his eyes began to soften.

"Are you sick?" she whispered at last, watching the final tremors fade away.

"I felt a fit coming on," he replied, his voice strained. "I get them, from time to time. They pass quickly. I did not want to wake anyone."

"I was worried when I did not find you in your room."

His eyebrows arched. "You were looking for me in my room?"

She realized how it sounded, and flushed. "I needed to talk to someone. It is almost dawn. Tyrus is coming. What do you think of all this? What Prince Aransetis told us? You always have strong opinions."

Paedrin breathed out heavily, pausing as he considered her. "How do we know we can trust him?"

"The prince?"

"No. Tyrus. Hasn't he misled us from the start?"

She was surprised to hear that coming from him. He was never one to wrestle with self-doubt. "I used to think that. But the more I have thought about this, the more I believe he was trying to protect us."

Paedrin lay still, his eyes far away.

"Are you all right, Paedrin?"

He flinched. "I am now. I wish you had not seen me like that."

She sighed and laid her hand on his arm. "No one expects you to be invincible." She sighed. The urge to tell him the truth gnawed at her. He deserved the truth, especially since he had disclosed his own weakness. It burned on her tongue. A secret is a weapon and a friend. It would give him power to hurt her. Sharing it might strengthen their friendship. She hesitated.

"I just wish I could fully trust Tyrus," Paedrin muttered softly. "If you look at it a certain way, he abandoned us to that Kishion. Those who stay with him have a peculiar habit of ending up dead."

Hettie felt a stab of concern at the way Paedrin was speaking. "He is my uncle."

"Are you sure he is?" Paedrin asked, staring at her. "Do you really know anything about him? Were you told by the Romani you were his niece? Are they trustworthy either?"

Hettie shifted away from him. "This isn't like you," she said with concern.

Paedrin frowned and shook his head, as if reproaching himself. "I'm sorry. All my doubts tend to come out at night. I will be…more myself…in the morning."

A chorus of trilling began just outside the window. The musical sound startled them and made them both start laughing. But on Hettie's part, it was nervous laughter. Something was different about Paedrin. Something wasn't right, but she could not decide what it was.

You have said enough. You planted doubts in her mind. You have done well, Paedrin. I applaud your efforts. Now be watchful. Look for the moment when you can seize the blade. We will appear suddenly, with enough force to distract Tyrus. My spies in the Druidecht camp say that he has it and that he disappeared this morning at dawn. He will meet you soon. You have led us to the end of the hunt. Soon you will be one of my Kishion. You will be very powerful in the realm. You will do great things.

The Arch-Rike's voice shriveled from Paedrin's mind, like a snake shedding skin. It was a horrible, violating feeling. It made him want to vomit. He stared at the ring on his finger. He knew he was betraying his friends. He knew he was betraying his race. He knew he was betraying the Bhikhu. If he could kill himself by removing the ring, he would have. All his life he had wanted to visit Silvandom. This act of treachery would never be forgiven. It would be better to die.

When he tried to will himself to remove it, his hands began shaking and would not obey.

"*Be cautious whose philosophy you choose to follow. It is not the punishment but the cause that makes the martyr.*"

– *Possidius Adeodat, Archivist of Kenatos*

XL

Tyrus produced the strange cylinder again. It was studded with gemstones and intricate carvings—either designs or a language beyond Annon's knowledge. It was an object tuned to the ways of spirit magic.

"What is this creation?" Annon asked, looking at his uncle curiously. "What do you call it?"

Tyrus pursed his lips. "All magic is spirit magic. The beings inhabiting the gems are not trapped but are bound in service. They do so willingly and can leave if the user desires something improper. One cannot bind these types of spirits by force. These are the Tay al-Ard. With this, I can travel anywhere instantaneously. They are powerful."

Annon stared at him in surprise. "Anywhere?"

"Anywhere I have been, specifically. Anywhere that I can imagine in my mind. I think of the place and the Tay al-Ard take me there. Anyone touching it or me will go with me. We go to the prince's estate. Hold it."

Erasmus stretched out his hand and grasped the cylinder. Annon hesitated. "Why can't I hear the spirit voices? Through my talisman, I should be able to."

"One of the properties of gemcraft, Annon, is to amplify power…to increase the effectiveness of their magic. It also results in silencing them. Some spirits, like the lights in the city of Kenatos, are bound by force and wish to be freed. Some serve us because of obligations they have made to our race." He glanced at Nizeera. "Her, for example. A talisman helps you begin to hear their voices. You must learn to hear them without it. That is when you will truly understand what they are saying."

Annon shook his head. "That made no sense to me, but I trust that it will someday."

Tyrus nodded and extended the cylinder. Annon clasped it.

The feeling was a jolt, a searing spasm of movement. There was an instant of nausea and dizziness. Annon found himself standing with Nizeera, Tyrus, and Erasmus in a strange room with a low table and cushions. The air was pungent with the smell of incense. He glanced around quickly, noticing the others in the room as well. There were Hettie and Paedrin. His heart leapt when he saw them and then sank when he saw Kiranrao brooding nearby, watching them. He remembered his insight from earlier—recognizing fully that Kiranrao was the one directing Hettie's actions. He knew the girl Khiara, who had healed him by Neodesha's tree. There was another Vaettir as well—Prince Aran—who looked like a Rike of Kenatos. The images blurred in his mind for a moment as he struggled with his thoughts and feelings. He needed to warn his uncle.

"Tyrus, wait," Annon said, but his uncle put away the Tay al-Ard cylinder and brushed him off.

"We do not have much time," Tyrus began. "The Arch-Rike will realize that I have moved again. He will try and locate me, but I must share what I know. It is critical."

"Uncle," Annon insisted, feeling his stomach bloom with panic. He saw Hettie's expression. She looked desperate. Paedrin looked ill. His mouth was twitching, as if he were trying to control his expression. Kiranrao said nothing, but his gaze was penetrating.

Tyrus looked at him, his expression hardening. "Trust me, Annon. Let me say what I need to say."

He stared at his uncle's eyes, his armpits stinging with sweat. The prince stood slowly, his expression turning into a scowl of distrust. The room filled with tension as everyone began looking warily at one another.

"My friends," Tyrus said, holding up his hands. "We are very different. We each have different goals. We have different motives." His eyes flickered to Kiranrao. "We even pray to different gods. But there is one cause which unites us, which binds us together." He strode forward into the room, his voice throbbing with emotion.

Nizeera stood proud by Annon's side, so near he could feel her fur brushing against his leg. She too was wary.

"Years ago, I took a band into the Scourgelands to defeat the Plague. We were killed. Destroyed. Murdered almost to the last one. I did not understand it then, but I do now. I know why we failed. We failed because we were betrayed by one man. There is a Romani saying. It is no secret that is known to three. Sadly, one of the three that I trusted with the full truth was the Arch-Rike of Kenatos. He has minions within the Scourgelands. He set them on us to defeat us. I think he was rather surprised that I survived. For years I have deceived him, hiding my knowledge of his betrayal. I was his prisoner in Kenatos, but now I am free. Now I am free to complete what I began."

He pointed a finger at Hettie. "I know why you came to Kenatos, Hettie. I know that Kiranrao sent you to deceive me."

Paedrin's breath came in sharply. The steely look on his face showed his anger.

Tyrus looked fiercely at Kiranrao, who was as tense as a bowstring. "I allowed her to bring you here. To get you here. Yes, Kiranrao. I need you. And you need me. The Arch-Rike plots to exterminate the Romani. He is using your people for his own ends, and they will be the next people to fall. He has his eye on Havenrook. It will collapse when the next Plague comes. He has a treaty with the King of Wayland to take over the shipping routes. Your people will be destroyed by the Plague he unleashes. I know this. I have seen the documents and know the signatures on the treaties. I know his plans. Your ring affirms that I speak the truth, so I will not waste more words trying to convince you."

He turned back to Hettie imploringly. "Child, you must know the truth. I am not your uncle. You were stolen from me as a babe, and I sorely regret it. But you are not my blood. You and Annon were twins. You were stolen by a Romani midwife as a baby. I could not save you then, but I *can* save you now. This is the moment you can earn your freedom. Whether or not I fail in my quest, the Romani will be hunted and destroyed with Plague. Because of your blood, it will not affect you. Your people will stop wearing the earrings voluntarily. This is the chance to earn your freedom. Help me in this quest. When this is over, you may reside in Silvandom, where Romani are forbidden. This is the freedom I promised you."

He turned to Erasmus, whose shoulders were scrunched, his mouth agape at the news so far. "This is why I summoned you away from Havenrook, my friend. I am certain you already realize that you will never be able to return to your wealth. You are smart, Erasmus. You understand connections. Think what will happen if we can end the Plague. Think of the prosperity it will unleash. The world will be reborn. Even you cannot calculate that."

Tyrus turned back to Annon. "Your mother saved my life. I would not have survived the Scourgelands without her. I seek to do her memory justice. To finish what we started. I need a Druidecht. I need you, Annon. We cannot succeed without you."

Annon felt a flush of pride. He nodded firmly.

Tyrus turned to the other Vaettirs in the room. "Khiara. We learned quickly in the Scourgelands that we should have brought a Shaliah with us. We were all wounded. Many were killed. With your skills, more would have survived. We need a healer. We need someone who can raise our spirits when we are depressed. Your family comes from ancient stock. You are strong in the *keramat*. You are also needed most desperately in this journey. There is much you can accomplish if your heart is true." Khiara nodded bravely but said nothing.

Annon looked at the stern-faced prince. His expression was hard, his look almost defiant.

"My friend," Tyrus said. "You were a lad when we last faced the horrors of the Scourgelands. You wish you had died with us. Instead, you have trained to be able to face the dangers this time. Your courage is without peer..."

"Say no more," the prince said, holding up his hand to forestall him. "I go."

Tyrus smiled, relieved. He turned at last to Paedrin, who had stood strangely quiet. Annon always remembered him as being jaunty and opinionated. He was staring at Tyrus with a look so intense it bordered on hatred. The look was confusing. It was not what Annon expected. Why? What had he expected? He felt a little growl inside of Nizeera.

"And you, Paedrin. Your master swore he would accompany me on the next journey, or train one to fulfill his vow. The Bhikhu Aboujaoude was from your temple and he perished on the journey. He died so that Annon and Hettie would live. I need you as well. Your master told me of a sword stolen by a pupil. A pupil known as Cruw Reon. I need you to find that sword and use it in the Scourgelands to defend us. With it, you can restore the Shatalin temple from the dishonor of Cruw Reon."

Tyrus breathed heavily, as if each word was a burden. "You are all already tangled in this web. The spider comes. Either we work together or we all die separately. The Arch-Rike will unleash all of his terrible power to stop us. Kiranrao—you must alert the Romani of the Arch-Rike's treachery. You will find evidence of the treaty in Wayland to prove my words. Then do what you must to disrupt the Arch-Rike's minions outside of the city. Annon—you, Erasmus, and Khiara must seek the oracle of Basilides as I told you to do. Gain the information I asked and return here. Hettie— help Paedrin claim the sword. You are a Romani. You have been trained to steal. The blade was stolen by Cruw Reon but it cursed him. He will no longer even touch it. You must steal it from the Shatalin temple."

He turned to the prince. "Our task lies south, in Stonehollow. Do you have the stones?"

"I do," the prince replied firmly. "We must depart at once."

"And what *is* your task?" Kiranrao asked, pushing away from the wall. "Tell me all, or I will have no part of this scheme. You have left a few pieces of the puzzle off the table."

Tyrus smiled grimly. "I did. It is not for you to know all the pieces."

"You seek another to join then? Or another magic to aid the quest?"

"It is the same. There is one with an ancient magic I seek. One more to join this quest."

"Who?"

"I cannot tell you."

Kiranrao scowled. His eyes were livid with rage. "Then take your schemes and perish in the wilderness. I serve no man. Either I am a full partner or I am none."

"I know your price, Kiranrao," Tyrus replied. "And it is not information." He reached into the folds of his cloak and withdrew a silver blade. It was the blade Iddawc. The moment it emerged, Annon heard its whispers fill the chamber, making him go cold. "If you join us, I will give you this. Even the Arch-Rike fears it."

Annon recoiled at the notion. The look that filled Kiranrao's eyes bordered on madness. He was mesmerized by the blade, his eyes suddenly feral.

Multiple emotions flickered across his face. "You tricked me," Kiranrao uttered with emotion. "You tricked me when I stole that blade for you. You never paid me what it was worth."

"True," Tyrus replied. "It is no good in my hand. It requires a special master. One who can tame it."

The feeling of blackness that washed over Annon made his stomach twist and his insides roil. The blade no longer spoke to him, begging him to take it. All of its efforts were being directed at one man. Giving the blade to Kiranrao was an awful mistake. Whoever held it would certainly go mad. He stared at Kiranrao in disgust and horror, saw the subtle transformation in his face. He wanted that blade. He had wanted it for years. It was just within his grasp if he accepted.

"I will join you," Kiranrao said in a hushed voice. Not defeated. He was satisfied with the bargain.

A popping noise filled the chamber. The sound was familiar. When Annon last heard it, they had been confronted by the Quiet Kishion seeking to kill Tyrus. This time, it preceded an avalanche of men. Everywhere he looked, there were those of the Paracelsus order, with gleaming necklaces and dark cassocks. Rikes of Seithrall as well. Soldiers wearing hauberks and carrying swords and shields emblazoned with the crest of Kenatos. There was no way to count so many quickly, but there were probably a dozen Paracelsus, holding cylinders, each bringing six or eight with them.

At the far door stood the Kishion, shrouded in an ash-colored cloak, and next to him stood another man, another Rike but taller and with short white hair. He wore the same black cassock as the rest, but his demeanor, the proud look on his face, marked him as a fierce man. It was the Arch-Rike himself.

"Kill them all," he ordered.

Annon raised his fingers and muttered the words to summon fire.

Paedrin lunged at Tyrus, quick as an arrow.

"There is no possible source of evil except good. It does not occur on its own. Good men become evil."

– *Possidius Adeodat, Archivist of Kenatos*

XLI

Paedrin reached Tyrus in an instant. Annon brought up his hands, ready to incinerate him with fire. His heart groaned with pain at the thought of destroying his friend. With the Dryad's kiss, he remembered every comment, every precept from the Bhikhu about injuring and not killing. How could he kill his friend? He knew that unleashing the fire-blood would not harm Tyrus, but Paedrin's skin would burn. How could he do it?

The hesitation unnerved him. The flames quivered on his fingertips, nearly guttering out.

Paedrin grabbed Tyrus's wrist, the hand that held the blade Iddawc, and quickly twisted it to force the weapon free. Tyrus's other hand chopped down and caught Paedrin on the neck, a stunning, forceful blow. He bunched his muscles together and then shoved Paedrin back with a maneuver hauntingly like the Bhikhu. Paedrin went back, but he was not down. He came at Tyrus again and Annon raised his hands to unleash the fire.

Suddenly Hettie was there, knives in hand, blocking the way to Tyrus. "Don't kill him, Annon. It's the Arch-Rike's ring!"

All it took was Hettie's word and the small ring caught Annon's attention.

The soldiers of Kenatos let out a battle shout and charged into their midst from every side. There was no time to think, let alone plan. Swords and shields converged around them. Shafts of light from the Paracelsus wove interlocking ribbons of color around the room and into the air, causing a net of energy to trap them inside the room. They were outnumbered and Paedrin was one of them. It was madness.

Kill him, Druidecht. I know he is your friend, but he has betrayed you. That blade will destroy us all. You must kill him! Nizeera shrieked in fury and launched at the nearest soldiers, terrifying them with her scream and slashing claws. Some butted her with shields, trying to protect against the ravaging fury she unleashed.

Kiranrao plunged into the midst of men, vanishing like a vapor of smoke only to reappear elsewhere a moment later, blade plunging into a soldier's side. The prince stood like a tree rooted in place and deflected attack after attack with his bare hands, crippling elbows and crushing knees. Even the girl Khiara fought back with a long tapered staff made of white oak, whipping it around and clearing the ground around her.

The Arch-Rike's voice thundered in Paedrin's mind. *Tyrus will not be taken easily. Cripple the girl and then come at him from above. Quickly now!*

Hettie slashed and swiped at Paedrin, trying to keep him back, but he was too fast for her. He caught one of her arms and kicked her hard in the ribs then smashed into her knee, dropping her. Even knowing the truth about her, it pained him to hurt her.

She grunted in pain but refused to cry out. Instead, she grabbed his tunic front and tried to wrestle him to the ground. She swore at him, but her words were lost in the commotion. He clubbed her neck, and she went limp; he shoved her down.

Paedrin whirled on Tyrus, sucking in his breath and floating up. Then exhaling sharply, he came down on him like a stone. He did not know how it happened, but Tyrus was no longer there. Paedrin slammed into the floor, seeing only a flutter of robes as the Paracelsus shifted away. Suddenly dazzling tethers of energy struck Tyrus from three sides at once. The blasts should have torn him to pieces, but the magic was absorbed by a gemstone embedded in an amulet around his neck.

Paedrin was still in a crouch and launched himself at Tyrus again, amazed at the older man's reflexes. He held up his hand and Paedrin saw a ring on his finger flash red. Paedrin remembered his earlier battle too late and found himself thrust violently backward, his own momentum suddenly reversing and spinning him.

"*Calvariae!*" Tyrus screamed in the Vaettir tongue. It was a word Paedrin had never heard before in context. It meant "place of the skull." It was an ancient term for a graveyard.

The word contained power.

Deafening explosions rocked the chamber, stunning Paedrin. Multiple thunderclaps, cracking stones, searing light as sharp and ferocious as the commotion of a thousand steel blades clashing with stone. The Paracelsus surrounding them were thrown back as their amulets and rings all shattered.

For a brief moment, Paedrin's mind was free. Then he heard the Arch-Rike begin to scream in fury in his head.

Spirits filled the prince's manor, wisps of violet and purple light, mingling with sparks and glittering ribbons of magic. Annon realized what had happened instantly. Tyrus had broken the bonds of their servitude, freeing them all at once and killing many of the men who had worn their charms. There was a frenzy of emotion and voices as the spirits, recognizing their sudden freedom, exulted.

"They are yours, Druidecht," Tyrus said to him, his grin triumphant. "They will serve you now."

Annon felt the first ray of hope. He did not even need to use words, for they responded to his thoughts, his desperate need. A flurry of spirits launched at the Kishion, swarming him with stinging pricks of pain and searing color. A blast of lightning came from one, blowing aside a team of soldiers rushing against Khiara and the prince. The fury of their magic was unleashed on the soldiers from Kenatos. Stabbing, stinging, blistering magic began to weave through the air at them. Annon stared down at Hettie and sent several to revive her, healing her damaged bones and restoring her strength.

The buzz of magic filled the room as the spirits darted throughout the chamber, unleashing their power on the mortals who had trapped them for so long. They focused on the Arch-Rike, turning their savage fury on him. Annon watched in horror as the Arch-Rike withdrew a cluster of black sticks and his hands turned blue with flames, igniting them into brands. Smoke began to fill the air from the sticks, and spirits began dying.

"Come to me!" he shouted to his men. "The smoke will protect you! Cut them down! We still outnumber them! Kishion, now!"

Hettie placed herself in front of Tyrus again. Paedrin batted away the blinding lights that dodged and taunted him.

"Paedrin, please!" she begged. "Don't make us kill you! Fight him! Fight him off!"

"Hettie, get away from him!" Annon warned. "Nizeera! Protect Tyrus!"

The Bhikhu had welts across his face, but he launched at Hettie again and found himself colliding with Prince Aran. The two faced off for only a moment before they fought, exchanging a dizzying series of blows and strikes, each one moving like twin whirlwinds. Feet, fists, elbows—all in a mesmerizing series of strike and defense, retaliation and leverage. Paedrin started to rise in the air, but some force drew him back down again, as if his abilities were being smothered somehow.

Annon watched the struggle from the corner of his eye, moving closer, gathering near Tyrus. He watched for his uncle to withdraw the Tay al-Ard again and wanted to be ready to disappear with him. It was their only hope of escape. If they did not touch his arm or the device, he would not be able to take them with him. Khiara saw his intent and moved closer as well, using the long reach of the staff to smash skulls and cripple knees. There were still too many soldiers and several Rikes leading them.

Spirits rushed this way and that, sending blasts of energy into the soldiers and Rikes of Seithrall, but the smoke from the firebrands was beginning to permeate the air. Soldiers grabbed them from the Arch-Rike and charged back into the room, waving them to spread the smoke. Most of the Paracelsus had risen from the original explosion, their chests smoking from where the amulets had been. Annon saw the death grimaces on their faces. Some were retching violently, unable to stand. Then he saw Erasmus, moving like a shadow from one Paracelsus to the next, dagger in hand, making sure each one was dead.

Behind you!

Nizeera growled in warning and launched at the Kishion, who appeared even closer now. The mosquito-like pests had not stalled him. He walked through their vapors without harm and closed in, bringing up a dagger to throw at Tyrus.

"Tyrus!" Annon warned, sending a blast of fire into the Kishion, knowing that it was hopeless, that not even Tyrus's flames had stopped him before.

Paedrin let out a roar of pain.

The prince torqued Paedrin's arm around, planting him face-first into the ground. The angle of his arm was excruciating. He tried to do a front roll to unwind his arm, but the prince dropped to one knee, making that impossible. His arm was locked and the rest of his body shrieked in pain.

"Cut off the ring!" Prince Aran said to Hettie. "Quickly!"

If they cut the ring, you will die. They will die. The ring will explode. Let them cut it. You will serve me best through your death.

Hettie's look was one of agony. "I'm sorry," she said, bringing the dagger up.

"No!" Paedrin said, his face contorting, his eyes wild with panic. "Don't...cut...it!" He tried to free himself. He felt the tears squeeze through his lashes. He tried to speak, but the Arch-Rike clamped his mouth shut. He tasted blood on his tongue. His entire body shook with pain, but he could not free himself from the prince. They were going to die because of him. They would all be killed. He looked pleadingly in Hettie's eyes.

She had tears in her eyes, but she took hold of his fingers and tried to pry them apart to get at the one with the ring.

Nizeera slashed at the Kishion, but he dodged her blows and planted a knife in her haunch. She shrieked in pain, scrabbling in spasms, and he shoved her away. He would be on them in moments, Annon realized. He tried to summon a spirit to heal her, but the hazy smoke was driving them to escape from the windows in droves. Annon saw the look of terror on Paedrin's face. The ring would not come off easily. Even if they cut it, what would happen?

There had to be another way.

"Wait," Annon said, rushing to her.

Tyrus shook his head in despair. "It's a Kishion ring. He cannot remove it himself without dying. Cut it off."

"No," Annon said, his mind whirling. A spirit hovered near him, whispering. He tried to make out the words amidst the commotion.

Neodesha warns you. The spirit ring. Someone else must release him from the trap. He has not shed blood yet.

It all came together in his mind, a flash of insight. In the woods of Wayland, he had seen many rabbit snares left by trappers. A rabbit would race into it headfirst and it would cinch around its neck. The more it kicked and tried to flee, the tighter the noose became until it strangled. He had freed several rabbits caught in such snares. The memory came to him as a whisper from Neodesha far away, but spoken through his mind in the form of a memory. They were connected somehow. Her wisdom seeped into him. Paedrin could not remove the ring from himself. He was the rabbit in the snare. But someone else could if he had not killed anyone yet.

Annon pushed Hettie aside and grabbed the Kishion ring. With a hard twist, he pulled it off of Paedrin's finger.

There was no explosion. It was yet another lie told by the Arch-Rike. The irony struck Paedrin bitterly. The Rikes and their rings were all a great lie. His imprisonment was a lie. His destiny as a Kishion was a lie.

Everyone stared at him, wide-eyed. Annon held the Kishion ring in his hand and jerked as if it scalded him. He dropped it to the floor.

The voice in Paedrin's mind was gone. He would never allow it in again.

Paedrin's eyes focused, a feeling of intense relief flooding him. "Thank you," he whispered. "Thank you, Annon."

Prince Aran released his hold and Paedrin straightened. He turned to the Quiet Kishion and launched at him like a spear shaft. He was free and it gave him energy and a sense of duty he had never felt before. Everything in Kenatos was a great lie. It was time for the truth to be shown.

The two were embroiled together. Paedrin observed everyone cluster around Tyrus, who withdrew the cylinder. "Gather round me!" Tyrus barked. "Hold my arm!"

Paedrin kicked and punched, using every technique of the Uddhava as well as his own violent passion. He wanted to humble this Kishion and teach him a lesson in pain. The Arch-Rike's treasured protector. Paedrin fought fast and hard and gave it his best. Master Shivu would have been proud. In the Bhikhu temple, he had never met his equal. The duel only lasted a few moments. He was kicked in the chin and then thrown across the room, skidding until he struck the wall and blackness took over.

Kiranrao appeared in a smoke-stain of magic next to Tyrus. "Give me the dagger, and I will face the Kishion next."

Annon stared at the Vaettir, full of distrust. "No," he warned Tyrus. "Do not trust him."

Kiranrao gave Annon a scathing look. "I can defeat him. Give it to me!"

Prince Aran glanced at both men and then confronted the Kishion as Tyrus hesitated. Prince Aran blocked the way, standing still as the Kishion advanced. If he defeated the Kishion then Kiranrao would not need the dagger. The two faced off silently, their visages grim. Annon had seen the Kishion up close once before, and the look of determination and murder in his eyes terrified him. He felt the last of the spirits abandon the room, one by one, their power fading as the stench of the smoke filled the air.

"Kill the others!" the Arch-Rike ordered. "They cannot harm you now. Go!"

The Kishion came forward and struck the prince in the stomach. It was a solid blow, enough to drop anyone, but the prince did not flinch. He struck back. Then the two traded rock-hard blows, meant to maim each other. The prince grimaced at the speed of the other man and deflected the next two. He struck the Kishion in the neck. He struck him again, to no effect. It was like striking rock. The Kishion was unstoppable. Several more blows were exchanged. A strike to the Kishion's abdomen. A blow to his collarbone. He did not even try to defend himself. He let the other hit him, to show him that he could not be harmed.

The prince's look filled with shock. "You are Chin-Na!" he breathed in awe and despair. The Kishion gazed at him coldly and struck him down in a single blow to the temple, delivered so quickly it could hardly be seen.

"Give it to me!" Kiranrao raged.

Tyrus's face went hard with frustration. Would nothing stop the Kishion? What protected him? Annon's heart raced with fear.

He watched as his uncle, the man he had always believed to be his uncle, handed the Iddawc to Kiranrao.

The look on the Romani's face. The look of surprise and pleasure. "Arch-Rike! You are mine!" he threatened, rushing across the room, leaving the Kishion unchallenged. Was he trying to draw away the Kishion to protect his master?

The Arch-Rike's expression shifted from fury to terror. He withdrew his cylinder and vanished. Kiranrao laughed in triumph. He looked back at them facing the Kishion, nodded in farewell, and vanished in a puff of inky smoke.

Nizeera! Annon pleaded. *To us! We must flee!*

I cannot, she replied, struggling to crawl to him. *Go, Druidecht!*

Annon's heart was ready to break. There was Hettie, Khiara, Tyrus, and Erasmus left. Their fighters had all been brought down. He searched his memory. Something to help them. Something that would save them. The quest could not end now, not when it had just begun. Dead before even entering the Scourgelands. His stomach shriveled in fear as the last of the spirits darted away. The fireblood could destroy the soldiers, but not the Kishion. He knew that if they left through Tyrus's device, then Paedrin, Aransetis, and Nizeera would be killed. They were all needed to survive the Scourgelands. It was an impossible choice to make. Annon did not know what to do. He turned to Tyrus in despair.

Tyrus pushed past Annon and lunged for the Kishion. He looked back once, giving Annon a desperate glance. "She's in Stonehollow," he said, reminding him. Pleading with him.

Tyrus's daughter—the missing linchpin.

He was handing the charge of the quest to Annon, and he was filled with despair.

When Tyrus struck the Kishion, they both vanished.

Annon turned to Hettie, raising his hands and facing the remaining Kenatos soldiers and Rikes. Hers turned blue as well.

"I have heard it repeated as an oft-favored quote of the Arch-Rike of Kenatos. One that was spoken a generation ago. He said it thus, 'Do you wish to rise? Begin by descending. You plan on erecting a tower that will pierce the clouds? Lay first the foundation of humility.'"

– Possidius Adeodat, Archivist of Kenatos

XLII

Paedrin awoke, his spirits revived and his body healed by the touch from the beautiful Vaettir girl Khiara. He did not know by what power she healed him, only that her hand brought the most deliciously warm feeling. He remembered her scent, the smell of jasmine, as he opened his eyes. She stood, holding the long tapered staff to rest herself.

The carnage in the room was horrific.

He stared up at Khiara, dipped his head to her in thanks, and found his feet. He scanned the room, looking at the bodies. Some writhed in pain. Others moaned. The dead, of course, were silent.

"Paedrin," Hettie breathed, rushing up to him anxiously. He stared at her warily, shocked at the rush of emotions—at the feeling of betrayal that poisoned the air between them. He jerked a curt warning to her with his head, a nod to forestall her words. He was unable to trust himself to speak to her yet.

"We cannot remain," Prince Aran said stiffly. "If the Arch-Rike could send men here once, he can do so again. We must flee."

Annon looked pale, as if he was about to be sick. "Agreed. To the woods then. Nizeera." The she-cat creature padded up to his side, obviously healed as well.

Paedrin gathered himself up and nodded in agreement. He approached Annon and gripped his shoulder. "Thank you. I owe you a debt." The freedom in his mind was absolute. It was like breathing air again when he had been used to breathing water. He could no longer feel even the shadow of the Arch-Rike's taint in his mind.

They abandoned the smoking chamber through a corridor to a door leading outside. The vivid richness of the garden flowers contrasted in Paedrin's mind to the spilled blood left behind. He was going to be sick himself. He clenched his jaw tight, willing the bile down. He searched every direction at once, wary of new enemies. His senses were as taut as a bowstring. He listened to each person's ragged breath. It was not clear to him why some strange mountain cat trailed next to Annon, nuzzling his hand, or why he had spoken to it like a person. Maybe it liked licking the scent of smoke from his fingers. Who could tell?

The gardens were a massive sprawl, extending beyond the reaches of the manor house, with hedgerows and sculpted trees and an intricate mosaic pathway that extended in a winding pattern, hidden away. The hedges loomed like a maze and the prince guided them inside, walking briskly to increase the distance. He said nothing, but occasionally glanced behind at the plumes of smoke coming from the wreckage inside.

The maze was vast and Paedrin found himself completely lost in its depths. He did not worry, because a Vaettir could always float to the top and bound from the tips of the hedges. But it would be useful in confusing any pursuers. Perhaps it was designed for that purpose.

At the end of a twisting path, they encountered an iron gate. The prince waved his hand over the jewel ensconced midway up the bars. The gate swung open silently and shut behind them. Paedrin was curious at the powers involved, but said nothing. There was a destination in mind. He saw Hettie walking near him but off behind him. She had been watching him. His stomach churned and he refused to look at her, feeling that sickening sense of betrayal again. She had been Kiranrao's puppet all along. That was her great secret. The curiosity he had felt for her earlier, his effort to convince her that she was truly free, made him sick inside. She had played him for a fool. Her look was chagrined, haunted even. Kiranrao had finally gotten Drosta's treasure. It was enough to make him ill.

She deserved to suffer.

The pathway suddenly opened to the interior of the hedge maze. Annon gasped in shock as a majestic oak tree loomed in front of them. The trunk was so vast it could not have been encircled if all of them had joined hands around it.

Paedrin stared at it, at the peculiarity and singularity of it. There were no lower branches and few higher ones, but each was wide and thicker than a human, all twisted and forked. The most striking thing about the tree was the enormous black maw, as if the tree had a mouth frozen in a wide scream of pain. The gap of the maw was taller than he was and it would take a Vaettir to float up and reach it. Moss covered the exposed tendrils of roots, which looked like serpents. Hardly any leaves existed on its barren branches, but higher up, amidst thick tufts of mistletoe, some sprays of green could be seen.

"That is the ugliest tree I have ever seen," Paedrin said aloud, unmindful of his host.

The prince and Khiara stared at him, offended, their eyes blazing.

"But it must be as old as the earth," he continued, shaking his head in amazement.

"Hold your tongue," Annon said, a smile crinkling on his face. "She can hear you."

Paedrin looked at him and the absurdity struck him. "The tree can hear me?"

"No, sheep-brains," Erasmus said. "The Dryad can."

Paedrin stared at the open maw on the tree, fascinated by it. It seemed to beckon him. He shook his head, feeling suddenly dizzy. "I have no idea what you just said, but pretend for a moment that I did and go on."

Annon turned to face him. "Remember when we were leaving the mountains of Alkire. Remember the Fear Liath when it hunted us?"

Paedrin nodded.

"We escaped through a tree. It was a portal to Mirrowen. That is the realm where the spirits come from. That portal took us to a grove of trees far away. Trees are the portals, you see. And those portals have guardians. The guardians are the Dryads." Annon stared back at the enormous tree, obviously not disgusted by its misshapen, hunchback look.

Annon turned to the prince. "She is ancient but beautiful."

Prince Aransetis nodded sternly, his face a mask devoid of emotion. "My family has been her protectors for centuries. The rest of the city of Silvandom does not know she is here. The maze is protected by spirit magic."

"My staff," Khiara said, clutching the tapered white-oak weapon, "was made from one of her boughs. It gives me knowledge as well as power."

Paedrin stared at it hungrily. It was much longer than the kind of staff he was used to, but he had been trained in the long staff since he was a boy.

Annon had a look on his face, almost a flush and a smile. He nodded softly, lost in his thoughts. Then he gazed at them. "She is amazing," he said, dumbfounded. He turned to the others, straightening his shoulders. "Tyrus shared some information with me that he has not shared with any of you. It is important that this information remain a secret for now. He gave each of us a task to complete that will aid in the journey into the Scourgelands. Do you accept your charge? Will you aid in this quest?"

He looked first to the prince, who nodded and said, "I go to Stonehollow."

Annon then looked at Khiara and Erasmus. "Will you both go with me to the oracle of Basilides? I could use your help. It is a temple the Arch-Rike has built away from Kenatos, in case the city should ever fall. It is still under construction, hidden in the mountains. But first we must find where it is."

Khiara cast a furtive glance at the prince, seeking a look from him, but he kept his gaze elsewhere. She nodded, saying nothing.

Erasmus scrunched his face and pondered it a bit. "I have lost every ducat I amassed in my bets. I am likely a wanted man in Havenrook, Kenatos, and probably Alkire if I were being honest. Knowing about the treaty of Wayland, I will probably be wanted there as well." He pursed his lips, muttering to himself. "The last group that ventured into the Scourgelands all died. I suppose the odds are great that most of us will as well." He shrugged. "But I could also argue that Tyrus has set the odds in our favor. I'm sure Basilides will give us some useful information about our chances for survival. It is a long gamble. Long odds. I like it." He smiled. "I'll go."

Annon turned next to Paedrin and Hettie.

He knew somehow that they would be last. He had been dreading it.

Before Hettie could speak, Paedrin took a step forward. "The Arch-Rike is my enemy and I will do all within my power to break his influence over the minds of the people. What I have not told you is that when I was locked away in his dungeon, he brought my master to me to disavow me. What my master said to me should have broken my heart, but I could see it in his eyes that he was trying to communicate with me without words. He told me the story of Cruw Reon. He was giving me information which would aid in the journey and hopefully lead to the restoration of the Shatalin temple." He sighed, nodding with enthusiasm, and said sternly, "I gladly accept the charge, but I will go alone."

He did not even bother to look at Hettie's face. He did not want to.

Annon looked at him curiously, but he did not object. He glanced from his sister back to him again, studying the two of them. Paedrin's ears felt suddenly hot and he prayed he would not start blushing. That would humiliate him.

Annon looked at Hettie once more. "Are you sure?" he asked her.

That caught Paedrin by surprise. He turned and found Hettie standing there defiantly, a look of revenge and malice in her eye. That same haughty look he had seen in the temple when he had tried to impress her.

"Paedrin can go anywhere he wants. I could care less. But Tyrus charged me to steal the blade. I accept."

He turned and looked at her, his rage beginning to blister the inside of his mind. "Haven't you stolen enough, Hettie?" he asked her mockingly.

She gave him a look of contempt. "I'm a Romani," she replied with a gracious bow. "How nice of you to have finally noticed."

"I am not going with her," Paedrin said adamantly. "I will do this alone."

"Alone?" she said. "As alone as you were in the Arch-Rike's prison? As alone as you were with the Arch-Rike's ring on your finger? Be thankful Annon got it off of you before I did it my way."

He was furious. His anger was ready to explode. But he would not let her see it. He would never let her have the satisfaction of unmanning him in front of her again.

"Go wherever you wish," he said coldly. "Better you go in secret. A secret is a weapon and a friend, after all." He thought the Romani saying was a nice dig.

Her gaze matched his. They stared at each other coldly.

Annon sighed deeply. Paedrin did not care.

"When we accomplish our tasks, let us meet again. I would suggest here at the manor, but the Arch-Rike knows where it is. So perhaps we meet in Canton Vaud. It is the seat of the Druidecht hierarchy and it is in Silvandom right now."

Paedrin shook his head. "The Arch-Rike has spies there. He knew you left this morning. We need another place."

Annon nodded. He looked at Khiara. "The other Dryad tree. The one that I saved. You know where it is. Can you explain the location to the prince?"

The prince nodded. "She told me its location already. It is being guarded. I agree with your choice."

"Thank you." He turned to Paedrin and Hettie. "It is in the forest west of Silvandom. The Bhikhu are guarding it. I will have spirits watching for you, and Nizeera can guide you to it. Agreed? Hopefully we will be ready to challenge the Scourgelands then. There is safety in numbers," he added. "Be watchful. I have a feeling the Arch-Rike will not be friendly to us after his defeat today."

"Do you think Tyrus is dead?" Hettie asked her brother. Her voice had lost its edge. She sounded as if she actually cared.

Annon sighed again, shaking his head. "I...I do not know. He's a clever man, but that Kishion could not be stopped. I do not know how he could have survived."

"What of Kiranrao?" Paedrin asked with a deliberate accusing tone. "He has the blade Iddawc now. He is a danger to our plans."

Annon looked thoughtful. "I think Tyrus always intended him to have it. I think he meant him to kill the Arch-Rike with it. If he does not go mad first."

Paedrin shook his head, amazed. "Then we part company here. You said this tree is a portal. Can it go anywhere?"

"Anywhere another portal exists. Why? Where do you want to go?"

"There is one place I must go," Paedrin replied. "My search for the Shatalin temple begins in Kenatos."

He enjoyed seeing the surprised looks on their faces. "My friends," he said with a grin. "Life is the Uddhava. The Arch-Rike's minions will be looking for a Bhikhu roaming the kingdoms. I will blend in with the city itself and can walk freely inside there. I must see my master. He can tell me where to start looking. The question, though, is if there is a portal inside or near Kenatos?"

Hettie surprised him.

"I know where it is," she answered.

"Some have accused the Arch-Rike of manipulation, intrigue, greed, and occasionally even murder. The weak always look to blame the success of the strong. The Arch-Rike is a powerful man. He is a wise man. He is also, to an extent, rather ruthless. But when you consider all the good he has done for the city and the surrounding kingdoms, we should thank him for his leadership and for being stronger than normal men. On a private occasion between himself and me, I have heard him say that his success was not to be attributed to what he has known or done himself, but to the faculty of knowing and choosing others who did know better than himself. Wise indeed."

– Possidius Adeodat, Archivist of Kenatos

XLIII

Annon didn't know if he should act surprised when Paedrin finally decided to join Hettie on his assignment. He could not understand their relationship. Only after verbally sparring did they finally agree to journey together to Kenatos. Once there, they would part ways. That was understood by both of them. Annon rather doubted it would happen. They were both uncommonly stubborn.

"The way through the portal is through that gap in the tree," Annon explained. "Think of where you would go, and you will emerge there."

"Will we sleep?" Hettie asked cautiously. "As we did when Drosta found us?"

Annon shook his head. "I do not know. I don't understand how this spirit magic works. Be careful, Hettie."

She smiled wryly. "I'm always careful. Be safe, brother." She reached out and squeezed his hand. He was not sure what she meant by the gesture, but it warmed him. She was about to pull her hand away, but he kept hold of it. He dropped his voice lower. "I trust you. I want you to know that. I also forgive you. You were being coerced as much as Paedrin was. I see that. This is your chance for freedom. I may be lingering in Silvandom myself when this is through. I would like us to always be friends. What happened is in the past."

Her look softened and she clung to him fiercely for a moment, pressing a little kiss against his cheek. "You have changed, brother. I am sorry, if that matters at all."

Annon smiled and touched her cheek, then fingered the earring. "It does. Be safe. I'll miss you."

When they turned, Paedrin was floating up to the gap in the tree trunk. Hettie sighed with impatience and then worked her way swiftly up the craggy surface. She was quite adept at scaling the tree.

Paedrin waited for her, his expression disdainful, and he looked down at the others and nodded.

"Be careful," Annon warned him. "But I pity the Arch-Rike your wrath."

"He does not deserve any pity," Paedrin replied. He nodded again. When Hettie reached him, they locked arms and entered the gap together.

Annon felt the shiver of magic rush through him and felt their absence immediately. It saddened him. Since the last time they had parted, so much had happened. Would he see them again? He hoped that he would, that Tyrus was right about them. He felt inadequate and wished the other two could have stayed with him as well.

Prince Aransetis approached the tree next. "I know my destination," he said. He paused, studying Annon slowly, as if memorizing his features. As if measuring him. The look on his face seemed to say that he found the young man lacking. He nodded once. "Be wise, young Druidecht. Tyrus has put much faith in you."

"So it seems," Annon answered. He bowed formally. "I wish I knew you better. I am sorry for the blood spilled in your home today. I know the Vaettir regard life."

The prince's expression softened. "You are indeed wise. Farewell."

Khiara was standing near, her eyes searching the prince's almost pleadingly. He looked at her, not acknowledging the unspoken request. He bowed stiffly to her and departed through the portal to Stonehollow.

That left Annon, Khiara, Erasmus, and Nizeera.

Annon sighed heavily, feeling the weight of the burden on his shoulders increase with each breath. His uncle had all but charged him with the burden of stopping the Plague. The enormity of the responsibility nearly choked him with despair.

"We seek Basilides," Erasmus said, shuffling his feet. He thought a moment, wriggling his fingers as he counted something in his mind. "It is the domain of the Arch-Rike. We will not find a passage to it unless we know generally where it is. What would be helpful is if we could speak to someone who did know its location. A Rike of Seithrall, for example. As it happens, there were several killed not long ago in the prince's manor." He looked at Khiara pointedly. "Do you know the *keramat* of raising the dead?"

She looked at him in surprise. "You are a Preachán from Havenrook. How do you know of the *keramat*?"

"Everything is bought and sold in Havenrook. Everything."

Annon turned to her in surprise. "I did not know it was even possible. What sort of magic is it?"

"We do not use it very often," she answered softly. "That *keramat* comes at a great sacrifice to the user. One exchanges a portion of his life force for another. Many who have this *keramat* do not reveal it except to close family, for they are the only ones that they would give up a portion of their own life for."

Annon stared at her in surprise, and Erasmus waved his hand impatiently. "You get what you pay for, Annon. A life for a life. There are those who sell a portion of themselves—a week or a month at a time. If they are desperate for money."

"A Vaettir would never sell this," she said with a touch of anger.

Erasmus pursed his lips. "I've seen it traded, my lady. Everything has a price in Havenrook. What I suggest here is not a severe sacrifice. Grant the life back to a Rike of Seithrall. Ask him what he knows about Basilides. We would not give him much of his life back. A fortnight, maybe. Do you know this *keramat*?"

"I do not. But the Shaliah who trained me does. He may be unwilling for one of the Arch-Rike's minions."

Annon was incredulous, but the idea had merit. "Regardless of whether we do this, it would make sense if we took their clothes at any rate. It would be easier to gain access to the place if we looked like we belonged. It seems that the prince shared that sentiment anyway."

Khiara nodded softly. "I will ask."

Annon looked at Erasmus. "You search the bodies. See if you can choose one who may be the most likely to know where we can find Basilides. Do you remember how many...?"

"There were eight," he answered curtly. "Three with brown hair, four with black, and one with fair hair. I think the fair-headed one may be our best man. He looked to be the old-est, the most experienced. He also seemed the most ruthless. I would imagine he was unhappy to die this morning." He turned to Khiara. "How long after death can this *keramat* be performed?"

"Up to three days," Khiara replied. "I will seek my mentor."

Annon nodded. "I will stay by the tree for a while. There is something I must do here. It is Druidecht magic, so I must do it alone."

Khiara nodded in deference to his desire. "Join us by the gate when you are finished."

As the two of them left, Annon turned back to the great oak, staring at it in wonder, and stroked Nizeera's fur. It was impossibly old. Was it as ancient as the oaks in the Scourgelands? The oaks they needed to penetrate to unravel the riddle of the Plague? He was awash in feelings in that moment, the terrible weight of the task. He was grateful for Erasmus's sharp thinking and Khiara's skills. They would both be so helpful on the journey.

Annon approached the tree humbly, bowing his head so as not to look at her. He knelt before the tree, feeling as insignificant as one of the many thousand ants scrabbling up her bark. He reached out and touched the tree.

"I do not know you," he whispered, keeping his voice low. "I am a stranger to you. But I would ask a boon. I would speak with Neodesha. I need her help. Or yours. Please."

Annon clasped his hands in his lap, keeping his eyes shut deliberately. Waiting. Breathing.

"I am here, Annon," she answered.

He looked up in surprise, his heart trembling with emotions. She smiled at him, that curious smile. It was a secret smile, one she only gave him. At least he hoped it was that way.

"Thank you," he said gratefully. "Thank you for your aid during the fight with the Arch-Rike's people. I heard the spirits bring your message. I did not know they could travel so fast."

She smiled and sat down in the turf near him, her dress a different color but the same style. "Of course I would help you, Annon. I did not want you to die."

He flushed, trying to control his feelings. "Thank you for saving my friend. I would not have risked removing the Kishion ring without that message you sent me."

"You will find that most prisons are forged in someone's own mind. And they invariably possess the key to their release if they could but think to use it. But some prisons are forged by others and it requires another intervening on our behalf to open the lock. Such is the case with the Kishion magic. It would not have worked if he had shed someone's blood. The ring would have exploded and killed you. What did you wish to ask me? Why did you summon me here?"

"I was not certain you would come," Annon answered.

"I cannot leave my tree for long. What would you ask me?"

"Two questions."

"Name them."

He nodded quickly. "I need your advice. I am not a leader of men. I am not a manipulator like Tyrus, who pretended to be my uncle. It is pretty certain that I'm young and inexperienced, yet Tyrus seemed to place the burden of leadership on me. You know the ways of mortals. Give me your counsel on how I may lead them."

She gave him an appraising look. "My kiss has certainly improved your thinking. A very good question. Will you hearken to my counsel, if I give it to you?"

"I will. I promise."

She nodded, satisfied. "Being a leader is not about rank or power. It is not even about skill or cunning. The best leaders, Annon, serve those they lead. You are united to a common goal. They will not follow you because Tyrus said so. They will follow you if they believe in their hearts that you care about them. That you sincerely desire their good regard. That you treat them with honor and respect and humility. The more of yourself you give away, the more they will flock to you. They will heed you. They will sacrifice for you. They will suffer with you." She smiled and touched his arm. "That is how to lead men. That is how to earn the respect of Mirrowen."

He nodded, remembering every word. "I must serve them. Be sure their needs are met. Show them that I care. I can do that, I think. A Druidecht believes in serving others."

"I know," she replied.

"I'm frightened," he confessed. "The Arch-Rike will send everything he can to stop us. I do not understand why, but I will do what I can to stop him. Without my uncle...I mean, without Tyrus, I do not know how much of a chance we stand."

She nodded sympathetically but said nothing.

"Thank you for your help," he said. "I do not think you would know where Basilides is, since it is within the Arch-Rike's sphere of control, and he does not control the woods west of Silvandom."

"You are right," she answered. "I cannot help you. Was that your second question?"

He shook his head. They had not known each other for very long, but he felt connected with her in a way that defied explanation. Their time together in the woods had created a bond. The thought of anyone damaging her tree again and banishing her from the world filled him with horror. He did not know how she felt about him.

He swallowed his nervousness. When the trouble with the Scourgelands was over, he hoped to be able to return to Silvandom. He hoped to learn more of her and of the spirits in the land. "Do you have any jewelry that you wear? A bracelet, say. Around your...your ankle?"

There was that smile again, a very personal smile. She looked pleased and a little startled.

Instead of answering, Neodesha smoothed the hem of her skirt away, revealing her bare feet. And bare ankles.

Tyrus's words floated through his mind, his memory perfect from her kiss. *When a Dryad chooses a mortal, she wears a brace-let around her ankle until the man is dead. It is an ancient custom. She does not choose a man very often.*

It was not lost on him that the Dryad chose the man. He stared at her face a while longer, knowing he would see it always in his mind.

"Thank you," he offered, hoping they would all survive the challenges ahead. Unlike Tyrus's previous group.

"While I was visiting one of the many orphanages in the city, I beheld an iron plaque on which was inscribed the following tenet: *Thou must be emptied of that wherewith thou art full, that thou mayest be filled with that whereof thou art empty.* The wisdom of the remark struck me. It is said that the orphanage, curiously, has produced a prodigious number of Paracelsus, including a very famous one known to all in Kenatos."

– Possidius Adeodat, Archivist of Kenatos

XLIV

The magic of the Tay al-Ard channeled Tyrus and the Kishion leagues away. Tyrus clenched his fists, preparing for the moment when the colors quit whooshing, his innards quieting at last. In a moment, the briefest instant, they were there and the struggle commenced. It was a small thicket of spindly evergreens, the ground overgrown with moss and rain-slick from mist. The churning rush of a waterfall enveloped them, pummeled them. Its pressure and force sent Tyrus spinning, uncertain which way was up. He lost his grip on the cylinder. He kicked against the Kishion as they thrashed beneath the foaming waters, struggling to reach the surface before he ran out of breath.

Tyrus tried to see, but the violence of the waters prevented him from understanding which way was even up. He kicked with his legs and groped, hoping to find the surface. His lungs burned with the want of air. He felt something snatch at his boot, a glancing blow. He struggled further, kicking and pulling, feeling his cloak a burden that was trying to drown him. He touched a jewel on his ring and felt the force of spirit magic propel him upward. Breaking the surface, Tyrus took in an enormous gulp of air and quickly cast around for the nearest way to the shore.

He felt the power of the Fear Liath instantly, a blind terror that made his mind cringe and quiver. But what was chasing him was worse than the demon hiding in the waterfall. Tyrus used the power of the ring to draw him toward the edge like a piece of magnet finding iron. The muddy bank clung to him, and Tyrus crawled forward, sputtering, trying to gain some strength again. It surprised him how tired he was already. There was little time. If he could get to Drosta's lair, he could hide beneath the stone, putting a solid barrier between him and the Kishion.

Gasping, Tyrus pulled himself to his feet and began running. The ripples of fear sent spasms of panic through him. He had to force his mind to accept that it was only the Fear Liath's power, nothing more. It would not be dusk for a long while. It would not be able to hunt him yet.

He sensed a presence behind him.

In that moment, all the terror of his experience in the Scourgelands returned. The naked fear. Desperation. All the intangibles of mortality rising like surf to overpower his emotions. He could sense the Kishion emerge from the pool and he knew, in his gut, that he was too far from Drosta's lair.

What to do?

He had gambled in that last moment. He had hoped the waterfall, the disorientation of a natural force—not magic, but a real force—would nullify the Kishion's power. A man would panic when faced with drowning. Tyrus had known where they would end up after their journey by the Tay al-Ard. The Kishion would not have known.

Tyrus's clothes were soaked and heavy. They were scant protection against a knife. He knew he would not be able to outrun his murderer. The little respite he had hoped for had failed. Wasn't that always the way of things?

He abandoned his plan, realizing by instinct it would not work. He needed to do another, to create one out of nothing. The strong gibbering fear of the monster inside the falls did not seem to affect the Kishion in the slightest. He approached, dripping wet, but his face was unconcerned.

"You left the Tay al-Ard in the water," the Kishion said, his voice low but clear. He had a rich voice. Tyrus wondered for a moment if he had ever been a performer or an orator.

"Did you drop your knives as well, by chance?" Tyrus responded civilly, backing up but preparing to fight.

The Kishion's face was clean-shaven. Multiple scars ran along one side. He had dark hair, nearly black, that was pointed like quills and dripping. He closed the distance quickly.

"I will not let you take me back," Tyrus said.

The Kishion's expression was placid. "The Arch-Rike does not want you alive."

"I can free you," Tyrus said. "I can free you from that ring."

There was almost a smile on the Kishion's face. Some inner chuckle. A flicker of contempt. He said nothing.

Tyrus closed his eyes, steeling himself for the pain. He opened his eyes again and began unleashing magic on the Kishion. He had rings and bracelets, charms and jewels. Each held a unique power. Each was bound in service until a single act would release it. He already knew fire would not harm him. He tried ice. He tried poison. He tried wind. He tried love. Spirit magic shrouded the Kishion in a multihued orb. Violet and orange, red and greens—dust and spirit and magic all weaving and thrusting, trying to overwhelm the Kishion's defenses. The man was immune to it all. He walked through the storm of colors as if it were nothing more than a drizzle.

Tyrus tried one more. It was a foolish notion, but everything else had failed. He opened a locket from around his neck and music emerged. It was a spirit song that was so haunting, so poignant, it never failed to make Tyrus weep. The melody invoked memories of his sister, long since dead. Of the parents he could no longer remember.

The Kishion stopped.

Tyrus stared at the man's face. The strain of the music filled the glen, overpowering the thrash of the waterfalls for a moment. A look in the man's eyes. The force of the music had halted him. Tyrus breathed, unable to know what it meant.

Then with a snarl of anger on his face, the Kishion rushed forward and jerked the chain from Tyrus's neck, snapping it. He kicked Tyrus in the knee, the pain excruciating and sudden. He lurched and stumbled, seizing the Kishion's shirt front to drag him down too. He would fight to the last breath. He would use his teeth, his fingernails, every stick or rock he could lay claim to.

Tyrus felt his arm jerk around, and the next thing he knew, he was chewing the dirt in agony. His arm was forced backward in an impossible angle and the pain startled him with its intensity. His wrist was on fire. He was hauled back for a moment, before a knee struck his groin. Every shade of torment imaginable. His stomach revolted at the pain. He would have vomited but the Kishion forbade it, punishing him further.

His thick hair was grasped by strong fingers and his neck exposed. The knife was coming next. He knew it. He struggled with his free hand, groping to find another charm in his pocket. His fingers closed around it, but he was too late.

The Kishion pressed a vial to his lips and poured a foul-tasting liquid into his gaping mouth. He tried to spit it out, but the Kishion had his head cocked in a way that prevented anything of the sort. He felt the liquid running down his throat, triggering his gag and drowning instincts.

Then the Kishion shoved him to the ground and he flailed and coughed. He could feel the poison working in him instantly. He could feel its magic turning into fire inside his skin. What was it? Monkshood? Banethrush? Villena? It had a sap-like texture and was bitter as yellow citrus.

Tyrus lurched for a stone, to try and plunge his abdomen against it, but the Kishion snatched him again, twisting his arm behind his back, jacking it hard. He screamed in pain, squeezing the stone in his pocket with his left hand. His fingers felt like they would snap.

The Kishion knelt next to him, his mouth near Tyrus's ear.

"Before we left Silvandom, you said, 'she is in Stonehollow.' Who is she?"

Fear.

It was worse than any he had known. He felt his mouth begin to move. He could not stop it. The magic of the potion forced him to speak.

"She is my daughter."

The Kishion paused, as if listening. "Where in Stonehollow is she?"

"I do not know. I left her in an orphanage run by a man named Winemiller. I have only been there once. I do not know where she is now."

He hated himself. He hated what he was saying.

"What is her name?"

"I do not know what they call her. I did not name her."

The Kishion was silent a moment longer. "Who was her mother?"

Dread filled him. "The Dryad tree...in the Paracelsus Towers. The Dryad is her mother."

The Kishion stiffened. "You left her unprotected then," he said venomously. His voice began to shift and change. He recognized the voice now. It was the Arch-Rike's voice. He could imagine him, sitting in his palace in Kenatos, using an orb to speak. "You sent Aransetis to fetch her. You sent the Bhikhu after Cruw Reon and the pup you pretended was your nephew to find Basilides. Know this, Tyrus Paracelsus. They will all die for aiding you. I know the Uddhava far better. I may not kill your daughter. I may bring her to Kenatos, as I brought your sister all those years ago. Kishion—go to Stonehollow and bring her to me. With his scent, you will find hers."

The Kishion pressed his nose against Tyrus's scalp. He struggled to unwind his arm, but there was no leverage and the pain only intensified. He felt the Kishion sniff his hair once.

"Kill him."

A knife plunged into Tyrus's back. It was a mortal wound. He knew it instantly. He had examined corpses that had been stabbed that way. The Kishion dropped him face-first into the scrub. His heart shuddered. Pain filled him, pinpricks all over his body. The sound of the waterfall was the last thing he remembered.

GLOSSARY

Aeduan: a race from the southern kingdoms of Wayland and Stonehollow. They are primarily fair-skinned with dominant and recessive traits for hair color, eye color, and complexion. Many consider the Aeduan as mongrels because of the variety of their physical characteristics. However, they have proven to be very adaptable and most resilient to the Plague. The Aeduan were the principal founders of Kenatos.

Boeotian: a race of tribes from the northern territories known as Boeotia. They have no central government, though they purportedly revere an individual known as the Empress. They are nomads with no permanent cities and live off the land. They are strong and typically have brown or black hair and are prone to fight amongst themselves, pitting tribe against tribe. Their skin is heavily veined and tattooed, giving them an almost purple cast. They have sworn to destroy the city of Kenatos, and occasionally unify for the purpose of attacking the island kingdom. Silvandom is the primary defense against Boeotia.

Bhikhu: a class primarily found in Silvandom and Kenatos. These are highly trained warriors that specialize in all forms of armed and unarmed combat and are trusted to preserve the peace and dispense justice. They cannot own treasure or items of value, and treat life with the greatest respect. They are often mistaken as being cruel, for they will punish and deliberately injure as a way of teaching their morality of painful consequences. The Bhikhu are typically orphans and nobility who have abandoned worldly wealth.

Canton Vaud: the seat of the Druidecht hierarchy, known as the Thirteen. These are the wisest of the Druidecht and they travel throughout the kingdoms to solve social and political problems and to represent nature in disputes over land. When one of the Thirteen dies, the remaining vote to replace that person with a promising Druidecht.

Carnotha: a small marked coin denoting the rank of thief. Showing it to another ensures cooperation in an activity as well as access to information and illegal items. There are purportedly only five hundred such coins in existence, and in order to acquire a carnotha, one must steal it from another thief. They are carefully safeguarded and hidden from authorities. There is one carnotha that identifies the location of all the others and can determine whether one is a fake. The bearer of this one is known as the Master Thief.

Chin-Na: a lesser-known class found in Silvandom and only taught amongst the Vaettir and usually only to nobility. In addition to the martial aspects of the Bhikhu, the Chin-Na train their bodies to exist on very little air and have learned to harden their bodies and focus their internal energy to the point where even weapons cannot pierce their skin. As such, they do not float, but their attacks are so focused and powerful that they can strike down an enemy with a single blow that damages internal organs. Only the most trusted and dedicated to Vaettir ideals are allowed to learn the secrets of the Chin-Na.

Cruithne: a race from the eastern mountains of Alkire. They have grayish-black skin, ranging in tones, with hair varied from pale blond to coarse gray. They are easily the largest of men, in terms of weight and size, but not slow or ponderous. The Cruithne are known for their inquisitiveness and deep understanding of natural laws and spirit laws. They founded the Paracelsus order in their ancient homeland and transferred its knowledge to Kenatos.

Druidecht: a class found in every kingdom except Kenatos. Those in Kenatos consider them superstitious pagans, though harmless. The knowledge of the Druidecht is only transmitted verbally from mentor to disciple. It teaches that the world co-exists with a spirit realm known as Mirrowen and that the spirits of that realm can be communed with and enlisted for help. A Druidecht cannot heal innately, but it can enlist a spirit creature that can. When a disciple has memorized the unwritten lore and demonstrated sufficient harmony with nature and Mirrowen, he or she will be presented with a talisman that will enable him or her to hear the thoughts of spirit creatures and communicate back. The variety of spirit creatures is diverse and so Druidecht often only stay in one place for a few years and then move to another place to learn about the denizens there. The Druidecht are the only outsiders trusted by the Boeotians to enter their lands unharmed.

Fear Liath: a spirit creature of great power known to inhabit high mountain country. Their presence causes fog and fear to disorient their prey. There are no recorded descriptions of a Fear Liath, but it is known that they cannot tolerate sunlight.

Finder: a class found in nearly every kingdom trained to search for lost items or people. They can track prints, discern clues, and are often hired as bounty hunters or guides. Finders trained in the city usually do not associate with those trained in the wild.

Fireblood: an innate magical ability possessed by a lost race. The race purportedly are the ancestors of the inhabitants of Stonehollow and are much persecuted. They appear to be a mix of Aeduan with some physical resemblance to Preachán, for most have red or copper-colored hair. Their race is impervious to the Plague, and for this reason they are distrusted and hunted during outbreaks and their blood dabbed on door lintels, which is commonly believed to ward off infection to the household. The real name of the race is unknown, but it is said they can conjure fire with their hands and that overuse of such innate ability renders them permanently insane.

Keramat: a Vaettir word for the innate ability to produce miracles, such as healing, raising the dead, traveling vast distances in moments, and calming storms. The secrets of the *keramat* are zealously guarded by the Vaettir and have not been disclosed to the Archivists of Kenatos.

Kishion: a class originating in the island kingdom of Kenatos. These are the Arch-Rike's personal bodyguards and administer the city's justice on those convicted of heinous crimes, such as murder, rape, and treason. Only Bhikhu and Finders are chosen to be Kishion and are given extensive training in survival, diplomacy, and poison. They are unswervingly loyal to the Arch-Rike and to the ideals of Kenatos.

Mirrowen: a concept and possibly a location. The Druidecht teach that the world coexists with a spirit realm called Mirrowen and that the inhabitants of each can communicate with one another. The realm of Mirrowen is said to be inhabited by immortal beings with vast powers. There is little belief in this dogma in the larger cities and they consider the belief in such a place trite and superstitious, a way of coping with the regular horrors of the Plague by imagining a state of existence where there is no death. The Druidecht suggest there is ample evidence of Mirrowen's existence and roam the lands teaching people how to become harmonious with nature.

Paracelsus: a class from Kenatos and Alkire. Enigmatic and reclusive, these practitioners of arcane arts study the records of the past to tame vast sources of power. Some Paracelsus excel at forging weapons of power to sell for profit in Havenrook. Others experiment with new sources of energy that they harness into powerful gems to be used by the ruling class. Most Paracelsus specialize in specific forces and phenomena and document their findings in great tomes that they contribute to the Archive of Kenatos. The Paracelsus Tower in Kenatos is the hub of their order, though many travel to distant kingdoms to continue unraveling clues from the past.

Plague: a terrible disease that strikes the kingdoms at least once every generation, destroying entire cities and decimating the population. There is no documented record of the origins of the Plague, and over the millennia the kingdoms have drawn closer and closer together for the preservation of their races. Documents discovered in abandoned towns and fortresses reveal that there are complete civilizations that have been wiped out by the Plague and races that used to exist which no longer do. The island kingdom of Kenatos was founded to be a last bastion for civilization and to preserve all knowledge and a remnant of each surviving race.

Preachán: a race from the trading city of Havenrook. They tend to be short, brown- or red-haired, and have an amazing capacity for deductive reasoning and complex arithmetic. They also have a deep-rooted desire for wealth and the thrill of gambling. They employ the Romani to execute their trading system and are generally devoid of morals. The Preachán take pride that there are no laws or rules in Havenrook. Those who rule are the ones who have accumulated the most wealth and prestige.

Rike: a class who lead the island kingdom of Kenatos. They are often mistaken as a priesthood of Seithrall, but in reality they are more like academics, physicians, and lawyers. While many believe them to possess magical powers, their power comes from the artifacts created by the Paracelsus order. With such, they can heal injuries and cure Plague victims. They are frequently dressed in a black cassock, but the most telltale sign is the ring that they wear. It is a black stone that purportedly gives them the ability to detect a lie spoken in their presence as well as to compel a weak-willed person to speak the truth.

Romani: a class that has no country or kingdom. Romani can be of any race. They control the caravan routes and deliver goods between kingdoms with the strongest allegiance to the Preachán city of Havenrook. They are forbidden to enter or to operate within Silvandom. Romani are known for kidnapping and organized crime. Starting at age eight, they are sold into service at ten-year increments. Their value increases in age and training and usually diminishes with age and disability. Each decade of servitude corresponds with an earring that they cannot remove under pain of death. Their freedom may be purchased for a single, usually large, lump sum.

Seithrall: a quasi-religion existing in the island kingdom of Kenatos. The term is a transliteration of the Vaettir words for "fate" or "faith," as one being under the *thrall* of one or the other. While the Rikes of Kenatos do not suggest that the term connotes a specific religion, the populace of the city have given it a mystical quality, as it is not possible to lie to a Rike who wears the black ring.

Shaliah: a class of Silvandom known for the *keramat* of healing. This ability is innate and comes from their closeness to nature and the ability to share their life force with others.

Sylph: a spirit creature of Mirrowen that is tiny and can travel great distances and provide warnings of danger and healing.

Talisman: a Druidecht charm, fixed to a necklace, which is presented to them by the spirits of Mirrowen upon achieving a sufficient level of respect usually achieved by the age of adulthood. The emblem is a woven-knot pattern, intricately done, and it purportedly allows a Druidecht to commune with unseen spirits.

Tay al-Ard: spirit beings of great power that possess the gift of moving people and objects great distances in mere moments. It is considered a *keramat* to be able to induce such spirits to perform this feat.

Uddhava: a Bhikhu philosophy and way of life. It centers around the observation and discernment of the motives of others, and then acting in a way that validates or rejects the observation. Life is a series of intricate moves and countermoves between people, and a Bhikhu who can make the observations and reactions faster than an opponent will win a confrontation.

Vaettir: a race from Silvandom that values life above all. They are generally tall and slender, dark-skinned, with black hair. They do not eat meat and seek to preserve life in all its various forms. Their magic is innate and the wise use and practice of it is known as *keramat*. When they inhale deeply, their bodies become buoyant and can float. When they exhale deeply, their bodies become more dense and solid and they sink.

AUTHOR'S NOTE

There are many sources of inspiration that writers draw on. For this story, it goes back to my college years at San Jose State. Being a medieval history major, I remember studying about the Black Death, the terrible plague that ravaged Europe repeatedly. I still have my college book by David Herlihy (*The Black Death and the Transformation of the West*) and have read it several times. I was also inspired by some of my ancient history classes, especially reading Julius Caesar's *The Gallic Wars*. There were many interesting descriptions in that book of the various "races" of Europe and also details about the Druids of Gaul, which I used to create the Druidecht.

For the development of the magic system in the book, I turned more to modern times. In fact, it was my experience working in a semiconductor factory at Intel that inspired it. The high-tech industry spends billions of dollars constructing factories that organize and exploit the atomic properties of certain elements. I grew up in Silicon Valley, and it has always amazed me how brilliant engineers can turn something simple—sand—into microprocessors that power enormous data centers. I worked for a while as a night-shift supervisor in the Ion Implant area of the factory (or "fab," as we call it in my industry) and was amazed at the machines invented to control basic atomic elements. The processes are so complex that experts exist in specific functional areas with strange-sounding names: litho, etch, diffusion, implant, thin films, planar. These folks are the modern-day Paracelsus. Learning about the technology and the small scale it operates on bends your mind. Granted, I'm not sure individual phosphorous or boron atoms are sentient and mind being trapped in silicon wafers, but that is how the idea came to me.

Only in a writer's imagination can ancient Roman history mix with mass epidemics and modern technology to create a new fantasy series.

I'm off to breakfast with Possidius at Mel's.

ACKNOWLEDGEMENTS

M any thanks to David Pomerico of 47North for discovering me. I gratefully dedicate this book to him for making my dream come true. Also thanks to my early readers for their priceless feedback and encouragement: Gina, Tony and Emily, Jeremy, and Karen. I also would like to thank Chris Cerasi, whose input and direction really improved the story and brought more life to the plot and characters. To my good friends Brendon and Rochelle, who for years told their kids many tales of the adventures of Paedrin and Hettie. And finally, to all the readers of Deep Magic who shared the world of Kenatos with me.

ABOUT THE AUTHOR

Jeff Wheeler is a writer from 7 p.m. to 10 p.m. on Wednesday nights. The rest of the time, he works for Intel Corporation, is a husband and the father of five kids, and a leader in his local church. He lives in Rocklin, California. When he isn't listening to books during his commute, he is dreaming up new stories to write. His website is: www.jeff-wheeler.com

Made in the USA
San Bernardino, CA
12 September 2017